SAFE AS CHURCHES

CATHY VASAS-BROWN

Safe as Churches
Copyright © 2013 by Cathy Vasas-Brown. All rights reserved.

First Print Edition: December 2013
ISBN-10: 1-4922-1147-8
ISBN-13: 978-1-4922-1147-1

Cover and Formatting: Streetlight Graphics

All rights reserved. No part of this book may be reproduced, scanned, or distributed in any printed or electronic form without permission. Please do not participate in or encourage piracy of copyrighted materials in violation of the author's rights. Thank you for respecting the hard work of this author.

This is a work of fiction. Names, characters, places, and incidents either are the product of the author's imagination or are used fictitiously, and any resemblance to locales, events, business establishments, or actual persons—living or dead—is entirely coincidental.

ACKNOWLEDGMENTS

Thanks to those who took time to pour over my pages and offer their editorial assistance. Every fresh set of eyes helps.

As always, profound gratitude to my husband, Al, for his unwavering support. There is no better partner to have on this journey. You are truly a gift from above.

DEDICATION

In loving memory of my mother, Helen, with heartfelt thanks for…
    reading to me
    making the best chicken soup ever
    coming to my high school band concerts
    working in the canning factory so I could have nice clothes and piano lessons…
    It's a long list. I miss hearing your stories and your laughter every single day.

PROLOGUE

SHE RECOGNIZED HIS VOICE IMMEDIATELY. A cultured British accent, words spoken in low crooning tones with a rhythmic cadence that could lull one into sleep.

"You're Opal's True Gentleman."

"I beg your pardon?"

Soothing. Refined. "Her True Gentleman. That's the name she gave you."

A deep chuckle. Then, "But you're not Opal."

"No, sweetheart. I'm Amber." Quickly she flipped through her notebook. "We spoke quite some time ago. And you can talk to me now. I'd like that very much."

A protracted pause. A small sigh. More nothingness. And finally, "You don't understand."

"Oh, but I do, darling. I understand a good many things. I understand that you need a special someone who shares your secret desires. I can make your dreams come true, but for that, you need to tell me what they are."

"I can't … I won't … I won't be unfaithful to Opal."

Unfaithful? To Opal?

Silence at the other end. Was he still on the line? There was no dial tone, so he hadn't hung up. What was he doing? She couldn't hear him draw even a single breath, so he wasn't doing *that*.

Then he cleared his throat. "Enough bullshit," he whispered, the sound harsh, like a death rattle. "Where … is … she?"

It was as if a puff of frigid air burst through the phone. Despite her layers of clothes and the steaming cup of tea she held in her free hand, she shivered. Still, Amber didn't want to lose him. For some reason, it had been a slow night. She glanced at the calendar. Long weekend. The married ones had gone away with their families. The single ones—God only knew.

How to play it? She kept her voice gentle, but sultry, like a coastal breeze. "Opal's gone, sweetie. But I'm here, and I'm all yours."

"Gone? What do you mean, 'gone?'"

Enough already. She wondered if she should just hang up. She needed a pedicure, and Jade didn't look busy. Remove the Petal Pink and try a deeper polish. Burgundy. Or deep plum.

"Gone. As in 'she's not here anymore.' But I'm more than willing to step in and take her place. Talk to me, honey. What have you got to lose, besides your inhibitions?" She rolled her eyes.

"Where can I find her? Tell me." The cadence was gone now, the voice flat, disembodied, impersonal. The British accent had disappeared, too.

"You can't find her, honey. Much as we'd all love to spend time getting to know you up close and personal, it's against the rules." A rule Amber might be willing to bend, but then, that's what rules were for.

Another chuckle, this one sending a chilling trio of notes through the phone line. "If Opal's not there anymore, then all rules are off. Now, I'll only ask once more. Where is she?"

Amber signaled in the air, caught the attention of the supervisor then tapped an index finger on her temple, the universal sign for 'psycho.'

More firmly than she'd intended, she said, "I don't know where she is. Opal's not even her real name." Damn. She shouldn't have said that. There went the credibility of the service, whose clients built their innermost fantasies upon a foundation of carefully constructed yet perfectly plausible lies.

Yes, of course I'm wearing stilettos and fishnets ... a rubber suit ... your mother's apron.

Yes, of course that orgasm was real.

I can't wait to hear from you again. You're the best.

Whatever they wanted to hear.

She tried to backpedal. "I know Opal was special to you, sweetie, but the thing you've got to do now is jump right back into the game. Best thing for you." She tilted her head back, relaxed her throat, closed her eyes and breathed into the sentence. "I know I can make you forget her. Won't you let me try?"

"No."

Amber sat up straight, eyes snapping wide open. A single syllable, yet it shot ice through her. The supervisor hurried over.

"I'll find her," the dead voice whispered into Amber's ear. "It won't be hard."

The True Gentleman's parting words sent the phone crashing to the floor.

"I already know where *you* are. Fat bitch."

CHAPTER 1

"Hey, God?" Paige Rowan looked past the jagged tops of Sitka spruce into the clear Oregon sky. "You need a woman in your life. Meet Mother Nature."

The morning sea fog had dissipated. A red-tailed hawk soared above the horizon. To the left, the Pacific surf was a blanket of low, white foam. In the other direction, a forest preserve, but the deer and elk were playing shy tonight. Paige breathed a deep lungful of evergreen-scented evening air and wasn't worried about anyone thinking she was crazy for talking out loud. In the state park, most of the hikers had already eaten their picnic suppers and gone home. Parker, her chocolate lab, was accustomed to her communing with nature and left her to it. While her parents had certainly spoiled church for her, among other things, they hadn't done enough damage to alienate her completely from believing in a higher power. She'd escaped before that could happen. Now she reasoned that if God did exist, He'd be out here, admiring the view.

Joshua repeatedly cautioned her about trudging through the forest alone. "I'm a careful hiker," she assured him. "I stay on the trails. I don't shortcut the switchbacks. I steer far wide of the cliff edges." That wasn't what he was worried about, he told her. To appease him, she carried a cell phone.

She was flattered Joshua worried about her. It could mean, as her friend Lani was fond of telling her, that their relationship might be stratosphere-bound. Still too early to tell, Paige told herself, but a nice thought to dream on.

"Besides," she reminded him after another of his lectures, "I'm not alone. I've got Parker."

"That hound? French kissing a criminal to death isn't my idea of protection."

Joshua had a point. Parker needed obedience school remediation. Though chocolate labs were reputedly an intelligent breed, Parker had missed out on something crucial in his lineage. His parents, Beauregard and Miz Lucie, must have been intellectually challenged too, a fact woefully absent on the pooch's pedigree papers. So the dog demonstrated the talent for which he'd been named—snooping—and Paige amused herself with Nosey Parker, forgiving the creature his frequent brushes with stupidity. Right now the canine had his muzzle buried in underbrush of wild fern where he'd probably get a snout full of another dog's poop. Paige tugged on the leash, and the pair made their way further up the trail.

At the viewpoint, they stopped. Paige sat on the bench and shot water from her squeeze bottle into Parker's mouth. Just over a mile out to sea stood Tillamook Rock Lighthouse. Terrible Tilly had been subjected to every form of nature's fury. She'd been flooded, hit by a tornado, and pelted by sixty-pound rocks that had broken off during a storm. Despite the assaults, Tilly still perched proudly on her basalt island, where cormorants and common murres now nested. She was a grand old thing, and proof to Paige that survival was indeed possible in spite of a terrible history of adversity. Let others wax poetic about Haystack Rock, further south. To Paige, this was the most beautiful view along the coast and she never tired of gazing at the lighthouse. Her lighthouse.

She checked the western sky. No sign of bad weather. Still, it was probably time to head for home. She would loop back on the inner part of the trail until she reached the Indian Point parking lot; at home, she'd barbecue a steak, then grab a book and read on her screened-in porch, where she'd probably fall asleep listening to the wind sing through the hemlocks.

She tucked her water bottle into the Velcro holder on her belt and rose. Though distracted by the occasional twitter of a wren in the distance, Parker remained obedient, the six-foot leash slack as the dog trotted alongside. Paige stepped cautiously. There were no erosive cliffs on this part of the trail, but the ground was humped with huge gnarled tree roots, prime ankle-twisting terrain. She could hear Joshua now. "See? Didn't I tell you not to walk alone?"

Paige rolled over plans in her mind for tomorrow, her day off. A bike ride along part of Route 101, maybe a little beachcombing for some razor clams. Grab an all-day breakfast in town and work it off with some weightlifting. Her vacation was coming up soon, an ecotour in the San Juans with plenty of kayaking and cycling, so she needed to keep herself in shape.

Parker's obedience was short-lived. He was whining now, straining at his leash, eyes riveted to a spot several yards ahead beneath a tangle of roots, mud and fern. A squirrel, Paige thought immediately, though she didn't hear any movement. A dead squirrel, then. Trust Parker to track it down. Several times the dog had broken his leash, on each occasion returning home an hour or so later with a baby chipmunk or rabbit between his teeth. Paige's back yard was a makeshift animal cemetery.

As they drew closer to the place where the path ended and the parking lot began, Paige caught sight of a patch of pale pink amid the muck near her Outback. A trio of black birds pecked at the mound. And the fresh air was tainted with something rancid. Spoiled meat. The dog was frantic now, yelping. Paige gripped the loop of the leash and dug her heels into the soft earth. "Steady, Parker. It's okay, boy."

But it wasn't. Parker broke away from his restraint and barreled for the pinkish patch, scattering the birds. "Parker! Parker, stay!" she cried out. "Dammit, dog!" In her mind, she was really saying *don't touch it, boy. Please God, don't touch it.*

The skin between her shoulder blades prickled, the sensation of thousands of minuscule ants skittering across her flesh. She felt her heartbeat accelerate, heard the rapid drumming in her ears as she inched ahead. *It's a scrap of fabric. Pink fabric. Or a section of fiberglass insulation.* Out here?

Parker's big body blocked her view. Not until Paige stood alongside her dog did she see what she wished she hadn't—a severed human foot.

CHAPTER 2

"Shouldn't be too tough to find the rest of her. Look at the circumference of that ankle. This was one queen-sized woman."

Paige burrowed her face more deeply into her dog's neck. She was sitting, knees hugged to her chest, under the protective umbrella of a Western hemlock, Parker pasted to her like a wet shirt. She tried to focus on the officer's questions, but felt herself inexorably pulled into the grisly observations of the forensic team nearby, circling her vehicle.

"If she's been bisected like a lab specimen, her parts could be all over the state."

A macabre image formed in Paige's mind, of a backpacker hiking his way through Oregon, strewing human limbs like seeds. Hot tears streamed down her swollen face. She ground the heel of her hand into her eyes, as if the pressure against the sockets would banish the disturbing vision. *Go away. Sweet Jesus, make it go away.*

The officer crouching beside her squeezed her shoulder, offered another tissue. His expression was kind, his grip firm, solid. "See any other people on the trail?"

"An elderly couple, about an hour ago. I passed them at the first viewpoint. Birdwatchers, I think. They had binoculars." Both had worn glasses and baseball caps, quilted vests—his navy, hers red.

He wrote on a ruled pad.

"I saw some surfers, too. On Indian Beach. Just after I pulled into the parking lot."

"How many?"

"Four." A hard swallow. "Yes. Four."

"Male? Female?"

Paige clenched her eyes shut, tried to remember. "I don't know," she said after a time. "They were far away, and wearing wetsuits, so they all looked pretty much the same." Like shiny, black seals. Shark food.

Crime-scene tape was being wrapped around the trunk of an ancient tree. One of the officers paced off a large rectangle in the parking lot, then wrapped more tape. Paige wondered if they'd have enough. Then she uttered a caution. The cop with the yellow tape was about to step where she'd thrown up earlier.

Klieg lights were erected. In a remote corner of the lot, headlamps were extinguished. Doors slammed. Then barking. Cadaver dogs.

Parker raised his head. Trembled.

"Can I go home now?" Paige asked. "My dog's upset. He thinks he's done something wrong."

The officer nodded. "I take it that's your tan Subaru?"

"Yes."

"I'll get you and your dog home. Your vehicle will be returned to you once we're done working the scene. Is there anyone you want me to call?"

She thought of Joshua. "No," she said. "I want to be by myself."

"Think some animal carried this thing here?" she could hear one of the other officers say.

"Minimal damage to it," came the reply. "Just some punctures from birds' beaks. Looks to me like some bastard put this thing here on purpose. Like he wanted someone to find it. Lucky thing she didn't smack right into him when he dropped it there."

"He's right," the officer told her. "That's one way to look at this. It could have been a lot worse."

Sergeant Carolyn Latham Holt came over, crouched down and clamped a reassuring hand on her shoulder. "You get going home, Paige. The Mad Magyar here will look after you. Anything you need, you just ask him." Paige felt some comfort by her presence. Joshua's sister offered a familiar face in a sea of chaos. Paige gave her a weak smile, stood and followed Carolyn's partner, Zygmunt Takacs—The Mad Magyar—back to his car.

In less than an hour he had seen Paige home, made strong espresso and settled her on a faded chintz sofa on the screen porch facing her rear yard. Parker was seconded to sentry duty on the sisal rug at her feet. "Great place," Sergeant Takacs said, admiring the densely forested view at the back of the property. "You don't mind being alone out here?"

"It's peaceful," Paige told him. "Cities make me nervous."

Takacs smiled. "I guess it's what you're used to. How much property do you have?"

"Twenty acres, give or take. It's my uncle's place. He's in a nursing home in Portland."

"Oh?"

"Stroke. He can't live on his own anymore. But I visit. Let him know how things are going."

"And speaking of going, I suppose I should be. Is there anything else I can get for you? You sure you don't want me to call someone? Sergeant Holt doesn't think you should be alone."

"I'm fine. Really. Thank you."

The sergeant pressed his card into Paige's hand. "You call me if you remember anything else. Or just call, period. You've had a helluva night."

"I wish I could have been more help." She guessed the police had heard that line a thousand times-plus.

"You did fine. It's up to us now."

As he was turning to leave, Paige said, "Wait. I just thought of something."

Sergeant Takacs spun to face her.

"It's probably nothing, but—"

"Sometimes those nothings can turn into somethings."

"Really, it seems so—" Silly, she had been about to say. But it wasn't silly. Not at all.

Takacs waited, his gaze steady.

"The foot," Paige said. "I—I was so upset, so sickened when I saw it, but now—what I mean to say is, I think I might know her."

"What?"

"The toe ring. I caught a glimpse of a toe ring. Someone I met in a class a few years back—a large girl—she had a ring similar to the one I saw. Her name was Bettina Reid."

Takacs wrote furiously in his notepad then shot her a quizzical stare. "How well did you know this Reid girl?"

"Not very well," she answered, eyes averted. "Like I said, we took a night class together. Had coffee during the break."

"When was the last time you saw her?"

"When class ended." Paige swallowed. "We exchanged phone numbers, promised to keep in touch but ..."

"Don't still have that number, do you?"

"I'll check."

Paige rooted in the kitchen drawer beneath her wall phone and produced a telephone directory. "Here it is." She gave the sergeant Bettina's home number.

"That paints this whole situation with a different brush. If it turns out that foot does belong to—" he checked his notes "—Bettina Reid, and you knew her, that's one helluva coincidence. Or maybe not."

Paige swallowed again. "But like I said, I just caught a peek. I could be all wrong. I hope I am. Bettina, from what little I remember, was really nice."

After Takacs had gone, Paige went to the kitchen and poured more espresso. She emptied the dregs of a brandy bottle into her demitasse then moved to her handbag where she'd kept a small atomizer of perfume. She sprayed the air, stepped ahead into the fragrant mist, but still the stench of death, of dank decay, lingered. The rank odor had permeated her clothes, her skin, her hair. It followed her from room to room, reminding her. Tears came again, burning her eyes. Her throat tightened, sorrow lodging there like a rough-edged stone.

Parker, awaiting her return to the screen porch, was warming her spot on the couch. She wriggled in beside him and felt the reassuring press of his big warm body against hers. Paige drank, patted her dog and, knowing sleep wouldn't come, picked up the newspaper she hadn't had the chance to read this morning. She skimmed a front page article about a group of Seattle area prostitutes who had gathered on the steps of city hall to protest the stalled investigation into the murder of Tammi Jean Flowers, whose body had been pulled from Elliott Bay nearly a year ago. Bodies everywhere.

Some time later, Paige realized she hadn't removed her gaze from the article—the paper was still in her hands. Her thoughts flashed like a slide show: a red-tailed hawk; a group of androgynous surfers; not-so-terrible Tilly, her beloved lighthouse. The final frame, frozen in her mind, beheld a fleshy, severed foot, a foot that had borne a distinctive silver toe ring with a tiny round blue jewel in the centre, and toenails polished in Petal Pink.

CHAPTER 3

AMBER HAD A MAGNIFICENT VOICE. It flowed like a river of melted chocolate, rich, seductive, and warm. She played it like the instrument it was, exploring its full range, unleashing her inner animal. She could mewl, bellow, purr, coo. There was always a pot of tea nearby, freshly brewed chamomile to ease the strain on her throat.

There were other strains too—on her back, on her feet, on her heart. To her clients, Amber was a petite Asian woman with ruler-straight hair, sooty lashes, full pouty lips and delicate, pale breasts that could be cupped in a small hand. In the flesh, Amber was nothing of the kind. She had stopped weighing herself once the scale tipped past three hundred. A bra had not been made that could support the heaving, pendulous breasts that, when she sat, rested in her lap. In warm weather, she slid puffy feet into Birkenstocks; when it got cold, she wore men's fleece-lined slippers. Outfits consisted of saris or muumuus, though Amber was neither East Indian nor Polynesian. In wet weather, she walked with a three-pronged cane; her doctor predicted she would be wheelchair-bound within the year. Her complexion was flawless, her hair lush, her eyes full of warmth and wonder.

She had long ago grown weary of hearing, *If you just lost some weight, you'd be a knockout.*

Amber was grateful for the work, almost always available, and immensely proud of the persona she had created. She had rid herself of the need to endure countless humiliating job interviews, rejection heaped upon rejection. So without apology or embarrassment, Amber became a seller of fantasy. On the telephone, she wielded power. She could prolong, *prolong*, prolo-o-o-ong, driving her clients to the point of near madness, and for Amber, the experience was delicious. Exhilarating. Talking to men on the phone and getting paid for it was the most exciting thing she had ever done. She was in no hurry to quit or look for other work. The men loved her.

And now she was dead. Paige had wrestled with memories for much of the night. Their first meeting—

"Hi, I'm Paige."

"And I'm morbidly obese. Pleased to meet you."

Visions of Amber's bare feet, perched on a plastic milk crate cushioned with an old phone book, with Jade, aspiring esthetician, rubbing sea salt into chapped heels between calls, following up with a rich slather of emollient. And Lani presenting her with that cute toe ring last Christmas, one she'd picked up in Seaside at one of the arcades on Broadway.

And in the midst of her haunted sleep, Paige was besieged with a kaleidoscope of horror—the scrape of a blade along a whetstone; a dump truck full of severed limbs tumbling toward her, their bloodied stumps plummeting to within inches of her face before veering off to either side; voices shrieking above a dozen ringing phones—*do me, just like that, you know what I want.*

She shuddered awake. An arc of morning sun crested above the horizon, a sharp sliver of orange. Eleven hellish hours since Parker had made his first plaintive wail. Eleven hours since she'd smelled that smell, almost tasted it as its noxiousness seeped down her throat.

Looks like some bastard put this thing here on purpose.

If he could get to Amber, he could get to her. Was that the message? How much danger was she in? And why?

She'd had to tell Sergeant Takacs she'd recognized the foot. It was the right thing to do. Amber's parents, regardless of how Amber felt about them, needed to know what had happened to their daughter, needed to put her to rest with all the decency and respect she deserved. But the lie about Paige not having kept in touch with Bettina had slipped out, and so easily. The police didn't need to know about the four of them, how their relationship had continued long after the university course had ended.

No. It would serve no purpose to tell the entire story. Best just to let them think her tears, her nausea, came about simply because she'd found that hideous thing near her car. Anyone would react that way. Especially, in afterthought, to realize that the foot may have belonged to someone she once knew. If Sergeant Takacs and Carolyn didn't believe in coincidence, then they would investigate and discover why someone had positioned that gruesome thing in plain sight for her to find. Meanwhile, her secret was still safe.

She would not, could not, betray her friends. They had so much to lose. Their pact was sacred.

Too, things were good between her and Joshua; the potential for a solid future was there. Messing with that right now wasn't something she was willing to do. Much easier to pretend she'd only been a passing acquaintance to the girl with the petal pink toes.

CHAPTER 4

SHE MUST HAVE DRIFTED OFF. Her next waking moment came on Sunday morning when Parker dropped a forepaw on her cheek. Paige squinted in the sunlight to where the dog was looking. Standing on her back stoop, peering through the screen, was Joshua, with two tall cups of take-out coffee and, she hoped, something sweet in the brown bag he carried.

She ground gritty sleep from her eyes, wished for a hairbrush and some mouthwash. "Hey there, you. Wait, let me get the door."

She stood up and unlocked the door. Joshua entered, laid the bakery goodies on the oval table and enveloped her in a hug. "I just heard. Why didn't you call me? At least you're finally locking your doors. And is it true? Did you really know her?"

Paige broke the embrace earlier than she would have liked. Too long in his arms, hearing the concern in his voice, and she would have crumbled, blurted out the whole story and told him how scared she really was. She returned to the sofa, Joshua following.

She kept her voice level. "I was fine, Joshua. Honest. I didn't call you because it was late. And I never said I knew her. I said I knew someone who wore a ring like the one I thought I saw. I could be wrong. I didn't take a good, long look. Obviously." She nudged Parker away with her stocking foot to make room on the couch.

Joshua sat next to her, thigh to thigh, and draped an arm around her shoulders. "Must have been awful. I really wish you'd called me. I would have been here in minutes. Made tea. Poured brandy. Whatever you needed. You know that."

"I poured my own brandy. But thank you."

"Damn independent women these days. Never give us guys a chance to be a hero."

In spite of everything, she managed a small laugh. Joshua was so good for her. They laughed often, in between all the kissing. And the great sex. "You're my hero if there's something fattening in the bag."

"See for yourself."

A multigrain bagel, his. And two mini-Danish, one lemon, one cherry. Because she could never decide. Between bites she asked, "How did you find out?"

As soon as the words were out, she realized how foolish the question was.

"Carolyn called me at home first thing this morning when she got in."

Carolyn was Joshua's twin, a whole ten minutes older, too, which she always insisted earned her bossing-around status. Joshua, who was executive director of "Friends for Families", claimed to have the more stressful job; there was never enough money, never enough volunteers, and the needy never stopped coming. The kids he and his staff dealt with were ripe for failure—socially outcast, intellectually challenged, psychologically screwed up. Friends for Families was pedaling as fast as it could, but what the kids really needed were parents who gave a damn.

Many days, Joshua hoped for a miracle. When one failed to arrive, he did what other harried and frustrated people did—he showed up at work anyway, unlocked the door to the timeworn Victorian building that housed his office and grit his teeth to face the day. His sister, he often teased, didn't know stress from schmess.

Carolyn was one of three patrol sergeants in the Cypress Village Police Department, with an eye on becoming lieutenant. Crime, in any form, didn't generally find its way to the artsy, upscale environs of Cypress Village. Until now.

"Sergeant Takacs told Carolyn you held up pretty well, other than the puddle of vomit."

"And here I thought the sergeant was a nice guy."

"He is, according to Carolyn. But he's not soft on crime. They call him the Mad Magyar at the station."

"Nice to know he's on our side. Have they learned anything?"

It sounded awful, being so cavalier, so chatty. They were talking about Amber. And someone had killed her, removed her foot, perhaps cut ... no, she had to stop this.

"Carolyn's not going to give away any cop secrets. What we learn, we'll get from the papers. But to leave that foot where anyone could trip over it? What kind of sadistic bastard is this? What if he's sending a message? 'Here's what I can do. Wanna see more?' All I heard on the news this morning was that cadaver dogs haven't turned up anything else. At least not along the trails in the park. And they covered a fair chunk of ground."

Last night's brandy rose up, sour. Quickly, Paige snapped the plastic tab on the coffee cup's lid and took a deep swallow of dark roast. Then another. She polished off the second Danish. Joshua stroked her hair. Parker sat on top of her feet, keeping them warm.

"I ... I really need to take a shower," she said, still queasy. "Do you ... could you stay? Just until I'm done?"

Joshua stood, took both her hands and pulled her up. "I'll do you one better. We'll spend the day together. Do something silly. Fun. Take your mind off ... well, you know. Unless you've got other plans?"

"No. But aren't you going to Mass today?"

"Fooled you. I went last night."

"But, Joshua, I can't ask—"

"Sure you can. Go get yourself cleaned up. I'll feed the mutt and take him for a quick walk to the end of the driveway." He planted a kiss on her forehead and followed her into the kitchen where she handed him Parker's leash.

"Maybe you should put some Vicks under his nose. I don't want him digging up anything else."

It was a feeble attempt at humor, but she had to start somewhere. Amber had died. Paige couldn't do anything for her now. Let Joshua's sister and the rest of the police use their brains and their science to help Amber rest easy. Perhaps then Paige could rest easy.

CHAPTER 5

THE VILLAGE WAS A BROWSER'S mecca. Art galleries, cafés and outdoor adventure shops were housed in strictly regulated clapboard or timber buildings along a stretch of cobblestone road accessible only on foot. Stores' signs were carved from wood or forged from iron; this was downtown, a six-block area adorned with overflowing flower boxes and planters, colorful gardens, and quaint courtyards. Shrub roses and ramblers wove among split-rail fences. Now that summer was past and the tourists had gone, locals meandered along the walkways, ducked into the bookstore, paused for a cappuccino. Except for the intermittently posted signs showing tsunami evacuation routes, Cypress Village was perfect.

Paige was looking at the village through different eyes this morning, eyes that had beheld a horrific sight. Despite her efforts, she thought constantly about Amber and what she must have gone through at the hands of the madman who had taken her. Paige hoped that whatever had happened had been quick. She couldn't bear to think that Amber, who had already experienced a lifetime of misery, could have been forced to endure more.

Joshua allowed Paige her faraway moments, but nudged her back to the present by gently pressing his body against hers as they walked. They ducked into a café, and though Paige wasn't hungry, she shared some of Joshua's poppyseed pancakes and broiled grapefruit. Then they headed to their destination, the kite shop, located across the street from "The Great Outdoors" where Paige worked, Tuesdays through Saturdays. The kite shop's manager, Arlen Dale, was a nerdy mid-to-late-twenties paleface, nothing like the usual athletic, wind-burned types that lived in the area. Though he clad himself in wide-wale corduroys and thick cable-knit sweaters, he still couldn't fool anyone with all that texture and bulk—he was a Popsicle stick. His face didn't have a single line, nor did it bear the nearly permanent five o'clock shadow that she loved on Joshua. Arlen's face was feminine smooth.

Paige and Arlen waved at each other every morning, either on the street, or from each others' store windows, and occasionally they stopped for small talk about how business was going or events in the village. Most of the time, though, it was pointless to shout a greeting at the man; lately, Arlen never went anywhere without an iPod.

If north-coast dwellers could count on anything, it was wind, and wind equaled kites. A dedicated employee, Arlen was eager to off show the store's wares.

"Nothing too fancy or tough to control," Joshua said.

Arlen stepped from behind the long wooden counter. "What you probably want is a single-line kite. They're easy to launch and they don't require a lot of know-how once they're in the air. We've got butterflies, parafoils, planes, deltas …"

"What do you recommend?" Joshua asked.

"Box kites are terrific. Great for high altitude flying. People like them because they're three-dimensional. And there's enough wind today to fly one. The elaborate ones are pricy though—"

"How pricey?"

Arlen pointed overhead to a beautiful kite, a chain of multicolored boxes suspended from the ceiling using fishing twine. "That one's close to two hundred dollars."

In the end, Arlen rang in a sale for Bubbles the Fish at $29.95 and wished them a smooth flight. "Always nice talking to you, Paige."

"You too, Arlen. Be seeing you."

On the beach, there were several kites aloft—an Aztec-inspired bird, a dragon with a long tail streaming in the wind, a dual-line stunt kite that was doing lazy figure eights in the air. It was a perfect day for kites, with onshore breezes just strong enough to rustle leaves and move bushes. Much higher in the sky, a Cessna—Mercer Wyatt, the dot.com millionaire, was leaving his weekend place to return to the Silicon Valley.

They took a moment to drink in the view—gargantuan monoliths to the south, a colony of puffins on the rocks to the north, forested headlands at their backs. The Pacific was jade green, the oncoming waves crested with white.

"Tomorrow will be better," he said.

She could only nod, a ball of emotion blocking her throat. Amber, since age nine, hadn't been to the beach, nor worn a swimsuit. And chances were good she'd never had a considerate guy bring her Danish or hold her hand when she needed it most. It wasn't fair. It wasn't right.

Paige braved a tiny smile and followed Joshua down the beach, away from the other kites. "Nothing worse than getting tangled in someone else's line," he told her. She watched helplessly while he removed the kite from its bag.

He studied her face. "Don't tell me you've never flown a kite before?"

"Nope," she said, finding her voice. "Very sheltered life."

"Well, here comes your first flight. They say a kite doesn't have any spirit until it's been flown, so let's breathe some life into Bubbles. Can't believe I let you talk me into this fish."

Joshua got her to stand, back to the wind and instructed her to hold the kite by its bridle point. He reeled out some line, she released her hands and the fish rose, high over the ocean, bobbing and dipping as it found the air current.

He handed her the spool. "Keep your hands at your sides. Raising your arms won't make it go higher."

"Am I doing it right?"

"Sure you are. Look at that fish. It's smiling." His arms wrapped around her waist.

"Joshua, I need to concentrate."

"Focus on the kite," he whispered in her ear.

When Joshua was close to her like this, she found it impossible to believe he'd once entered the seminary, intending to become a priest. He was openly affectionate, a skilled lover, with a raucous sense of humor. But she also knew his faith was still tremendously important to him. He attended Mass every Sunday, went daily during Lent. A St. Christopher medal was affixed to the sun visor in his Jeep. He would have been an excellent priest, with his warmth, his compassion, his ability to bring out the best in people. A congregation of believers would have done anything for him, just because he asked. And so would Paige.

At once he broke his embrace and said, "Oh, shit. Wait here." Then Joshua was running down the beach toward two young boys clambering along huge logs that had washed ashore on wet sand.

Killer logs, Paige could hear him shouting, warning the boys to get off. A rogue wave was strong enough to pick up even the largest of those logs, roll it over on top of one of the boys. Even the smallest logs could be saturated with enough water to make them weigh tons. In seconds, an innocent adventure could turn deadly.

Paige tried to reel the kite in, steadily, slowly, resisting the urge to pull too firmly, but the kite had a mind of its own and Bubbles made a few nosedives toward the surf before Paige managed to bring the kite to the sand. A clumsy landing, but not bad for her first solo flight.

During lonely childhood moments, she would often fantasize about flying, soaring above the clouds, touching down on castle turrets or tops of bridges.

You can't catch me here.

She dreamed of growing up, quickly, immediately, and having the most wonderful, fancy-free life, working for an airline, or on a cruise ship. Her parents, as she'd once explained to Joshua, were "out there"—an oddball, quirky duo who sought to cloister Paige from a world she yearned to experience. They had fantasies of their own, a utopian ideal that Paige could never understand. She hated the clothes they made her wear, hated that they didn't have a television, hated that they scrutinized her schoolmates so closely that eventually none came around. None except Lani, her best friend since the third grade and the only one who didn't think Paige was weird, the only one who didn't call her names. Paige didn't think Lani had ever flown a kite either.

Lani Hollis's world had been one of starched collars and pinstripes. At night her parents retreated to their den to pore over their law books, leaving Lani to dream alone. She gravitated eagerly to Paige's parents, to their utopian ideas and their strong belief that prayer and sacrifice were the ways to salvation. She adored them. Too much. That adoration had nearly cost her everything. Even now, despite Lani's well-rehearsed independent act, Paige still sensed a frightened, fragile creature, one grasping at empty air in a desperate attempt to find a lifeline. A role Paige had come to assume. For Lani, she would march into hell. Lani had already been there.

Paige crouched and picked up a smooth pebble and aimed it horizontally at the water. She heard it plunk then it disappeared. She had never learned how to skim stones either.

When Joshua returned, he was shaking his head. "Parents drop their kids at the beach with no lifeguard while they go shopping in the village. Nice, huh? But I scared them with a sneaker wave lecture."

"Sneaker wave? What's that?"

Joshua told her that no one should ever turn a back to the ocean, that sneaker waves could erupt at any time without warning, often surging toward shore with a cruel force. Even on calm days, the killer surf was difficult to predict and a sudden powerful wave could sweep an unaware beachcomber into the water. "You really were sheltered, weren't you? How can a girl raised in Oregon not know about sneaker waves?"

"I didn't know how to fly a kite either, but look at Bubbles." The fish rested peacefully on the sand. "Safe and sound. He got a little wet, though."

"It's okay. Fish are supposed to be wet."

She laughed then felt guilty for laughing, for enjoying herself. For forgetting about Amber, even if only for a while. She wondered if she could make the feeling last, just a few moments longer. She remembered the feel of Joshua's arms around her. "Take me home," she said at once, the meaning clear.

They were quiet on the ride back, the atmosphere in the Jeep charged with excitement. Anticipation. From time to time, they stole looks at each other, caught themselves at it, giggled nervously. Paige was conscious of his breathing, his strong fingers stroking the soft palm of her hand, the inside of her wrist, sneaking under the cuff of her jacket. She heard him swallow. Sigh. He traced a gentle line up the inside seam of her jeans, stopping just short. His eyes focused on the road, but he was smiling. By the time Joshua steered into the gravel road that led to her log cabin, Paige was already working the buttons of his jacket. They raced from the vehicle, but instead of using her key to enter the front door, Paige hurried behind the cabin, pulling Joshua after her. "Come on."

To the right of the screen porch was a decades-old hemlock. Beneath the canopy of the tree, Paige kicked off her shoes, slipped quickly out of her jeans and spread her jacket on a carpet of dried leaves and needles. She tugged at Joshua's belt then his zipper, and lay down on her jacket while he let his own jeans drop. Their movements were frantic, desperate, Joshua covering her body with his. She reached down, stroked, guided him.

"People have been arrested for this," he murmured, sliding inside her.

She let out a whimper as he filled her. She arched her hips upward, matching his rhythm. "No one could make the charge stick."

"Okay. Now shut up."

But they were vocal lovers, each motion and thrust eliciting groans that crescendoed, prompting a skittering among the leaves from a nearby squirrel. And Paige loved every sound, every tweak at her nerve endings that let her know this was powerful, this was real. Making love with Joshua, wherever, whenever, however, was one of the things that kept her breathing. The sound of his release filled her with both a feeling of ecstasy and profound loneliness, as if the act of his pulling away was too great a distance between them. When he cried out, she wrapped her legs tightly around him, keeping him inside her.

He looked intently into her eyes then kissed her deeply, lips moving firmly against hers, then more tenderly, ending with feathery brushes across her mouth. He burrowed into her neck.

In the months that they'd been together, his afterplay had always been as good as what happened before and during. Without exception. They hadn't used the L word, and Paige wouldn't rush it. Whenever

Joshua was ready to declare his feelings was the right time. Meanwhile, none of this was too shabby.

"We gotta go inside," he said. "My butt's freezing."

"Too bad," she told him. "Parker happens to think that's your best side. Look." Paige gestured toward the cabin, where the chocolate lab had his snout pressed against the screen.

"See? Told you we'd get caught. They've sent the K-9 unit."

They stood, gathered clothes and ran, half-naked into the cabin. Once inside they dropped their jeans and shoes at the door, then Joshua took her by the shoulders and spun her to face him. He took her face in his hands, touched his mouth gently to hers, trailed his lips along her jaw toward her ear. His breath was hot. "Paige?"

A delicious shudder across her shoulders.

"What just happened out there ... I think—" A nibble. Another hot exhale of air. "Well, there just might be more where that came from."

She could only manage a moan as he led her to bed.

Afterwards, there was a tumble of words, a rush of emotion that swelled in her heart even as they lay together, limbs entangled. They breathed in unison. They dozed. They awoke, sleepy-eyed, kissed.

The jarring ring of the bedside phone shattered the bliss. Paige picked up. "Hello?"

"Hey, baby, miss me?"

CHAPTER 6

She could hear Joshua slamming kitchen cupboards, opening the fridge, having excused himself to give her privacy on the phone. Paige wrapped a quilt tightly around her, as if the person at the other end could see her naked. "Nicholas?"

"None other. Good to hear your voice again, babe."

"I told you to stop calling me. How many times do I have to say it?"

"Until I'm convinced you mean it." He laughed. "Then again, maybe that won't stop me either."

"You're wasting your money on all these long distance calls."

"Not any more. I'm closer than you think."

"You're not in Europe?" He was joking, Paige thought. He'd been calling her from France on and off since she left.

Please, let him still be there.

"Uh-uh. Been back for a few months now, scouting around the Northwest for a place to settle down. So guess where I am?"

"I don't want to guess, Nicholas. I don't even want to talk to you."

His selective hearing had already kicked in. "Portland. A mere ninety minutes away. I'd sure like to see you, do some catching up. Maybe you could come here. I've bought a place, babe. Great view of the river. You'd love it."

Paige glanced at the bedroom door, remained quiet, listening for more activity from the kitchen. A clatter of cutlery bought her more time. "No way. Forget it. In fact, forget you ever knew me. I've already forgotten you."

She prepared to hang up. His words stopped her. "Cypress Village is a pretty small place, babe. You won't be too hard to find. So keep a candle burning."

The click at the other end of the phone reverberated like a gunshot. She replaced the receiver, noticed her hand trembling. This couldn't be happening. It was a joke. A cruel joke. Nicholas was still in Chamonix, drifting from job to job, getting drunk. He wasn't in Portland. He had no reason to be in Portland.

Joshua, wearing boxer shorts, peeked in the doorway, making sure she was off the phone. He carried a tray of odds and ends he'd salvaged from the refrigerator—some fruit, a wedge of brie, two glasses of milk. He looked at the way she was bundled up.

"Let me find you something to wear." He set the tray on the bedside table, moved to her dresser and slid open the second drawer from the top. It tugged at her that he knew where she kept her nightclothes, and that he was so comfortable being in her house. It was a good feeling. She tried to hold onto that.

He came toward her with a mannish striped pajama top and matching shorts which he helped her into. "Gotta cover that body before I'm overcome by the urge to go exploring again." He smiled, pressed his lips to hers and she clung to the kiss. "Hey," he whispered. "Cut it out. We've got to come up for air sometime."

They burrowed under the covers, decided the food could wait. Lying in Joshua's arms, Paige could almost forget the phone call, forget the voice of Nicholas Bissonette, forget that he was within creeping distance.

"Know what I hate?" Joshua asked.

Her cheek rested on his chest, his heart pulsing in her ear. "What's that?"

"Mornings without you. And afternoons ... nights ..."

"So you like me?"

He raked fingers through her hair, laughed softly. "Very much. Any bad habits I need to know about? Leave your pantyhose hanging on the shower rod, anything like that?"

"Are you kidding?" she said, though she couldn't meet his gaze. "I'm perfect."

It must have been her tone of voice. Joshua was no fool; he picked up immediately that something was left unsaid.

"That phone call. Is everything okay?"

"Everything's fine, Joshua. It was nobody important. Nobody at all."

CHAPTER 7

PAIGE USUALLY LOVED MONDAYS. SHE had the day off and often passed the time on her bike, in her kayak, or on her feet, hiking with Parker at her heels. Hiking, though, had been spoiled for her, and that was an understatement; she had no energy for it or anything else today. With Joshua at work, she felt as though the two-bedroom log cabin was a cavern—way too large and way too isolated. Yes, definitely too isolated. Every scamper of a squirrel through the fallen leaves startled her. Parker sensed her unease as well and barked at unseen predators in the wooded tract behind the cabin. Nature's sounds weren't peaceful today.

"Fine pair we are," she told her dog and patted her thigh, signaling him to follow her in from the screened porch. She brewed some Chai tea and settled in her living room where she tried to narrow her thoughts to only Joshua.

Any bad habits I need to know about?

Gosh, just one small one. I used to talk dirty for a living. And I haven't told you about it. Does that count as two bad habits or is it all part of the same black spot on my soul?

After her parents' death, Paige had inherited their ten-thousand-dollar debt. When the bank came knocking, her Uncle Spence bailed her out but she was determined to pay him back. But with what? The phone sex business would be temporary, a quick means to an end. Harmless, or so she thought. Now Amber was dead and Paige was keeping secrets from a man she cared deeply for. The situation had the word "implode" written all over it.

Skulking in the wings was the large black shadow of Nicholas Bissonette. Why was he still calling her? It had been seven years since they'd shared that horrid little room plus bath plus hotplate in Chamonix, seven years since she'd left him in the middle of the coldest January night, passed out and snoring heavily. She'd fought like hell to forget that time, to forget that she could have ever been so vulnerable, so desperate, so stupid. That trip to Europe, a graduation gift from her only uncle, had bought her precious freedom. She had finally escaped from Seraphina Greene.

She hated the name she had been saddled with. Seraphina. Paige had been named after the highest ranking of the angels in heaven. More ardent than archangels and cherubim, the seraphim were noted for their zealous love. To Paige's schoolmates, Seraphina was simply a weird name and another reason to make fun of her. Once they'd found out that the seraphim had six wings and four heads, it was open season. Paige spent her recesses alone and lonely, with classmates running in the other direction, warning others that to look upon her face meant instant destruction.

Though they eventually tired of the games, Paige continued to feel the sting of their cruelty. Leaving Oregon when she was eighteen had been easy. There'd been nothing to stay for.

In Europe, she became Paige Rowan, so grateful for the opportunity to sever the chains that bound her to her mother and father. The opportunity her uncle had given her.

But celebrating her freedom had been fleeting, short-lived. Nicholas must have seen the need all over her face, perhaps even smelled it, and swooped in, fangs bared.

She had been in France for a year, working as a tour guide, making just enough money to buy food and pay rent for a cramped room over a cheese shop. She spotted Nicholas on the street one day, drawing a caricature of a young girl, a delightfully silly rendering of the tyke sharing a roller coaster ride with an elephant. Paige laughed. Nicholas bought her coffee. Coffee led to drinks, and drinks led to dinner. A month later, they moved in together.

In Nicholas, Paige had seen what she wanted to see—a deep thinker, an underappreciated intellectual who had yet to discover his niche. Like Paige, Nicholas had escaped to Europe to discover life on his terms. He wanted to make a name for himself but in what realm, he did not know. She remembered those sad eyes, deep mocha pools she felt she could lose herself in. She cringed.

It had nearly happened. She *had* nearly lost herself. In subtle ways, Nicholas began to sculpt, reshape, reprogram. At first she was grateful, awestruck at what she thought was his superior wisdom. She was only nineteen. There was so much she didn't know, but Nicholas, nine years her senior, could see everything so clearly. Her parents had repressed her—he would free her.

Just a little thicker on the eyeliner, babe. And maybe some brighter lipstick.

You'd look great as a redhead. Why not give it a try? For me?

Not a huge deal, the clothes he'd made her wear, the new hairdo, the bold make-up. She made herself over every evening so that when he came through the door, he would be pleased.

Instead Nicholas smoked up. Nicholas drank.

During the day, he set up his easel in the street, selling corny souvenir paintings to tourists. He sketched family pets, famous French landmarks, whatever paid the rent. And always the caricatures with pen and ink, until Nicholas complained he was becoming a caricature himself.

Paige sympathized. It was only a matter of time until Nicholas would discover what he was meant to do. She dismissed his constant jibes that he could make more money selling dope. She encouraged him to take classes, get a diploma, but diplomas, Nicholas said, were unnecessary scraps of paper, framed on the walls of those too insecure to believe in their own brainpower. He was a grown man, for God's sake, and already as smart as he needed to be to make his way in the world.

In her weekly emails to Lani, Paige wrote that everything was fine. She bragged about Nicholas, their life together, their prospects for the future. She described the beauty of the French countryside. The latter, at least, was true.

Paige spent as much time as she could outdoors, leading hiking tours along the glacier, her face scrubbed, her flaming hair hidden beneath a woolly toque. The big money would come, Nicholas told her. Then she could quit her job. He knew people who knew people who knew people. There was always something big in the works.

In the blackest part of the night, Nicholas retreated to a grotty room in the basement of their apartment building to work on his art. There had been a resurgence of the pulp detective magazines popularized in the forties and Nicholas was trying to hone his skills by designing covers for some independent publications. Paige, determined to be very French and *très moderne,* respected his privacy. He would steal from their bed after a feeble attempt at dismal sex and she began to feel secretly grateful for his nocturnal descents to the cellar.

Nicholas of the 5-second erection, she'd come to think of him toward the end. His problems, of course, were her fault. She still hadn't broken the vise grip of her parents, wasn't freeing herself to experience the thrill of the *avant garde*, the supreme satisfaction. Until she surrendered the bindings of her past, she would be imprisoned. Meanwhile, Nicholas complained that being with her was like fucking a plank.

Paige noticed the good-looking women entering the building by the side door, knew they were making their way down the dimly lit staircase to the basement where Nicholas would be waiting. He admitted he sometimes painted nude portraits. Women occasionally wanted that special gift to present to a husband or lover. The money was good, he said. Paige told herself that all great artists had paintings of nude women in their collections. Nicholas was simply following in their footsteps. It didn't mean there was anything more going on.

She endured several more weeks of godawful gropes after dinner, then the fumbling stopped altogether. Paige had just celebrated her twenty-first birthday. She had done everything Nicholas had said, had worn what he liked, had become what he asked, and still he had shut her out.

The parade of women continued. Occasionally there were two or three at once. And sometimes men, too. Paige became jealous. And angry. And curious.

She found the key to the cellar hideaway one day when Nicholas was visiting a client who was commissioning a special portrait of his daughter. Nicholas said the job would earn him a good chunk of change. He would return for supper.

The key was tucked under the insole of a smelly running shoe. Without guilt, Paige plucked it from its hiding place and skirted the building to the side entrance. Her relationship with Nicholas was in trouble and she needed to know what demons she was battling. If Nicholas was having affairs, she had to find out.

The stairs to the basement listed to the left, the half-rotted wood springy as she stepped. Overhead, ancient copper pipes sweated and dripped. Her shoes crunched on crumbling pebbles of mortar that had eroded from between the bricks. She felt that at any moment, the entire structure would collapse and bury her.

Ahead were four doors, two on either side of the narrow corridor. The first room on the right was already open. A monstrous cast-iron furnace growled in the corner. The rest of the room was bare, save for some antiquated skis and a pair of Lange racing boots. Opposite the furnace room was a makeshift storage area for the building's few tenants. Labeled boxes piled against the far wall—*Le Duc, apartement* 1B; *M. Plante, numéro* 2E—a rusty lawn chair, three fat-tired bicycles and a dressmaker's dummy, still wearing the beginnings of a long-abandoned sewing project.

Paige tried the key in the next door on her left and the portal squealed open. She fumbled for the light switch. A naked bulb overhead cast a yellowish glow over Nicholas's props—a large brass bed, a Bentwood chair, a velvet *chaise longue*, a stripper's pole, a wooden swing hanging from a thick ceiling beam. There were costumes as well—shelves with top hats, bow ties, walking sticks, feather boas. There were racks of corsets and period lingerie. For the more adventurous, contained in a humpback trunk in the farthest corner, was an assortment of bondage gear. Paige backed away, noticing then the large rusted rings affixed to the wall, the leather restraints still looped through them. And the brownish flecks spackling the walls. Please, let it be paint, she thought. It had to be paint.

Another room, off to the left, had a battered wooden door reminiscent of one from a castle in the Carpathians. Her flesh prickled but she moved toward the door anyway. It opened smoothly, the hinges well oiled, well used. The light switch was by her right shoulder. Mounted on every available wall space was Nicholas's collection of boudoir paintings. There were scantily clad women, as Paige would have expected. But as her gaze moved from left to right, the series degenerated into a horror show of hard-core porn. She caught only a glimpse of a trio of women draped across the chaise, their network of hands and tongues eagerly giving pleasure to the lone man in the picture: Nicholas.

Paige turned to flee, stopped short by the sight of a life-sized color poster on the back of the wooden door. One of Nicholas's magazine covers. Red letters emblazoned the message: "She Met Her Match." On it, the woman had been eviscerated, a coil of gray entrails cascading onto the floor. Her mouth was agape in a mute scream. Her legs appeared broken, painfully spread to expose a shaved pubis and blood red labia.

Paige felt her gorge rise. Her body quaked. In the left foreground loomed a grainy silhouette of a predator, the outline of a curved blade poised in the air. His handiwork had been thorough. The victim's eyes stared lifelessly at the grisly scene from within a glass jar.

Paige bolted from the room, raced down the dingy hallway and up the crooked stairs into the bitter, winter air. Tears froze to her face but she gulped the frigid air greedily, realizing a terrible moment later that she needed to return to the cellar to lock the door to her lover's chamber of horrors.

He arrived home ten minutes later. Paige managed to serve him a huge bowl of *boeuf bourguinonne*, and it took no coaxing for him to finish two bottles of Chambertin on his own. She endured a half-hearted few minutes of clumsy fondling before he passed out. His loud snores continued as Paige packed her meager belongings into a worn canvas satchel. She left behind the eyeliner, the lipstick, and the wardrobe of slut clothes. Four days after her return to the States, she was a blond again and standing on the threshold of her uncle's cabin, weeping and asking for his help.

Her uncle was crying too. Where had she been? He had been trying to contact her. Her mother, her father. Gone. And Lani—oh God, Lani.

Paige was plunged into a nightmare. She attended her parents' funeral, the media microphones following her from the two caskets to the gravesite then to an awful, surreal wake in a church basement where stale sandwiches and syrupy fruit punch were served by a group of women Paige had never seen before. While mourners pressed clammy hands to hers, Paige wanted nothing more than to dash from the place, to be at the hospital with Lani, who needed her more.

The nightmare lasted for months. Uncle Spence relieved her of the burden of going through her parents' papers, of accompanying him as he spread their ashes in the woods behind the cabin. The media was not as empathetic. They hounded her about her parents. What did she think of their new brand of religion? Did she think the car accident was part of a conspiracy? Why did she move to Europe? She answered no questions, granted no interviews. Her time was devoted to Lani, to getting her well, to helping her heal.

Paige did not want to be reminded of that time. But now Nicholas was here. Too close. And her uncle was in no position to help her.

Perhaps she was jumping the gun, worrying for nothing. If Nicholas was determined to pay her a visit, she would just tell him what she hadn't bothered to write in a farewell note. Summed up? Get lost. She didn't need her Uncle Spence for that.

Nicholas had done his best to sound ominous. Threatening. Paige knew voices. But she also knew that behind Nicholas's menacing bravado lurked a spoiled, overgrown boy-child who talked big, dreamed big, and spun his wheels straight to nowhere. Nicholas Bissonette was mediocre at best, both in terms of his talent and his lovemaking. If he was living near the water in Portland, then he was doing better now financially and probably wanted to show off, especially to the foolish young thing that had dumped him. Paige wouldn't give him the chance.

If anyone does the leaving, Paige, it'll be me, he'd told her once during a late-night call. So many years later, Nicholas's ego still couldn't bounce back. He needed to impress, to show Paige what she was missing. From where Paige sat, the only thing she was missing was being held hostage by a man who hated women. That much was clear from the horrific tableaux she'd come across in that dingy cellar in France.

Half of her day off had been wasted on obsessing over a call from a former lover, and a shitty one at that. Perhaps she could salvage the afternoon, get on her bike, or go for a long walk ...

That private musing brought her full circle and crashing toward the foreboding thoughts that had already crowded her morning. Someone had killed Amber, sliced off her foot, yet left the toe ring intact. Why not remove it? Take the toe, if need be.

The ring was an identifier, and the killer was sending a message, just like Joshua had said. *I found her, I killed her, and I don't care who knows it.*

Worse, Amber's foot was left by Paige's vehicle. Not a coincidence. What if the intended message was: I killed her and I want Paige Rowan to know it?

She struggled with the *why* of it well into the evening. When gray shadows deepened to black, Paige was still searching her memory, recalling conversations with Amber, casual comments that may have had no significance then, but could be vital now. The more she tried, the farther away her memories slipped. The *why* was important, she knew. But the *who* was crucial.

CHAPTER 8

WHEN HER PHONE RANG AT 7:00 p.m. Paige nearly shed her skin. Joshua had already called to check on her and to tell her he wouldn't be able to make it out to the cabin. Someone had broken into the charity's office and had made off with a CD player and portable television. The filing cabinet had been pried open as well, so Joshua needed to make sure all his files were still there.

Paige got to the phone on the third ring. *Nicholas, if it's you again, I'll—*

She picked up the receiver.

"Paige Rowan?"

A female voice. Relief washed over her. "Yes?"

"Fallon McBride. *Clatsop County Examiner*. I understand it was you who found that woman's foot in the state park. Mind if I ask you a few questions?"

"Actually—"

"We could do this over the phone, or we could meet for coffee if you'd rather."

"I told everything I know to the police."

Except how well I knew Bettina Reid. How easily she had concealed the truth. How sick it made her feel.

"Yes, but I'm much more interested in how you're doing, how you're coping …"

"I have no comment, Ms. McBride," she replied stiffly, feeling the muscles in her neck tighten.

"Yours is an interesting story, Paige. I know my readers would benefit from the human aspect, the tale of a woman alone and how she handles a crisis, keeps her head despite her terror ..."

"I'm hanging up, Ms. McBride." And she did.

Fallon McBride exercised her redial option. The phone rang persistently for the next half hour, and it was many minutes after Paige removed the receiver from its cradle that she was able to loosen the tension that had crept into her neck and shoulders. Fallon McBride had the dubious reputation for creating more stir than story and she had amassed a sizeable list of detractors. Paige didn't like her either, particularly since the woman had once shared a few dates with Joshua.

It hadn't been serious, Josh had told her. Fallon had approached him when he had first come to town four years ago. She'd done an article on Joshua and his charity for the *Examiner*. A few statements for the paper turned into a meeting over Irish coffee, then a casual lunch date several days later. Fallon may have been interested in more; Joshua was not. Good, sensible Joshua.

Paige scanned the TV listings. "Cold Case Files." "Criminal Minds." "CSI: Miami." She was surrounded by crime. She felt another clutch at her throat as a fresh thought of Amber intruded. Amber had been rigorously stashing away most of her earnings, saving for gastric bypass surgery. She had already bought a pair of size 14 jeans, had hung them on a hook just inside her kitchen door. A great motivator, she'd said. Something to shoot for.

Dammit, Amber. What happened? Who did you meet?

Fantasy could be a dangerous thing, particularly when its parameters blurred. Both Amber and Lani had spoken about clients who claimed to have fallen in love with them, who believed heart and soul in the lies they were told. Lani thought of her lovestruck client as nothing more than a desperate loser. Amber was different. For her, the declaration of love was a rush, a heady experience and a mainline injection to the ego. All she had to do was talk, and *wham*. She had reached someone, touched something deep within and he had responded. Her Thursday man began depositing gifts in her post office box—a bottle of champagne, a book of poetry, and a cuddly stuffed koala bear, her favorite animal. Amber began to believe, *needed* to believe, that she and her caller had much in common, that he really did care.

Over time, she grew to anticipate his calls and began working from home on Thursday nights. She prepared for their telephone dates by styling her hair, doing her nails, applying make-up, and lighting scented candles. She kept a bottle of Evian on her bedside table, along with a selection of perfumed oils, some feathers, and a vibrator. She invested in a top-of-the-line cordless phone with 90 MHz; there was less static than on her previous model and this one rested more comfortably between her shoulder and ear, allowing both hands to be free.

Amber bragged about her devoted client, a Dr. James Lowrey, she claimed, until the three of them were sick of it. Desire, Dory had told her, was rooted in curiosity and mystery. Take that away and Amber would never hear from her caller again.

But Amber argued. Her weight wouldn't matter, she told them. He truly loved her.

The line between Amber and Bettina became hopelessly muddied. She let her guard down. Amber told her Thursday doctor that she didn't actually look like the picture posted on the website, that in reality she was a rather hefty girl. With coaxing, she described her heaving boobs, her flabby thighs, her dimpled derrière, every square inch of her vast flesh, her voice rising above the groans of the devoted doctor's cataclysmic orgasm. Lowrey continued his Thursday calls, and Amber boasted they were hotter than ever.

See, Dory? she'd said. Maybe all men aren't scum after all.

When they had begun, the four had made a pact—to rendezvous with a caller was *verboten*. They'd sworn—never, never, never, never. Others before them had ignored the rule. One had been beaten, another raped. But nothing like what happened to Amber. They had all manufactured more physically and socially perfect versions of themselves. Had Amber risked all? Had she consented to meet one of her callers face to face?

Paige wondered how long it would be before the police discovered who Bettina Reid really was. Carolyn was a great cop. She'd learn soon enough, without Paige's help.

Excuse me, Officer, but your dead woman, Bettina Reid? She was a phone hooker.

I see. And how do you know this, Ma'am?

It takes one to know one.

Even if news of Paige's former profession didn't make the papers, Carolyn would know. Which meant Joshua would know. And she would lose him. She couldn't let that happen. She loved him. Amber had been thrilled that Paige had found a decent guy, too.

Don't blow it, Paige. Not because of me. Let the police do their jobs. They'll find out who did this to me.

Nice rationalization, she told herself as Amber's imagined words faded. Luckily there wasn't a mirror nearby.

Perhaps there was still something Paige could do for Amber. She reached under her sofa and grabbed her notebook. Settling at one end of the couch with Parker's big head on her lap, she began thumbing through the pages. She would look for a name, a margin note, anything that might spark a memory of a conversation with someone who had struck a false chord. Paige knew it would be like looking for a pin among a heaping pile of pins—as much as the women misrepresented themselves, so did their clients. A truck driver could pass himself off as a millionaire; a millionaire could claim to be a truck driver. In the world of fantasy, anything was possible. And none of it was real.

What if she located that person who sounded the wrong note? What then? An anonymous call to the police, a far-fetched tip that they would be obligated to chase down—she would be just one of the dozens of crackpot callers they would get in the coming days.

Though it was tearing her apart, she hadn't admitted how well she'd known Amber. Couldn't. Lani and Dory would never forgive her. But maybe there was something she could do to make things right. If Amber had spoken to her killer, maybe Paige had too.

She opened her ruled notebook. Paige's list was alphabetical. She began with Angus, who really did speak with a heavy brogue and had a penchant for hearing her spank herself, which she mimicked by slapping a plastic ruler hard onto her coffee table. Angus was good fun—imaginative and humorous. There were three Bills—shy Bill, married-with-four-kids Bill and Old Bill, a client who claimed to be in his seventies, and judging from the tremor in his voice, was probably telling the truth about that. There had been men she'd loathed speaking to—women-haters who spoke of their hands around her throat, who loved to hear her cry out in pain until her voice was hoarse. Orson, a particularly loathsome caller who claimed to be an insurance adjuster, fantasized about placing a plastic bag over her head. While he moaned and grunted, she had to describe the vivid blues and purples her face was turning as she suffocated. Hardly possible if she was really suffocating.

It's the quiet ones you have to watch. Perhaps that was also true in the phone sex arena. The real evil might not lurk in the blatantly perverse, but in the customer who spoke with cool, measured tones. A polite caller. A gentleman.

She had to talk to the others. She was reaching for her phone when it rang. Dory was frantic. "We have to meet. Something's wrong."

"I was just about to call you."

"I'm worried about Amber."

"It's too late for that. Haven't you seen the papers? Call Lani. We've got to talk."

At the other end of the line, Dory sobbed but managed to choke out, "In the village. Paisano's. Half an hour."

CHAPTER 9

PAISANO'S WAS A CONGENIAL BISTRO in the heart of the village that specialized in wood-oven pizza and homemade pasta sauces. Dory had likely chosen the spot because it was always noisy and whatever conversation the three of them would have wouldn't draw a blink. Plus, it was kid-friendly, and Dory would be bringing Sebastian, her six-year-old who loved magic tricks, riding horses and just happened to have Down's Syndrome. It was how Dory always described him, listing all his strengths and likes, mentioning his condition as a mere fraction of the whole, an afterthought.

Though Paige lived the farthest from the village, she was the first to arrive and was directed to a round booth the back of the restaurant near the kitchen. She ordered coffee and wondered what Dory knew. Dory hadn't read the papers—never did—so she hadn't seen the screaming headline in the *Examiner* about the grisly discovery in the state park.

Dory still worked the phone lines, but these days she worked from home, allowing her to be present when the bus dropped Sebastian off after school. She was able to make him supper, read him a story and help him with his schoolwork. Once she tucked him into bed, she became Dallas, a big-haired, busty blonde who never refused a call, never hung up on a caller. In the flesh, Dory was a slender brunette with no visible curves who lived for nothing more than to see her son smile. Sebastian, she said, was the only man she could ever count on.

Lani burst through the door clad in head-to-toe funk. Paige flagged her down. Dory and Sebastian arrived moments later, and the six-year-old had warm hugs for his mother's two friends. He thought Lani's lime fishnets and black miniskirt were cool but thought she should quit smoking because it made her smell bad. Dory shot Lani an apologetic look and distracted her son with a dish of spumoni and a package of crayons. The paper tablecloth soon became a kaleidoscope of color, with the young boy tracing circles around the salt and pepper shakers, expanding the circles to join with others he'd formed around the coffee mugs, sugar container, and teaspoons.

"What is it?" Paige heard the panic in Lani's voice. "What's happened?"

From the inside of a huge handbag, Paige pulled a section from the *Examiner*. Dory and Lani read together. "You found a foot?" Lani's voice rose higher. Even the restaurant's din couldn't muffle her words.

"Worse. It's Amber's. I know it."

"Amber's dead?"

"Who's dead, Mama?" Sebastian set his crayon down. "Do I know her?"

"No, sweet pea." Dory smoothed a cowlick, wiped ice cream from her son's face. Her touch was tender, and she stroked his face long after the traces of the ice cream had disappeared. "Mommy and her friends are just playing a game. It's a mystery game, okay? Can you color me another picture?"

"Sure," Sebastian said, his small face beaming. "What should I draw?"

"Flowers," she told him. "Lots and lots of bright, cheerful flowers." To Lani she said, "Remember the rules of our game. Watch your language."

Sebastian worked on what looked like a basket of tulips. "Yeah," he said. "No swearing."

Paige explained the events surrounding her walk, couching her words in the presence of Dory's son. "I should have called you both yesterday. I'm sorry. But I needed to run away from the awfulness of it, even if only for a day."

She was having trouble forgiving herself for that. And a lot of other things. So many sins.

"You knew it was Amber?" Dory asked. "How?"

"The toe ring Lani bought her. Remember? She was still wearing it."

A small sob escaped from Lani, but Sebastian continued drawing. The tulips now kept company with daisies and patches of blue and orange that Dory told him were magnificent.

"If Amber's been killed, then—"

"Easy, Lani," Dory said, glancing deliberately at her son, "there's no point in getting anyone upset, is there."

Once Lani appeared to have composed herself, Dory continued. "He phoned me. Less than an hour ago. The True Gentleman. He's still looking for Opal."

Lani's face, already pale, went chalk white. "Did he say that?"

Paige added, "Did you tell him Opal doesn't work anymore?"

Dory nodded. "It doesn't matter to him. He wants to find her. Won't stop until he does. Says she's his soul mate, his savior, the love of his life …"

"Okay," Paige said, "so he's got an obsession going. It happens once in a while. No need to panic. Eventually he'll grow tired of the pursuit, find another girl to talk to who revs him up as much as Opal did and he'll move on."

"I don't think so." Dory's voice dropped to a whisper. While Sebastian colored rainbows and dragons beside her, she stroked his fine black hair, praised his artwork, kissed the top of his head. Paige watched how Dory looked at her son, as if she was sending him every ounce of her warmth.

"Why do you say that?"

"He said finding Amber was easy."

Oh God, Paige thought. This was bad. The worst. The True Gentleman had bought the fantasy, was hooked, and intended to stay. Opal was the prize and he wouldn't rest until he got her.

"Did he call Amber too?" Lani said. She tugged at the belled sleeves of her sweater. "Looking for Opal?"

"That's what he told me," Dory said. "Then he said I should read tonight's paper."

Paige directed her gaze at Dory. "The True Gentleman. You think he did this? It didn't sound like a bluff? A hoax?"

Dory's mouth formed a straight line. She glanced down at her son who had completed his masterpiece and was leaning against her, in half-sleep. "No bluff."

"How could you tell?"

"He didn't call me Dallas," she said simply. "He called me Dory."

"Oh, God," Lani whimpered.

Dory inhaled deeply and added, "Then he asked me how Sebastian was."

CHAPTER 10

MULTNOMAH FALLS IS THE HIGHEST waterfall in Oregon, the second or fourth highest in the United States, depending on which guide book a person read. The two-stage chute was created by natural springs and melting snows from Larch Mountain. The scenic area is surrounded by miles of hiking trails, one beginning at the stone lodge at the base and climbing to Benson Bridge, a span which allows visitors to cross the falls between the upper and lower cataracts. Those with good knees could continue upward along steep switchbacks to a lookout above the cascade. In summer particularly, an avid photographer would have to grapple with busloads of tourists in order to get a decent shot of the falls, often having to hang precariously over the railing to avoid capturing a snapshot of a stranger's elbow or nose.

During autumn weeks, with thinner crowds, a backpacker might be afforded more privacy. Equipped with a water bottle, a container of gorp, and decent hiking shoes, someone could make his way to the top of the lookout and have the luxury of an unobstructed vista of the falls below. Seeing no one on the trail or on the bridge, he would be able to remove a green garbage bag from his pack, make sure the plastic twist tie was firmly secure, then toss his cargo over the falls and watch it drop six hundred and twenty feet into the churning pool below. Which is what Sergeant Carolyn Holt determined probably happened. Some time later a local hiker plucked the bag from where it had caught on a fallen tree limb and opened it to discover that it contained a human head.

Paige was grateful for the return to work on Tuesday. Too much time alone had her spooked at shadows, made her dread the phone's ring. She'd slept with the light on, but the ghosts came anyway—specters of Nicholas, her parents, Opal's True Gentleman. And that awful severed foot. Dory had been spooked, too. Normally unflappable, Dory's voice had trembled when she told them what the caller had said, how he'd called her by her real name, asked about her son. Then she had become angry, realizing that Amber, with whom she'd argued a week earlier, had sold her out, had given the caller her real identity. Her address. What else had Amber revealed?

Opal had to stay buried. She should never have been created. Like the myth that surrounded the October gemstone, Opal was bad luck. The persona had inflicted serious damage, an accident that *did* happen. The True Gentleman could not, must not find her.

When Paige entered the store, her co-worker was already reorganizing a display of DEET, snake bite kits and army knives. Seeing her, Lukas Rush dropped several packages of tent pegs and hurried over. "So it's true? You really found that foot? Cool."

Oh, God. She took a deep, measured breath. "Actually, Luke, it wasn't. It was horrible." More than you know, she could have added.

"Yeah, sure, I mean—it's awful that someone's dead, but man, Paige, a *foot*. All I find when I go walking are rusty pop cans and used condoms."

Luke had been hired to work at "The Great Outdoors" a year ago. He had come from Seattle, having been a regular fixture on the grunge music scene there, but Luke also knew everything there was to know about kayaking and cycling. He liked climbing mountains too, and called himself the freakiest of nature freaks. Store owner Harry Washburne insisted he be less freaky on the job, so Luke's dreadlocks were always neatly gathered in a ponytail, his Nirvana and Blind Melon T-shirts traded for oversized Henleys that he tucked into faded Wranglers. Customers liked him and so did Paige, though she found his fascination with all things gruesome tough to take. Despite occasional pleas from Washburne, Luke couldn't be persuaded to surrender a large silver skull ring, a gift from a Goth girlfriend who slept in a coffin.

"I'd really like to forget about the weekend, Luke. Stay busy, you know?"

Luke wasn't finished. "Could be worse, Paige. You only found a foot. What about that guy who found the head?"

"What?"

The floor spun out from beneath her. She clutched a steel clothes rack for support.

"Came on the news last night at eleven. Harry's got a copy of the paper."

Harry Washburne was bent over accounting ledgers in the back room when Paige entered his office on shaky legs. Harry set down his mechanical pencil and said, "Rough weekend, I take it. You okay? You look a little green."

"Is it true? Someone found a head?"

"Poor bastard," Harry said and peered closely at her. "Better sit down before you fall down. I'll get you a coffee."

Harry rattled cups, told Paige he'd already thrown the newspaper in the recycling bin. "I don't think you should read the damn thing anyway. No sense upsetting yourself any more than you have been."

He handed her a mug of tar black coffee and she drank greedily, the strong brew sending a jolt through her that seemed to steady her wobbly legs. Thank you, Harry.

Her boss was a trim man in his mid-fifties who favored preppy clothes, close-cropped hair and long-legged women who didn't mind hoisting a sail. Divorced for twenty years, Harry claimed to prefer his life as a single, but Paige wasn't always convinced. At times, she'd caught her boss during quiet moments of deep introspection, a mask of profound melancholy etched on his face. When questioned, Harry always claimed he was fine. He kept his private thoughts private.

"Better?" Harry asked.

"I will be," Page answered, and hoped it was true.

"Well, here's something to distract you. How'd you like to rub elbows with an honest-to-goodness multi-millionaire?"

"You've lost me, Harry."

"The ecotour," he said. "Mercer Wyatt will be joining you. I'm surprised Luke didn't already spill the news."

"I think Luke's got other things on his mind. Mercer Wyatt? Coming on the trip? He's been a recluse for years."

"You don't have to pinch yourself. It's true. Told me himself it's time he got on with the business of living. Said he's not the first to have a rebellious son run away, and he won't be the last. Poor bastard, though. Even though he's got all those pots of money, I couldn't help feeling for the guy."

Paige recalled reading about the dot-com millionaire in an issue of *Time* a few years back. Wyatt had made his fortune the way so many other entrepreneurs ahead of him had—by logging in eighteen-hour days, seven days a week, sacrificing all to build an empire. With success had come tragedy. Wyatt's wife, Brooke, was diagnosed with uterine cancer. Their only son, Taylor, fourteen years old at the time, kept a bedside vigil while his father shuttled from hospital to office, micromanaging both camps. When Brooke died, Taylor had held her hand. Mercer Wyatt was chairing a meeting with investors from Japan.

For the next four years Taylor existed in a state of nocturnal anarchy. He ingested drugs of every description, slept in alleys, ate discarded food from restaurants. Yet during the day, he always managed to get himself to school. Mercer, bereft at the death of his wife and at a loss as to how to deal with his son, plunged deeper into running his company. Then Taylor disappeared. The photo in *Time* showed a grim Mercer Wyatt reading his son's farewell note.

Dad,

Don't worry. I'm off to look for who I am. When I find me, I'll let you know.

The crackerjack head of security for Wyatt Enterprises helped the millionaire search for his son, but Taylor didn't want to be found. He had, quite simply, vanished. Eight months later, Wyatt purchased a few acres of land on a secluded wooded hill just north of the village and began flying up on weekends to supervise construction of a country getaway, determined, if too late, to strike a balance in his life.

And now he was coming on a wilderness adventure. Paige wondered how much of himself Wyatt would reveal once the campfire was lit. "Well, good for him," she told her boss. "I guess. Should make for an interesting couple of days."

"Be great for business, too. Both mine and Bill's."

Bill Washburne, Harry's brother, owned the *m/v Madrona*, a 1920s wooden boat once chartered for fishing excursions. Now, beautifully restored and updated, the *Madrona* was like a floating lodge that carried ten passengers around the San Juan Islands. The trip that Paige, and now Mercer Wyatt, were booked for, combined cycling, kayaking and hiking. Paige was looking forward to the vacation, and now, it couldn't come too soon.

She added milk to her coffee and returned to the front of the store. Arlen Dale was just opening up across the street, his ear buds glued in place.

"What do you supposed that guy's listening to?" Luke asked. "I'm guessing opera. He strikes me as the theatrical type."

Paige shook her head. "I'm thinking more like 'learning Spanish in ten easy lessons.'"

"*Sí. Es verdad.*"

It was a slow day, customer-wise, so Paige and Luke were able to cart the last of the summer equipment into the basement and do general housekeeping. Paige did the same at home. After walking Parker down her long driveway to get the day's mail, she straightened up her living room, changed the bedding and made sure she had beer and wine in the fridge. Joshua had called while she was still at work and was coming out with pizza and his pajamas.

She donned an old jacket and headed out her back door to where she kept a stack of firewood under her screened-in porch. A crisp chill was in the air, a great night for a roaring fire, some mulled wine and great sex. A few feet away, a startled chipmunk darted across a carpet of dense, dry leaves. As Paige grabbed an arm full of logs, she heard tires crunch on the gravel out front. Parker barked. Paige smiled then wondered why Joshua hadn't tooted on the horn as was his habit. When she returned indoors, she called out, "I didn't hear your horn. And since when do you wear pajamas?"

She entered the living room and saw him sitting on her sofa. At once, her arms turned to water and the logs thudded to the floor.

"Hi, babe. Your front door was open."

CHAPTER 11

Nicholas Bissonette had changed. In the years since she'd seen him, he had eschewed his starving artist uniform of black denim and baggy sweaters in favor of more mainstream attire—khakis, a dark blue shirt, a suede blazer. The shoulder-length hair was gone, too, but he still bore the look of smug arrogance he'd reserved for her during their final weeks together. Now the sneer was permanently etched on his face, the corners of his mouth curving upward as though already mocking her.

Paige directed a steady glare at him. "Get out of my house."

He rose from the sofa and came toward her. Parker, sensing a threat, stood alongside her and emitted a low growl. "Easy, boy," Nicholas said. "Paige, call that mutt off. I just want to help you with the firewood."

She made no move to call off the dog. "I don't need help. What I need is for you to leave."

"Be reasonable, babe. I drove over here from Portland just to see you. What's it gonna hurt to spend some time catching up? Besides, things are different now." He lifted his chin toward one of the long multi-paned windows on either side of the fireplace. Outside was a silver Porsche Boxster. "I'm different now. See? Two hundred and twenty-five horses under the hood. Isn't it a gem?"

Paige gave the sports car a cursory glance then turned to face him again. "Great. You can ride all two hundred and twenty-five horses out of here."

He was deaf to her dismissal. "You look good, Paige," he said, eyeing her curly blonde hair, her cargo pants, her Kodiak boots. "Very outdoorsy."

"As I recall, you never much cared for outdoorsy. You were more into that come-to-the-cabaret look. But none of that matters now. I've never been a fan of history. Especially ours. So go."

Parker growled again.

"Not until you at least agree to have dinner with me."

"There's no bargaining here, Nicholas. This is my house. You're in it. I didn't invite you."

"Guess you don't remember who you're talking to." He took a step toward her.

She planted her feet, stood firm. "Don't you dare try to bully me. I'm not nineteen anymore. Now in case you're hard of hearing, I've asked you to leave. Twice. Call it trespass, harassment—I'm sure the police won't have any trouble coming up with a name for what you're doing when I call them, which I plan to do right now."

Paige fixed her gaze on him but moved toward her phone. Nicholas held up a shaky hand. "Don't get your thong in a knot, babe. We'll do this some other time. Count on it."

It shouldn't have been that easy. Nicholas had always been accustomed to the upper hand. During their two years together, Paige had never won a single argument. His vote always counted double—*we'll go to this movie, we'll have this for dinner, we'll have sex now and in this position*—and Paige usually went along. It was easier, and she always rationalized that she would pick her battles, save the quarrelling for when it was really warranted. Why then, when Nicholas had driven over an hour to see her, was he knuckling under so quickly?

Police. A common, six-letter word, yet the mere mention of it had been enough to propel him toward the door.

What are you afraid of, Nicholas? What have you done?

Through the front window, Paige saw Joshua's Jeep pull up. He didn't sound the horn; the sight of an unfamiliar vehicle, a Porsche no less, would give him pause. Joshua stepped from the Jeep carrying a pizza box and looking puzzled.

"Something you want to tell me, babe?" Nicholas said over his shoulder.

"Not a thing," she replied. "Bye."

There was no way to prevent it. Nicholas opened the door and the two men stood face to face. An awkward, sour silence hung in the air, and both men waited for Paige to end it with an introduction.

Instead, she rushed over to Joshua and planted a kiss on his cheek. "There you are! Come on in. I'm starved." To Nicholas, she said coolly, "Good luck. I'm sure you'll meet with continued success." In an efficient series of moves, she tugged Joshua inside by the sleeve of his jacket and used the door to nudge Nicholas out of her house. Seconds later the Porsche spun on gravel as it screeched off.

"What the hell was that about?" Joshua said. "I've never seen you treat anyone like that." He looked over at the scattering of fire logs on the floor between the kitchen and dining area. "What went on here?"

Paige was already setting the pizza down on the coffee table in the living room. "I'll explain, but I need a drink first." She brought Joshua a beer and poured herself a full glass of Australian shiraz, not caring about giving the wine breathing space in the goblet's bowl. She took her time lifting slices of pizza onto stoneware plates, returned to the kitchen for napkins and the bottle of wine, made the trip again to retrieve the logs and set them on top of the kindling already in the hearth.

Joshua drank his beer from the bottle, lit a trio of pillar candles on the table, but Paige felt his gaze on her as she flitted about, stalling for time, selecting her words. Then there was nothing more to do but settle onto the carpet, cross-legged beside him and tell the story.

"I told you I spent a few years in France. After high school."

"Yeah. Your uncle sent you. I remember. Sounds kind of glamorous."

"I thought so too. For quite a while. The man you just saw was part of that time." How she hated the sound of that. "Joshua, have you ever wished anything undone? I mean, wished it so much you could almost believe it had never happened, that it was really someone else's story?"

"We've all got those crappy memories, Paige. That's why you won't catch me at any high school reunions. I don't want reminders of what a horse's ass I was."

He smiled, and she knew he was trying to lighten the moment for her. She watched him press the beer bottle to his lips, longed to feel those lips on hers and forget that Nicholas had ever existed. When she was with Joshua, she could almost believe it. Could almost believe she'd never come across that monstrosity in the basement of their apartment building that winter day. Could almost believe that the man who had drawn such grotesque work had never touched her bare flesh.

Between nervous sips of wine, she told Joshua about Chamonix, about the first few months and what they had represented to her—freedom, adventure, romance. At first it had been good between her and Nicholas, but the relationship began to deteriorate about the same time as his frequent descents into his basement studio. What initially seemed to be Nicholas's artistic temperament soon metamorphosed into a constant darkness of mood, one in which accusations were hurled too easily and too often. "I was never pretty enough, never sexy enough. And he was painting portraits of so many women wearing next to nothing. I knew there had to be more going on. I felt so crummy about myself, which actually seemed to turn him on. Thank God I got out." She couldn't bring herself to speak about the hideous visions she encountered in the dim light of the cellar.

"So what's the guy want with you now after all this time? Is he stalking you?"

Paige shook her head vigorously, perhaps to convince herself. "Nicholas is a big kid. I think he came here to strut his stuff, to show me he's moving up in the world. He probably thought I'd be impressed and fall all over him and his Porsche. Now that I haven't, he'll leave me alone."

"Let's hope so." He refilled her wineglass and took a sip from it before handing it to her. "Paige, if this guy becomes trouble, you'll tell me, won't you? I mean it. Don't hide anything from me. Deal?"

Here was her chance. She could tell Joshua everything. That being with Nicholas wasn't the worst decision she'd ever made, that she'd taken a seedy job because she needed cash, and more foolishly, simply to feel that for once, someone was listening to her. She thought once more of Lani and Dory, and the domino effect her coming forward would have on their lives. She could swear Joshua to secrecy, if indeed he ever spoke to her again. She could beg Carolyn not to question her friends, and insist that they had no helpful information to offer about Amber's killer.

She took a generous sip of wine and privately rehearsed what she would say. For a moment, she tried to appreciate the robustness and the smoky aroma promised on the wine's label, but could discern neither. The words she intended to say got stuck, along with the wine, somewhere in her throat. Instead she said, "Deal."

She bit into a slice of pizza but it was already stone cold.

CHAPTER 12

DON'T HIDE ANYTHING FROM ME.

Long after Joshua had drifted off to sleep, Paige heard his words echo in her mind. She tried at first to lose herself in the rhythmic lullaby of his breathing. She pressed herself against his back with her bent knees tucked firmly behind his, felt the warmth of his bare skin next to hers. She struggled to bring details of their earlier lovemaking forward, hoping the resurrected pleasure of it all would ease her into sleep, but the memories would not surface, not as a complete movie. She only glimpsed disjointed scenes—a kiss, a caress, a murmur—voyeuristic snapshots out of sequence that roused her to a state of pop-eyed wakefulness. In the dark, she knew why both sleep and pleasant memories eluded her—she had hidden things from Joshua. So many things.

Why had she concealed the horror she had seen in that dingy cellar? She had been young when she moved into that dismal apartment with Nicholas. Naïve. Impressionable. She couldn't have known the monstrous ideas that lurked in Nicholas's imagination. Or what a monster Nicholas had become. *We've all got crappy memories, Paige.* The type of person she was then no longer existed.

But what of her more blatant omission? *Joshua, I meant to tell you, but somehow it slipped my mind. I worked as a phone actress for a year.*

Loyalty to her friends? Absolutely. But she had selfish motives too. Joshua would leave her. The man who'd come so close to being a priest, might find her ... sullied. Unworthy. As dirty as she felt when she thought about it all.

Phone actress. A euphemism for phone whore. That's what Dory used to call them, and she was proud of it. It was all a game to her, and she often boasted of drilling her clients to the last drop, maxing out their credit cards and still have them dialing for more. Dealing with the occasional violent calls was a temporary, necessary evil. Job stress. And besides, if callers were venting their hostilities via the telephone, then they wouldn't be enacting their fantasies in real life. According to Dory, the phone whores were vigilantes.

It had begun innocently enough. Wasn't that what people always said before they embarked on something reckless?

I didn't mean it, honey. It just happened.

It was a lark. Who got hurt, really?

Four young women, taking a night class in Women's Studies, a second-year sociology course, four women who gathered for coffee during the break and shared tales about their miserable lots in life. Dory, trying to complete her degree part-time while raising her child; Bettina, saving for surgery, finding it tough to land a job because of her size; best friend Lani, aspiring romance writer, estranged from her upper middle-class parents and needing money; and Paige, who was determined to pay back the person who meant the most to her, her Uncle Spence. So on a February night, when sleet made the roads slick and Dory's liqueur-laced hot chocolate went down too smoothly, the quartet was born. Amber, Dallas, Laurel and Opal.

They approached their new venture as if starting their own business. They investigated the different types of phone sex operations, zeroing in on those that were widely advertised in several men's magazines over the course of many months. This, according to Dory, was a reasonable indicator that the company was more legitimate and likely to be around for a while. Eventually, after much discussion, deliberation and many glasses of wine, the women decided to go with a 900 service. In the industry, 900 numbers were considered to be an antiquated type of operation which was what made it the most appealing to the four of them. The 900 numbers were heavily regulated by the Federal Communications Commission; while indecent speech was protected by the First Amendment, obscene speech was not. In short, the women working the lines couldn't discuss anything illegal. No talking about rape or sex with minors or incest scenarios. The four thought such a service would help weed out the kinky customers.

They did other research too, watching porn videos together and making notes, testing their racy vocabulary on each other until words rarely spoken by them became second nature. They read erotic stories on the Internet, which Lani really enjoyed. They rehearsed every conceivable fantasy and scenario, sometimes sickened by what another had invented, sometimes collapsing in fits of laughter. By the time they applied for the jobs, they felt well seasoned, as though they'd heard it all. They hadn't.

They had steeled themselves for the cross-dressing fantasies, the fetishists, the bondage freaks, the callers who wanted a domination/submission scene played out. Paige and Lani refused to speak with anyone interested in torture or mutilation. Both knew that the longer they stayed in the game, the fuzzier the boundaries became between what would be refused and what would be tolerated, so they promised each other—no trespassing into dark territory. Bettina and Dory, more desperate for quick cash and plenty of it, were less discriminating.

The four stood resolute about the client-operator relationship. It was strictly business. No freebies, not even for birthdays or for those claiming to be between jobs or on their deathbeds. And definitely no leaking personal information.

The True Gentleman began phoning in March. Opal created stories for him about candlelit evenings in chilly castles, her wearing a flowing velvet gown, her tiny bosom heaving over a low-cut neckline. Over the course of their meal her breasts would strain at the taut fabric until they were fully exposed. Unable to resist any longer, he would sweep her into his arms and carry her up a wide, winding concrete staircase. Their lovemaking took place in a massive canopy bed, with the gentleman lifting layers and layers of skirts and crinolines to expose pale white legs and labia that glistened with desire. Opal enjoyed conversations with her romantic gentleman and, like Amber with her Thursday doctor, began to anticipate his calls. Her mistake was in telling him so.

Paige was the first of the four to abandon the phone lines. At first, she found the job boring. The money wasn't all she'd heard it could be, there were no benefits or bonuses, and the hours were brutal. Later it became depressing. She began to wonder whether everyone she saw on the village streets withheld some dark fantasy. What about the mechanic who'd winterized her car, the waiter who'd served her at the diner, the guy who'd bagged her groceries? Did everyone with a Y chromosome secretly want to wear lingerie, share two women, screw a midget?

In the end, the whole scene was just plain scary. The supervisor grew impatient with Paige, told her she would have to accept more challenging calls, that it wasn't fair for the others to shoulder all the tough customers. By the time her first three-way call came in, she was already cleaning out her cubicle. For what was proclaimed to be a progressive, liberal industry, the phone sex business, to Paige, was nothing more than another ultra-conservative method to keep women subservient and dependent. Wasn't that what she'd been running from?

One month after Paige quit the lines, she received a call from Lani.

"Paige? Can you come? I've done ... something's happened."

Lani lived in a one-bedroom apartment at the south end of the village. The door was unlocked by the time Paige arrived. The place was dark, save for a slender shaft of yellow that stretched across the living room rug. Paige hurried toward the light. Inside the bathroom, she witnessed a scene of carnage, the horror before her making her faint, dizzy. The bathtub was a vat of blood. Arterial spray dotted the tiled walls. It was as if a mad butcher had been turned loose and had used the room as his abattoir. Lani, completely naked, sat on the toilet seat, knees pulled up to her chest, her bare feet having left a trail of crimson footprints across the white floor. A heap of bloody towels lay at the base of the pedestal sink. Her arms, wrapped in more towels, hugged her knees, the direct pressure of her wrists against her legs apparently stanching the flow of blood. Lani's skin was the color of snow.

"It ... really hurts, Paige."

Oh, no, Lani. Not again.

Lani refused to go to the hospital. "I'm all right. Now that you're here. You always know what to do."

"But I don't, Lani. Not this time. I need help."

In the end, Paige used her knowledge of first aid and improvised as best she could until paramedics arrived. She grabbed a fresh towel to apply gentle pressure to the wound and forced herself to keep her supper down when she saw the jagged cuts along her friend's wrists, the spidery network of hesitation wounds. She swaddled Lani in flannel pajamas, tugged thick socks onto her cold clammy feet and guided her into the living room where she made her lie down with feet and injured arm elevated, to wait for the ambulance.

At the hospital, Lani was treated for shock and Paige paced the waiting room floor, relieved when she was told her friend would be just fine. A psychiatric assessment would follow in the morning. Paige was given permission to visit with Lani and she sat alongside her on the bed, crooning that everything would be all right. She promised that she wouldn't call Lani's parents. Lani's mother was a judge, up for re-election. The Hollises didn't need the headlines, and Lani didn't need yet another lecture on what a disappointment she was. Eventually Lani dozed off and seemed, for a time, at peace.

During the quiet night, Paige returned to her friend's apartment and scrubbed the bathroom, spending hours removing the traces of the ghastly havoc that had taken place within the tiled walls. When Lani was released, Paige took time off work and brought her to the cabin, made soup, played soft music, waited. Finally, the story came.

A client. He'd seemed harmless, just another run-of-the-mill lonely guy who wanted to feel less lonely. That was what the supervisor told Lani, so Lani took the call.

She tried to read his signals, give him what he wanted but he complained that nothing was working, that the right mix wasn't there. After a time, Lani grew weary and frustrated, wanting nothing more than for the caller to swear at her and hang up. Then it happened.

A child's voice. *"No. I don't want to play."*

"Guess what I have in front of me?" the caller asked.

"Hey, look, I don't do—"

"She's about four, isn't that right, sweetheart? With lovely red ringlets and a shower of freckles across her fat little cheeks. And I've got something else you'd be interested in."

"We're not allowed to—"

"It's a cross. A wooden cross. And how about that? Here are some nails."

There was a thunderous bang and an ear-splitting scream.

"You sick fuck! Stop!"

Lani heard another crack, a hammer pounding hard on wood. And another high-pitched scream that went on forever, kept playing in her head long after she'd slammed the phone down.

Paige felt her stomach turn over, but kept her emotions hidden from Lani who whimpered as she struggled to get the story out. "You ... you told the supervisor, of course."

Her friend nodded. "Said she'd check it out."

Paige said nothing, knowing the agency wouldn't follow through. She had never heard of any caller being barred from the lines, nor was she convinced that the supervisor and the orange-haired security guard would act on Lani's or any other operator's behalf. It was a promise made, never kept.

"It wasn't real," Paige said at length. "The caller used a tape recording of a child's scream. Probably pounding nails into a plank in his garage. Don't you see? Your fear ... your revulsion. That's what he was counting on to get himself off. It wasn't real, Lani," she said again. "None of it."

And they weren't real either. Not Amber. Not Dallas. Not Laurel. Not Opal. They were cardboard, cartoon cut-outs—women who lied for a living, women who, if they weren't careful, could be subjected to the worst kind of mindfuck. And it had worked on Lani, almost costing her everything. The pale, lightning-bolt scars on her wrists were superficial reminders; the damage done by the sadist cut much deeper, etching ugly marks on her very soul.

Paige wondered as well what effect the work had wrought upon her. When half-truths were uttered so easily and parts of her were so skillfully concealed, could she really say she had left the job behind? Wasn't she still the same phone whore, showing Joshua a more perfect version of herself and revealing only what she was certain he would approve of, what he would desire?

Joshua was in the deep-breathing stage of sleep, his arms curled around his pillow. Paige drew the blanket over his bare shoulder and crept from the bed, stepping over Parker who was stretched out on the rug. She grabbed a crocheted afghan from her living room sofa, wrapped it around her and went out to her screened porch. The night air was cold but it helped clear her head.

There *was* still something she could do for Amber. She had to confirm for the police how Bettina Reid paid her university tuition and her rent. They had to know about the True Gentleman.

She would call Carolyn in the morning. Once she came forward with the information, everything would be all right. It had to be.

CHAPTER 13

THE LOCAL NEWS THE NEXT morning put a hitch in Paige's good intentions. She and Joshua were having orange juice and croissants in bed when the television news anchor declared that the remains found in the state park and below the falls had been conclusively identified as belonging to Bettina Reid, 24, of 145 Chilton Way, Portland.

Paige swallowed hard and said, "Oh God, it really is her."

"You were up and around last night." Joshua set his glass on the bedside table and reached for her hand. "Did you get any sleep at all?"

"Not much, no."

Lani called first. "One of the bastards killed her. Poor Bettina."

"I'm going to the police," Paige told her.

"You can't," Lani wailed. "They'll cut me off without a dime, you know it."

No more scandals, Lani's parents had threatened. Any hint of impropriety and they would strike her from their will.

"I won't involve you. Won't mention your name. Dory's either."

"It'll come out. Once Fallon McBride gets wind of this, we'll be front-page news. Phone Hookers Linked to Killer. Paige, you *can't*."

"It's Joshua's sister we're talking about here. You don't know the position you're putting me in."

"I'm begging you, Paige."

Dory's call came fifteen minutes later.

"You're going to the cops?" she shrieked. "Are you out of your mind? You really want me to lose Sebastian?"

"I can keep you out of it. But they've got to know."

"Know what? That some guy killed Amber? It could have been anyone. We can't prove it's the True Gentleman or any of the other callers."

"Come on, Dory."

"Paige, I mean it. I'm on my third strike. If the courts find out how I'm making extra cash, they'll take Sebastian. I won't let you do that. You promised."

So to Sergeant Carolyn Latham Holt, Paige admitted only that she knew Bettina well. She was a nice girl with a huge crush on Johnny Depp. She was frustrated with her history of yo-yo dieting, and had mentioned something about the possibility of gastric bypass surgery.

"That procedure's supposed to be a last resort," Carolyn said. "Expensive, too. Maybe that explains why she had ten grand in the bank. Where do you suppose she got that kind of money?"

Paige took a deep breath. "Bettina worked the phone lines. You know, phone sex." Paige was glad she had decided to call Carolyn at the station, glad Joshua's sister couldn't see her face which she was sure was now flushed red. "Maybe one of the callers was some kind of kook," she added.

"Okay, Paige," Carolyn said, her voice hesitant. "Every little bit helps. How are you doing, by the way?"

"Still a little shaky."

"Understandable. Get that brother of mine to take good care of you, and Paige? If you remember anything else, you know where I am."

On Thursday night, Dory Getz was drying the last of the supper dishes, shuffling her feet to the "Shoop-Shoop" song on the radio. Sebastian sat at the kitchen table and added a school of brightly-colored speckled fish to his undersea drawing. Dory had already explained how fish breathed under water, what they ate, how they protected themselves from their enemies.

"Mom?"

"What is it, Bear?"

"I've got polka-dot fish and striped fish." He examined his artwork. "Is there any such thing as plaid fish?"

She gave him a wide smile. "In art, anything is possible."

Sebastian placed three crayons side by side—one pink, one lilac, one lime green. "Would these make a good plaid?"

Dory folded the hand towel, tucked it into the handle of the fridge and walked over to where her son sat. She planted a noisy kiss on the top of his head. His giggle was irresistible. "I think your other fish will be jealous of how handsome the checkered guy will look."

Her portable phone rang, one short, one long. Dory frowned then picked up. "Hello?"

"Is this Miss Dallas?" A soft voice, the trace of a southern accent.

Dory looked at the wall clock. 7:00. Dammit. What kind of snafu was this? She didn't go on the clock for another two hours.

She glanced over at Sebastian who was adding what appeared to be bunches of pink and purple cauliflower to the bottom of his drawing. Coral, she decided.

"Yes, but—"

"Oh, go-o-o-od," the voice drawled, oozing North Carolina. "Because I just *love* talkin' to you."

Wait a minute. A joke. That was it. "Ben, you rotten bugger ... "

Sebastian looked up, wagged a shame-shame finger at her.

"Sorry, sweetie," she said, placing her hand over the mouthpiece. "Mommy was wrong."

Ben Fahey was one of two males who worked at the agency. He had a melodious voice, had played in dozens of area dinner theatre productions, and masqueraded on the phone lines as Mistress Patrice, a much-in-demand black dominatrix. Ben was artistic temperament personified, his moods swinging widely from lovable jokester to sarcastic harridan during a single late-night shift. Dory never knew which face he was going to show, so during those months she'd worked in the phone room, she usually steered clear. She thought Ben would have forgotten about her by now and guessed that Thursdays must be slow for black dominatrices.

"Look Ben, this isn't funny. You know I spend this time with my son."

"I surely do," came the answer, "but I do believe you've got me confused with someone else. And how is that delightful boy of yours? He really is quite a little artist, isn't he?"

Talons of fear raked her back. She glanced out her kitchen window, the blinds still raised from when she'd let in the afternoon sun. Beyond the blackness was an apartment building, with dozens of yellow rectangles facing her rear yard.

"Honey," she called gently to her son, "why don't you take that drawing into the other room? You can put the TV on."

"Neat!" Sebastian packed away his crayons, dropped a few on the floor, spent agonizing moments picking them up and returning them to the box. He took more time tearing his drawing away from the large pad of manila paper before finally leaving the kitchen.

Dory reached over to shut off the radio. Along the top of her son's picture, he'd printed in red crayon: I ♥ U MOMY.

Her throat threatened to close, a swelling of emotion so great she feared she couldn't speak. Quickly, she turned the drawing over. Control. That's what she needed. She was the phone expert, not this crazy bastard.

"You can drop that Grand Ole Opry accent, you sick son of a bitch. I know who you are."

"Do you really, Dory, my dear?"

British now. Gentleman, my ass. And he called her Dory, not Dallas.

"I believe we've clearly established that I know who *you* are. And *where* you are. But what, really, do you know about me?"

"Well, now, why don't you just tell me a little about yourself?" She was Dallas now, her voice taking on just enough of a haughty edge.

I'm in charge, you miserable, pathetic fuck.

"I vas born in small village in Croatia, son of simple, honest peasants. They vanted me to be priest."

She heard his soft chuckle, and something else. Metal scraping metal. Again she peered through her window to the apartment building beyond. *Which one, you shit? Where are you?*

"Enough with the accents," she said, willing the tremor from her words. *Come on, Dallas. Strut your stuff.* "Or is that all part of it? You're too scared to show me who you really are, so you hide behind—"

"Scared? Oh my dear Dory, it seems you don't know me well at all. Very little frightens me. I couldn't say the same for your friend Amber, though. Or was it Bettina? How confused you all must be at times. Do you know why I cut her up?"

Oh God, oh Christ, what was this?

"Because I couldn't lift her. My word, she was huge, wasn't she? E-fucking-normous!"

His laughter peeled through the phone, pierced her heart. Yet she steeled her jaw, squared her shoulders and said, "This is such bullshit. You can't even speak to me in your real voice. There's nothing real about you, is there! You think you can call people up, spout a bunch of shit that anyone can learn from a newspaper—"

"Oh my, Dory, it won't help to get angry, now will it? The police always keep a little something back from the press. But you and I know that Amber wore a ring on the second toe of her right foot. A silver ring with a blue stone. I left the ring on when I removed her foot."

She barely made it to the sink. Supper came up, sour and hot. At the other end of the phone, the low, amused chuckle.

"But that's old news," he said when he sensed she was through. "Let me offer you another incentive. Then perhaps you'll answer the one simple question I've put to you previously."

Dory heard the sound of something tearing, then a quiet whimper. Like a woman gone mad, she raced into the hall, relieved to see Sebastian sitting knees to chest in front of the television.

He's not in the house. What were you thinking?

Then: "Dallas?"

The voice was feminine, familiar. Where had she heard it?

"It's Jasmine."

From the agency. Jasmine was a middle-aged blonde who had been working the phones for years. She remembered that Jazz preferred the cubicle farthest from the ceiling vent, claiming the air conditioning dried out her contact lenses. Dory struggled to gather a complete image of the woman, but all she could recall of Jasmine was that she was unremarkable.

Again: "Dallas? Amber never liked you and me. She told him who we are."

"Jazz, where are you? Who is the bastard?"

She heard a strangled cry, then the dulcet tones of the gentleman in the background. "My, this could become quite unpleasant. Be very careful now, dear Jasmine."

"Tell him, Dallas," she urged. "Tell him I don't know who Opal is. Or where she is." There was a strangled sob. "*Please*, Dallas."

"Jazz? A name—quick!"

"I—"

She heard a loud crash followed by a thud, then, "Oh my, didn't that make a mess on my floor. Can't have Jasmine giving away all my secrets, now can I?"

"Leave her alone!" Dory's heart hammered in her chest. "What do you want?"

An eternity passed, Dory hearing nothing but her own rapid breath, the tinny laughter coming from the television in the next room. When he spoke again, his voice was whisper soft. "You know what I want. Where's Opal?"

"I already told you," she pleaded. "I don't know."

"How sad," the True Gentleman sighed. "That won't bode well for poor Jasmine when she comes to. And her having a sick mother to care for. Such a shame."

"None of this is real. You're not real. You're just a fucking psycho! Get yourself some fucking help!"

Sebastian stood in the doorway, a look of alarm clouding his small face.

Once more, the quiet British voice crooned in her ear. "Remember your friend Amber? I'll just let her wish you pleasant dreams, Dory."

She heard a click followed by the sound of a door opening and closing.

"Stop! I'll do anything!"

No, no, *no*. Amber's voice. He had recorded Amber's voice.

"I—"

There was a raw, straight-to-the-soul scream, then something worse. Silence.

"Mommy!" Sebastian cried out as Dory hurled the phone through the window.

CHAPTER 14

Harry Washburne shoved aside a cold cup of coffee and spread *The Clatsop Examiner* out on his desk. Lukas Rush leaned over his boss's shoulder and read. Fallon McBride had captured the front page scoop.

Both men looked up as Paige entered the room. "TGIF," she said, but neither responded. "What's up?"

"You haven't seen the paper, I guess," Harry said.

Paige's boss looked haggard, as though he'd paced the floor all night with a colicky infant. His eyes were hauling king-sized luggage and his face seemed to sag with the weight of some dark worry.

"No. Why?"

"Another body." Luke's eyes sparked as he told her about the surfer who'd made the grisly discovery as he'd carried his board down to Short Sands Beach, following the same trail as thirty-some-odd other surfers had done that same day, hoping to catch some decent waves. "Says here he just happened to turn to his left, thought at first he was looking at an old burnt log then he noticed her hands. Couple of birds were snacking on her pretty good."

"No need for that, Luke." Harry, in his advanced state of fatigue, clearly wasn't in the mood for Luke's fascination for the macabre this morning. Paige wasn't up for it either.

"Short Sands Beach. That's in Oswald West State Park. Just south of here. You won't catch me surfing at Shorty's anymore."

"The police aren't concluding it's the same killer."

"This one wasn't cut up," Luke said. "Different signature. Different pattern. They're saying this one was suffocated."

"They already know that?" Paige said.

Luke nodded. "Suffocation, like with a pillow over the face, doesn't leave much trace evidence for the medical examiner. None of that cyanosis or petachial hemorrhaging unless there was a major struggle."

Paige blinked hard. "How do you know all this stuff?"

"Call it a hobby," Luke replied.

And too much CSI, Paige thought. Harry must have agreed because he said, "Luke, that new shipment of sunglasses needs to be displayed in the front case. And call Freda MacIntyre and tell her the kayak she wants is back-ordered, but she'll still have it in plenty of time for Christmas."

"I get the hint," Luke said and moved toward the door.

"No flies on you," Harry said.

When Luke was gone, Paige sat down on the chair in front of her boss's desk. "Do they know who the woman was?"

Harry traced a finger down the newsprint. "Sarah Lydell. Forty-five years old. Cashier at a supermarket up the coast. Seems she cared for her mother who's in a wheelchair. The mother got worried when her daughter didn't show up with her supper after work, which she always did."

"How awful."

Harry nodded. "Never used to be like this around here."

Oregon's homicide rate, according to Carolyn who was a walking statistics whiz, had been declining steadily over the past decade. The smallest county, Multnomah, in which Portland was situated, had a disproportionate number of murders, a whopping forty percent of the state's total. Last year, their own county had only three homicides. Though it was still three too many, residents continued to feel they were living in a safe environment and that these were the good old days. Now, in less than two weeks, two women were dead.

Paige was eager to leave the room before Harry began waxing nostalgic, but as she rose from the chair, she felt her gaze drawn to the upside down view of a grainy photo on the paper's front page. She spun the paper to face her.

"Pretty lousy picture, I'd say," Harry told her. "You'd think someone could have found a more flattering photo. This one looks like a mug shot."

Sarah Lydell. She looked older than forty-five in the picture, her blonde hair styled in a bushy spiral perm that made her already large head appear enormous. She was frowning, almost scowling, as though the photographer had caught her before she was ready but clicked the shutter anyway. Paige stared at the Lydell woman, mentally erased the perm and imagined a sleeker bob. It couldn't be. Yet Paige knew she had seen that scowl before, only briefly, but she'd seen it. When Sarah Lydell got a deadbeat on the phone, a caller who tried to schmooze and charm his way into a freebie, she wore that look.

But Paige only knew her as Jasmine. Cubicle 8. The worker who'd handed her disinfectant spray for her phone the first night on the job.

"Paige, is something wrong?" Harry was staring at her, his expression full of both curiosity and worry. "You don't know her, do you?"

"No, Harry, I don't know her." She folded the paper. "It's just sad, that's all. The mother in the wheelchair and everything."

Harry said nothing but continued staring.

"You get some sleep tonight, Harry."

Paige rushed from the room. She had to call the others.

CHAPTER 15

"GODDAMN! DID YOU HEAR THAT?" A rotund and balding racquetball player stepped from the shower stall and wrapped a towel around his waist. Seconds later there was another ominous rumble overhead, punctuated with a deafening clap of thunder. "Storm season. You'd think I'd be used to it by now."

Joshua thought of Paige's dog, who was now likely cowering under the bed with its huge paws over its eyes. Parker didn't like storms either.

The rain had forced Joshua indoors. He and Carolyn intended to go for a quick morning kayak ride, but they postponed their plans for calmer weather. It wasn't so much that they minded getting wet—that's what wetsuits were for, but they were justifiably leery of the southerly winds that were a harbinger of unstable conditions. High clouds had gathered in the sky this morning, too, and the telltale ring around the sun signified the arrival of a front. An adventure would be one thing—suicide quite another. Judging by the crowd inside the health club, others' plans had been foiled, too, and there were line-ups at almost every weight machine.

The twins' battle of the abs had been no contest today, Carolyn only managing to complete half as many pull-ups as her brother. Josh claimed he wasn't counting, but his sister was clearly suffering from too much caffeine and too little sleep. Or something else. Physically, Carolyn had been moving like a rusty robot lately. Finding the Lydell woman had dumped a tremendous burden on her shoulders and her body was buckling.

"Probably get a case of raging warts from these floor tiles," the stout man complained, drying off then tossing the towel into a metal bin.

Joshua ignored the man's grumbling. He dressed quickly and towel-dried his hair. It was still too early in the morning and he didn't have the patience for locker room chat.

Minutes later he was sitting in the health club's small café with two glasses of orange juice and a couple of whole wheat bagels. Carolyn was emerging from the women's change room. Judging from her appearance, a workout and bracing shower had done little to invigorate her. Josh thought his sister would benefit more from a tranquilizer dart and three days in isolation.

"Two victims," he said. "Making any headway?"

"Depends on what you mean by headway." Carolyn spread strawberry jam on half her bagel, marmalade on the other half. Long moments were spent with her appearing to consider which to bite into first. "Reid was a twenty-four-year-old student. She lived in Portland. Lydell was late-forties, worked at the Safeway in Seaside. No evidence they knew each other. At least, not yet. Of course, the Reid girl didn't have a large circle to begin with. Landlord never saw her with anyone. We've got a list of classes she was enrolled in at the university so we're tracking down her profs to see if they remember anything about her other than her size."

"Did Sarah Lydell have any connection with the university?"

Carolyn shook her head. "Had a small apartment over on Prescott. Walked to work. Took the bus to and from her mother's place every day. Salt of the earth, so everyone said, but then again, aren't they all?"

"Lydell wasn't cut up."

"Small woman. Stood about five-one, one hundred and fifteen pounds. Easy enough to carry. Different story with the Reid girl."

Joshua recalled the television photo of Bettina Reid, posed beside, of all things, a bright red Mini Cooper. Someone's idea of a joke, posing her beside that puny car.

"Must have been tough on her, being that size. Physically and emotionally."

"Yeah, and what would you say if I told you she talked dirty for a living?"

"Where'd you hear a crazy thing like that?"

"Paige called me. We're checking it out."

He lifted his glass of juice and took a long drink. "Hard to imagine, yet it makes sense. Hiring plus-sized people costs companies too much in health benefits. And the perception is that they take too many sick days."

"But working the phones, Reid can pass herself off as a slim buxom whatever and no one's the wiser. Perfect job for her."

"And she told this to Paige?"

"Apparently."

"Wonder why Paige didn't mention it to me?"

Carolyn shrugged. "Friends don't rat each other out. How's she doing?"

"Some trouble sleeping. I've been keeping a close eye on her."

"I can imagine," Carolyn said, the first trace of life appearing in her smile.

"Knock it off."

As quickly as the smile came, it disintegrated. "Oh, shit." Carolyn set her bagel down and wiped a glob of jam from the corner of her mouth.

"What?"

"I've got Fallon McBride in my sights, twenty paces behind your left shoulder and bearing down steadily. Double fucking shit."

Then she stood before them, close enough for Joshua to see the scattering of freckles across her pale skin. Her straight black hair was gathered into a messy topknot. A well toned, bare midriff teased him at eye level.

"I'd say funny running into you both here," she flashed a blinding smile, "but where else is there to go on a miserable morning like this?"

"Ms. McBride," Carolyn said.

"Hi Fallon."

She directed another 100-watt smile at Joshua then turned her attention to his sister. "You've certainly got your hands full these days, Sergeant. Any leads on either of those murders?"

"You've spoken with our media rep, Ms. McBride. You got your story."

"But there must be something else. You guys always hold something back."

"That's why it's called 'holding back.'"

Joshua couldn't resist a grin. "She does have you there, Fallon."

"Fair enough. For now. You'll both be watching my television debut, I hope?"

"What's that you say?"

"An hour-long documentary for the local cable network." She was having a tough time keeping the pride from her voice. "Cults. Specifically, the Greenes."

"Not Jerome and Millicent Greene?" Joshua was stymied. Why would Fallon McBride or anyone in Oregon still be interested in those two? They were old news, their story over before it had really begun.

"None other. The New Order of Angels and Saints."

"Why, for God's sake?" Carolyn echoed what Josh was thinking. "Cult activity's been pretty quiet around here. Why stir up the Greenes?"

"Are you kidding? The timing's perfect. We've got two women dead, not far from each other, within the span of a few weeks. I'm not hearing about any suspects being brought in. And from what I'm picking up, this could be the beginning of a serial killer spree. The state is full of transients, faceless backpackers hiking through our woods. What if you don't get your man, Sergeant? What do you think that'll do to people's mindsets around here? The world is a big, bad place. Nobody knows anybody else, people don't go to church, don't sit on their front porches. The atmosphere is rife for another cult to start up, some fringe group who will save the disenchanted and disillusioned from the evils around them."

"You're reaching, Ms. McBride. Nothing else newsworthy coming across your desk?"

"With the two murders, there's plenty to write about. But you're forgetting something, Sergeant." Fallon inhaled deeply, deliberately, her chest straining behind form-fitting Lycra. "We've still got Seraphina Greene living right here in Cypress Village."

Paige had been through enough lately, Joshua thought. She didn't need some ambitious reporter stalking her about her parents and their wackadoo band of followers. "Leave well enough alone, Fallon," Joshua said. "There's no story there."

With that, the reporter turned toward him and said, "There's always a story somewhere, Joshua. Anyway, it's been a pleasure seeing you. Coffee sometime?" She didn't wait for a reply.

Several in the room studied the sway of Fallon McBride's taut behind as she made her exit. When the reporter was safely out of earshot, Carolyn said, "Whew! Did you get a whiff of that?"

"What? Perspiration?"

"No, lust. I could cut the smell of it with a knife. She wants you, Joshua. Still."

"You know that's not gonna happen. Why do you suppose she's resurrecting the Greenes?"

"You know how Fallon likes to dig up old stuff, dust it off and try to make something huge out of it. And let's face it, around here people still talk about the Greenes. No disrespect to Paige, but Millicent and Jerome Greene were class A loonies. That car accident nipped their fanaticism in the bud, thank God. We can only hope that the kids they tried to recruit are living normal lives again."

"This is going to be tough on Paige. She left the country to escape her parents, and even though they're both dead, she still can't get away from them."

"But you'll provide the necessary diversions, I'm sure. And may I say it's nice to see you in a relationship that's lasting longer than three hours."

After leaving the seminary, Joshua had played a wide field, and to his shame, he hadn't always played fair. Making up for lost time, he reasoned. Getting in touch with his inner adolescent. He stole away from beds in the dead of night, not wanting any part of the morning bathroom routines, moony-eyed cuddling and breakfast chatter that seemed to go along with sleeping over. But now there was Paige, and not even Fallon McBride's finely tuned parts and humming engine could sway him from the thought of getting home to Paige at the end of a day and staying there.

He tossed a crumpled napkin at his sister's head. "Get that goofy look off your face."

"I'm happy for you, Josh. Paige is good for you."

"What about at your place? Any progress on the baby discussion?"

Carolyn's husband Gregg was a prosecuting attorney who loved nothing more than being waist-deep in work.

She shook her head. "Tough to make a baby when the one with the sperm is never home."

Carolyn's face was veiled with sorrow, regret, and it made Joshua sad for her. He knew how much his sister wanted children.

"Things will turn around," he told her. "At home and with the investigation."

"Think so?"

He nodded. "Believe it."

Carolyn sighed. "Wish I could."

CHAPTER 16

LANI HAD ADDED ANOTHER DEADBOLT to her collection. As Paige stood in her friend's foyer, dripping water from her raincoat onto the doormat, she counted. The newest lock brought the grand total to six. Ridiculous. And yet Bettina and Jasmine were dead. What precautions had they taken? And would it have mattered? Did they even see the end coming?

"No luck, Paige." Lani jammed arms into a slicker, laced up old green high-tops. "Either at home or on her cell. Where would Dory be on a night like this?"

She should be at home, working the phone lines, Paige thought. It was 10:30, Friday night, and Sebastian would have been tucked in hours ago. "That's what we're going to find out."

They hurried through the pelting rain to the Subaru parked down the street in the visitors' lot. Paige's feet were already soaked and her insides trembled with cold. She started the engine and waited for the heat to blast through the vents. Despite the full-out run to the car, Lani's cheeks were ashen. "It'll be okay, Lani," Paige told her. "We'll swing by Dory's, find out her cell phone needs a new battery and Sebastian's dropped her cordless into the washing machine again. You'll see. And Dory'll have the biggest laugh at us."

"You don't really believe that." Inside the car, Lani's voice was hollow.

No, I don't. Dory needed the phone to make money. She wouldn't allow her cell to run down. And she'd have purchased another phone if something happened to her portable. Two of the operators were dead, and neither Paige nor Lani had been able to reach Dory since the news about Sarah Lydell had made the papers yesterday morning. Paige's heart thudded with dread and she pressed harder on the accelerator. "Think good thoughts."

The wipers thwacked at full speed against the greasy windshield. Paige squinted through the rain, road signs a blur, pavement slick and inky black. The tires fought for traction. Dory would not take Sebastian out on a night like this. No one should be out on a night like this.

She gripped the steering wheel while Lani remained mute, arms hugged to her chest. The storm raged around them. In the distance, forked lightning split the sky.

It was another fifteen minutes before they found themselves at the curb in front of Dory's bungalow. The place was dark, nearly invisible in the tangle of overgrown shrubbery that Dory had always intended to prune.

"Come on." Paige flipped the hood of her jacket over her hair and yanked on the drawstring. Lani did the same and moments later, both were running from the car toward the house. Lani pounded on the front door while Paige squeezed between a thatch of dense yews, shielding her eyes to peer through the living room window. She could make out shadowy contours of furniture but no more. If something moved inside, she couldn't see it.

"Around back!" she shouted to Lani above the wind.

They raced around the garage, following the narrow sidewalk to the rear of the house. Paige reached over a wooden gate, sprung the latch and Lani followed her through to the back door. Here, more light was afforded from the apartment building and its parking lot behind, enough for both to see that the kitchen window had been shattered and was now boarded up.

"What the hell's going on here?" Paige hammered her fist against the door, then against the sheet of plywood where the kitchen window had once been. "Dory! Sebastian!"

"They're not here," Lani wailed. "Now what?"

"Look! There's a light on at the neighbors'. Maybe they know something." Without waiting for an answer, Paige ran to the front of the house again, then across the lawn to another bungalow, awash in welcome light. From the porch she could see an elderly woman rise from a lounge chair and squint through the window. She came to the door, left the chain on, and through the crack said, "Yes?"

"I'm sorry to be bothering you so late, but we're friends of Dory's, your neighbor? We were wondering if you knew where she and Sebastian might be. We can't seem to get in touch with them."

"Friends of Dory's? My goodness, come on in. What a horrible night."

The chain slid, the door opened and now Paige found herself dripping onto another entry mat. Lani stood behind her and peeked over her shoulder while Paige introduced her.

"I'm Harriet Foster. I babysit Sebastian sometimes when Dory's in a bind. What a sweet boy he is. Would you like some tea?"

"No, thank you. Do you have any idea where Dory is?"

"She's gone."

"Gone?"

"Left about nine last night. Had a couple of suitcases with her. Asked me to watch her house."

"Did she say where she was going? Or how long she'd be gone?"

"No. She was in a hurry. But Sebastian told me he and his mommy were having a 'venture.' Isn't that cute?"

CHAPTER 17

They were inside the Subaru again, following the coast road with less urgency now. Dory and Sebastian were long gone, so Paige saw little sense in crashing her car into a tree.

The Foster woman had no explanation for what had happened to Dory's kitchen window. She'd met with her reading club last night and had only noticed the boarded up window when she'd gone into her own kitchen for her medication around nine thirty. By then Dory had already left, so there'd been no one to ask.

She was in a hurry. Harriet Foster had been taken aback, hurt even, at Dory's abruptness when she'd shown up at her doorstep. "She wouldn't wait long enough for me to give Sebastian a cookie," she lamented.

He had called her again. That had to be it. The True Gentleman. Looking for Opal. What had he said to make Dory run?

A threat. He would harm her. Or Sebastian. Or both of them.

Paige mentally erased the thought. They'd all received threats before. It was the beastly nature of the business. Verbal threats were generally shrugged off as part of the fantasy, part of the game. Callers got off on threats. And Dory's skin was as tough as leather. Everything rolled off her.

Unless it was no longer a game. If the True Gentleman somehow knew where Dory was, had indicated the danger was real, that would make her bolt. Her son would not end up like Amber or Jasmine.

If the escape failed, if Dory was caught, then what?

She would protect Sebastian. At all costs.

And the True Gentleman would come after Opal.

Sodden hair dripped down the back of her neck. Her toes puckered and shriveled inside her saturated socks, but the icy chill that stabbed through her, nucleus-deep, had nothing to do with being wet. Paige was rigid with a fear so palpable she could taste it, acrid and coppery in her mouth. Lani, silent beside her, was entombed in her own dark thoughts.

As the street lamps of Cypress Village came into view, Paige managed to say, "Strength in numbers?"

Lani nodded, her wide eyes darting from the passenger mirror to the roadside to the hood of the car, as though expecting the True Gentleman to leap from the darkness and ambush the vehicle.

"Bunk in with me for a few days. At least until we find out about Dory."

Another nod. "I'll try her cell again."

Paige heard the solemn beep, beep, beep of numbers being punched in. Then nothing until Lani clapped her phone shut.

"What if he's got her? Or that sweet little boy?" Her voice was child-like, tremulous.

"We've got to keep it together," Paige said, summoning control from some mysterious place within. "If we fall apart, we can't think. Then we're useless. Besides, we still don't know that anything is wrong."

Another dubious talent from her phone actress days wove its ugly way into her real self—she was capable, at a moment's notice, of uttering complete and absolute bullshit.

CHAPTER 18

Outside the diner, gale winds howled but Sebastian barely noticed. He was channeling his concentration onto his latest masterpiece, the scene from his favorite movie, *The Wizard of Oz*, with the flying monkeys swooping down into the Haunted Forest to capture Dorothy and her supporting cast. In her son's drawing, Dory could make out what she assumed was Toto, being snatched up into the sky by one of the simian creatures.

Sebastian had seen the DVD fifteen times. With cues from Dory, he could sing "If I Only Had a Brain" and he especially enjoyed the song's finale, alternating the lines with his mother.

"If I only had a brain."

"A heart."

"A home."

"Da noive."

Dory wondered about art lessons. Or music lessons. Sebastian had a wonderful singing voice, high and cherubic. Whatever it took, she vowed, to enable him to be the best he could be.

Sebastian. Such a big name for such a little boy, her neighbor Harriet Foster had once said. But Dory hadn't wanted a babyish name for her son. St. Sebastian, someone had told her, was the patron saint of soldiers. And that's what she wanted her son to be. A brave soldier.

The diner was half full of people like Dory pulling off the road to warm up, dry off, and get a break from the hypnotic effect of the pounding rhythm of the rain against their windshields. They all looked alike, a unisex crowd of drenched people, visors from their ball caps dripping as they bent over what the menu proclaimed to be real home cooking. The owner of the place made the rounds with the coffee pot, shaking his head when a customer spoke about an overturned truck, its cargo of dead chickens all over the road. "Awful night," Dory heard him say more than once. Cups rattled in saucers. Spoons rattled against cups.

When he reached Dory's table, he said, "That your purple VW out there, Miss?"

Dory peered through the window. Sheets of water cascaded down the glass but she could still see the pale mauve of her Beetle, the car Sebastian loved because it reminded him of a great big candy. "Yes, it's mine."

"You might want to think about moving it. That tree you're parked beside is pretty old. No telling what'll happen in this wind."

She glanced at her son, now finished with the haunted forest and working on what appeared to be his version of Glinda, the Good Witch.

"I'll watch your boy for you," the man said. He was a lanky, aging hippie with a wide open smile and friendly crinkles around his eyes. "Bring him a refill of milk, if that's okay. On the house. Might even scare up a chocolate chip cookie to go with it."

That got Sebastian's attention. He put down his blue crayon, looked up and said, "Is the cookie on the house too?"

"Sebastian," she said. "If you want more milk ... and a cookie, we'll pay for it." Dory hesitated, scanned the diner then looked carefully at the owner.

"He'll be all right here, Miss. Take you just a second to move that car."

Outside, there was a loud thunderclap and a split second later, a jagged bolt of lightning pierced the black sky.

"Go save Gumdrop, Mommy," Sebastian said, his eyes earnest. "I'll be okay."

She hesitated again then relented, rising and leaning across the table to kiss her son's forehead. "What are the rules?"

"No leaving my place," Sebastian recited, "and no talking to strangers."

"I'll watch him like a hawk, Miss," the diner's owner repeated. "Uncle Mike won't let anything happen to him."

Dory sidled off the vinyl bench, removed her raincoat from the hook at the end of the booth and put it on. She raced outside, fingers gripping the car keys in her pocket. Rivulets of water ran from her hood into her eyes, blurring her vision. When she started the car, the radio blared on, nearly scaring the piss out of her. She clicked off the switch, her heart well north of where it should be, choking off her gasps for air.

Steady, Dory, steady. Just move the damn car and get back inside.

With wipers slapping the windshield, Dory maneuvered into the last angled space, farther away from the diner and farther away from the floodlight that beamed down from the corner eave. A massive Dumpster hulked against a peeling white fence. Sebastian hated Dumpsters, though he'd never been able to tell her why. Now Dory didn't like them either. Or storms. Or out of the way places full of strangers.

Or running from a nameless, faceless son of a bitch who watched her through her window.

She killed the engine, yanked her key from the ignition and flung open the car door, her feet landing squarely in a pothole full of water. Once more she plunged headfirst into the storm, moving toward the promise of light, warmth, and Sebastian. Inside, a full glass of milk and a cookie rested on the arborite tabletop, but her son wasn't in the booth.

No! she heard her silent scream. She'd only been gone two minutes! Two fucking minutes! She hurried across the room. Mike met her halfway.

"Easy, ma'am," he said softly. "Look."

Sebastian crawled out from under the table, an orange crayon clenched in his chubby fist. Oblivious to everything else, he scooched himself back onto the bench and continued coloring. When Dory reached him, he had a big smile ready.

"Did you have a venture outside, Mommy?"

"Quite an adventure," she told him, feeling her heartbeat return to normal. "And Gumdrop is safe now."

She drank her next cup of coffee in contemplative quiet, her gaze alternating from the storm beyond to her son's drawing. Glinda's gown was a glittery pink and her magic wand was topped with a gleaming gold star. Inexplicably, Dory found the drawing disturbing and she repressed a shudder.

Three taps with the ruby slippers. *There's no place like home.*

Tonight, home would be a seaside inn, hundreds of miles from where they lived, away from ringing phones, prying eyes, and a whispery lullaby voice that breathed death.

CHAPTER 19

COLD TO THE MARROW. RUNNING from the warmth of the Outback into the storm once again brought fresh chills. It was a mere twenty steps from the vehicle to Paige's covered porch but even at a run, she felt the wind wick away her last vestige of body heat, leaving her a quivering mass of sodden flesh. Lani looked blue-cold.

They rushed inside and Parker barreled over to greet them. They began peeling off sopping outer layers, removed waterlogged shoes and socks, and took turns petting the dog. Then Paige heard a throat clear. Joshua was standing near the fireplace. When they turned to face him, he said, "Thought I'd better announce myself before more clothes came off. Paige, you picked a helluva night to go out." To Lani he said, "Hi, I'm Joshua."

Lani gave a small nod then responded with, "I'm Lani." This was followed by an awkward silence.

"Lani," Paige said, "why don't you grab a hot shower or bath? You know where everything is. I'll bring you some pajamas and a cup of tea. By then I should have Joshua caught up."

Lani gathered her pile of wet clothes and moved toward the main bathroom just off the living room. "Nice to meet you, Joshua," she said nervously, sending an apologetic look across the room. "Paige has told me tons about you."

Joshua's raised eyebrow indicated, *I don't know a darn thing about you*. Once Lani had left the room, Joshua said, "I'll get the kettle boiling. You dry off and change then I'll give you a hug and see if it helps."

Paige retreated to the master bathroom, toweled excess water from her hair, and changed into fleece-lined sweats and the thickest socks she owned. She took warm nightclothes in for Lani. When she returned to the living room, the tea was steeping and Josh was throwing a huge log onto the fire. Parker sprawled on the carpet nearby. Lani emerged wrapped in a plaid robe, took the mug of tea Joshua handed to her then said, "I'll leave you two alone. Again, nice to meet you, Joshua."

"Pretty shook up," he said after the door to the guest room closed. "Problems, I take it?"

Paige nodded then stepped in for her hug. "Lani's been going through some stuff. I didn't think she should be alone." She thought that would be enough, that Joshua would respect the confidence shared between female friends, but just for a moment, Paige forgot she was talking to a cop's twin.

"So you've brought her here for what ... a couple of days? Without so much as an overnight bag, her own toothbrush? Must have had to leave in a hurry."

Joshua often came across kids on the run, fleeing from horrendous situations. Desperate, afraid, they traveled light. And in the dark. In all kinds of weather.

Paige wriggled loose from the embrace. "There's no abusive partner, if that's what you're thinking."

"That's what I'm thinking, yes. Are you two okay? I was really worried."

Paige settled onto the couch, Joshua beside her, holding her cold hands in his. If he was disappointed in how the evening was turning out, he wasn't showing it. He handed her tea, rubbed her arms for warmth, repeated how much he'd been concerned, wondering if she'd had an accident. Now here she was, with a frightened girlfriend in tow and as yet, she hadn't explained anything. Like rapid-fire, Paige rolled the words around in her mind.

"We used to work the phone-sex lines."

"One of the callers is looking for Opal, and we can't tell him who she is. We just can't."

"So two of the operators are dead. Dead. Dead. Dory is missing. And we don't know who's next."

She could hear the words tumbling out, mixing together in an incoherent mess of story that no sane person would understand. And his response would be what?

You did what for a living? For how long? Been a slice. Gotta go.

She needed to give him more credit. He was a better person than most. Maybe her past wouldn't make a bit of difference. And if it did? She loved him too much to lose him. How much did he love her?

Paige had dug a deep hole, delaying telling Joshua the truth. Now, with Lani in the next room, the timing was all wrong. Coming forward about her past filled her with dread; not coming forward filled her with something far worse.

Joshua interrupted her thoughts. "You're pretty terrific, jumping in to help a friend like this. She sure looks skittish. Anything I can do to help? I don't want to pry."

"No, I'd be curious too. We went to meet a friend of ours," she explained. "To talk out some of Lani's problems. When the weather turned bad, it was just easier to bring Lani straight here instead of stopping by her place. It'll only be for a couple of days, Joshua. And I'm sorry if I worried you."

He sat down and turned to face her. "Hey, I'm just glad everything's okay. Well," he glanced over at the room Lani occupied, "relatively speaking, anyway. I also know how much you like coming to the rescue." His mouth softened into a smile.

She knew what he was thinking. On one of their first dates, they had hiked through Cape Lookout State Park, intending to explore the tidepools at the base of the cape. They had come across an injured rabbit and, unable to leave it there, Paige had sent Joshua back to the car to get a cardboard box so they could safely transport the creature to the emergency vet clinic. She had paid the bill, returned to the clinic when the animal was ready to be re-released and insisted on doing it herself, taking it back to the very place where they'd found it. Paige swore that before the rabbit hopped away, it hesitated and looked up at her, as if expressing gratitude.

Joshua gave her hand a squeeze then stood and moved to the hall tree by the front door. He retrieved his jacket from the hook.

"Where are you going?" Paige asked, rising and hurrying toward him. "Lani won't cramp our style. You can stay."

He shook his head. "If she's messed up about something, she'll need a full-time friend tonight and she's lucky you're volunteering for the job. I'll only be in the way here. Besides," he smiled again, "your bed squeaks."

"Josh, please don't leave. It's horrible out there. You were worried when I was out driving in that mess, now I'll be worried that you're out in it."

He wouldn't be persuaded. "I'll take it slow. And I'll call you when I get home. Oh, I almost forgot. Your favorite person, Fallon McBride called. Wanted to know whether you've reconsidered being on that documentary she's airing."

Paige rolled her eyes. "That's got to be the sixth time she's asked me. What will it take to get that woman out of my life? As if my present isn't bad enough, with me finding that awful foot, now Fallon wants me reliving my past too? What did you tell her?"

"Said I didn't presume to speak for you, but that when you say no, you generally mean no."

"Thanks," Paige said, but she knew that wouldn't stop McBride whose specialty lately was being a thorn in Paige's ass.

Joshua broke her unpleasant train of thought by putting his hands on her shoulders and drawing her close. "Let's just hope your friend Lani is a quick healer. A guy can get pretty lonely on these stormy nights. Selfish bastard, aren't I?"

Paige wondered again about bringing the truth forward, but the words got stuck. Instead she let Joshua run his hands through her still damp hair then she tilted her face upward for a brief kiss. "Sure you won't stay?"

"Call me when the coast is clear," he said. "I hope everything works out for Lani. But remember Paige, you can't save 'em all."

CHAPTER 20

Their room at the Tidewater Inn came with a turret and a view of the ocean. It was more money than Dory wanted to pay, but she'd promised Sebastian an adventure and the minute he'd spotted the tower through the foggy car window, his eyes had widened at the prospect of sleeping in a castle. Finally, hours after his bedtime, Dory was able to coax him from the turret window and tuck him in. He dozed peacefully under a down comforter, eyelids fluttering in childhood dreams that Dory hoped magically carried him far away from the storm and all other harm. Especially all other harm. She kissed his forehead for what must have been the tenth time, smoothed his hair from his face and allowed herself a smile at his favorite pajamas, bright red flannel and covered with Dalmatians. Yes, one day, she promised him, they would have a dog.

Dory sat in the chair her son had vacated, the only light coming from the adjoining bathroom. Beyond the semi-circle of windows, the weather was being a real bitch. The wind whistled and shrieked around the tower. Pellets of rain did a frenzied dance against the glass. We're safe here, she thought, in our castle by the sea.

For the first time since learning of her pregnancy, Dory craved a cigarette. And a brandy. She yearned to relax, yet she knew she couldn't. She needed every nerve ending, every sense intact. Some adventure. She had no plans for tomorrow, or the day after. She had no idea how long they would have to run, nor how far. How many school days would Sebastian have to miss?

She had some money in the bank, enough to last them a little while, but that cash had always been meant for emergencies. For Sebastian's care. Deplete that and she'd have worked all those years on the goddamn phones for nothing. It was bad enough she'd broken the kitchen window. Impulsive and stupid and expensive. And it had frightened her son. Her explanation was close to the truth. A bad man was playing mean tricks, trying to scare people. Mommy shouldn't have broken the window. It wasn't nice to break things, but she had learned her lesson and would have to replace the glass soon.

This adventure had to end. But she couldn't call the police. She hated them, and they hated her back. No one could know about this. If she was in danger then that meant Sebastian was in danger, and the cops wouldn't be sympathetic. Not a second time. She had lost her son once, had fought like hell to get him back. She wouldn't lose him again. She was a good mother, a fit mother. And she could handle this situation.

If she had anything to say about it, Sebastian would be back in school, hopefully as early as Monday, and they would be home. Modern cops had techno-everything at their disposal. They would find Amber's killer—maybe they were closing in on the bastard this very second—and the hunt for Opal would be dead in the water. Until then, whatever it took, Sebastian would not see her fear. They would fly kites, eat hamburgers and pizza, shop for storybooks, and play "Sorry." It would be a mini-vacation. Nothing wrong with that. Quality mother-and-son time.

For that she would need her rest. It was nearly one a.m. For a moment, she wondered how her regulars were doing. Chuck D usually dialed in around midnight on Fridays, Cowboy Bob closer to one thirty. The cowboy could always be counted on—he was pleasant, full of ideas, and always appreciative. On Christmas and Valentine's Day, he sent cards and perfume to her post office box. On April 16th, which she'd told him was her birthday, he'd sent an anthology of erotic verses. That had been going on for three years. Tonight he would be talking to someone else. She wondered what the cowboy would think of that. She wondered why it mattered.

Dory was an expert at keeping them on the line, adept at creating a vivid, visual image in the minds of her callers. She spoke slowly, spun minute details about what her tongue was doing, where her fingers were. She stretched each vowel to create an atmosphere of prolonged sensuous tension. A poet at work.

She talked to attorneys and professors who worked late, long-haul truckers, one or two ministers and once, to someone reportedly burgling a house. No counseling, no moral judgments, no asking where their wives were. Her job was to get them off then move on to the next one.

Job stress? Plenty. Paige had sized the gig up perfectly. The hours were crap, the benefits, nil; the talk often repetitive. Dory heard from a foot freak about twice a month, and had to stifle a yawn when describing the shape of her toenails, how high her arch was, whether her feet sweat in the summer, dried out in the winter. What lotion she used on them. How many pairs of shoes she owned. What they looked like. Sometimes there weren't enough adjectives. But generally, feet men were the nicest of the bunch.

Some callers were out-and-out shits and when Dory got stuck with one, she thought about the money. That she could work at home. That she could keep her clothes on. And that one more course would earn her a degree and her options would change.

She snapped her eyes open, looked at her watch. Another half hour had passed, the storm mesmerizing her into gray numbness. To bed, she told herself. Tomorrow, weather permitting, she and Sebastian would fly his new diamond kite and feast on pancakes and sausages somewhere. It would be great.

Then the bedside phone rang. She lunged at it, caught it before it could wake her son. Who the hell? At this time of night? Some drunk and a wrong number.

"Hello?"

"Good evening, Dory. Imagine you still awake. Storm keeping you up?"

No. Not possible. The lilting voice traced a hair-thin line of fear along the back of her neck. In the dark she shivered. Dropped the receiver. Raced to the door. Made sure it was locked. Tugged the drapes across the windows, frantic. Grabbed the phone again.

"Pardon, Dory? I can't hear you. Not like you to be at a loss for words, is it? How ironic—silence from someone who makes her living saying all the right things."

"How ...?"

"How did I find you? Your naiveté comes as something of a surprise. Don't you know you can't hide from me? None of you can."

"Jazz," she whispered. "You—"

"All gone," he crooned. "Don't you read the papers? Poor Jasmine. Pity, really. I only wanted one thing from her. A simple thing. These complications aren't necessary."

Murder. A complication. "You sick son of a bitch."

"Now, now. Name-calling won't help. Tell me, Dory. Where's Opal?"

She swallowed, set her jaw. "Haven't got a clue."

"We both know that's not true. I feel it only fair to tell you that my patience is wearing thin. Quite thin."

"Then give up." Dallas's voice was coming forward, dominant, all business. "Turn yourself in. Get help."

From the other end of the phone, his soft laughter crawled over her like a fat maggot. She shook it off. She was still in the game. Wasn't she?

"You *will* tell me where Opal is, won't you, dear Dory?"

"Can't tell what I don't know."

A small sigh. "Very well then. Perhaps you can tell me how your son likes his new crayons."

She felt her brow furrow then at once she was cloaked in sticky sweat. Her pulse drummed in her ears. The drawing of Glinda. The glittery pink gown. A package of eight sparkly pastel crayons she'd never seen before.

"You ... in the diner ... when I moved my car ...?"

Another dry chuckle oozed its way into her ear. "You see, Dory, how close I am? How close I can get?"

Hot tears ran down her cheeks but somehow she managed to grasp one final sinew of composure, kept her fear at bay and summoned anger. "You stay away from my son!"

She slammed the receiver. Sebastian stirred under the coverlet. Would he remember what the man looked like? Had the True Gentleman spoken to him?

A diner filled with people. Dory remembered baseball caps. Brimmed rain hats. Soaking wet hair. Everyone hunched over steaming cups of coffee and gravy-saturated food, each traveler looking much like the next. He could have been sitting at the lunch counter. Or in the booth behind theirs. Why hadn't she paid more attention?

She thought they were safe. Her guard was down. She had been a fool, a stupid naïve fool.

You can't hide from me. None of you can.

Dory reached out to touch her son's shoulder, longed to gently rouse him awake to seek answers to her questions, even pack up to run again, but in his sleep, Sebastian was smiling. Sweet dreams.

She let him have them. It would all be clearer in the morning. When she was calmer. To Sebastian, it would be another adventure, a contest.

Remember the crayons? For every thing you can tell me about the man who gave them to you, I'll buy you a picture book.

Morning wasn't so far away, she reasoned, looking at her watch. In real hours, only five away. But she knew in her heart that time would pass slowly, that she would lie in the dark and remember that horrible voice, aware that the True Gentleman had passed within inches of all that was precious to her.

He would do it again. Or much worse. All because of Opal.

Dory eased herself on top of the covers and snuggled behind her son, tucking his small body against hers. She longed to clutch him tightly to her, fiercely protect him with every muscle and bone within her, but she knew he might awaken, be alarmed, feel her terror. Instead, she gently draped an arm across his waist and hoped that, while he slept, he knew how much she loved him.

CHAPTER 21

H E WASN'T THERE YET BUT he was close. Soon he would be united with Opal and everything would be perfect. He would reveal himself to her, pledge his everlasting devotion and the two of them would find a sunset to sail into. He could be such a romantic.

He had already selected the church they would be married in—a tiny white chapel in Washington State. They would shop together for an engagement ring, though he was certain she wouldn't need anything ostentatious. Opal wasn't materialistic. Simply being with him would be enough. She had already told him so.

He was pleased she had left her job. He knew how much she loathed talking to other men, that she would have preferred speaking only to him. In their conversations, some stretching as long as two hours, they had traveled the world. In Paris, they had made love under one of the bridges that spanned the Seine while *bateaux-mouches* full of tourists cruised lazily by. In London, they'd pressed themselves into a dark corner of St. Paul's Cathedral, their moans, gasps and murmurs of satisfaction echoing in the whispering gallery around them.

One of their favorite places had been Nairobi, where they'd stayed in a luxurious hotel nestled in the treetops. Jungle breezes caressed their bare skin, their lovemaking a gourmet treat for the senses, each of them squeezing tropical fruit juices onto one another's bodies, tongues meandering along mounds and crevices to lap up the nectar. Their orgasms roused sleeping creatures awake, the chatter of monkeys and shrieks of birds competing with their own rapturous cries. They'd revisited Kenya often. Both blushed when they thought of it. Opal giggled at how naughty he'd been.

If she only knew. He had, over the years, thought and said terrible things, done worse. He would never, could never share his unspeakable deeds with Opal. His blackest thoughts, he did, however, confess. She, unlike the other girls, did not excuse him, did not tell him what she thought he wanted to hear.

Moral fiber. Inner goodness. That's what Opal had, and he fell in love with her the second she refused to participate, even verbally, in what he referred to as his "purple game." It was too dangerous, too sadistic, too easy to lose control.

You don't need to get off that way, she'd said. Let me show you other ways.

And she did. Talking with Opal, listening to her sweet voice aroused him in ways he never imagined possible. His desire for the purple game, while never completely gone, could be suppressed, diluted, contained, as long as he had Opal. She was the only one who could keep his darkness from taking over again.

Their last conversation had been so special, so … perfect. They had gone to the Galapagos, spent a wonderful day holding hands and walking among the penguins and frigate birds before returning to the sailboat they'd rented to drink champagne and make love, their naked bodies sweat-soaked and glistening in the sun. Opal had taken control that night, described herself straddling him on the deck of the boat, rocking to the stroking rhythm of her own hand. He was made to watch for nearly an hour while she brought herself pleasure over and over, fingers probing, hands running across her firm breasts, erect nipples. Only when he finally cried out in agony did she allow him to enter her and still she withheld his release, halting her sliding motion completely until he thought he might go mad. Finally he gripped her firmly and thrust into her, exploding in a rush of milky heat.

The sun disappeared beyond the horizon and their bodies cooled.

"I love you, Opal."

"I love you too, my fine gentleman."

"I would do anything for you."

"No one's ever told me that before."

"I'd even kill for you."

And now someone had.

CHAPTER 22

With the morning came a rainbow, the first one Sebastian had ever seen. He pressed his nose against the tower window while Dory packed their bags.

"Where does it begin and end, momma?"

"What, Bear?"

"The rainbow."

She had passed a harrowing night staring at the room's doorknob for a telltale wiggle and watching the space below the door for shadowy footsteps. Dory couldn't defog her brain enough to bring forth the scientific answer to her son's question. "Maybe rainbows have no beginning and no end," she said, lifting her son's folded pajama top to her cheek briefly before packing it. "Maybe they just go on and on."

"Like God?"

"Yes," she smiled sadly. "Like God."

She zipped the duffle bag and went to sit beside her son in the tower. One last look at the rainbow, a sign that everyone would be safe. The storm was over.

"The picture you colored last night, Sebastian," she began. "Of Glinda. You put her in such a pretty dress. Where did you get those sparkly crayons?"

"They were on the table." Sebastian's gaze remained fixed on the rainbow. He pointed, his index finger jabbing in the air as he counted the colors.

She pulled the crayons from her purse. "But you didn't have these before we got to the restaurant. Who gave them to you?"

Sebastian shrugged.

Dory fought for patience. "It's important," she told him, repositioning her chair so she sat between her son and the rainbow. "If someone's given you a present, we have to thank him. What did the man look like?"

Her son's eyes filled up. His lower lip quivered. "I'm sorry, momma. I would have said thank you, but I didn't see him."

"You must have. Come on, Bear. Think."

He shook his head. "I was coloring. I just looked up to pick a new crayon and they were already on the table. Did I do wrong, momma?"

He started to sob and Dory gathered him into her arms, rocked him forward and back until he calmed down. "It's okay, sweetie. Somebody else just thought you were as cute as I do. And an excellent artist, too. Tell you what. We'll go back to that restaurant, see if Uncle Mike remembers anything about the man."

Sebastian wiped his nose with the tissue Dory handed him. Then he said, "Is there such a thing as cookies for breakfast?"

"There is today," she told him.

A black Mercedes followed them from the inn for about five miles, the car staying far enough back so Dory couldn't make out the driver's face. But at Gold Beach, the car pulled into a service station. If anyone was tailing her now, he was doing a good job of it.

Mike Driscoll, owner of Driscoll's Diner, where she and Sebastian had taken refuge and eaten the night before, brought juice, fresh fruit and cereal to their table. Plus two oatmeal raisin cookies, still warm from the oven. He assured Dory that no one had approached her son during the short minutes she'd gone to move her car, but that plenty had passed by the booth on the way to the cash register. Any one of them, he supposed, could have surreptitiously placed the package of crayons on the table. He hadn't noticed.

He sensed her frustration, her urgency, and Dory could see the man was frantically replaying the events of the previous night—a face, a gesture, some detail he'd overlooked. He shook his head, apologetic.

Dory thanked him, paid the bill plus twenty percent, and hustled Sebastian out to the car. Their adventure had ended badly. The True Gentleman had been right—she couldn't hide from him. Nor could she protect her son.

Call the police? And say what—that someone's been calling, frightening her senseless, giving presents to her son?

What kind of presents, ma'am?

A box of sparkly crayons. Very scary. With her rap sheet, she'd be lucky they didn't laugh in her face. Or worse—take her son away again. With her being connected to two women who'd been murdered, she knew what would come next.

The four words she never wanted to hear again. Ward of the court.

Once she heard the click of Sebastian's seatbelt, Dory started up Gumdrop and headed back up the coast toward home. She would make spaghetti and meatballs for dinner, tuck Sebastian into his own bed, send him off to school on Monday with barely a ripple in their routine. No more disruptions, no more adventures. She had worked too hard to turn things around.

The next time the True Gentleman telephoned, she knew what she would say.

CHAPTER 23

Lani dropped Paige off at work on Saturday, determined to keep busy with errands and stay in very public places with plenty of people around. No way was she going back to her apartment alone. Even as Paige watched her pull away from the curb, Lani triple-checked both her rearview and side mirror. Extra cautious. Paige heard the snap of the Subaru's automatic door locks and wondered whether Lani, in her jumpy state of mind, should even be behind the wheel of a car.

It'll only be for a few days, Joshua. A few days, and the gentleman caller—no, gentleman killer, would be caught and the quest for Opal would end. *Come on, Carolyn, Ziggy and the rest of you. Do your jobs.*

Across the street and right on schedule, was Arlen Dale, and when he spotted her, he broke into a wide grin and removed his ear buds. "Some storm last night, huh?" he called out.

She shot him an exaggerated nod and pointed at his earphones. "Who are you listening to?"

"The Dixie Chicks. Gotta start the day with something upbeat."

Paige would have bet on Arlen being more into Dvorak than Dixie, but as always, appearances were deceiving.

"Have a good one," he hollered then turned the key in the lock and entered his store.

Lucky Arlen. A few up-tempo tunes and he was ready to greet the day. Two people Paige knew were dead and two more were missing, one a sweet-faced six-year-old who happened to have Down's Syndrome. When Dory and Sebastian were found safe and the killer was locked up, perhaps her own face might finally relax into a smile. Until then she made an uneasy peace with the tight-lipped image that had stared back at her from the bathroom mirror earlier. More challenging was living with a stomach that felt weighted down with ball bearings.

She managed to fake a half-cheery good morning to Harry Washburne. "Plans for the weekend?"

"What happens happens," was her boss's enigmatic reply.

Luke entered just in time to flip the OPEN sign in the store window. Unlike Harry, Luke was in a talkative mood. "Ever dance with the Green Fairy, Paige?"

"English please?"

"The Green Fairy. *La Fée Verte*. Absinthe."

Luke educated Paige in the art of absinthe consumption, how pouring cold water over a cube of sugar on a slotted spoon would dilute the absinthe and mask its bitterness.

"Why would anyone drink something that doesn't taste good?" she asked.

"If it was good enough for Baudelaire, Lautrec and Hemingway …"

"A few glasses of a fine cabernet wouldn't be exotic enough?"

Exotic, be damned. Absinthe, Luke whispered, was once illegal in the States, which Paige was certain was part of its allure for Luke. He told her the FDA banned all spirits containing thujone, the chemical said to be responsible for absinthe's mysterious effects—the clarity of thought, the full-body high. According to Luke, he and his friends were drinking the real thing, smuggled in by a guy who knew a guy. There had been plenty of thujone-spiked discussion about literature, some poetry readings, and insightful discussion about world politics—all very fin-de-siècle Parisian salon, a gathering of youthful intelligentsia—but if any world problems had been solved by those under the influence of the potent wormwood liquor, Luke couldn't remember. It was the general experience, the buzz of like minds coming together, that he remembered. Specific details were a little fuzzy. So much for clarity of thought.

Paige tried to keep her conversations with Luke on a need-to-know basis. She definitely didn't need to know the number of ways he skated around the law, but his absinthe adventure made her wonder what else he could be up to. And with whom.

She was grateful for the arrival of a customer, a mid-thirties male with thinning hair and a soul patch that jutted below his lower lip like a hairy talon. He was dressed all wrong for Saturday in the village, his tweed sport coat, cashmere vest and leather oxfords too stuffy and expensive for the casual weekend crowd. He was a novice hiker, he said, and in the market for a pair of boots.

Paige had him sit down and she brought him a selection of entry-level boots.

"These will keep your feet warm and dry without adding extra weight." Paige used a shoehorn to slip the boot on. ""These should be fine for your needs. The boot's spine is designed to facilitate a cushioned heel strike with rear foot stability. Feel how it cradles the middle of your foot?"

The man looked skeptical. "Shouldn't I get something more heavy duty? I have weak ankles."

Something about his voice made Paige's jaw tense. It was whispery and babyish, and he hesitated over some syllables, as though grappling with a stammer. She was reminded of one of her former callers, a bad little boy-man who deserved a good spanking. The four had talked about this, the fear that one day, any of them could bump into a phone client, that the sound of a voice or turn of a phrase would trigger a memory of another conversation, one each of them preferred leaving faceless. Paige searched her memory but she couldn't put a name to the voice.

"The lining will mold to the shape of your foot, just like a custom boot." Quickly she tied the laces, felt his penetrating stare and spoke faster. "Walk around a bit and see how much flex is in the forefoot."

He stared at her another long moment before rising then he ambled around the store, his fingertips brushing across a display of women's wool sweaters.

She thought once more of Dory and Sebastian. Where were they? And what had happened to Dory's kitchen window?

If the True Gentleman knew who Dory was, what else did he know? How close was he?

"They're quite comfortable." The customer had quietly slid in front of her again and sat down, his gaze fixed, she thought, at the base of her throat. She wondered if her heart throbbed there and if it showed.

"Very few seams inside—" she told him, hearing her own speech falter, "—less chance of abrasion."

He looked down as if he didn't know what she was talking about. After another walk around the store, he decided the boots were perfect and he would purchase two pair of hiking socks as well. He paid cash, his hand grazing hers when he handed her the money. She recoiled which seemed to amuse him and heaved a relieved sigh when he exited the store.

Luke glanced toward the door. "What was with the professor? He's no more a hiker than I'm a Sunday school teacher."

Paige shrugged. With the arrival of her next customer, Paige forgot about the weirdo with the weirder soul patch. She recognized Mercer Wyatt from his picture in *Time* magazine. He wore a chambray shirt and jeans, and for a man in his late fifties who'd been welded to a desk for most of his life, Paige thought he was remarkably fit. He was letting his hair go gray and he still had all of it. But there was sadness in his eyes, a look that spoke of regret. Paige knew that look.

"So we're going to be shipmates soon," he said when she introduced herself. "I admit I'm a neophyte when it comes to the outdoors, but it's time for me to come out from hibernation." Wyatt handed Paige an itemized list of outdoor adventure gear that included brand names, models, sizes.

It's how the rich get rich, Paige thought. By paying attention to detail. "You're making my job much too easy, Mr. Wyatt."

"Mercer. Please."

Paige looked at the sheet he'd handed to her. "We'll have you hooked in no time," she said.

She stuck faithfully to Wyatt's list, making an exception only on his choice of backpack, substituting one that had a dry bag option, with clear panels inside to make finding supplies easier. He appreciated the suggestion. "Until awhile ago, you couldn't even coax me to walk to the mailbox. I hope I don't hold anyone back."

At this Paige smiled. "We'll all help each other."

"Maybe there's hope for me yet."

"Of course there is."

When quitting time came, Lani had the Subaru idling curbside. She had gone around to the passenger seat, so Paige slid behind the wheel and glanced over to the store where Luke was flipping the sign from OPEN to CLOSED. When she waved, Luke frowned. Perhaps the aftereffects of the absinthe had taken him hostage. He looked as green as the liqueur.

As Paige pulled away, Lani said, "I thought I'd seen the last of that place. I dread going back there."

"Back there" was the phone room where they'd both worked, a charmless square space equipped with three dozen used study carrels, an assortment of leased chairs, and a pair of single-line telephones in each work station. The supervisor, known to them only as Jean, perched on a raised platform, commanding a clear view of all the operators, though usually only half the cubicles were occupied.

"We won't stay a second longer than necessary," Paige assured her. "We'll talk to Jean, find out if anyone else has been bothered by the True Gentleman, see if she's heard from Dory...." Paige, like Lani, was no more eager to revisit the dingy room where tawdry porn movie posters were taped to grayish walls.

The night watchman, Phil, sat behind a modular workstation in the lobby of the eight-storey office building, his face registering surprise at seeing them. "What has it been? A year, I'll bet."

"Give or take," Paige said. "You look good, Phil."

Lani had already signed the register and was handing the pen to Paige. Now there were two barely legible signatures that, if printed, would look suspiciously like Laurel Canyon and Opal Kadett.

"Not going to the sixth floor, are ya?"

"Phil, I think I left a spare set of keys in my desk. Can't think of where else they'd be. I've looked everywhere."

"I'll take you up," Phil said. "Gotta make my rounds anyway. But I guarantee you won't find your keys up there. Been a lotta changes."

They followed Phil. The elevator groaned then shuddered to a stop on the sixth floor. As they moved down the hall toward 626, Lani leaned close to Paige and said, "Don't take this the wrong way, but sometimes I wish we'd never met Dory and Bettina."

Paige knew what she meant. If they hadn't gone for coffee after class, the quadruple threat of Amber, Dallas, Laurel and Opal would never have been born.

"Likewise."

Room 626 had a new door, and it was wide open. A rolled-up carpet, still sheathed in plastic, lay near the entrance. On a radio, playing at ear-splitting volume, some rapper was dissing his bitch. Two workers were inside, applying moss green paint to the once gray walls.

The thirty-six cubicles, supervisor Jean, and the telephones were gone.

CHAPTER 24

Carolyn's sciatica was working overtime today. She'd popped a couple of anti-inflammatories earlier when her lower back had started aching, but now her left hip was sending a bolt of searing pain down her leg. She knew it was impossible, yet a small part of her believed the condition was aggravated short minutes after entering Kent Marland's office on campus on Monday morning. She wasn't impressed with the professor; it was enough that the professor was impressed with himself.

"Bettina Reid was a student of mine, yes," Marland said, spoken as though he were trying to rid his palate of the taste of cheap wine. "Bettina and about three hundred others."

"Ever notice anything peculiar during your lectures? Someone staring at her or always sitting nearby, anything like that?"

Marland shook his head. "To the best of my recollection, she usually came in alone and left alone. Once I start lecturing, it's just a swarm of faces in front of me. What happened once she or anyone else left the lecture hall, I have no idea. And as to anyone staring at her, well, pretty much everybody did. She had a tough time getting around." As if Carolyn couldn't put the pieces together, he added, "She was ginormous."

Carolyn sized up the professor—hair beginning to thin, facial muscles more spongy than taut, a stomach with the six-pack on the inside. She suspected the professor still saw a trim, thirty-something in the shaving mirror, though he was a good decade and several pounds beyond that. Carolyn also suspected he insisted his students address him as *Dr.* Marland.

Ph.D. in pomposity. People like Marland made her stomach twist. What made her sicker still was the knowledge that if she'd known Bettina Reid, she would have stared too. Then looked away. Then sneaked another peek when it was safe. Wonder how she could have let herself become so unhealthy.

It could be a superficial world and Carolyn was no different than many, forming snap judgments based on appearances, not something she was proud of. But right now she needed to discover what Bettina Reid could have said or done to get herself killed.

She was rising to leave Kent Marland's office when another question struck her. "I had a crush on my biology professor once. Anything like that ever happen to you?"

Marland affected a modest look but didn't quite pull it off. "We've all got our occasional war stories," he said. "Thankfully, most crushes last about as long as a snowflake on the tip of your nose."

Carolyn smiled. "'Suppose Bettina ever had a thing for you?"

Marland took a moment to think it over, his gaze wandering to a shelf full of weighty books to his right then said, "She always sat in the front. Came to my office once in awhile to say how much she enjoyed a particular class." He shrugged. "Possible, I guess. But I've never crossed that line. With any student."

And certainly not someone like Bettina Reid.

Carolyn wished the professor a good day and thanked him for his help. Leaving campus, she noticed the flag at half mast and felt that if Bettina hadn't been acknowledged in life, at least her death was getting her noticed.

In the glove compartment of her car was a stash of ibuprofen, and Carolyn swallowed two caplets dry. The pain burned down her leg, beyond her knee. Her foot felt stuck full of pins. The good news was that her leg hurt so much she didn't feel the back pain anymore. Another cheerful thought was that, unlike her late father, she'd not yet lost control of her bladder. Carolyn needed rest, but couldn't afford to take it. Stretching and strengthening exercises would help, too, but there wasn't time for those either. She had another stop to make.

The three-bedroom raised ranch Bettina had grown up in was still occupied by her parents. Wally Reid, who was using a walker, ushered

Carolyn inside. They went straight into the kitchen where his wife Kay was rolling out pastry on a flour-dusted countertop. The aroma of apples and cinnamon scented the air.

Carolyn expressed her condolences.

"Didn't want our girl moving out," Wally said. "She had everything she needed right here. Why would she want to leave?"

"I'm baking her favorite pie—apple custard," Kay said. "I just can't believe she won't be coming in that door asking for a big slice with ice cream." There was a slight chuckle. "Don't guess it'll go to waste, though. Me and Wally do like a good pie."

She accepted a cup of tea but nixed the offer of coconut cookies, lemon-cranberry bars, marble cake. Kay rooted in the cupboard for a teapot and a plate for the pastries. "Have a little something," she urged. "We seldom get company."

She let the Reids walk her through Bettina's life. It was a short biography revolving around excellent report cards and saxophone lessons. There was no talk of birthday parties or outings with friends, no seaside summer holidays or trips to camp. Nor was there mention of cruel schoolyard taunts or a lonely adolescence. But then there wouldn't have been. The Reids, cloistered in their little sugar house, were in deep denial. If Bettina had ever confided her misery to them, they would have smoothed things over with a pat on the hand and a slice of chocolate cake.

Carolyn asked about Bettina's living expenses, how she was making ends meet.

"We gave her money for tuition, books, a food allowance, and first and last month's rent." Wally Reid dumped spoonfuls of sugar into his tea. "We were sure she would want to come home, but that backfired. She must have got some kind of job, because we never paid for a thing after last November."

"But she didn't say what kind of job?"

"Never said, we never asked."

"Did Bettina ever mention anything about having surgery?"

Kay stopped rolling dough. "Why? She wasn't sick."

Carolyn explained gastric bypass and that she'd heard Bettina had been saving up for the procedure. Kay grimaced as though a pubic hair was stuck to her tongue.

"What would she do a fool thing like that for?" Wally said.

"Bettina had a healthy appetite." The rolling started up again.

Carolyn spent a miserable hour in the Reids' kitchen. Their daughter had died tragically and they were grieving in their own fashion, losing themselves in the comfort of food. They loved Bettina, at least in the best way they knew how, but they didn't have a goddamned clue about what went on in her mind.

By the time Carolyn left, her sciatica was raging. There had to be more to Bettina Reid than a plus-sized wardrobe and too many calories. Carolyn needed to know her. Nobody else did.

CHAPTER 25

It was all part of his game. Dory was being played, just for sport, and she knew if something didn't give soon, she would absolutely lose what was left of her fucking mind. Scarce moments passed that she wasn't haunted by Amber's screams, by Jasmine's begging for her help. But the True Gentleman hadn't made contact and it had already been four days since she had aborted her adventure with Sebastian.

She grilled her son daily when he got home from school. Were there any visitors in the building? Anyone waiting for you to get off the bus? She even asked about substitute teachers, certain the man who'd killed Jasmine and Amber would use any ruse to get to her through her son. Her heart never resumed its normal resting rate until she met Sebastian at the curb at 3:30. Even in their tiny bungalow, she couldn't bear having him in another room. If she could see him, he was safe. Tonight she'd given him three goodnight kisses, had trouble tearing herself away from his bedroom when she'd turned off the light.

Jean had called late on Saturday night after Dory and Sebastian had returned home, the jangle of the telephone nearly rocketing Dory from her chair. The business was moving, given what had happened.

What had happened? "They were *murdered*, Jean. That's what happened. It's that Gentleman bastard looking for Opal. How does he know who we are? Who leaked the information?"

"Easy, Dallas," the supervisor said. "We don't know that's what went on."

"He called here, Jean," Dory said through clenched teeth. "Used my real name. Threatened my son. He's watched me. Followed me. And Paige found Amber's *foot*."

She heard Jean sigh. Not her concern that a serial killer was preying on the women at the agency. The priority was to get the service up and running again quickly. Welcome to show business.

"Consider this my resignation," Dory huffed and hung up. Fifteen minutes later she signed on with another agency up the coast as Crystal.

When her phone rang at nine p.m. that same night, she dove at it.

"Dory, where the hell have you been?"

She swallowed hard. "Oh, hi Paige."

"Oh, hi Paige? That's it? Lani and I have been insane with worry."

Enter Crystal. "Worried? What for?"

"Couldn't reach you by phone. Came by your house Friday night and saw your kitchen window boarded up. Your neighbor said you left in a hurry. How's that for starters?"

"Oh, hell. I'm sorry, Paige. Sebastian and I decided to treat ourselves to a little getaway. Found a great B & B down the coast. Amber, and now Jazz—well, I needed a break. You know how it is."

"And your window?"

"Neighborhood kids broke it, the little bastards. They've been on a real tear around here."

Paige said nothing.

Don't overexplain, Dory told herself. Don't fill the silence with chatter. She'll know you're lying.

Eventually Paige said, "We *were* worried. And why didn't you at least activate your cell?"

"Dammit, Paige, I said I was sorry. But what do you think the word 'getaway' means? No phones, no television. God, I haven't been interrogated like this since the night before I ran away from home."

"Pardon me all to hell for thinking something might have happened to you. Two people we know have been murdered, you disappear, and your window's been smashed to ratshit..."

Dory let the silence hang, partly to allow the lump in her throat to clear and partly to figure out what she would say next. This was torture. She played the chant in her head. *Paige ... Lani, you're not my friends anymore.* It was the only way.

When Paige spoke next, her voice was quieter. "Dory, are you okay? He called you, didn't he."

"No," she said firmly, "and I don't want him to. I'm getting an unlisted number. I'll let you know what it is as soon as I get it."

She was about to sign off, maybe make one more stab at an apology, her final one, but Paige wasn't through.

"The phone room is gone," she said.

"You're kidding. Really?"

"Lani and I went there. Tried to find Jean, see if the True Gentleman's been hassling anyone else about Opal. The place is cleaned out."

"Hmm. Typical in that business. You know that. Anyway, it doesn't matter to me. I quit."

"You did?"

"I've got enough to live on until I finish my last course. Plus I've already got some job interviews lined up."

Shut up, Dory. You're talking too much.

"Hey—that's great. Well, it's good to know you're safe. Sorry if I pissed you off before."

"Me too."

"Kiss Sebastian for me."

"I will."

That had been four nights ago, and she'd hated herself since. *We're not friends anymore*, she kept repeating, sometimes aloud. She scanned the Wednesday night TV listings, knowing she'd be wide awake again tonight.

At precisely one minute after midnight, her phone rang.

CHAPTER 26

Mrs. Ava Lydell lived on the second floor of a modern condo in Sunset Beach. It was modestly but neatly furnished with enough space for her wheelchair to maneuver smoothly between the furniture. Dominating the living room was a 54-inch television, a birthday gift from her daughter Sarah.

"You were very close to your daughter, weren't you, Mrs. Lydell."

Carolyn accepted a cup of strong coffee from Sarah's mother who nodded then swiped away fresh tears.

"I can't seem to turn off the waterworks," she said. It had to be her third apology since Carolyn had arrived some ten minutes earlier. A box of tissues rested in her lap. "I've always thought of myself as independent, Sergeant. Now I'm not so sure. Sarah made my life easier, bringing me dinner, hiring a cleaning lady to come by once a week…"

The police had already accessed Sarah's bank records. Carolyn figured Lydell would be in hock up to her earlobes, but the killer's second victim had incurred no debts. She lived frugally. She didn't own a car. Her apartment was a bachelorette and the view from the minuscule balcony commanded views of other minuscule balconies.

Carolyn did the math. Large screen televisions didn't come cheap, and neither, she assumed, did a weekly cleaning woman. Sarah Lydell was a cashier in a supermarket. Where had she found the money to finance such niceties for her mother?

"I can't believe it's only been a week, Sergeant. Without Sarah stopping by, the time crawls. I dread the supper hour, eating alone, watching television alone, just waiting for my eyes to get heavy, praying that when I finally fall asleep, I won't wake up."

Carolyn had an aversion to growing old, each day a contest to see which body part would ache the most. She did not look forward to the impatience of the young, their pitying glances. Worse than growing old was growing old alone. Ava Lydell was doing both from a wheelchair.

"Is there someone you can call, someone who can come over and sit with you, keep you company?"

Mrs. Lydell plucked another tissue from the box and blew her nose then stuffed the balled-up Kleenex into the cuff of her cardigan. "I have good friends, Sergeant, and of course, they'll visit. But sometimes an old woman just needs to be alone with her sorrow. Are you any closer to learning who—?"

"We're working very hard on Sarah's case, Mrs. Lydell." And getting nowhere fast, but she kept that comment to herself.

"Yes, that's what Sergeant Takacs said when he was here last week. Such a nice man."

Carolyn nodded, envying Ziggy who, when delivering tough news to worried or grieving families, always seemed to get the words right. "Did your daughter socialize a lot? Have a steady boyfriend?"

"She never mentioned anyone specific, but yes, she had dates. Went to the movies and dinner with people from work, too."

Carolyn had taken a tour of Sarah Lydell's apartment, looked in the single clothes closet. Work basics—some jeans, a few shirts and blazers, but no high-heeled shoes, no little black dress. Not the wardrobe of someone with a heavy social life.

On the end table beside the sofa, Ava Lydell had a framed picture of her daughter. Sarah's brown hair was styled in a fashionable blunt cut. She wore a denim skirt and a pale green sweater set. In the photo Sarah made a concerted effort to strike a carefree pose, but clearly she didn't enjoy having her picture taken and the camera didn't like her much either. Sparrow eyes were nearly lost on her large, square face. Her lips were thin, her shoulders broad. Somehow Carolyn doubted that Sarah's dance card was full.

She flipped open her notepad, a gesture that seemed to bother the elder Lydell. Yes, Carolyn thought, your daughter's death has become business. Nothing I can do about it. "Any names that you can remember?" she asked as gently as she could.

The police had already questioned many of the cashiers at the grocery store. Yes, they'd known Sarah, liked her, had a few cups of coffee and conversation with her during breaks and lunch, but there'd never been any after-hours get-togethers. Sarah, at forty-eight, was older than most of them and besides, she'd always been in a hurry to leave once her shift ended.

Mrs. Lydell sniffed, used another tissue to dab at her nose. "I'm terrible with names. But Sarah just loved her job and the people she worked with. She said everyone in the office treated her with such respect."

Carolyn fought to keep her eyeballs in her head. "Office?" She flipped back through her notepad. "Mrs. Lydell, I'm given to understand that your daughter worked at the Safeway on Duane Avenue in Astoria. What office are you referring to?"

Ava Lydell shook her head. "I can't understand why everyone's so mixed up. The papers, the television news people ... Sarah hasn't worked at the market in years. She could never have afforded to buy me this condo on a cashier's wages. Sarah works for a legal firm, and she does very well, too."

"Legal firm? In Astoria? Which one?"

"I don't know exactly," Mrs. Lydell said, flustered. "I told you I'm no good with names. All those companies sound the same. Somebody, Somebody, and Somebody Else, Incorporated."

Carolyn wasn't prone to headaches. Most of her pain radiated from her ass on downward, but now she felt tightness creeping up the back of her neck. Two women dead. With more money floating around than either of them should have had. Sarah Lydell had lied to her mother. Bettina Reid didn't need to lie—her parents hadn't asked. But both women were into something they didn't want their families to know about and Carolyn didn't think it was delivering junk mail door-to-door. The story Bettina Reid had told Paige about her connection to a phone sex service was true. She would bet on it.

Ava Lydell wheeled ahead of her to the door. She was crying again. Another lonely evening was approaching, and Sarah wouldn't be bringing dinner. She took the woman's hand and held it. "We're gonna solve this thing, Mrs. Lydell. Then you'll sleep easier."

Through her tears, she sent Carolyn a grateful look then shifted her gaze to the wall on her left. "Do you like that painting, Sergeant?"

It was a botanical print, beautifully framed in gold with an ivory silk mat. "Yes, very much. Another gift from your daughter?"

"Yes," she said wistfully. "Her favorite flowers. They're jasmine."

CHAPTER 27

Paige talked to Joshua every day—sometimes twice—but their phone conversations were a poor substitute for being together. His deep voice wrapped around her, making her weak. She missed him, told him so, and promised again that Lani's stay would only be for a little while. Right now, she didn't feel she should leave her alone.

"You're being a good friend, Paige," he said. "I hope Lani appreciates it."

She continued to tell herself that honoring the pact was the right thing to do, that loyalty, especially now, might save their lives. She hoped that loyalty to Lani and Dory didn't cost her a future with Joshua.

She swallowed hard. "You're being great about all this."

From an early age, Joshua had majored in magnanimity. During storm season, he used to urge his father to drive through the downtown streets of Portland so he could distribute blankets to the poor. Eventually the entire family jumped on the charitable bandwagon, with Carolyn making thermoses of hot chocolate and Joshua's mother handing out scarves, hats, and mitts knitted by a group at church. The *Oregonian* had written a column on the Lathams. "It's all Joshua," Patrick Latham boasted to the press about his nine-year-old son. His mother added, "We're hoping he'll become a priest."

"Sure this isn't some kind of female ploy?" Joshua asked her.

"How do you mean?"

"You know, get me missing you so much that when we eventually see each other, I'll be insatiable. Lovesick. Realize how hopeless I am without you."

"Is it working?"

"Absolutely."

Lani, bundled in a thick robe, entered the kitchen carrying the rest of the dirty dishes so Paige switched from love talk and asked about Carolyn. "Are the police any closer to finding Bettina's killer?"

"Haven't heard of any new developments," Joshua said.

Paige shook her head at Lani who'd looked momentarily optimistic. When she saw Paige's signal, she hung her head and left the room.

"I'm sure Carolyn's on top of it, though. Once that woman clamps her jaws onto something—"

"Sounds like her twin brother."

"I have been busy," he admitted. "Prepping for the year-end, getting a presentation ready for the board ... but not too busy to miss you. That guy hasn't come around again, has he?"

Nicholas. Paige's stomach turned over. "No. I think he got the message that he wasn't welcome here."

"How long were you with him again?"

"We managed to just make it to our second anniversary. Two years too long," she said, "but no one could have convinced me of that at the time. I thought he was exotic. Now I know he was just a creep."

"You didn't know him as well as you thought you did?"

"You can say that again. By the end, I think I knew him too well."

She wondered why Joshua was asking about Nicholas. Was he jealous? Probably in the same way she was jealous of Fallon McBride. It didn't mean anything, it was over long ago, but still ...

Soon there would be no secrets between them. She would tell him about Amber, Laurel, Dallas and Opal, too. A clean slate. But Joshua was signing off. "Got a call on my other line, Paige," he said in a rush, "and I've been waiting for this one. Talk soon."

Paige heard the click at the other end, the loneliest sound ever. For so many reasons, she hated the telephone.

She was assaulted by a maelstrom of emotions. She longed to be with Joshua, already feeling a separation anxiety after just days apart. She bore the crushing weight of her secret past, the guilt she felt at keeping the truth from Joshua.

Then there was the fear. The True Gentleman hovered around every other thought. Who was he? Where was he? What was next? She knew what he was capable of, fought constantly against disturbing, terrifying visions of Amber's final moments. She deeply regretted the conversation that propelled her and the others into a murky realm about which they knew essentially nothing. And during the past day, she found herself growing angrier at Lani for being so helpless, so needy, so damn romantic and foolish. Paige saw her cuddled up on the living room couch with Parker, fighting a raging case of the flu. She couldn't even manage her illness on her own. Paige had been fetching ginger ale and crackers since she'd arrived home from work, but Lani hadn't kept it down.

"Something's not sitting right," Paige said, forcing back her temper. She sat on the edge of a chair facing Lani.

"Yeah, my supper. Was that Joshua on the phone? I hope I haven't messed—"

"Yes, that was Joshua, but that's not what's bothering me. I can't stop thinking about Dory. It's been five days since I talked to her. Why isn't she returning our calls?"

"Busy, I guess," Lani said weakly, looking yellow. "She's a single mom raising a kid. Neither of us knows what that's like."

"I'm not buying it. Amber and Jasmine are dead. Instead of banding together, which is what friends do in a crisis, she seems to be cutting herself off from us. There's more to this and I'm going to find out what. I'm tired of sitting around waiting for something to happen."

Paige sprang from the chair and went to the front closet for a jacket.

"Where are you going?" Lani sat up, eyes wide.

"Dory's. I won't be long."

"I'm coming too."

"Forget it, Lani. You're sick, it's cold out, and I don't want you throwing up in my car. Stay here with Parker."

"I don't want to be here by myself."

Paige heaved an exasperated sigh. "Look, Lani, I said I won't be long. Just sit tight. I'll close the curtains and lock the door. No one knows you're here except Joshua."

"We can trust him, right?"

Paige bit hard on her lip. "I'll pretend I didn't hear that."

She spun away from Lani, yanked the living room curtains shut then opened the front door. A gust of chilled night air rushed at her and she inhaled deeply. It was all getting to her—finding the foot, Amber and Jasmine's murders, Dory's mysterious flight down the coast, Lani's moving in. Nicholas, back in the States. And no Joshua lying beside her at night, telling her everything would be all right.

Paige locked the door, feeling guilty for leaving Lani alone inside, sick and scared, but she was desperate for a break. And Dory knew more than she was telling.

She tailgated an out-of-state yellow Focus along the coast road, her foot jerking from gas pedal to brake as the driver slowed to check street signs at each intersection. Paige was tempted to pull out and pass, even though it was a no-passing zone. Had the pavement been dry, she would have gone for it. To her relief, at the next street, the car signaled and got out of her way. Normally, she was a careful driver, but tonight she was short on both traffic manners and patience.

When she turned into Dory's driveway this time, all the lights were on except the one in Sebastian's bedroom. Paige glanced at the clock on her dash. 8:30. A school night. Dory would have tucked her son in, read him a story and sat beside him on the bed until his breathing grew heavy.

Paige killed the engine, stepped from the Outback and locked it. Dory met her at the door with a mobile phone attached to her ear and a surprised, unpleasant expression on her face. She stepped aside and let her in anyway.

"Honey, you're just terrific," she purred into the receiver. "Guess you could tell that, couldn't you. Now you go rest up for next time and be sure to call Crystal real soon."

She disconnected the phone and said, "What brings you by, Paige?"

"I thought you said you quit."

"I did. With the other service. I'm working for someone else now."

Paige nudged by her and moved further into the room but remained standing. "You led me to believe you were no longer in the business.

'Interviews lined up,' I think you said. You knew the phone room was gone before I told you, didn't you."

Dory leveled a gaze at her and shrugged. "Maybe."

Paige was staring at a stranger. Dory's jaw was set in concrete, her lips pressed into a thin line. "Listen, Dory, I know what you're doing. You're scared. He *did* call you."

"What the hell are you talking about, girl? I already told you he didn't."

"And I don't believe you."

"Well, then you can go fuck yourself."

Paige exploded. In a swift move her hands flew at Dory's shoulders and she shoved her backwards. "Dammit, Dory! Cut the bullshit. He called you. Don't bother denying it."

Dory glared at her. "So what if he did."

"That's why you ran. He threatened you."

"He played me a tape recording, Paige. Of Amber screaming." Her voice broke. Dallas and Crystal had vanished, leaving a quivering, frightened Dory. "I dream about it. I hear those screams. Do you have any idea what that's like?"

Paige shook her head.

"There's more," Dory said, her face a collage of agony, helplessness, terror. "He let me talk to Jasmine. Before he—" She winced, closed her eyes, squeezed back tears. It was long moments before she could continue. "Jazz begged me, pleaded with me to tell him she didn't know who Opal was. Then there was an awful noise—" Dory clamped hands over her ears. "And the next thing I knew, she was dead."

"But you ran away, Dory. To stay safe. What made you come back?"

Dory's mobile phone rang.

"Shut it off," Paige said.

The air between them was thick with tension. Dory did as she was told but left Paige's question unanswered. A poisoned silence hung in the room.

Forcing gentleness she did not feel, Paige said again, "Why did you come back? Dory?"

There was an audible swallow, then, "He found us. Called me at the inn. Was with us when we stopped for a meal at a roadside diner.

Left a new set of crayons for Sebastian. He knows every move we make, Paige."

"He broke your window?"

"I did that. He was watching us. Knew Sebastian was sitting at the kitchen table, coloring. I lost it. Threw the phone through the glass. Packed and ran."

Paige tried to process it all. Dory and her son, fleeing, pursued by the True Gentleman who had one goal in mind, to locate Opal. He wanted Dory to know she couldn't hide, that her son was easy prey. "You've been back in town since Saturday, Dory. That's five days. And you haven't returned my calls. My guess is you're keeping your distance because you can't look me in the eye. He's called again. Since you've been back."

Dory's gaze focused on the small rug below their feet. "He's called once."

"When?"

"Tonight. About an hour ago."

Fear squirmed along the back of Paige's neck. "Look at me, Dory." And then she knew.

"Oh, God, you told him. Didn't you. About Opal. Everything."

"*I don't like you anymore.*"

Both Dory and Paige turned to where the sound was coming from. Sebastian stood in the doorway of his bedroom, glaring at Paige. "You pushed my mom. I saw you. And you made her swear."

Paige crouched down, wanted to go to him but knew it was no use. She had committed the unforgivable. "I didn't mean for you to hear us, Sebastian. I'm so sorry I woke you. Mommy and I were having an argument. Friends have fights sometimes, right?" She looked up at Dory, whose eyes were moist.

"No. I don't like you," he said again. "You're making my mom cry. You shouldn't stay. You're wrecking our special day."

"Sebastian, I'm sorry. I—"

"Wait," Dory cut in. "Sebastian, why is today special?"

"My lunch," he said, insistent. "You put a cupcake in my lunch. You only let me have dessert on special days."

Dory's hand flew to her mouth. Quickly she recovered then went to her son. She gave him a kiss on the top of his head then turned him toward his room. "You scoot back into bed," she said gently, "and I'll be right in. Because it's a special day, I'll read you another story."

The young boy looked over his shoulder at Paige. "Is she going home now?"

"Yes," Dory said, following his gaze, "she's going home."

Sebastian disappeared into the bedroom, his pajama bottoms dragging on the floor.

When Dory turned to face her, her eyes were slits, her voice a low rumble. "Now do you get it?"

Paige shook her head. She hadn't meant to upset Sebastian. "What did I miss here? What was that stuff about a special day?"

"The *cupcake*," Dory said. "I didn't put a cupcake in Sebastian's lunchbox. But we both know who did."

"Oh God."

"Better get home, Paige. Do whatever you need to do to keep Lani safe. I did what I had to do. Given a choice between a phone whore and your son, what would you have done?"

CHAPTER 28

From the cell phone in the Outback, Paige punched in her home number. Lani picked up on the first ring. "Paige, thank God."

"Lani, listen. I'm on my way. I should be there in five minutes—"

"What happened? Did you talk to Dory?"

Paige threw the car into reverse, squealed out of Dory's driveway. Next door at Harriet Foster's, the living room sheers parted.

"I'll explain when I get there. Sit tight. And don't open the door. Not for anybody."

"Paige, what's going on?" Lani's voice shot through the phone, panic rising. "What aren't you telling me?"

"Be home soon, Lani. Hang in."

"Shh. Quiet a minute." There was an interminable silence then a whisper. "Please hurry, Paige. I think there's someone outside."

She disconnected the phone and pressed the accelerator to the mat. If a police car was nearby and spotted her speeding, she would put on her four-way flashers and make the cruiser follow her home, siren blaring. She shouldn't have left Lani alone. Not for a second. If anything happened, it would be her fault.

I'll never leave you again, Lani. Not ever.

Paige had made that promise once before, when she had flown home from Europe on the heels of an urgent phone call from Mrs. Hollis. "Seraphina, you've got to come. You're the only one she'll talk to. Please."

Lani, in the hospital, her wrists swathed in layers of gauze, cried a steady stream of I'm sorrys. Paige had been doing so well in France, and with every letter she received, Lani had grown more despondent, more lonely. She struggled against her feelings of abandonment, accepted dates to the country club dances at her parents' insistence, agreed to give up her foolish aspiration to be a writer and apply to law school instead, following the Hollis family tradition. Her desolation grew. Her parents told her to snap out of it. Eventually Lani found herself gravitating to Millicent and Jerome Greene. They became the parents she wished she had, and spending time with them was like keeping a small part of Paige with her. In the company of the Greenes and their little group of saints, Lani felt she finally belonged somewhere, that someone was listening.

Then the Greenes committed the unforgivable. They died. Short hours after news of their deaths broke, Lani took her father's razor blades and drew herself a scalding bath. Her mother committed the unforgivable by finding her.

Retreating in a swirl of shame and embarrassment, the Hollises essentially turned Lani over to her best friend, washing their hands of the daughter that just wouldn't conform. No harm could come to Lani, Paige thought. Not now. Not after everything she'd been through, the battles she'd fought and was winning.

There were few cars on the road, but Paige would have given anything for some traffic. It had been a warm day, and now a sea fog blanketed the hood of the Outback. Ahead, there were no other taillights to guide her, only gray and more gray. She was alone out here, and Lani was alone, too.

She hoped. Had Lani really heard something outside? Or were her senses in overdrive? Since the conversation with her final client, the one who'd plunged her into another suicidal miasma, Lani had run from her shadow and everyone else's. She told Paige of furtive glances from strangers, too many wrong numbers, the reappearance of familiar faces at the grocery store, the dry cleaners, her morning coffee stop. In the three months since Lani had quit the phone lines, she'd become a walking textbook case of paranoia. Paige had tried to be supportive and compassionate, but her friend's need proved to be more than she could handle. Her patience was gone. Now Lani had good reason to be paranoid. And Paige had every reason to feel guilty.

She nearly missed the turn into her driveway, seeing the painted white post only when she was almost upon it. The gravel drive was cloaked in fog, swirling and curling in the Outback's high beams. Ahead, she barely made out a hazy yellow glow from the porch lights that flanked the front door. The rest of the cabin was dark.

Paige's fingers tightened around the steering wheel. On the porch, silhouetted in the half-light was a man, trying to peer through the separation in the living room drapery panels. Off in the murky shadows and camouflaged by the fog, was a silver Porsche.

Paige yanked her keys from the ignition and climbed out of the car. "What the hell do you think you're doing?"

Nicholas Bissonette turned and seemed relieved to see her. Then he grinned. "Hey, babe! Anyone mention you need some lighting for that fucking driveway of yours? It's like driving into the mouth of hell."

She strode up onto the porch. "Why are you skulking around in the dark? Looking in my window?"

"Who's that in there?"

"None of your damn business. Get away from that window. Better yet, get off my property."

"Brought you something."

Nicholas reached into the inside pocket of his jacket and produced a 4" x 6" faux moiré card bearing elaborate calligraphy in deep garnet ink. An invitation. To the opening of Atelier Bissonette. 319 Surfside Boulevard.

Two blocks away from where Paige worked. She'd seen the work being done on the building that used to be a pet boutique. She'd even asked Harry and Luke if they knew anything about the renovations and who was moving in. Harry had heard something about an art gallery but didn't know the owner. Arlen Dale and some of the others across the street didn't know either.

"You're opening a gallery? Here?"

"Thought you'd be surprised. It's going to be fantastic."

No, it wouldn't be. What delusions was Nicholas harboring? Their relationship had been disastrous for much of their last year together. What memories had he exaggerated in his mind?

She searched her own memory, and from its recesses, snatched what she recalled of the voice she'd once used with her submissive clients. "Nicholas, you didn't have to drive all the way out here with this. Most normal people use a stamp and a mailbox. And don't hold your breath waiting for me to come to your gallery."

"Paige, if you'd just give us a ch—"

"There is no 'us.' I left you, remember? Put an ocean between us. Why don't you swim back to where you belong?"

"I don't blame you for leaving. Back then we barely had ten cents between us. But all that's changed. I'm raking in six figures now. You'd never have to work—"

"You think that's why I left? Because we were poor? Oh, Nicholas, you're too much."

His brows knit into a V. "If not the money then what?"

"Let's just say I don't share your taste in art." She let the pause hang there, but he still didn't get it. "I'm with someone else," she added, "and did I forget to tell you his sister is a cop? The last time I mentioned the police, I got the distinct impression it made you nervous."

Nicholas tried to bluff, but again, Paige saw the shift in expression. The cocky sneer was gone. She came at him again. "And stay off my property. That's for your own protection. Out here, late at night, I could easily mistake you for a rabid animal and shoot you."

His eyes narrowed and he took a half step closer. "You'll be sorry, Paige. Really sorry."

She fixed him with a glare that stopped him. "A threat now? Just another thing for me to document. There are anti-stalking laws nowadays, Nicholas. The way I see it, you're this close to crossing the line. Why are you still here?"

He turned toward his car and Paige heard the click of the Porsche's keyless lock. When he reached the driver's side door, he cast another glance in her direction and she held up the invitation he had brought her and tore it in half. The car rumbled on and Paige remained on the porch until she saw the last trace of red from the taillights disappear down the driveway.

She unlocked the front door and flicked the light switch. Lani cowered at one end of the sofa, her eyes red and swollen. Nicholas's footsteps on the porch outside had reduced her to a quivering mass. Now Paige was about to shove her over the edge.

"Get dressed. Throw your stuff in a bag. You're leaving."

"What's going on?" Lani was already kicking off the afghan. "Who was that out there?"

"Who that was doesn't matter. The True Gentleman got to Dory. He knows who Opal is."

Lani began to whimper.

Paige cut her off mid-sob. "Don't you dare fall apart on me! We've got to get moving!"

Opal's caller was growing desperate. It wasn't enough to keep her from his grasp. If the woman of his fantasies could not be found, it wouldn't be long before he would hunt down the others. Amber and Jasmine were dead. Dallas was being terrorized. Soon, Laurel wouldn't be safe either.

Paige had to call Carolyn. She had to tell her everything she knew, why the women were dying. She would look through her journals again, try to remember voices, clues, anything that might give the police a leg up on their investigation.

Lani reappeared in jeans and a turtleneck, her meager possessions packed into a duffle bag. She stared at the front door as if a slavering ogre waited beyond. "What if he's already out there? That guy with the Porsche. How well do you know him?"

Nicholas? The True Gentleman? No. It couldn't be. But his *timing*. It all fit.

Amber had been killed at the beginning of September. Nicholas had phoned Paige a day later. He'd been back in Oregon for several months, he'd told her vaguely. Long enough to phone Opal, build an entire fantasy relationship with her. If there was one thing Nicholas knew plenty about, it was fantasy. Paige recalled the costumes she discovered in the basement, the clothes he'd made her wear, the horrific artwork she'd stumbled across. And the drugs. Always plenty of those around. To Nicholas, the world was a better place when he had a fat wallet and a little something to take the edge off.

Dory had admitted the True Gentleman had phoned her earlier this evening, and that she'd told him who Opal was. Within an hour, Nicholas was in her driveway, peering in her window.

The invitation to the gallery opening—a ruse. He needed to account for his being on her porch. And it wasn't Paige he wanted a relationship with, it was Opal.

Paige shook away all thoughts of Nicholas. Lani's paranoia was contagious. Just because the pieces fit didn't make it so, and there wasn't time to sort through it all now.

"We can't just hang around here," she told Lani. "Come *on*."

"I hate Opal," Lani declared, slinging the duffel over her shoulder. "I really hate her."

Suddenly Paige stopped, scanned the room, moved toward the kitchen, the screened-in porch at the back of the house. "Lani, where's Parker?"

"He took off."

"What?"

"He needed to pee. I needed a smoke. I put his leash on, took him out back but as soon as I opened the door, he broke away. He'll come back, won't he?"

CHAPTER 29

He had imagined Victorian furniture, heavy draperies, fringed area rugs and plenty of sentimental clutter, but Opal's apartment left him stunned and frankly, disappointed. The décor was retro-kitschy, a mélange of pink, black and white '50s and '60s memorabilia. He inhaled deeply, hoping to catch a lingering floral scent but detected instead a trace of pine-scented air freshener and stale smoke.

The entrance door was decorated with a battalion of shiny new dead-bolt locks. He smiled. A girl couldn't be too careful.

It was already past eleven but Opal was still out. Another disappointment. Tomorrow was a work day for most. He hoped she wouldn't keep him waiting much longer.

He moved purposefully into the bedroom where more retro-glop waited—an Art Deco dressing table and matching stool upholstered in pink fur; a pair of bedside lamps with prowling panther bases; a nightmarish bedspread in a hallucinogenic pattern. He scanned the top of the dresser, the window ledge and the bedside tables for photographs but saw none. Opal was still a mystery to him.

In her closet were several pairs of slacks, jeans and short skirts slung carelessly on hangers. Most of the garments were wrinkled and stank of cigarette smoke. Her dresser drawers were filled with tank tops and cropped sweaters. A T-shirt and a pair of flannel boxer shorts had been tossed on the rug beside the bed. Sleepwear? He rooted through more drawers for delicate lace, sensuous silk or satin, but found only sports bras, cotton camisoles and some thong underwear. He slammed the drawers and went to her nightstand. In the cupboard below was a collection of period erotica mixed with more raunchy contemporary stuff, plus some how-to manuals on talking dirty. In the drawer above she kept a pack of Virginia Slims and a box of condoms.

More disappointment waited in the bathroom. Opal's perfume was "Poison," a pricey fragrance but much too heady a scent for the woman he knew. "L'Air du Temps" would be more appropriate. He made a mental note to buy her some.

There were black towels. A pink heart-shaped bath mat. Mold on the grout between the tiles. The medicine cabinet contained whitening toothpaste, a nearly full bottle of Zoloft, some spermicidal jelly and a diaphragm.

He wondered if he had entered the wrong apartment. He pulled the slip of paper from his pants pocket and rechecked the address.

Once more his gaze was drawn to the diaphragm. He imagined being with Opal, offering to help her insert it and her refusing, saying she wouldn't be needing birth control with him. She would welcome his children, as many as God would grant them. He reached out and plucked the diaphragm from the shelf, cupped it in his hand and squeezed, then watched with fascination as it swelled back into shape. He held it gently, imagined holding a delicate breast in just this way, feeling smooth warm skin beneath his touch, the vital pulse-pulse-pulse of her heartbeat, a firm nipple rising to meet his fingertips.

He lifted the diaphragm to his face and breathed in, hungry for the musky scent from deep within her, smelling only rubber. Tentatively he ran his tongue around the rim, felt throbbing and stiffness between his legs. From a distant corner of his mind he heard a moan. He probed his tongue deep into the centre, poking, teasing, prodding. He didn't bother to wipe the ejaculate that dampened his underwear. Better still, he tucked the diaphragm over his soaked penis. Opal wouldn't need the device anymore. The spermicide either. Or her supply of antidepressants. He grabbed these and shoved them inside his jacket.

It was after midnight now. He wasn't pleased. But he needed his sleep. Once more he entered the furry pink and black nightmare bedroom but this time he turned down the gaudy bedspread and slipped between the sheets, one of Opal's foam pillows tucked tightly between his legs.

CHAPTER 30

PAIGE SAT UP HALF THE night waiting for Parker. Each creak of the porch floorboards had her sprinting for the front door but the dog never appeared. The lab had escaped once before, breaking free of his leash to chase a squirrel through the woods, only to return an hour later with a contrite expression on his face and a snout full of burrs. Eventually Paige fell asleep on the couch, but when the first rays of sunlight shone through the windows, she grabbed binoculars and a dog whistle and walked the gravel drive to the roadway, calling aloud. Periodically, she blew the whistle and listened but the bark she longed to hear never came. She repeated her calls in the back yard, standing at the edge of the woods. "Parker! Come on, boy!" Several times her voice broke and her eyes welled up. More than once she cursed Lani, blamed her for being careless, blamed her for needing a cigarette, and blamed her for not running after Parker when he'd first escaped. Instead, Lani had curled up on the sofa feeling sorry for herself.

After showering, Paige called Joshua who told her he would come by later to help her search. "We'll get him back, Paige. Don't worry."

Her nearest neighbor, Stan Gardner, lived two miles away, but Paige called him anyway, woke him up and told him Parker was loose. In a sleepy voice, he promised to keep a lookout. Paige had only spoken to Stan a few times, but he was a lifelong friend of her uncle's and when he heard the quiver in her voice, he told her he would take a walk later and look for the dog. "That's what neighbors are for," he said.

Paige's phone rang, and it was Lani, telling her she'd arrived in Vancouver and was waiting for her connection to Halifax. From there she would rent a car to get to her cousin's place in Wolfville. "I'm paying cash, Paige," she told her. "No paper trail." As an afterthought, she asked about Paige's dog and mumbled an apology before hanging up.

As she drove to work Paige scouted for some sign of Parker bounding along the side of the road, or worse, stretched out and still on the pavement. At the store, both Harry and Luke offered consolation. "You spoiled that dog rotten, Paige," said Harry. "He'd be a fool not to come back."

"But maybe he can't come back," she replied. "What if he's hurt? Or what if someone's taken him?"

Luke made her coffee. "He's off making canine love with some French poodle. Once he's had his way with her, he'll come home."

That made her smile, but soon she was frowning again. She had called Carolyn and was meeting her for lunch, telling her only that she might have relevant information on the murders of Bettina Reid and Sarah Lydell. Between customers she mentally searched for the right words and rehearsed what she would say to Joshua's sister. She thought, too, about the True Gentleman. Where was he now? Her mind formed the image of a man cloistered away in a cobwebby attic, plotting his next line of attack.

More terrible was the thought that the True Gentleman was not in some cobwebby attic, but at work, like everyone else, blending in and chatting up colleagues during coffee breaks, asking what their plans were for the weekend. He could be anywhere. He could be anyone.

When Paige arrived at the Surfside Café just after twelve, the place was already full. She spotted Carolyn at a small round table near the front window nursing a glass of 7-Up. She greeted her, told her Parker was missing and listened to her reassurances. After a hasty glance at the menu, they both ordered the meatloaf.

Joshua's sister, not one for small talk, said, "Okay, give me the goods. What do you know?"

Paige told her that not only had she known Bettina Reid, she'd also been acquainted with Sarah Lydell, the second victim. "But I knew Sarah only as Jasmine. We called her Jazz."

Carolyn said nothing, just flipped open a notebook and scribbled Sarah = Jasmine, and underlined Jasmine twice. She thanked the waitress when the meatloaf came.

"Bettina used the name Amber," she continued then the rest tumbled out—Dory, Lani, the True Gentleman, the search for Opal.

Carolyn didn't interrupt. When Paige was done, she said, "So Lani's left town? And she's this Opal the caller is after?"

"Yes. When Lani quit the phone lines a few months ago, this guy went crazy. Started asking everyone else if they'd seen Opal, if they knew where she went, when she was coming back. Then somehow he found out who some of the operators were—you know, their real identities—where they lived and ... you know the rest."

"Not all of it. What does this guy want with Opal?"

"He thinks he loves her. So I suppose he's thinking marriage, kids, baby animals frolicking in the back yard. Who knows?"

"And Opal never set him straight?"

Paige shrugged. "Give the customer what he wants to hear. That's the job description."

"In other words, she encouraged him."

"She looked forward to his calls. It can happen."

"So he's not the reason Lani ... Opal quit the business?"

"No." Paige explained about the sicko, the caller who'd driven Lani to a second suicide attempt by involving her in a scenario that Lani thought was real. She described the child's words, her screams, the sound of nails being driven into what Lani believed to be a cross. Then she told Carolyn how she'd found Lani and the grisly scene at her apartment, her friend's hospitalization and convalescence at Paige's cabin.

"Mother in heaven," Carolyn said. "Give me a minute to process this." She took a deep breath and cut her meat into bite-sized chunks, each fork full of meatloaf taking a dive into a scoop of mashed potatoes before being lifted to her mouth. She ate that way for quite some time and jotted illegible scribbles onto her notepad while Paige picked at her food. Eventually she said, "You told me you and Bettina met in a university class."

"Two years ago." Paige felt her face go warm. The bad part was coming.

"And this Sarah ... Jasmine? Was she in the class too?"

Paige sighed and set her fork and knife on the plate. "I think you already know the answer to that. I worked the lines too, Carolyn. Two years ago, I was Laurel. I met Jazz on the job."

Joshua's sister let a few heartbeats go by. Then: "Has this guy called you at home? Used your real name? Asked for Opal?"

She shook her head. "Not yet. Dory blew Lani's cover, but not mine."

"If you can believe her," she muttered. "Where's Lani now?"

"East. At a cousin's in Nova Scotia someplace. Waiting it out until the killer is caught."

"She's safe there, at this cousin's? No one followed you after you left the cabin last night?"

"I didn't notice anyone. And Lani called this morning. She made it to Vancouver in one piece."

Carolyn frowned. "Seems too easy. This guy was able to follow Dory and her son down the coast in a rainstorm, terrorize her with a phone call in her hotel room and come within breathing distance of her son, yet when the object of his obsession becomes known to him, his surveillance skills fall apart? It doesn't compute."

The waitress came, cleared plates and brought two mugs of dark roast along with the bill. Paige grabbed it. "Please. Very small compensation for my not telling you about my involvement in all this earlier."

"And you didn't because ...?"

"I guess I thought some things stink so much they should stay buried."

"Phone sex isn't illegal, Paige," Carolyn said, making no move to fight her for the check. "So you kept quiet because you were ashamed?"

"There's some of that, sure. But I made a pact with the others, Carolyn. I believe in keeping my promises. Lani and Dory had so much at stake. If social services knew Dory was doing any kind of work in the sex trade industry, she could lose her son. And a scandal could cost Lani's mother the election. Imagine the headlines. Judge's daughter caught up in phone-sex ring. Lani's relationship with her parents is already hanging by a hair. We agreed to protect each other."

Carolyn nodded. "I take it Joshua doesn't know?"

"No. But he will. Tonight."

Carolyn grew quiet once more and made more scribbles on her notepad, a time-filler, Paige realized, because after all, how does anyone react to being told she's sitting across from a phone whore? One who's dating her twin brother?

Paige left a decent tip for the waitress and asked to have her half-eaten meal boxed for take-out. She might be hungry later, though somehow she doubted it. The little she'd managed to swallow had sunk like granite. "What will he think, Carolyn?"

She let out a sigh. "Joshua? All I know is that Josh cares about you. I also know secrets and lies have a way of biting you in the ass, so get this thing out in the open, but quick. And explain why you didn't tell him earlier."

"It won't be easy."

"Listen Paige, I hope you two can work this out. Really. Meanwhile, I'm going to get over to your friend Lani's apartment and see if she's had any uninvited visitors. Obsessed guy looking for the love of his life is bound to show up at her place sooner or later now that he knows where she lives." She glanced at her notes. "I'll pay Dory Getz a call, too. And Paige? I'll want to see that phone journal of yours."

Paige nodded. Carolyn was right. Secrets did have a way of biting you in the ass.

"One more thing," Carolyn said. "I want you to exercise much more caution until this guy is caught. Any suspicious phone calls, you tell me. Anyone acting strangely, no matter how harmless it seems, you tell me."

"I am being careful, Carolyn. Don't worry."

"Paige, you think only reckless people get themselves killed? That foot was put by your car for a reason. Maybe Dory didn't blow your cover, but someone else sure as hell knows your connection to all this. If this guy is picking off phone-sex workers to get to Opal, then there's no way you're safe. And the only reason he hasn't made contact with you yet is because he has something else in mind. And that should scare you as much as it does me."

CHAPTER 31

WHEN JOSHUA KNOCKED ON HER door at seven o'clock, Paige didn't even pause long enough to kiss him.

"Joshua, there's something I need to tell you."

They'd spent too many nights apart and, as much as she wanted to leap into his arms and make everything else go to hell, she feared losing her nerve if she didn't follow Carolyn's advice.

Get this thing out in the open, but quick.

I hear you, Carolyn.

"You found Parker?"

"No, but—"

"Then maybe we should talk later—" He touched his lips to her cheek "—and look for him while we've still got some light. And bundle up. It's windy."

Paige tried again to speak but he silenced her. The weather was turning nasty. Soon they wouldn't be able to hear Parker if he was whimpering for help somewhere. They took flashlights and headed into the bush behind the cabin. Paige called out at frequent intervals to no avail. Her voice was swallowed by the wind.

Earlier, Stan Gardner had knocked on her door. As promised, he had gone to search for her dog as well, combing the wooded acres behind his property but he saw no sign of Parker roaming on his land. He would keep looking. Paige had stopped by the animal shelter en route home with a picture of her dog, but he hadn't been turned in, nor had any dog matching Parker's description been taken to a veterinarian's or been hit by a vehicle. It was like he had been beamed up, carried skyward on the howling wind.

She and Joshua walked for close to two hours, their flashlights sweeping wide arcs through the dense underbrush. Paige stopped to fasten the top button on her jacket, feeling the night chill rip through her. Josh turned up her collar, landed another soft kiss on her forehead then they continued on. They spoke little, more concerned with listening for a dog's bark or howl. Way off in the distance, an owl hooted, but otherwise they heard nothing, not even a squirrel or chipmunk skittering for shelter. Paige prayed in the only way she knew how—*be safe, Parker. Better yet, come home.*

They made their way back to the cabin in the pitch dark, both of them cold and dejected.

"He's wearing a collar and he's microchipped, Paige. Someone'll turn him in. Don't lose hope."

She barely felt Josh's protective arm slip around her shoulders. Hope? It had deserted her days ago and now, on top of everything, she was mourning her beloved and loyal pet. She forced the image of Parker's face from her mind. There were other issues pressing in on her.

Joshua got a fire going while Paige made hot chocolate, adding a generous shot of Cointreau to each mug. Would the liqueur relax her? Put the right words in her mouth?

It seemed so harmless at the time, Joshua.

I was a different person then.

I needed work.

She gazed at the alcohol in the bottle. There wasn't enough of it.

They settled close together on the couch and Paige steeled herself. "I had lunch with your sister today."

"Really?" Josh set his mug on the coffee table. "She didn't haul out my naked baby pictures, did she?"

When she didn't smile, he said, "What's on your mind, Paige?"

"Opal. It's all about Opal."

"Who?"

As she had done with Carolyn, Paige repeated everything she knew about how Lani, as Opal, had tapped into the True Gentleman's fantasies, and how because of his delusion, his obsession, two women were dead and Lani was on the run.

"She's tried to kill herself before, Joshua. Twice."

"I'll be damned," he said. "That scared little rabbit I met worked the sex lines? She doesn't seem the type."

Paige swallowed then plunged into deep water. "What about me, Joshua? Do I seem the type?"

The room went quiet. Interminable minutes ticked by.

She knew it would be bad, her admission jarring in itself, her delaying the truth making it that much worse. She had envisioned scenarios—a screaming match, some foot stomping, a litany of curse words and a dash for the door—but she knew none of these were Joshua's style. He simply stared at her as if seeing her for the first time.

When she could bear the silence no longer, she said, "Well, do I?"

"No, Paige, you don't seem the type. But then, how well do I really know you anyway?"

She reached out for his hand but he kept his folded. "You *do* know me, Joshua. I worked the phone lines for just under a year. Then I quit. I couldn't pretend anymore. I was in therapy … after Nicholas … trying to figure myself out. My life with Nicholas had been a sham, with me reinventing myself to please him. I realized the phone-sex business was keeping me disguised too. I needed to find my way back to who I really was. I wanted to have a real life."

Joshua frowned and gazed at the rug. "I want a real life too. With someone I can trust."

"You can trust me. There are no more secrets."

She explained about the promise the four had made, the loyalty she felt she owed the others and her reasons for keeping her secret for so long. Her parents' debt, her desire to pay her uncle back quickly.

"You could have told me sooner."

"Yes, I could have. I should have. But honestly, at the beginning of our relationship, I didn't think my past was any of your business. It's not like I slept my way up and down the coast. My having worked the phone lines wasn't going to impact you."

"Are you sure? Who really whispered to me when the lights went out? Was that you, Paige? Or was that some actress with a script."

She half expected the comment but it stung like hell anyway. Her eyes welled up, but she blinked the tears away. "Maybe I deserved that. And you can choose to believe me or not, but I never, ever acted when I was with you."

"But all those men ... the things that were said ..."

"Role-playing, Joshua. Just like at the movies. Only not face to face. And yes, there were some real creeps, but there were nice people too." She told him about Andrew, a youngish-sounding caller, who only wanted advice about girls. He was twenty-one, he claimed, and had never been on a date, didn't know the first thing about approaching a woman and was petrified at the prospect of having to make conversation with one. Paige had walked him through a few ice-breaking scenarios, then a first date scene. *You just practice that awhile, Andrew, and when you're ready to move to first base, call back, ask for Laurel, and we'll talk again.*

"So now you're telling me you provided an essential service. Maybe I should hire you as a counselor at 3F House."

Paige sprung up. "Okay, Joshua. If you're angry, I can understand that. You want to imagine every conversation I ever had with a stranger, you go ahead and do that too. But if you're going to sit there and preach from your pulpit about the error of my ways, then you know where the door is. I was always afraid of losing you over this, but I won't let you throw my past in my face every time we're together." She began walking toward the door, thinking he would follow her, that this would be the last time she would see him. When he didn't pursue, she whirled around and in spite of herself, said, "By the way, must be nice, to have lived a perfect life with no regrets."

He stood then and went over to the fire. He added more wood and stared into the burning flame, his elbow resting on the huge wooden beam that served as the mantelpiece. After a few moments, he said, "You're right. I'm handling this badly, but you've thrown me for a loop, Paige. I didn't see this coming."

She returned to the sofa and sat. "I know. And I'm sorry."

He had more questions for her. "Does the caller know who you are? What has Dory told him? Where's Lani now?"

She answered each in turn then Joshua echoed Carolyn's words. "Are you sure you weren't followed to the airport?"

"Reasonably sure."

He shook his head. "Reasonably sure isn't good enough. If this bastard is out there, killing women to get to Lani, then ... I want you safe, Paige."

"Carolyn and the police will catch him, Joshua. You said it yourself. Carolyn's the best."

More silence followed. Joshua ran his hand along the coarse beam of the mantel. Paige gave him the space to gather his thoughts. She picked up mugs and the liqueur bottle and took them into the kitchen. When she returned she said, "I'm exhausted. I'm going to bed."

He turned to face her. "I'll stay here until the fire goes out."

And then? She couldn't ask.

"I won't leave you alone. Not while that bastard is on the loose. I'll just bunk on the couch."

She nodded, understanding, but her expression must have registered pain. Disappointment. Worry.

"I haven't stopped caring, Paige," he said softly. "I just need some time to get my head around all this."

"Goodnight, Joshua." She retreated to her bedroom and closed the door. It had begun to rain. Icy pellets tapped against the window. Parker was out there somewhere, and so was the True Gentleman. Paige disrobed and climbed into bed, rolling to the side where Joshua usually slept, the covers pulled tightly under her chin. She felt sorrow laced with dread, missing her pet, wondering where the True Gentleman was and what he was thinking, what he was planning.

She clung to one filament of hope, Joshua's reassurance. *I haven't stopped caring, Paige.* For now, it was enough.

CHAPTER 32

"OPAL WASN'T THERE."

His voice sliced through her like a newly sharpened ax. Dory rushed to her kitchen window, repaired earlier in the day, and closed the blinds. *No more, you bastard. Not one more call. You promised.*

"I gave you what you wanted, you prick," she replied, sounding like Dallas and Crystal, feeling like shit. "I don't keep tabs on what Opal does or where she goes."

"Such language, Dory," he whispered. "Are you so certain you want to anger me?"

"Look," she said, softening a little, "I'm just frustrated, that's all. And scared. I answered your goddamn question, told you who Opal was and where she lived. I kept my end of the deal, fair and square."

His low chuckle oozed through the phone line, coiled around her and squeezed. "Fair and square," he repeated, his tone mocking. "You didn't call Opal yourself, of course. Warn her, perhaps cause her to leave town …?"

"Are you nuts? Why would I? She's not my friend. I've got my child to think of."

"Ah, yes. Dear Sebastian. He looked so nice this morning in his bright red Fair Isle sweater. A proper little man."

Oh God, no. Where had he seen him? Was he watching her son board the bus? Had he been parked somewhere on their street? She hadn't noticed. She hadn't looked. This was supposed to be over.

"Did he happen to tell you how his day went?"

Had she asked him? Yes. She always asked Sebastian about his day. He had told her it was fine, mentioned something about learning a new song, one with actions to go along with the words. When he'd tried to sing it for her earlier, he'd gotten the gestures all mixed up.

"He had a good day."

"Isn't that just like the little man of the house, not wanting to worry his mother? I suppose he didn't mention being tripped at the bottom of the slide by one of the older boys."

Dory hated the world outside her door. Hated it, hated it, hated it. Predators lurked behind every tree trunk, in every dark corner. They were on the bus and in the classrooms. At recess, their numbers multiplied as a whole school full of them rushed outdoors, just waiting for someone like Sebastian to happen by, a true innocent on a planet overrun with bullies. Damn them straight to hell. "No, he didn't say anything."

"I could have beaten the red-headed rat bastard who hurt your son, Dory. Twenty footsteps and I would have been on top of him, throttling the last breath from his throat. Poor Sebastian. He really does arouse one's protective instincts, doesn't he?"

Twenty steps away. *Sebastian, you must have seen the man. You'll tell me when I ask. Think. Remember.*

"Schools can be terrible places, can't they? Full of teasing and cruelty and humiliation. I would spare Sebastian that, remove him from all of it. I almost did."

Dory thought of Parkview School, with its L-shaped playground where six hundred children skipped and screamed and tagged each other every day while two harried yard duty teachers laughed at students' corny jokes, wiped runny noses and broke up fights. They couldn't be everywhere, couldn't see everything.

"Stay away from my son."

"I'd love to, Dory," came the awful lilting voice, "but I'll need something in return. And you do have something for me, don't you."

"I don't know where Opal is! Fuck!"

The caller cleared his throat. "She hasn't been in her apartment for almost a week. The milk in her fridge is sour. She ordered food from Ming's on September 7th. The leftovers are still there. Where did she run, Dory? Who's protecting her? One more name and you'll never hear from me again. You have my word. As a gentleman." There was another soft chuckle. It reverberated up her spine, bristled her scalp.

She killed the lights in the kitchen. Somehow it made the telling easier. "Try Paige Rowan," she said quickly and slammed the phone down.

Paige Rowan. When he heard the name, he smiled.

It was almost funny, imagining the outdoorsy, wholesome-looking Paige working the phones. Yet it fit. Her voice was so distinctive. It reminded him a little of that chanteuse, Edith Piaf, and for a moment, he was able to conjure an image of the athletic Paige clad in a sequined red dress, vamping it up on top of a Steinway, belting out a tune in a smoky room.

He traced his memory—all the calls, all the conversations—and finally came up with a name: Laurel.

Paige had been good on the phone—not like Opal, because Opal was real—but steamy nonetheless. The single time he'd spoken to her she had gone the extra mile, but as hard as she tried, she had never really gotten through to his core. She'd played the purple fantasy game with him, but when he called again, she'd hung up. He hadn't forgiven her for that. Indeed, it made him furious each time he thought about it.

He could call her now. It might be fun, hearing the fear creep into her voice. Where's Opal? She would lie—they were all good at that, weren't they? Paige would protest—she didn't know any Opal. He would remind her of Amber, of Jasmine, and she would miraculously recall that yes, there was an Opal. She would beg.

Please don't hurt me.

Calling Paige would be against the rules. And foolish. He saw no sense in setting off alarms in her head that might frighten her into taking flight. It was enough for now that she'd found Amber's fleshy foot. It had sickened him when he'd heard about it, but he realized then that he couldn't undo what had been done. His soul had already been sold. Instead, he focused on the end game, his life with Opal.

Soon she would be his and together they could go anywhere, away from all the killing.

Paige would tell him about Opal. Soon, the perfect opportunity would present itself and he would step from the shadows. When he was done with her, she would tell him anything.

CHAPTER 33

THE 1960S APARTMENT HOUSE THAT the infamous Opal called home was a low-rise shoebox, one of three in a complex called Westmore Terrace at the north end of the village. Years ago, the buildings had been faced with orangey-red brick, but someone had jumped on the renovation bandwagon, covering the crumbling brick with stucco the color of Dijon mustard. Shortly afterward, the money had run out, so each unit still bore Italianate balconies of curlicued white wrought iron. Joshua drove by the complex every morning on his way to work and said the sight of the place spoiled his breakfast. Carolyn agreed with her brother—Westmore Terrace was hideous.

Lani Hollis lived in building C, so Carolyn followed the winding drive around until she spotted the faded gold C etched into the transom over the entryway. She pulled into a visitor's parking space, used the dregs of her 7-Up to wash down a couple of heavy-duty muscle relaxants, then got out of the car and stretched, every inch of her sciatica-ridden body feeling like an old woman. She located the apartment's super, who was running a vacuum over a threadbare carpet in what passed for the lobby. The ring attached to the bald man's belt held at least fifty keys. Carolyn's hip ached just looking at it. She flipped the super her ID, explained the nature of her visit in the vaguest terms and was ushered into a wood-grained elevator that reeked of beer and bleach. The super, who introduced himself as Ben Stayner, made small talk about last night's windstorm and excused himself when he didn't quite manage to squelch a burp. At apartment 302, he jangled his key collection until he found the one to open Lani's door.

"I'll be in the lobby," he said, tipping an invisible hat. "Buzz if you need me."

"Will do."

As Stayner turned to leave, he pointed to the door and said, "Jumpin' Jesus, will you look at all those locks? What was she afraid of, do you suppose?"

"Whatever it was got in anyway. Door's been jimmied." Carolyn directed his gaze to three vertical gouges in the door frame.

Stayner assured her he'd seen nothing, heard nothing, and none of the tenants had reported anything amiss. "Wife and I are always home. We don't miss much." He told Carolyn to pull the door tight when she was done.

Carolyn tugged on gloves and looked closely at the pry marks. Way overdone. If Opal had vacated her apartment, her battery of deadbolts wouldn't have been engaged. A credit card could have opened this door. Why overdo the effort when a flick of the wrist would suffice?

Sadistic bastard. He wants Opal to know he's been here. Doesn't care one ounce of shit if the cops know it too.

Let's see what other clues you've left behind, you sick son of a bitch.

Investigators were on the way. They would go through the apartment, take a cast of the door jamb, dust the place senseless, but Carolyn already knew there would be no prints. Parquet floor and ceramic tile meant no carpet indentations either.

She switched modes. She had to stop thinking like a cop and come at this like a killer, an obsessed, lethal predator who had one goal in mind—to find Opal. And if not find her, at least get closer to her. The bedroom would be first. Intimate. The object of his sick desire slept there, pressed her bare skin against fresh linens, removed bras and panties in that room. He would want to feel, to smell.

Opal's telephone, a pink one, was on a bedside table. Had he picked it up, knowing this was the phone she had whispered into? Made his fantasies come alive? She made a note for the forensic team.

Carolyn opened dresser drawers. Impossible to tell whether Opal's things had been rifled through or if anything was missing. She rooted through the crammed lingerie drawer; the garments were soft, supple to the touch. She noticed boxer briefs and a T-shirt on the floor by the unmade bed and felt these as well then held them close to her face, inhaled a hint of smoke and perspiration. In the closet Carolyn spotted a slew of trendy clothes, some bearing designer labels. She knew it often took plenty of cash to look bad and thought some couturiers had a conspiracy going to make women look ridiculous. The conspiracy was alive in this closet.

The apartment's décor was quirky, too, but it would have cost Opal a few bucks to put the look together. Carolyn scribbled a memo to herself. *Ask Paige about Lani's financial status. Talk to parents?* Perhaps even Stayner, who said he didn't miss much, knew something about the tenant in #302.

The bathroom was neat, like the rest of the apartment, and the cupboard below the sink, aside from toilet paper and Sani-Flush, held the usual feminine stuff—tampons, bubble bath, a hot wax kit, a curling iron. Carolyn tried to recall what she crammed into her small vanity at home. Perfume, Q-tips, nail polish remover, raspberry-scented deodorant. Opal had all these items as well; if something was missing, Carolyn didn't know what it was. But the bastard had been here. She could feel it, as if he had left a rancid streak of his pheromones behind.

She toured the rest of the apartment, opened the fridge and examined the leftovers, checked the kitchen drawers and the hall closet, groped around under the chesterfield cushions, thinking the son of a bitch might have left a souvenir, some small token of his love. *I've been here, Opal. Right where you live. Where you eat. Where you sleep. I've touched your things. Can't you feel me everywhere you go?*

Carolyn went toward the linen closet where Opal kept a neat stack of towels and washcloths. A glass bowl of peach-scented potpourri rested on top of a brand new pink blanket. Carolyn ran her flat gloved hand between the folds of the blanket then did the same with the towels. She groped behind a pile of sheets, shoved aside a portable heater. The bottom shelf was allocated to cleaning supplies contained in plastic bins: Windex, Mr. Plummer, Lemon Pledge. She rummaged in there, too, but found only a crisp-dead centipede.

She abandoned the linen closet and returned to the bedroom. She was missing something. Her gaze was drawn to the unmade bed, a standout in an otherwise organized, tidy living space. Opal could have left in a hurry, of course. It was a possible explanation. But Carolyn knew before she folded back the bedspread and before her latex-sheathed fingers patted the whitened crusty patches on the pink pillowcase that forensics would find a treasure trove of the True Gentleman's DNA.

Stayner was still in the lobby when Carolyn emerged from the elevator. The super was squirting what smelled like vinegar on the large picture window at the front of the building. "Get what you came for?" he asked.

Carolyn gave a noncommittal shrug. "What can you tell me about Lani Hollis? Come and go much? Boyfriends?"

Stayner put down the squeegee. "From what I could tell, she stayed in most nights. Shy young thing. Always friendly enough, but didn't go out of her way, you know? Went to class during the day, drove a new white Cabrio convertible. It's still in her parking space out back."

"Nice car for a student," Carolyn said.

"I thought so, too. 'Remember when I was going to school. Drove a 12-year-old Corolla that I was almost too embarrassed to pick up a date in."

"Don't suppose you've seen anyone hanging around, trying to strike up a conversation with her, that sort of thing?"

The super shook his head. "I never saw her with any men, just one girlfriend with blond curly hair. Is everything all right with the Hollis girl? I mean, we've been following those murders in the papers ...."

Carolyn assured Stayner that Lani Hollis was just taking a vacation and ducked out of the building before the super thought of more questions. She called Gregg from the car and let him know he should go ahead and eat without her. It didn't sound as if it mattered much.

During their early dating days, she and Gregg could spend hours on the phone, often meeting afterwards for a late night coffee so they could talk some more. Carolyn's voice would be hoarse the next day, her throat never sore enough to postpone another date with the man she knew she would eventually marry. She wondered now if love could be measured by how long couples spent communicating at a stretch. The conversation Gregg had just hung up on had lasted three minutes.

Carolyn sighed. No time to think about that now. She still had to pay a visit to Dory Getz. Twenty minutes later, when she strode up Dory's front walk, a woman appeared on the porch next door. "She's not home," the woman called out. "I'm picking up her mail for a few days."

After crossing the lawn which earned her a frown, Carolyn produced her ID again. "I'm Harriet Foster," the neighbor said, wiping her hand on a checkered tea towel before shaking Carolyn's hand. "Dory's taken Sebastian on another adventure. That's all I know. Took off out of the driveway like nobody's business. That poor boy of hers was half asleep, too. I don't like to butt into anyone's life, but another break in his routine can't be good for him. Still, I keep my opinions to myself."

Carolyn thought about calling home again to tell Gregg she'd be home for dinner after all, but instead, decided to grab a meal in town.

CHAPTER 34

WHO THE HELL ARE YOU, Paige?

The question resounded in Joshua's mind for much of the weekend, chanting like an off-key chorus between his temples. Paige had worked the sex lines, yes. Not illegal, he kept telling himself, but since she'd confessed to him, he'd repeatedly cast her in the role of phone whore, his fertile imagination injecting a cynical edge in her voice, a bored-with-the-world expression on her face. He fought like mad against it but found himself replaying the sounds of their lovemaking, wondering how many others had heard those groans and whispers, how many had paid to hear them. He hated the way he was thinking, hated that it bothered him. What was it exactly that he found so disturbing—was it the number of clients? The anonymity? The cash? That perhaps Paige had been good at it? And if she was so convincing with the others, what about her time with him? How much was real?

He'd always thought of himself as open-minded and a good listener but he'd sure proven that point of view wrong last night with his reaction to Paige's news. Her admission had to have been hard on her, and he'd made things worse with his questions, his imagination running amok. Much easier to be compassionate and understanding when the bad shit doesn't hit your own fan, he reasoned. Had he stayed in the seminary, he might have become an average priest, but now he was proving to be a lousy boyfriend. He wondered whether some of his father's bitterness and distrust was rubbing off on him.

Joshua's mother had run off with her dance instructor, leaving behind a twenty-five-year marriage. The pain of that desertion had chafed and burned through his father's soul for years afterwards.

Those in the old man's inner circle whispered that he'd never been the same after that. There had never been a divorce in the Latham family, or heart trouble either, but a massive heart attack a few years later robbed Joshua and Carolyn of their beloved father.

Now Joshua had inherited his father's distaste for deception and found himself obsessed with learning as much as he could about Paige, one way or another.

His curiosity drew him to his laptop. Joshua did a Google search on Nicholas Bissonette and discovered his website, an amateurish bit of promotion for his artistic talents. Joshua wondered how designing a few detective magazine covers and drawing caricatures at children's birthday parties could earn someone a Porsche and concluded there was much more to Bissonette than Paige was telling. Another deception?

Paige, in the six months they'd been together, had told him about her childhood, but most of those discussions had been cut short, with Paige saying only that she never felt close to her parents even though she realized they always had her best interests at heart. She had found their over-protectiveness cloying, their fanaticism embarrassing. They had attracted a clutch of devotees during the time Paige was in Europe, Lani Hollis among them. While Lani grew closer to the Greenes, Paige sought to cut all ties to her parents, leaving Seraphina Greene behind to become Paige Rowan, taking her uncle's surname. Her stay in Europe had been about trying to form her own opinions, make her own decisions, though jumping into a relationship with Bissonnette only made it clear that she'd traded one kind of control freak for another. So she'd fled France too. Upon returning to Oregon, Paige/Seraphina added another moniker to the mix. Laurel.

It was a lot to take in. Too much. It ate away at his gut.

He went to Mass, but couldn't hear the priest's homily over the chanting husky voices in his head—Paige's voice, and another man's. Then two men. And a third.

Joshua drove to his office, looking for a distraction. He turned down a lunch offer with one of his staff who'd shown up to organize the last of the files that had been misplaced during the break-in. He wasn't hungry and he didn't feel like company, but his short-tempered refusal made him ashamed. He apologized twice but felt that still didn't cover it. Several times during the afternoon Joshua had his hand on the phone, ready to punch in Paige's number and offer some excuse for not stopping by later. He was up-to-here with work—not a lie. There was always something to do. She would understand.

He needed time. A break. A chance to decompress. Not an outrageous request. Perfectly reasonable, in fact. Yet once his work day was done, he steered his Jeep in the direction of Paige's cabin.

He belonged there. Where else would he go? Home to an empty apartment that would feel emptier because she wasn't in it? He loved her. That much he knew. He even loved her dog, and Parker still hadn't come home. He had to get past his wounded feelings and rally to Paige's side. She was miserable without her dog, and she needed his support. Too, there was a killer preying on women who worked the phone lines. He wasn't about to leave Paige alone.

Paige appeared on the front deck in a weather-resistant jacket and hiking boots. She carried a flashlight and a paper bag of kibble.

"Guess this means no luck at the animal shelter." He gave her a chaste kiss on the forehead. Her eyes were red and he felt helpless. "Come on," he said, taking her arm. "Tonight's the night we'll get him. I know it."

"He must be getting hungry by now." Her voice was quivery, the life drained from it.

They searched the woods again, traveling ground they had already searched, the rattle of the kibble in the bag sounding forlorn, lost in the vastness of the woods.

When darkness descended they returned to the cabin. Paige hurried to the washroom and Joshua heard the tap running. When she emerged he went to her. "It's okay, Paige. Maybe some nice family's looking after him."

"I put an ad in the paper. No one's phoned." She swiped at an escaping tear. "Sorry, Joshua. It's all getting to me. I know I can't undo any of it, but isn't there a way to make it better somehow?"

He wanted that too. Joshua gestured toward the sofa and they both sat, close but not touching. "Time, I guess," he told her. "Carolyn will catch the killer, Lani will come home safely, and so will Parker."

"But *us*, Joshua," she sniffed. "What can I do to make us better?"

He knew he was waiting too long to answer, that he should have said they were fine. It was what she needed to hear and he felt her painful stare bearing down on him. Instead he bit firmly on his lower lip and eventually said, "Same thing, Paige. Time."

She gave him a resigned nod. "If you want to get to know me better, maybe you should watch this." She dug the television remote out from where it had wedged itself between the sofa cushions and clicked.

CHAPTER 35

On camera, Fallon McBride looked trim and professional in a serious dark plum suit. Her black hair was slicked back into a twist, revealing her only jewelry, a pair of small gold hoop earrings. She introduced each of her guests, who were seated in a semi-circle of tub chairs to her right.

Reverend William Buchan, a robust man with a full gray beard and twinkling eyes, was an Episcopalian minister from Salem. Beside him and a good head shorter, sat Dr. Farukh Khan, professor of world religions at the University of Oregon at Eugene. Farthest from Fallon and looking waif-like and ill at ease was Cassie Pepper, a former member of the New Order of Angels and Saints.

Paige's stomach knotted. What would Joshua think of her once he learned about her parents and their wackadoo church? The Greenes had flown under the radar. Little was known about them other than a short article that had run in the paper months before their fatal accident. Their merry band of worshippers had dispersed and the New Order of Angels and Saints appeared nowhere on the Internet. Now Cassie Pepper, former disciple, was going to spill some serious beans. Paige stole a glance in Joshua's direction, but his expression was unreadable. If he was privately salivating over former fling Fallon McBride, Paige couldn't tell.

Fallon directed her first question to Dr. Khan. "What is your definition of a cult?"

Khan pressed his fingers to his lips and cleared his throat. "A *destructive* cult," he began, "at its root, has two fundamental purposes: to recruit new members and to fund-raise."

Fallon inclined her head toward Reverend Buchan. "But many altruistic groups fund-raise, Reverend, and so do established religions. Where is the line drawn between 'religion' and 'cult?'"

"There are many distinctions between the two," Buchan said. Even when speaking about something serious, the man's eyes sparkled. His voice was rich yet gentle. "Often the fund-raising done in cults is superficial. Rather than raising money to better the human condition, the funds acquired serve to increase the personal wealth of the cult leader. These leaders quite often claim to hold the key to some greater truth, but members are kept in the dark as to what this truth is."

The camera zoomed in on Khan who nodded, adding, "With mainstream religions, there is informed consent. A person examines and evaluates the beliefs, then makes a commitment to join the faith. With a cult, the follower often isn't sure what he is getting involved in. Information is dispensed on a need-to-know basis."

The reverend stroked his beard thoughtfully. "Also, traditional religions endeavor to help their believers live in the world, not remove themselves from it."

The person behind the lens now closed in on Cassie Pepper whose wrinkled cotton dress and long braids put her at odds with the polished calm of both male guests and the broadcast's host. Fallon McBride said, "Cassie, you were once a member of what some might consider a cult. How did Jerome and Millicent Greene recruit you for the Order?"

"They didn't," came the answer.

There was a pause, an expensive silence in terms of on-air dollars then the breathy voice spoke again. "I worked with Jerome Greene at Pacifica Nurseries. He was always so nice to everyone, and he really knew his plants. He could make anything grow."

"So he approached you at work?"

"No. He had a philosophy—live simply so that others may simply live, and I really respected that. Our group grew, not because of any recruiting the Greenes did, but because of the kind of people they were. A few of us started to gather at their house for meals, prayer, discussion. It was a wonderful time. We could stay up all night, just talking."

"How often did the group meet?"

"Whenever we felt like it. There wasn't a rigid schedule. If your evening was free, you were welcome at the house."

McBride wasn't satisfied. "Once a week? Twice?"

"Sometimes twice. Sometimes more. But I went because I wanted to. It was peaceful. I felt happier when I was with them."

"Love bombing," Khan interjected. "Typical of cults in their early stages. The recruit is provided with intensely pleasurable emotional highs so that eventually he or she comes to feel there's no other place to be. It's done subtly, in almost invisible baby steps—no hard selling, more like a seduction—until the recruit becomes a social isolate. Eventually other obligations to family, friends, even one's job, are in peril."

"It wasn't like that," Cassie said, miffed. "I came and went as I pleased, saw who I wanted. All of us did."

Khan didn't appear convinced.

McBride addressed the minister. "What Cassie's describing, her feeling of contentment with the group—isn't that what everyone wants? A sense of belonging?"

Reverend Buchan sat straighter, hands resting assuredly on his knees. "Of course. Everyone is looking for community, and we all need to be comforted, supported and strengthened by those around us. But cults promote zealotry, a dangerous fanaticism whereby intolerance for those outside the group becomes the norm. Over time, cult followers commonly demonstrate a lack of compassion and empathy. Their allegiance and obedience is directed to a messianic authority figure as individual conscience becomes irrelevant and eventually disappears. As Professor Khan alluded to earlier, there comes a great degree of paranoia about outsiders as well."

"Yes," said Khan, "and the 'talking all night' that Ms. Pepper referred to earlier is just one of the coercive systems used to break down a recruit's former set of beliefs and increase his suggestibility. Sleep restriction, a low-protein diet or fasting, other forms of sensory deprivation or restraint can induce a trance-like state. The recruit becomes more malleable and compliant, thereby allowing the reshaping of his reality and values. The threat of social ostracism, economic loss, fear of being ridiculed by other members ... these are also methods of coercion, but the recruit may not even be aware, for years afterwards, that such methods were employed."

"I can only speak for our group," Cassie Pepper said. "We weren't some mind-numbed bunch of freaks. There was never any intimidation, never any punishment, and at no time were we asked for money. Nor were we restricted in what we spoke about or to whom. We were simply a group of like-minded people who were looking for a better way to live."

Paige cringed at the sight of Cassie's wrinkled dress, the floral pattern faded. *I looked exactly the same when I was a child,* she thought. *And the kids at school pointed and laughed and called me a loser.* Cassie was in her late twenties, and there wasn't a blush of makeup on her. She wore white ankle socks and Mary Janes. The uniform of a schoolgirl.

Paige swallowed, felt a chill come over her. Perhaps Cassie didn't feel like a freak, but Paige did.

Fallon McBride spoke to the camera. "In established religions, there are rites of passage to announce a candidate's full membership in the church. Confirmation, Bar Mitzvah ..." She turned once more to Cassie Pepper. "Cassie, was there any type of rite or ritual the members performed, to demonstrate loyalty to the Greenes or the group?"

On camera, Cassie Pepper appeared to cave in on herself. She didn't like Fallon's question. The young woman's voice struggled for authority. "We were never forced to participate in any ritual that wasn't of our free will, and certainly not to show any loyalty to the Greenes."

Fallon smiled. "And that ritual was?"

Cassie stared at a spot on her lap and there was more dead air. Finally she said, "Some of us volunteered to be indoctrinated. And it was a beautiful experience."

"Can you describe the indoctrination rite for our viewers?"

"The initiate would be blindfolded and taken to a secret location. There, the blindfold would be removed and the candidate would climb by rope ladder into a deep hole. We were given enough bread and water for three days, a flashlight and a Bible. From Friday evening until Sunday night, the person would stay in the hole and experience the purest form of life, having only these meager items. I came away from the indoctrination completely changed. Material possessions mean nothing to me now. I no longer worry about little things that don't matter. I know it's possible to live simply and I'm grateful to the Greenes for teaching me that." Then she stressed, "I was indoctrinated of my own free will."

Fallon stared directly into the camera. "New religions. Salvation? Or snake oil...." Then she added, "Seraphina Greene, daughter of cult leaders Millicent and Jerome Greene, declined to be interviewed for this broadcast."

Paige stood. "That's because Seraphina Greene is dead." With that, she turned and went into the bedroom.

Joshua appeared in her doorway some time later. Paige was lying in the dark, struggling to banish Fallon McBride's telecast from her mind. She propped herself up on an elbow. "What time is it?"

"Little after eleven. And Paige? It wouldn't matter if your parents were from Neptune."

"There were times when I thought they were."

They both laughed at that.

"Feeling kind of restless," he said, bending over her and smoothing tendrils of hair from her forehead. "Think I'll take another look for Parker."

"I'll get dressed."

"No. You stay here. Get some rest. I won't be long." He closed her bedroom door.

Then Paige heard the front door shut and felt despair wash over her. Joshua was still avoiding her, her bed a forbidden zone. Perhaps this was how their relationship would end, with him pulling away in calculated stages until she grew lonely enough and hurt enough to declare it over. He was trying his best to be understanding, but she had kept her secret for too long and now the truth hung like thick orange smog between them.

She dropped back onto the pillow and tugged the blankets tightly around her. *Come on, delta sleep*, Paige thought. *I'm so tired.*

She drifted into a fitful half-sleep, disconnected images plaguing her. Cassie Pepper, in her little girl outfit, her face shape-shifting, becoming Paige's. Her parents' car, still smoking, flipped on its roof, her mother's body partway through the windshield. Amber's foot, severed above the ankle, a glimpse of white shiny bony protruding from the cut edge. Then sounds. The voices of men, urgent, thick with desire and need. Each image, each sound, replaced by another.

She rolled over, squinted as pale light bathed the top of her blanket. Dreaming. Impossible. Joshua had closed her bedroom door.

Then a dark shadow whispered her name.

CHAPTER 36

She reached for the bedside lamp.

"Carolyn? What are you doing here?"

"It's Parker," Carolyn said. "Joshua found him."

Paige scrambled out of bed, pulled her jeans from the closet door knob and yanked them on. "Where are they?"

"Easy does it. They're heading to the emergency vet clinic in Portland. Looks like your dog may have broken some bones. And he's dehydrated."

"I should be with him, Carolyn! Parker is my dog. And I still don't get why you're here."

Carolyn, like her brother, had perfected the stony face. "Come into the kitchen and I'll explain."

They sat at the kitchen table and Carolyn pulled a spiral-bound notepad from her jacket pocket and flipped it open. Carolyn wanted to know how long her uncle had owned the property.

"Uncle Spence bought the place as an investment. He's owned it as long as I've known him. Why?"

She recorded the name and address of the nursing home in Portland where Paige's uncle was staying. "How old is he?"

Paige thought for a moment then said, "Sixty-seven. He had his stroke just after his sixty-third birthday. I'd been back from Europe for about three months. Carolyn—"

"Just a few more questions, Paige. Did your uncle ever mention anything to you about this property? Anything strange?"

"Like a buried family treasure or something?"

When Carolyn didn't laugh, Paige said, "No. He just said I could use the cabin, that it would be mine someday anyway."

"Is he of sound mind now, do you think?"

"That's it." Paige was beyond irritated. "Why all these questions? My dog is hurt, Joshua's taken him to the vet's without me, and you're here in the middle of the night. What's going on?"

"You've never noticed anything unusual on the property? When you were trekking around in the bush?"

Paige expelled an exasperated breath. "More questions. No, Carolyn, I've never noticed anything unusual. Just trees and more trees. A patch of poison oak that I stay clear of. Why? Where did Joshua find Parker?"

Carolyn hesitated then replied, "A bomb shelter. Really not much more than a crudely built bunker. The door leading to it consisted of a few flimsy wooden slats across a four-foot hole. Perhaps your uncle was planning to install a stronger door later, one that would withstand a bomb blast, but the boards that lay across the opening were spongy. Completely rotten. That's where Parker fell through."

A bomb shelter. Paige's parents and her uncle had been members of the Duck and Cover Generation. Her father had told her about the paranoia of nuclear attack that had its peak in the '50s, how air raid sirens had sent students diving under their school desks, their bodies coiled and their heads shielded by folded arms. They had been shown newsreels of Hiroshima and the devastation wrought by the A-bomb. Somehow that doomsday mentality prevailed in Paige's uncle. He had once instructed her that if a bomb hit, she would have less than ten seconds to protect herself. Drop. Curl up, he'd said. Once the heat and blast wave passed over, her best defense would be to press up against the nearest building, preferably one faced with concrete, because concrete didn't strip away like brick. Crumbling debris and broken glass would fall in front of her. At that point in the lesson, Paige's mother had entered the room and admonished her brother. The world was frightening enough. She didn't need him making it worse by giving his niece nightmares.

Paige wasn't surprised to hear about the bomb shelter. Uncle Spence would have seen it as purchasing peace of mind. What did surprise her was that he hadn't told her about it.

She massaged her brow. There were still pieces missing. "What haven't you told me? Finding my dog in a bomb shelter still doesn't explain why you're here."

"I'm here because of the shelter. And what was in it. Along with your dog."

"You've lost me."

"In a few minutes, the area will be sealed off." Carolyn eyed her curiously. "It's a crime scene, Paige."

Cold fear passed over her. She felt Carolyn's steady gaze on her as she fought to make sense of her immediate world tipping over into madness. "It can't be. I've been here for almost four years. There's been nothing going on ... I haven't heard anything ... seen anything suspicious. What kind of crime are you talking about?"

Carolyn refilled their mugs, took a long swallow of scalding black coffee before responding. "There are bones in the shelter, Paige. Human bones."

CHAPTER 37

PAIGE'S REUNION WITH PARKER WAS more bitter than sweet. The sight of her lab's forepaw in a splint and sheathed with gauze was almost more than she could bear; watching Joshua carry the injured creature inside and seeing it hobble about the cabin was agony. She wanted more than anything to protect her pet from more stress, but that hope was dashed with the arrival of Fallon McBride.

The long driveway was already lined with vehicles. The coroner, the sheriff and an army of forensic investigators had been on the property for almost an hour, and now McBride's white Ford Escape pulled up close to the front porch. Another woman hoisting a camera emerged from the passenger side and panned the front of the cabin. Fallon followed closely behind, pointing. Paige remained partly hidden by heavy drapes and hoped they wouldn't knock on the door. This had to be delicious for Fallon. She could almost read her mind.

Lots of bodies dropping around your girlfriend, aren't there, Josh? Didn't she find that foot in the state park? And now, scarcely two weeks later, a skeleton shows up on her property? You know what they say about smoke and fire.

Fallon was trespassing. Paige knew she could poke her head outside and tell the woman to bugger off. One less thing for the police to do. But she also knew Fallon's buddy with the camera only needed seconds to capture a picture and that if there wasn't a story to be dragged out of Paige, Fallon would create one. Paige remained behind the curtain. Overhead she heard the thwacking rotor of a helicopter.

Fallon spotted Joshua's Jeep and frowned, looking once more at the cabin. She started to walk toward the porch when something more important caught her eye. Paige followed the newswoman's gaze to the east, where a group of investigators were carrying evidence bags across an expanse of grass.

One of the uniformed officers was politely ushering Fallon out of the way, inclining his head toward hers. They would be as cooperative as they could be, tell her just enough for her to wrestle out a few paragraphs for tomorrow's paper, then hopefully send her packing.

Carolyn came striding across the driveway and knocked before entering. "Paige? Do you want to talk to the press? Fallon McBride is here from the *Examiner*. I'd advise against it."

"Get her out of here."

"Atta girl."

Within moments, McBride's Escape was backing up to turn around in the driveway. Paige could see her gesturing to the camera person, pointing in the direction of Stan Gardner's property. That would be next, of course—Fallon zeroing in on the neighbors, though she didn't think even Fallon McBride would awaken Stan at this hour to find out what he thought of having Seraphina Greene living next door, especially now that human remains had been found on her land.

"It could be crazy like this for another day or so, Paige," Carolyn told her. "We have to document and photograph everything thoroughly before we can remove those bones from the hole and seal up that bunker so no one gets hurt. Our criminalist will be back at daylight and hopefully, your place will be de-skeletonized by the end of tomorrow." It was a feeble stab at humor and Carolyn was the only one who braved a smile.

They went through two pots of decaf, with Carolyn picking up steam with each passing hour as though she had been drinking high octane. She repeated her questions to Joshua. How had he come across the bunker? Had the dog barked? What had made him go outside in the first place? And how, if he and Paige had searched for Parker on previous nights, had they not heard him bark or found the bunker?

He couldn't sleep, he said. He missed the dog, knew Paige was upset and wanted to try to find him. He'd gone to a different section of the property from where they'd searched before. It was heavily wooded and untracked. The walking was difficult and Joshua had the scraped legs to prove it. Parker hadn't barked, but Joshua heard him whimpering, the high pathetic mewling of an animal in pain. He followed the noise, found the hole. Looked inside and saw the chocolate lab lying beside an intact skeleton. Called Carolyn on his cell phone.

If he'd have been trapped in the hole with that thing, he'd have been whimpering too, Joshua told her.

Carolyn had more questions for Paige as well. Since she'd moved onto her uncle's property, had there been any prowlers? Maybe some high school kids having a bush party? Had she ever found any empty liquor bottles or beer cans on her walks with Parker? Condoms? Roach clips?

No, no, no. She would have screamed her answers aloud, her exhaustion, her frustration, every damn thing getting to her, but Paige had questions of her own.

How long had those bones been there? What did the police think happened? Carolyn could answer neither. Other questions ran through Paige's mind, ones she didn't utter aloud. Why this place? Why me? And when will my goddamned life be normal again?

Carolyn left at four a.m. Paige sent Joshua home immediately afterwards, insisting she would be fine, that she just wanted to be with Parker, to give her pet the attention it was craving.

And I'd like to feel sorry for myself too. So much easier if you're not around.

As promised, the criminalist returned at dawn, with Paige watching his comings and goings from her living room window. She emerged from the house only once, to walk down the driveway to pick up the newspaper from the box near the road. An *Examiner* truck was parked at the foot of the drive, far enough away to escape the No Trespass rule, but close enough to be obnoxious. The same camera woman that Paige had seen on her property the previous evening sat behind the wheel, waiting to capture a picture of someone carrying a body bag containing old bones or to snag a photo of Paige herself. Paige kept her head down, adjusted the hood on her jacket and turned quickly, spoiling the shot, she hoped.

Despite successfully avoiding having her picture taken, Paige didn't win the final battle with the press. She had made the front page, under the headline "Skeleton Found on Local Property." Bad enough that someone had died on her uncle's land, and bad, too, that Paige would have to endure yet another round of questions and curious stares from the people she knew. "In an intriguing twist on an already intriguing story, the current resident of the property is Paige Rowan, who some years ago, changed her name from Seraphina Greene. Ms. Rowan is the daughter of the late Millicent and Jerome Greene, co-founders of the New Order of Angels and Saints cult featured in a recently broadcast documentary by this reporter."

Damn you, Fallon.

Fallon's bombshell had other reporters slithering out from beneath rocks as well. Paige deflected calls from the *Daily Astorian*, the *Headlight-Herald* from Tillamook, the *Register-Guard* from the Greenes' home town of Eugene. Paige was polite but terse. She had no comment. There would be no interviews. It wasn't until Fallon McBride tried to get through for the third time that Paige finally burst into tears, but not before slamming the phone on the *Examiner's* new star. She hoped Fallon went deaf.

When Monday morning came, Paige felt ripped in half. Parker shadowed her from room to room looking small and vulnerable, and she hated the thought of leaving him, even if only for a few hours. Joshua was at work and, at a loss for who to call, she punched in Luke's number. Since the weather was lousy, Luke had made no plans for his day off and was more eager than most to dog-sit on a property where a body had been found. Paige needed to see her uncle and was glad Luke spared her the questions she knew must be swirling in his head.

"I should be back by suppertime."

"Don't sweat it," Luke said. "Parker and I will be fine. And you will be too. Soon."

Nothing in her life was fine, Paige thought bitterly as she closed the door to the cabin and headed for her Outback.

Wellington Lodge, where Spencer Rowan resided, was a hexagonal-shaped nursing home in north Portland. Paige's uncle had a large corner suite on the third floor with a nice view of a courtyard garden. He had outfitted the room with his collection of outdoorsy memorabilia. An antique fishing rod and a pair of black rubber boots were propped in the corner near the entrance. A creel hung on the wall, stuffed with rolled up magazines. Wooden duck decoys perched on a deep window ledge. There were times when Paige wondered if her family had altered her birth certificate and she was really Uncle Spence's daughter. Once, on an outing with her uncle when she was nine, she asked him.

"No, Angel Heart," he told her, "but I wish you were my daughter. I love you that much."

She remembered being disappointed, fantasized for years afterward that Spencer had withheld the truth from her because he'd thought her too young to hear it. She'd always felt closer to him than to her own parents, who were more wrapped up in God than their daughter.

Uncle Spence was sitting in a wooden rocker near the window. Paige recognized Vivaldi's "The Four Seasons" playing on the mini-system. She was overcome, as always when she visited, with the urge to pluck her uncle from the rocking chair and whisk him back to his beloved cabin. She wanted to take care of him. There had to be a way to make it work. This arrangement was all wrong. Her uncle in this place was all wrong.

"It's me, Uncle Spence," she said.

He turned and smiled. "Hello, Angel Heart."

Since his stroke, Paige's uncle had problems judging distance and fell frequently. Frustrating to his caregivers but also typical of right-hemisphere stroke survivors was his insistence that he was fine, that he didn't need a walker for balance, and could probably still drive a car if given a chance. Yet his impaired spatial awareness turned buttoning shirts and tying shoes into Sisyphean tasks, which in turn, made him depressed. Spence, who had always thrown himself eagerly into life, was now dwelling in a confusing and hostile world, one that Paige wished she could save him from.

His short-term memory was shot, too, but Paige was less concerned that her uncle couldn't remember what he had eaten for breakfast. His recollection of the past was as sharp as ever and that was what she'd come to see him about.

"How's my favorite man?" she said, planting a kiss on his right cheek.

"Better now," he answered and reached out to adjust the volume on the CD player. His fingers closed on air and it took several tries before he managed to find the knob. Paige pretended not to notice as she dragged a nursing-home-issued armchair across the floor and positioned it opposite her uncle and slightly to the right.

"Uncle Spence, I need your help. Again."

"Something wrong at the cabin?"

"The cabin is fine, but …" She paused then took his hands. The post-stroke spasticity that had tightened his muscles was nearly gone. His hands relaxed in hers. "Car running okay?"

"The car's great. Uncle Spence, what can you tell me about the bomb shelter on your property?"

His laugh was hearty and long. In this place, Paige would ordinarily rejoice to see her uncle laughing, but today she didn't welcome the sound. Every corner of her life was a shambles and now a skeleton had been found in a hole on her uncle's land. Nothing was funny.

"Oh, that," he said, calming down.

"Did you have it built?"

"Not me," he said. "That thing wouldn't save a person from a loud fart. People who owned the place before me put it in. Don't know why they didn't make a better job of it."

"When was the last time you went down there?"

He cast his eyes toward the ceiling. "Only been in it twice," he said, focusing again on her face. "Once just after I bought the place then again to show it to your folks."

"Mom and Dad knew about it?"

A wave of dark fear swept over her. She didn't want to hear this, yet somehow she knew it already. Beside the bones, Carolyn had told her there were other objects found in the pit: three plastic water jugs, a flashlight, and a Bible.

"Took them down on a rope ladder. Surprised me, your mother not being the adventurous type, but she seemed really interested in that shelter."

"Uncle Spence, have the police been in to talk to you?"

"Police?"

A struggle. If Carolyn or one of the other officers had been in to question Paige's uncle, it would have been yesterday. He wouldn't remember.

"Why would the police want to talk to me?"

Would it do any good to tell him? Her uncle had nothing to do with the skeleton. But Paige knew who did. And it made her sick.

"What do you remember about the church they started, The New Order of Angels and Saints?"

Her uncle didn't blink at the abrupt shift in topic. "Wasn't all that much of a church, I don't think. Just a gathering of impressionable kids trying to find their way in the world and making the mistake of thinking my sister and her husband could help them." He rolled his eyes and sighed. "There was a write-up in the paper about it once, then a big deal was made of their car crash, but on the whole, nobody paid much attention to them."

Which is why they were so dangerous, Paige thought. And which was why Fallon McBride was so eager to revive Seraphina Greene. Especially now. Someone needed to be accountable for those fragile bones found in the shelter and who better than the daughter of the two fanatics responsible for the death of one of their loyal followers?

"Did I do wrong, Paige?" Her uncle's face was twisted in a grimace of worry. "I knew you were being stifled, that as long as you stayed with your parents, you'd learn nothing about the real world or the people in it. But I didn't want to cause trouble. I didn't mean to break up your family."

Paige gave her uncle's hands a gentle squeeze. "I think the family was broken long before you gave me that trip to Europe." She released his hands and wrapped her arms around his neck. "And I love you so much for giving me my life."

She felt his grip on her forearms, strong and reassuring even as he eased her away from him. He looked deeply into her eyes. "My sister and her husband, did they hurt someone? Is that why you asked me about the police?"

He remembered. Paige swallowed hard and said, "There've been some bones found in the shelter. And a Bible. The police are investigating."

"Sweet Jesus," Spence said and buried his face in his hands. It took him some minutes to compose himself and Paige hoped she hadn't made a mistake in telling him. Still, better this than for him to read about it on the pages of the *Oregonian*.

"I knew Millicent had some strange ideas," he said, his voice hushed, "and I knew she worshipped that husband of hers, but even though they raised you differently than most and their beliefs were extreme, I can't, not for a single second, believe my sister could have been a killer."

And until Carolyn had told Paige about finding the Bible in the shelter next to the pile of bones, Paige wouldn't have believed it either.

CHAPTER 38

To locals, the trail was known as Cardiac Heights, an eight-mile, lung-busting bike path with an elevation gain of 1250 feet. If heart and legs were up to the challenge, a rider might still end up in an ambulance headed for the nearest hospital. Poison oak grew rampant along the trail, so Joshua and Carolyn were prepped for battle, outfitted in long-sleeved shirts and long pants tucked into socks. Cardiac Heights was one of their favorite rides, and well worth the hour-plus drive to get there.

"Race you to the top?" Carolyn said.

"You haven't got a chance, old woman."

They pedaled across a flat section of scrubby grass for mere minutes before switching into granny gear to manage the uphill climb. At the first junction, they took the left fork and cycled up an old gravel road, Joshua grateful for the overcast sky and gentle wind that cooled sweat from his brow. At the four-mile mark was a hand-painted sign: Wimps Need Not Apply. Carolyn stopped and steadied herself by anchoring a foot to a rock. She tilted her head back and squirted water down her throat. Joshua grinned and pedaled past her. "Feel the burn?"

"Not even a pinch," she shouted after him.

He veered left again through a rusty metal gate and searched for the well-concealed, hard-packed path ahead that led to the final grunt-inducing ascent to the top. Someone had marked the turnoff to the single track by painting a white rectangle onto a tree trunk. Joshua steered onto the narrow trail and caught a glimpse of his sister struggling well behind him, her bike wobbling with her effort. He shifted gears and slowed down.

The reward at the top was a patch of forest with a clearing that afforded a spectacular view of Mount Hood. Someone, at some time, had used a 4-wheel drive vehicle to transport a picnic table up to the spot and Joshua headed for it, leaned his bike against a tree and guzzled water.

"What'd you do that for?" Carolyn gasped, dismounting from her bike and joining him on top of the table.

"Do what?"

"You slowed down. On purpose. Because I was too far back. Not like you to be chivalrous, especially if you've got a chance to do some serious gloating."

He took another long swig from his bottle and stared straight ahead at the view of Crater Rock, a lava dome beneath the summit of the mountain that rose some five hundred feet above the crater like a deformed head. "It most certainly is like me to be chivalrous. No fun racing against someone with an obvious handicap. How bad is your sciatica?"

"How long have you known?"

He shrugged then leveled a gaze at her. "How bad?"

"Some days are agony. Today is merely excruciating."

"So what was the point of the ride?"

"To see if I could."

"Going down'll be easier. You can coast off-saddle. Does the chief know?"

Carolyn shook her head. "Are you kidding? I love my job. I'd like to keep it. And so far, there's been no interference. When I've been called, my body has cooperated."

"Or you've bitten back the pain. How's Gregg with all of it?"

"When he's home, you mean?" Carolyn sighed. "He makes me the obligatory cup of tea, plumps my pillow like a dutiful husband then hits me with a look that lets me know what a disappointment I am as a wife."

"Any hope of things changing?"

It was Carolyn's turn to shrug. "We haven't slept together in eight months. How much longer do you give it?"

"What the hell's wrong with the guy?"

"There's no one to blame here, not really. Gregg works with beautiful, intelligent women all day. Feminine types, with high heels and skirts and jewelry. Then he comes home and finds me with sock dents in my legs, putting my gun in a drawer and hoisting my weary aching body into bed. I'm not sure I'd sleep with me either."

If his brother-in-law was here, Joshua would flatten him. His sister, his twin sister, was honorable, and smart, and good. Too good for the likes of Gregg Holt. Their father had said as much when the engagement had been announced. Carolyn so badly wanted to prove him wrong, and she confided to Joshua that often she felt her father watching over her, saying he'd told her the marriage would be a disaster. "You're not tough to look at, Carl," he said, using the nickname he used to tease her with when he claimed to wish for a twin brother. "Don't let Gregg make you feel second-rate."

"You're just saying that because we shared a womb."

She was hurting, and it made Joshua hurt twice as much. He knew Carolyn wasn't worried about the women, plural, who circulated in Gregg's job world, but about one in particular—a recent addition to the law firm where Gregg worked. "Are you going to leave him?"

Her face was a veil of indecision. "Old habits are damn tough to break," she said finally. "Who'd have thought I'd be so traditional? Irish Catholics don't divorce, do they?"

"Don't use the church as an excuse to be miserable."

"Fine one to talk, you are. How's Paige?"

He returned his attention to Mount Hood off in the distance. "Okay. I guess."

"Meaning you don't know. Haven't seen her, haven't called her, am I right?"

"How does conflicting schedules sound?"

"Like bullshit. What's going on?"

"You know what's going on. Too much getting in the way. It's complicated right now."

"What's bothering you the most—that the Greenes could have been involved in a murder and that Paige was their daughter?"

Joshua remained silent.

"Nope, I don't think the Greenes are your problem. My guess is that it's the phone-sex thing." Carolyn leaned forward to engage eye contact but Joshua fixed his gaze straight ahead. "Tough to get around the fact that your girlfriend talked dirty with all those strangers, isn't it?"

"If you're so smart, then why'd you ask?"

"She's a good person, Joshua. And you're good together."

"I just need a little breathing room. Time to sort through this."

"And while you're taking the time to get yourself figured out, Paige is hurting. She's got a dog with a broken leg, for starters. She found a foot, a *severed* foot, by her car. A foot that was probably placed there deliberately to scare her. Now we've raised a bunch of bones up from a hole on her property and she's got the press camped out wherever she goes, implying that Seraphina Greene might be as unhinged as her parents. How'd you like to go through all that with no one to lean on? You go ahead and take your time, Josh. Sort yourself out. And while you're doing that, I'll use my stopwatch to see how long it takes for Paige to fall apart."

"She's made of stronger stuff than that."

"I'm sure that's exactly what she wants you to think."

"So I'm a shit. Is that what you're saying?"

"If you love her, then yes, you are a shit. A mega-shit. Did you ever bother informing Paige about all the conditions you'd placed on the relationship, Father Latham?"

"That's low, even for you."

"I'm just getting started."

He could feel his jaw tighten, his shoulders hunch up close to his ears. "Maybe you ought to lay off, Carl."

"The hell I will. There's someone out there stalking and murdering women who worked the phone sex lines, specifically those employed by the outfit that hired Paige. How long I can keep that information from the likes of Fallon McBride, I don't know. But that's the least of my worries."

She tugged Joshua's sleeve, made him turn to face her. "See if you can get your head around this. This killer won't stop until he finds Opal. He knows Paige was protecting her, and that she knows where

Opal is. How long before he comes after Paige to get the information he wants? He's killed two women already. Is Paige next on his list? I don't know. But she's definitely on the list."

Joshua buried his sweaty face in his hands. "Dammit."

"Double goddammit. Paige is spending the next five days kayaking with a group of strangers and there wasn't a thing I could say to change her mind."

"Maybe the change of scene will do her good."

"Sure it will. If the killer stays away from her."

Joshua went silent but Carolyn wasn't ready to let him off the hook. "Getting back to you and Paige, did you ever stop to think how tough it was for her to 'fess up about her past, especially to a holier-than-thou ex-seminarian?"

"I'm not holier than anybody."

"That being true, then why are you separating yourself from Paige, making her feel she's not quite good enough?"

Their ten-minute age difference felt like ten years. Joshua hated being told off by his sister, hated even more that she was right. When he looked over at her, she was half-turned around, glancing back at the steep trail they'd just cycled. "What are you looking at?"

She pivoted to face him. "Just seeing if there was a psychiatrist pedaling up the hill. Maybe a good shrink could tell us why you're ready to throw away a perfectly decent relationship, while I hang on to one that sucks."

CHAPTER 39

THE M/V MADRONA WAS BUILT to last. The 90-foot vessel was constructed of teak, white oak and Alaskan yellow cedar and had been lovingly restored to her 1920s heritage by Bill Washburne. It was a floating lodge for adventurers and nature enthusiasts, and Paige could see that Captain Bill was justifiably proud of his boat. As she entered the spacious salon, she was greeted warmly by the captain and his wife, Denise, who was both the chef and naturalist for the excursions.

"Don't say it," Bill told Paige.

"He hates it when people talk about his resemblance to Harry," said Denise. "Bill thinks he's much better looking than his brother."

Paige heard herself laugh and was glad all over again she hadn't cancelled her trip. She couldn't remember when she'd laughed last. She extended her hand. "Both you and Harry are very handsome."

"She has to say that," Bill said in his wife's direction. "Harry pays her salary."

Bill had his brother's paper-white hair, but he wore his longer, curling just past his upturned shirt collar. He was leaner than Harry and his skin was ruddy and dry from years of exposure to wind and sun. "Great to have you aboard," he said, finally releasing her hand. "You're in cabin 2, almost directly below where you're standing. You can stow your gear, get familiar with the boat. I'll look after putting your bike in the locker, but that's all the pampering you'll get." Denise gave him a playful slap on the arm. "Lunch is in the galley at noon then we'll all gather on the foredeck for a safety meeting and orientation."

Paige shook Denise's hand, hoisted her duffle bag and went below. Her cabin was wood paneled like the salon, and cozy. As she unpacked, she already felt some of her tension slide away. She would be cruising around the San Juans, two hundred miles away from that bomb shelter and its terrible secret, far enough from Fallon McBride and anyone else curious to know about Seraphina Greene. She had locked her cell phone in the glove compartment of the Outback, eager to leave all connections to civilization behind.

Carolyn had begged her to reconsider but Paige refused. Canceling the holiday would have been unthinkable. For a few blessed days, she could escape and perhaps find a measure of peace. She would keep company with harbor seals, herons, otters and perhaps some Dall's porpoises. There would be seven other passengers, along with Captain Bill, Denise and an engineer.

"I've got to go," she told Joshua's sister. "If I stay, I'll go mad. The phone doesn't stop ringing. Fallon McBride is everywhere and customers are coming into the store just to gawk at me like I've got three sixes on my forehead. When news of the phone-sex operation comes to light, my life will be a complete hell. At least for a little while I can be Paige Rowan, outdoor enthusiast. Not Seraphina Greene and not Laurel. I deserve this time away. I've earned it."

"There's a killer all around you, Paige," Carolyn had said. "He wants what you know. I can't protect you out there."

She was adamant. "I'll be safer on a boat with less than a dozen people than I'll be in the village or at the cabin."

On the morning she'd left, Joshua tried to talk her out of the trip too. "I want you safe, Paige. I'd feel better if you were closer to me. We can stay at my place in town."

Her mind was made up. Once she heard the diesel chug of the engine and felt the boat slip away from shore, she knew that would be the moment when civilization would truly begin.

Joshua was house- and dog-sitting, so Paige didn't need to worry about Parker or any nosey interlopers stealing onto her property for a glimpse at where the skeleton had been found. She felt awash in sadness thinking about Joshua, remembering that although he'd stayed at the cabin on Monday night, there'd been no intimacy. Again. Both Seraphina and Laurel had come between them, and she wondered what it would take to recapture what they'd had. Perhaps this time apart would prove to be good for their relationship. Perhaps Joshua, wandering around the cabin, would miss her. Or he might realize she was a complication he could do nicely without.

Get up on deck, she told herself, and stop thinking so much.

Mercer Wyatt was stowing his bike in the locker outside her stateroom when Paige opened her door. "Looks like we're going to be neighbors," he said. "I'm in number 4, across from you."

"We're all neighbors down here," she told him. "There's nowhere to hide on this boat."

"I'm really looking forward to this trip, aren't you?"

"And then some. See you up top."

Arlen Dale was just coming aboard when Paige reached the covered aft deck. Despite his skinny frame, he was managing his gear with ease, the top tube of his Trek bike resting on one shoulder, a khaki canvas tote slung over the other. Paige was disappointed when Harry told her Arlen had booked the trip at the eleventh hour, snagging a cabin that had come available because another passenger had cancelled. She would have preferred a boat full of strangers. She hoped Arlen wouldn't be too chummy because they knew each other.

He had offered to drive Paige to Port Townsend in his van but she had politely declined. True, the drive yesterday had taken her five hours and she'd been exhausted by the time she checked into her hotel room, but she couldn't see herself making small talk with anybody for that amount of time, and then repeat it all on the return trip, especially if Arlen was as intrigued about her life as everyone else seemed to be. A little fatigue was a small price to pay for the autonomy of listening to her favorite CDs in the Outback, being able to stop for a snack and a pee without asking anyone's permission, and the complete absence of questions about her parents, the bones in the bomb shelter, and the severed foot. Enough already.

The lunch buffet was both generous and delicious. It would take a lot of kayaking and cycling to work off Denise's platters of grilled chicken and roast potatoes. As everyone seated themselves on a pair of long benches flanking a rectangular table, introductions were made.

Shawn and Gaby Ellison were newlyweds from Calgary. Paige guessed they were in their early thirties and had done some serious working out in the gym in anticipation of their honeymoon trip. Hardy Litton, seated beside the Ellisons, was their exact opposite—a paunchy, forty-something with skin like vanilla pudding. Hardy had difficulty making eye contact with anybody, and he spoke like someone with serious adenoid problems. Paige detected a trace of an accent, too. He freely admitted he wasn't the adventurous type, but he'd traveled the world on organized tours and was sick to death of jumping on and off buses, especially when many of his traveling companions seemed to be well-intentioned seniors who had just the perfect eligible relative for him to meet. "It's challenging traveling as a single," he said, looking at Paige.

Paul Kuzemchak was an architect from Petaluma, California, who'd decided to come on the trip a month ago. He'd neglected to make a hotel reservation and arrived in Port Townsend at midnight only to learn he'd have to sleep in his car. He planted himself next to Paige, making it difficult for her to sneak another look at him, but when he'd entered the galley, she felt she had seen him somewhere before. Perhaps he'd passed through Cypress Village at some time, or had even been a customer in the shop. She would have to ask him. If she could get a word in. Paul had already regaled the passengers with the tale of his bitter divorce and the repercussions the split had on his two teenaged sons who were living with their mother and were completely screwed up. He hadn't seen the oldest one since the split occurred five years ago, though Paul's biting tone of voice made it sound like the divorce happened last week. Paige was grateful when Arlen cut into the monologue.

Chloe Grier, another last-minute shipmate, introduced herself after Arlen. She was a striking blonde, nearly six feet tall, with legs that reached her ears. The *Madrona's* tattooed engineer, Rafe, was doing his best not to notice. Mercer Wyatt was simply "Mercer," and if anyone recognized the millionaire, no one let on. On this trip, everyone was part of a team, all equal. Nature would be laid out at their feet, for them to experience at their leisure and not as part of some rigid itinerary. At least, that's what it said in the brochure.

CHAPTER 40

HER VOICE WAS LIKE THE tender caress of a soothing breeze. With each sentence, each word, he loved her more. And she loved him.

In a rare moment of doubt, he had said, "You'll stay with me forever?"

"You are the love of my life," she told him. "Now tell me what you'd like me to do for you tonight."

With the others, it was always so much fucking and sucking, but Opal wasn't like that. Every conversation was a mind-blowing journey, a rapturous sensory excursion into the sublime. Soon he wouldn't have to be content with only the sound of her voice. He would know the warmth and smoothness of her skin, explore every curve and crevice, feel her body respond to his touch. The magic was within his grasp.

Paige Rowan held the key. Opal had stayed with her for a few days. That much he'd learned. But now Opal was gone and Paige knew where she went. She would tell him, of course. He wouldn't give her a choice.

Everyone knew that Paige was really Seraphina Greene, the daughter of a couple of cult crazies. Even in Eugene, hippie haven and gathering place for non-conformists, the Greenes had stood out. Though Paige claimed to have been estranged from her parents, there were several who'd come forward and painted her with the same weird brush. Former schoolmates had vicious quotes for the paper, recalling Seraphina as an odd kid, one on the fringe who never quite managed to shake the image. From where he watched, he could see that even on her vacation, Paige was reflective, despondent, and even better, he knew she was afraid. Later, when it was all over, passengers would undoubtedly remark that Paige was preoccupied and moody, choosing to spend time alone hiking in the wilderness, easy prey for the madman who was stalking women in the Pacific Northwest. Poor Paige.

On the first day of the voyage, the *Madrona* crossed the Strait of Juan de Fuca, headed for Lopez Island. Everyone cycled the flat backroads, doing the customary wave at the passing motorists, browsing the galleries and shops in friendly Lopez Village and generally doing their best to unwind from whatever had brought them on vacation in the first place. There was a relaxed camaraderie and spirit of conviviality. Even Paige seemed to loosen up. Tomorrow it would be Orcas Island—hillier terrain and more strenuous cycling. Some of the group would certainly forgo the rigorous ride to the top of Mount Constitution and head for a bookstore, pottery studio or spa. He figured Paige would pedal up the mountain.

Even with the group split up, he wouldn't make his move. That wasn't the plan. A much better opportunity would present itself on the final night of the trip. There was to be a moonlight clambake in a sheltered bay on San Juan Island, likely with plenty of reminiscing about their adventures and plenty of alcohol. He had to exercise patience. Only three more nights.

CHAPTER 41

THE WATER LAPPING AGAINST THE *Madrona's* hull failed to rock Paige to sleep. She was haunted by relentless visions of more severed limbs, grinning skulls, and a young man, clawing at the sheer sides of an underground bunker from which there was no escape. Paige felt as if the backs of her eyelids had been injected with air. She climbed the steps to the salon and saw Mercer Wyatt seated on a banquette and staring out at Deer Harbor, a glass of red wine in front of him.

"No sleep for you either?" she said softly.

He turned and smiled. "I'm still pumped from that ride up the mountain today. And my muscles haven't forgiven me."

"For someone who says he's not much of an outdoorsman, you did all right. Mind if I join you?"

He gestured to the bench opposite and Paige sat down.

"Good to be out in the fresh air," he said. "And the group seems nice."

"Yes. Most of them."

"I'm sensing a 'but.'"

Paige hesitated then said, "Between the two of us, that Paul guy is driving me crazy. He's sticking to me like Velcro. Every time I turn around, there he is."

"He's probably got a crush on you."

Paige rolled her eyes. "Please. I've got enough trouble."

Mercer nodded. "I don't envy your limelight these days, that's for sure."

Thanks to Fallon McBride, Paige had become the hot topic of conversation in coffee shops and beauty parlors. The reporter had been relentless to the point of near cruelty in trying to snag an interview with Paige. She had called her at home every night since the skeleton had been found. She showed up on Paige's doorstep one morning with coffee and muffins and had even made an appearance at The Great Outdoors, only to be escorted out of the store by Harry Washburne. Fallon's article in Monday's *Examiner* carried the headline: "Seraphina Greene—Woman of Mystery." It contained broad hints that the only child of Jerome and Millicent Greene might know more than she was telling about the bones found in the hole and possibly other skeletons, real or figurative, in the Greenes' closet. Paige's reluctance to grant an interview was deemed as conclusive evidence of her complicity. Like witnesses to a fatal car crash, people descended on the store hoping to catch a glimpse of the enigmatic Seraphina.

"I don't suppose there's a soul in the Pacific Northwest who hasn't heard about me and that skeleton." She rubbed the back of her neck, tried to ease the tension that had gathered there. "Mercer, I always knew my parents were a couple of flakes. But I've tried to envision them as ruthless killers and I just can't."

"You saw Fallon McBride's documentary, heard about the indoctrination ritual …?"

"I know. The Bible. The water. But I also know my parents and there's a big difference between being kooky and being cruel. There's got to be some other explanation for whatever happened to that person in the bomb shelter."

"I'm sure you're right. And take heart. All this media attention will die down soon and that bottom-feeder McBride will be off stalking someone else. Even better if the police find out your parents had nothing to do with that skeleton. Then you can go back to being Paige Rowan."

"You have no idea how badly I want that."

"Must be terrible for you, aside from the media scrutiny, I mean. That skeleton on your property, not to mention finding that foot—how are you keeping it together?"

"I'm not sure I am. I'm here, aren't I? Trying to get away from it all, even if only for a few days."

"And listen to me, talking about it when that's probably the last thing you need. Sorry." Mercer tapped his flat palms on the table. "How about some wine?"

"I'd love some."

He sidled out of the banquette and went to the galley's fridge, stepping softly so he wouldn't disturb the crew below. He returned with a glass for Paige and a half-full bottle of South Willamette pinot noir. He poured wine and said, "Maybe this will help us both sleep."

He touched his glass to hers. "To new beginnings," he said. "And to healing."

"You betcha."

Mercer took a long drink and sighed. "Five years ago tonight, Taylor ran away. And it just doesn't get any easier."

Paige swallowed hard. "I ... I can't imagine how you must feel, losing your only son. Are you still trying to find him?"

The man winced, his brow creased with pain. "What would be the point? He's outrun every investigator I've hired and there have been a string of them. When one would tell me the trail had grown cold, I'd hire another one. Finally gave up about six months ago. It hurt too much, watching their faces as they tried to break the news that maybe Taylor doesn't want to be found, not by me. I get postcards about once a month from all over—New Orleans, Miami, Atlanta, Boston."

"He writes to you?"

"For what it's worth. I get two-line generic notes. 'Hope you're well.' 'Hiked the Appalachians.' 'No one sleeps in Vegas.' He could be writing to anybody."

"Still, it's something to hold on to, knowing he's all right."

He seemed to struggle with that. Mercer Wyatt would be used to dealing in the concrete realm—give him the facts, show him the numbers. Until Taylor stood in the same room, Mercer wouldn't believe his son was safe.

"Of course I'm relieved, but it still kills me to know he's out there somewhere, seeing the country and having a far better time than he would with me around. And I admit it, Paige. I was a piss-poor father for a lot of years. When Taylor was young, I was building my business.

Parenting was Brooke's job. Then when she died, I let the live-in help do what I didn't make the time for—they looked after my son."

Oh God, she thought. Joshua was the social worker. He would know what to say. She didn't.

"I drove him away," Mercer said. "I understand why he ran. But he's been gone for five years. And still he can't make his way home? Or even call? I thought there were plenty of second chances to go around. Shows what I know."

Paige fought the urge to take his hand. She didn't know Mercer Wyatt. It wouldn't be appropriate. And it might make everything awkward tomorrow morning. Instead she said, "When we're young, it's so hard to see the other side. Everything is extreme, magnified, and we're ultra-sensitive. When I was Taylor's age, I did some pretty stupid things, too."

And she was still paying dearly. For the first time since boarding the *Madrona*, she thought of the True Gentleman and felt a chill.

"You okay?" Mercer asked.

"What's that they say? 'Someone walking on my grave.' I'll be fine. And Taylor won't be lost to you forever. Once he gets whatever demons he has out of his system, he'll be back. You care so much—he's got to feel that, wherever he is."

"Nice of you to say so, Paige. It helps." Mercer drained his wine glass and stretched his arms overhead. "Maybe I'll be able to sleep now. Kayak orientation is at six, right?"

"See you then. With any luck, my shadow, Paul, will sleep in."

"There's always hope," Mercer told her.

As she descended the stairs to her cabin, Paige wondered if that were true.

CHAPTER 42

With only a few hours' sleep behind her, Paige thought six o'clock came too early. She was the last one in the galley, and the only remaining seat was beside Paul who was already moving his water bottles from the bench to make room for her. Mercer, sporting his own under-eye circles, sensed her urgent need for caffeine and had her coffee poured before she reached the table. Paige stashed her dry bag against the wall with the others, a cheerful assortment of bright yellows, oranges, and lime greens, and edged in beside Paul. Mercer shot her a knowing look from beneath the peak of his baseball cap.

Everyone was clad in various versions of water-resistant clothing. Most, like Paige, opted for layers of polypropylene, fleece, shorts with padded seats, and loose-cut Kokatat jackets with plenty of ventilation. Hardy Litton, not confident anywhere near water, was wearing a full wetsuit reluctantly provided by the Washburnes and Paige knew that within an hour of kayaking, Hardy would be sweating buckets and regretting his decision. When she looked more closely, she noticed that Hardy had fastened a small silver pin to his borrowed suit. WWJD. What would Jesus do? Well, Hardy, He wouldn't be wearing that wetsuit today, that's for sure.

Paige breathed in an unpleasant mix of sunblock, Paul's aftershave, bacon frying, and the distinctive stench of wetsuit booties badly in need of a good airing. Adding to her discomfort was the feeling that others were trying to snatch glances at her but not get caught at it. She was still an anomaly, even here, still the daughter of a couple of kooks, still the one with a skeleton on her property and the one who'd found a human foot just a month ago. These were the people who would have sat beside her in class, made fun of her clothes, run in the other direction at recess. Only now they were adults and trying to be discreet.

While they feasted on a carb-loaded breakfast, the *Madrona* chugged the two nautical miles north of Orcas to Sucia Island, from where they would launch their kayaks. Denise held the tide tables in her hand and presented the group with an overview of the island and how they would pass their day. Everyone would be paired up in high performance, stable Seeward kayaks. The Washburnes would paddle in solo kayaks so they could split up and act as separate guides, one leading, the other following the group. Both Bill and Denise were trained in CPR and first aid; they also had their certification papers in BCU, the British Canoe Union, which meant they had superior paddling skills and coaching ability. Hearing this made Hardy Litton's shoulders sink back into place.

"How about it, Paige?" Paul said. "Be my tandem partner?"

Mercer looked about to speak but long-legged Chloe piped up, "Paige agreed to paddle with me last night."

Thank goodness for you, Paige thought. "Sorry, Paul. But the women have to stick together."

The honeymooning Ellisons comprised another pairing. Arlen would paddle with Paul, leaving Mercer with Hardy.

The Washburnes showed a video on paddling technique and how to right an overturned kayak. Over a final cup of coffee, there was more talk about safety. Everyone was cautioned to drink before they became thirsty, eat before they became hungry. They would all be wearing Type III PFDs—personal flotation devices to Hardy—with 15 ½ pounds of buoyancy, enough to keep an adult afloat in the water, yet comfortable enough to paddle in. They were reminded to reapply sunscreen and to wear their sunglasses. They were told to not grip the shaft of their paddle too tightly and not to slouch in the cockpit. Sore wrists and an aching back would spoil a wonderful trip.

The *Madrona* entered Echo Bay through a narrow passage along one side of South Finger Island, anchored at one of the buoys, and everyone prepared to disembark. Mercer tugged Paige by the elbow, holding her back. "Thought you should know. The skeleton they found on your property. It made the news again this morning. I heard on the radio that the skeleton doesn't match any Missing Person reports, and no one's come forward to lay claim to the ... remains."

"So that's why everyone was staring at me during breakfast."

Mercer nodded. "And the police have released more information about the bones, hoping it will trigger someone's memory. Apparently, the right fibula had been fractured at some point, maybe in some kind of athletic accident or fall—skiing, they're guessing—there was a bump in the bone at the fracture site, just above where a ski boot would end. No way of knowing how old the injury was and there were no pins with serial numbers to help identify the victim. Police are questioning as many former members of the New Order of Angels and Saints as they can find, figuring that eventually they'll get a name."

Paige sighed. "Even out here, my life catches up with me."

"Sorry, Paige, but I thought I should tell you. I didn't want you to hear anyone whispering. There's something else, too."

What more could there be? Paige pinched her lips together, whether in anger, or frustration, or to keep from crying, she wasn't sure.

Mercer continued. "That barracuda McBride has dug up information on those two dead women. Radio quoted her headline, 'Victims Linked to Phone-Sex Operation.' So now there's a panic surrounding the possibility that a serial killer is targeting women who work the phone lines."

Paige felt the bottom drop out of her stomach. Carolyn had been right after all. She shouldn't have come on this trip. If the True Gentleman knew who she was, she wasn't safe anywhere, not even out here on the water, where anyone could be watching. Waiting. Until the True Gentleman found Opal, he wouldn't stop killing.

A bubble rose in her throat and she must have whimpered because Mercer Wyatt covered her hand with his. "Easy, Paige. I know finding that foot was awful, and you'll be a long time getting over it, but there's nothing you can do for that poor girl. And it's not like you had any other connection to her."

She felt the urge to blurt everything out, that yes, she was connected to Bettina. And Sarah. And Opal, who was at the heart of all the horror. But she heard the voices of the others, already disembarked and calling for her.

"So try and let it go for now," Mercer said, "and let's get out on that flat water."

The word "sucia" in Spanish means "foul" and the island was so named because of the many rocks and reefs along the shoreline. Advice from the parks ranger to all mariners was "when you think you've gone far enough to miss a reef, go farther." The island, as Denise had told them, was really an archipelago of eleven islands with a history of illegal smuggling of Chinese laborers, opium traffic and rum-running. To Paige, Sucia Island was one of the most beautiful places on earth. While most of the San Juan Islands were made of dark volcanic basalt rock, Sucia was formed from blonde sandstone which had been quarried in the early 1900s, the bricks used to pave the streets of Seattle. As she and Chloe paddled along the shoreline, she marveled at how the erosive sandstone formed intriguing honeycombed patterns in the rock walls. They rowed past a steep gravelly beach and through a kelp bed toward a spectacular view of Mount Baker. Chloe was an expert rower, edging to turn as rocks jutted out in the water, engaging her large muscles to give her strokes more power. For most of the morning the two women were content to paddle in silence and enjoy the peace that surrounded them. Then Chloe, in a deep voice that reminded Paige a little of Mistress Patrice, said, "Don't let all that stuff in the news get you down, Paige."

"Thanks," she replied. "I'm doing my best, but it's hard."

They rounded the northern rim of the island at the head of the bay, paddling through the Cluster Islands then along a shoreline of forested bluffs and steep cliffs, each view more magnificent than the next. At Shallow Bay, they beheld an eerie sight, a graveyard of dead trees rising just beyond the marsh, their silvery branches beckoning like ghostly fingers in the mire.

Paige glanced behind her. Mercer and Hardy were keeping pace in their kayak, running parallel and further out on the strait; Paul and Arlen were well behind.

At Little Sucia Island, Chloe pointed to the top of an old Douglas fir; on it perched a mature female bald eagle, distinguishable by her regal white head. Yellow eyes scanned the water vigilantly for signs of salmon. In the distance they could hear the repeated distinctive whistle of the black oystercatcher, a goofy-looking shorebird that used its laterally flattened bill like a crowbar to pry open mollusk shells. Eventually they made their way back to the outside horn of crescent-shaped Echo Bay where the surf was gentle and they could alight without much fanfare or drama. They unsnapped the spray skirts that had kept their laps dry, climbed from the kayaks and dragged them further onto shore. Everyone was thirsty, ravenous, and thrilled with what they'd seen on their morning paddle. Hardy's pudding face was glowing, especially when his tandem partner, Mercer, called him Admiral Litton.

"Handled the surf like a pro," he said, clapping Hardy on the back.

The *Madrona's* engineer had been busy setting up for a picnic. Rafe had a single burner camp stove and on top of it was a small fuel-efficient convection oven. An array of oils, condiments and spices had been collected in labeled 35-millimeter film containers and were hanging from a pouch near the stove. With everyone pitching in, it wasn't long before a meal of steamed mussels, crusty bread and cinnamon-baked apples was set out on plaid cloths on the beach. There was plenty of red wine to go around then a pan of brownies was marched out bearing a single lit candle while everyone sang Happy Birthday to Arlen.

In the afternoon the group split up. The Ellisons wandered off in search of a secluded cove and some romance. Arlen was content to enjoy a book on the beach and listen to his iPod. Hardy was eager for another cruise in the kayak so Denise agreed to go out with him while her husband and the engineer cleaned up. Everyone else made for the trails, with Mercer choosing the challenging trail to Ev Henry Finger. Denise told him to watch his footing but that he would be rewarded for his efforts with a dramatic view of Orcas Island and Mount Constitution, where they'd cycled yesterday. Paige, damned if she was going to let fear ruin her holiday, headed solo to the east side of the island and Ewing Cove, a jackknife tucked into her pocket. She followed the bluffs along the bay, and on the trail saw thick patches of sword fern and a tiny rabbit hopping in the brush. She hoped it would escape the talons of the golden eagles who were fierce hunters.

At another time, she would like to return to Sucia with Joshua, bring Parker along to hike these trails. She wondered how they were doing. And how much sleep Carolyn was getting, juggling her time between trying to identify the skeleton and investigating the murders of Amber and Jasmine. The police had to be exhausted. And frustrated.

At least out here Paige was far away from bones and phones. She chuckled quietly at the rhyme. What was the True Gentleman doing now? Who was left for him to torment? The service had moved. Everyone had certainly been given new phone numbers. Dory and Lani were gone, and Paige was up here in the middle of nowhere. His links to Opal were disintegrating. What would that do to him?

Paige hoped it would send him leaping from a high ledge.

"So here's where you're hiding!"

Paul stepped into the clearing.

Paige was pissed and didn't bother concealing it. "Yes, here's where I'm hiding. At least I was until you came along."

"Wasn't that kayaking great this morning?"

"Yes." She turned deliberately from him to stare out at Wiggins Reef in the distance.

He came closer, stooped and prepared to sit on the rock beside her when she said, "Look, Paul, don't take this the wrong way, but I really want to be alone a while. I'll catch up with everybody later."

"Oh, sure," he said, straightening up, his disappointment plain. "I just don't think it's safe to hike alone, so I followed you. Especially since the last time you went hiking, it didn't turn out so well."

"I'm a big girl. Besides, the odds are pretty slim that I'll find another foot, don't you think?"

"I didn't mean—"

"It doesn't matter. I need some space. That's why I took this vacation."

Paul gave a huff but no apology. Quickly he muttered, "Whatever you say," then turned around and sprinted back onto the trail and into the forest. Things would be strained around the campfire tonight, but

Paige didn't care. Paul had insinuated his way near her every chance he could and it was driving her mad. She hadn't spent good money to come on a holiday only to have to use all her energy avoiding some creep.

Another crunch of twigs. Chloe stepped out of the brush. "You okay, Paige? I saw Paul following you and wasn't sure if you two were getting a thing going—"

"Let me stop you right there. Paul and I definitely do not have a thing going, and any effort you make to keep us apart is greatly appreciated. Thanks for jumping in to be my paddling partner this morning. If I'd been stuck with Paul, I might have slit my throat by now."

"So he's just a cling-on?"

"Probably gets laid on every vacation, figures this one would be no exception."

"Gee, wonder why he didn't pick me?" Chloe said.

"You're too tall," Paige shot back and laughed.

"He sure looked pissed when he walked away."

"I'm sure the wrong kind of popular these days."

Chloe sat down on the rock beside her. "Must be rough, huh? Everyone staring at you like you've sprouted an extra nose. Maybe Paul just wants to protect you."

"Put bluntly, I don't give a shit what Paul wants."

"What about you, Paige? What do you want?"

Good question. The list seemed to grow longer with each day. She wanted the True Gentleman caught. She wanted Dory, Sebastian and Lani to be safe. She wanted Parker to heal quickly and she wanted the skeleton in the bomb shelter to be nothing more than some unfortunate trespasser who'd stumbled onto the property and paid a deadly price. And she wanted her past to go away, but knowing that it couldn't, she wanted it not to matter. Because she wanted Joshua. How many of those wishes would she be granted? Or had too many sins and secrets erased the wishes she had coming to her?

"Maybe I should start with something simple. I want to enjoy my vacation. That shouldn't be too much to ask."

"Want some time alone?" Chloe rose but Paige stood with her.

"Not from you," she said. "You're good company. How about showing these trails what we're made of? We've still got plenty of time to hike over to Fossil Bay and work up an appetite. Tonight, we'll eat and drink everyone under the table."

Chloe smiled. "I like the way you think."

They made their way back toward Echo Bay where Arlen was still listening to his iPod on the beach. He told them he hadn't seen Paul or Mercer. Denise and Hardy were visible far off shore in a tandem kayak, and Bill and Rafe were on the boat. Paige told Arlen that she and Chloe were heading to the other side of the island, and that when he saw them next, there had better be drinks waiting. He saluted and wished them happy hiking.

After the cycling of the past two days and the morning kayak ride, Paige's body was beginning to tire. She prided herself on being fit and thought three strenuous days in a row shouldn't be wearing her down this much. She stopped often on the trail and drank, vowing to take it easier tomorrow.

Must be the stress, she thought. It was all catching up to her, sapping her dry.

Chloe was letting Paige take the lead. She stopped when Paige stopped. Complained when Paige complained. Paige's legs ached. Chloe's butt was sore.

Paige was glad Chloe was on the trip and that she'd been in the kayak with her this morning, allowing her those precious hours of quiet. She was glad to be hiking with her now, and wondered if the long-legged blond would be sympathetic to her situation with Joshua. Paige needed a female friend. Dory had loathed men, and Lani, gone for who knew how long, had been too needy. What would Chloe think if Paige told her how she'd once earned her living?

There were a few moments along the trail when Paige was tempted to tell her. She held back. Too much had already gone wrong because of secrets, yet Paige knew that some secrets were still better kept. Yes, Chloe seemed sympathetic. She seemed friendly and understanding and was giving Paige the space she'd needed. She wasn't pushy. She was behaving the way a good friend should.

Suddenly Paige was suspicious. When everyone else was introducing themselves, Chloe never mentioned what she did for a living. In fact, she hadn't offered much information about herself at all, except to say that she was from Oregon. Perhaps Chloe Grier wasn't a friend at all, but a very clever, very patient reporter following the story of the year around Sucia Island.

CHAPTER 43

SHE HAD SAT STILL FOR too long and had the backache to prove it. Carolyn stood and walked around her tiny office, braced herself against her desk and did some cat stretches to try to relieve the inflammation. Branding-iron pain radiated down the back of her left thigh. She needed to keep moving. While she paced in front of her desk, she felt glad at least that Paige had kept excellent records. Carolyn had spent the last two hours going over her phone-sex journal, reading and rereading Paige's notes in case she had missed something.

The clients were listed alphabetically according to their first names, since most didn't furnish a surname. Paige had provided physical characteristics: 6' 4", muscular, well hung; 5'9", mustache, lots of body hair. The men's sexual fantasies were described in a form of hieroglyphic shorthand that Carolyn struggled to decode. PPR, she concluded, stood for "peeper." WU signified the client's preference for women's underwear. A few of the entries were still a mystery. Beside the name Gerry, Paige had written the letters WD. Weird? Wired? Widowed? And someone named Orson was a PBAG, whatever that meant. Several clients, including Orson, had stars beside their names, the code explained on the journal's first page. * = MG. Mega creep. Paige's least favorite calls.

Paige had listed the dates of every call and had even recorded customers she'd hung up on and why. "George B., Aug. 12, pedophile." "Jon J., Sept. 4, animal freak." And Orson, the PBAG guy, had called again on September 30.

Nowhere in the journal was there mention of a gentlemanly caller, nor one who had called asking for Opal. If the caller had indeed made contact with Paige/Laurel, he had presented her with a different persona. Carolyn, after poring over the notes, was no further ahead. The True Gentleman could be anybody.

Carolyn returned to her swivel chair, lifted her feet onto her desk and kneaded the sore muscle behind her leg. It would be another two hours before she could take another muscle relaxant. Too, she felt a cold coming on and knew the coughing and sneezing would send pain through the top of her head. She reached for her thermos of tea and filled her mug.

Lani Hollis hadn't kept a journal and her apartment yielded no clues as to her fantasy lover's identity. Carolyn had two female officers working for different phone-sex operations, posing as both Laurel and Opal, but neither had yet reported hearing from anyone remotely resembling a gentleman. She would have to pull them from the lines soon. There weren't enough officers to go around, and the chief was making big noise about FBI involvement. Carolyn balked at letting the feds come in. A few more days, she pleaded and she got her way. This was her investigation, and her best chance to escape the humiliating memories of the incident that had earned her the hated nickname "Rambette." She had to do right for her career, and she had to do right by Paige.

So many things were falling apart. Her health. Her marriage. Couldn't she just win one battle?

Last night, Carolyn had taken Chinese food out to Paige's cabin, preferring to dine with her twin brother instead of her husband. Gregg was barely speaking to her after she'd canceled out on attending a charity banquet with him earlier in the week. Two women were dead, she said—more were in danger and there was a skeleton in the morgue that still waited for a name. She needed to work. He told her to go to hell.

Joshua listened to the latest chapter on the bleak state of her marriage and encouraged her to seek counseling even if Gregg refused to go. "I'll think about it," she told him, "if you agree to try and put aside whatever's eating you about Paige's past." She looked him square in the eyes and added, "You love her, Josh. And you miss her."

He didn't argue, but Carolyn knew his overwrought imagination hadn't yet finished tormenting him with images of all those horny callers.

Tonight Carolyn would be late getting home again. She had interviewed Cassie Pepper earlier and was fed the same nicey-nice lines the girl had spouted on Fallon McBride's televised documentary—the Greenes were benevolent, the Greenes were sincere, the Greenes could never have harmed anyone. But Cassie had also given Carolyn some names of former saints and several she had spoken to on the phone weren't as charitable. She was seeing another member of the Greenes' church in fifteen minutes. Time enough to brush her teeth, splash water on her face and gulp down a couple of painkillers.

At exactly 8:30 a man looking to be in his late twenties was ushered to her desk. His blonde hair was cut military short and his face was freshly shaven. Carolyn shook his hand, thanked him for coming and invited him to sit. She offered him coffee, water, a soft drink, but he declined.

Eric Bowden had been a member of the New Order of Angels and Saints for nearly six months. Yes, he knew Cassie Pepper; they'd even gone for coffee a couple of times, but they were just friends. Then he left the Order. Cold turkey.

"Why?" Carolyn asked.

"Just wasn't my thing," he said. Eric's voice was high-pitched, soft, girlish. "The kids in the group were nice, and the Greenes were okay but some of their ideas were whacked. I couldn't see how I'd be a better person after spending a weekend in a hole."

"The indoctrination ritual," Carolyn said. "The one Cassie spoke about on television. Did you feel pressured to participate? Was that it?"

"The Greenes weren't into pressure. They said I would know when the time was right. But some of the others were talking about the experience like it was the best high on the planet. I guess I got curious. Didn't want to feel left out."

Bingo. The Greenes wouldn't need to apply any pressure when they had their followers do it for them. "So you went through with it? You went into the shelter?"

Bowden nodded. "The Greenes took me there. Blindfolded. I didn't know where the hell I was going. It was exciting in a way—listening to the road noise, trying to figure out what direction we were traveling—but creepy too, you know? We got out of the car and walked for about twenty minutes. I could feel soft ground under my feet. I couldn't hear any traffic."

Carolyn imagined being led across Paige's property in the dead of night wearing a blindfold and being at the complete mercy of two near-strangers. She would panic, wonder if she was going to be shot, tortured, left to die. She would doubt the testimonies of the others who'd told of their religious epiphanies. She would smell a trap. She would yank off the blindfold and run.

How screwed up did a person have to be to consent to such a bogus rite of passage?

"Jerome went into the hole first, then Milli removed my blindfold and told me to follow. I climbed down a rope ladder with wooden rungs while Jerome shone the flashlight so I could see. Then Milli came down."

"They told me the shelter had reinforced concrete walls and ceiling with forced-draft ventilation. It was about eight by ten feet and there was a turn at the entrance passageway that was supposed to stop a lot of the heat flash and radiation from a bomb blast. All I knew was that I was underground and those walls were closing in."

"Could you have changed your mind? Told the Greenes you didn't want to go through with it?"

"I never asked. I didn't want to look weak, you know?"

Bowden, with his smooth face and high voice, had likely been called much worse during adolescence. Carolyn figured him to be grateful for the Greenes coming along and accepting him.

"They showed me where my bread and water were, what I could pi—use for a toilet, then they both hugged me, told me they loved me and that they'd see me Sunday night."

"As soon as they lifted that ladder out of the hole I started crying. I was so scared. Off in the distance I heard their car drive away and all I could think of was that something awful would happen. I imagined the shelter filling with water and me drowning. Or else there'd be a mudslide and I would suffocate."

"At any time during the weekend, did either of the Greenes come to check on you?"

"Not once." Eric's voice broke. "And no one else knew I was down there. We had to volunteer privately for the ritual. To make sure our motive was pure and not just for group recognition or acceptance."

Eric Bowden had not experienced any kind of religious epiphany in that hole. Judging from the tremor in his hands, he still bore the scars of what he remembered as three days of horror. "Nightmares?" she asked him.

"Plenty. To this day. It was so damn quiet down there. And I had no concept of time. We weren't allowed to take a watch with us. I was afraid I would die there, that the Greenes would forget about me. Then I began to think that they'd brought me to the shelter because they were angry and punishing me."

"Could you think of anything you'd done wrong?"

"I wracked my brain, but no."

"And they didn't forget about you, did they."

"No. They lowered the ladder on Sunday at sundown just like they said. They threw down the blindfold, I put it on and climbed out. I didn't know whether to kiss them or kill them."

"How did they treat you?"

"They bought me a steak dinner that night, told me how proud they were, said I was a true saint and knew what it meant to stand up for my beliefs. They asked me about my experience in the shelter and I made up a bunch of bullshit. They drove me to my apartment, hugged me again, and that was the last time I saw them."

"You quit then?"

He nodded. "Just too weird for me. Sometimes I still wake up sweating. And I don't like closed spaces much. Or the dark."

"But you were never coerced into the ritual?"

"No."

"Hypnotized? Drugged?"

"No."

"Eric, think carefully. At any time, did you see either of the Greenes angry with a member of their church? Did they threaten to punish? Humiliate? Ostracize?"

He sighed. "No. Never. Like I said, the Greenes' hearts were in the right place. Just too freaky and intense for me."

"And yet we found a skeleton in that hole. Water jugs, a flashlight, a Bible. What do you think happened?"

He was silent for long moments, and Carolyn wondered if he had once again descended into that black pit. At length he said, "I think someone volunteered for the ritual. Just like always. Except this time, instead of coming with the ladder on Sunday, the Greenes cracked up their car."

Not murder. An accident. One that claimed the lives of Millicent and Jerome Greene, plus one other victim who had yet to be identified.

CHAPTER 44

At five-foot eleven, Chloe Grier could look down on most of the *Madrona's* passengers with disdain and, with a slight lift of her chin, reduce men to whimpering dogs. Off the boat and in the everyday world, she wouldn't condescend to glance in his direction. Like so many of them.

He was headed for trouble again. Having Chloe in his sights resurrected the Dark Thoughts. He had already imagined her perfectly coiffed head thrashing from side to side, her flawless complexion turning purple as she struggled for breath, those Tina Turner legs kicking out at dead air. The purple game.

At first, The Dark Thoughts were episodic, descending on him like a seasonal hailstorm. In the early days, he had been disturbed by them and sought to understand the fantasies that plagued him. Were there others out there who thought as he did? And what were they doing about it? He read books by the dozens, examined underground newspapers, surfed the Net and chatted with other asphyxiophiles on-line but found nothing that eased his mind. To distract himself, he went on a fitness jag, tried kayaking, racquetball, cycling. Took a carpentry class. Made a bookcase, a footstool. The thoughts persisted.

He grew tired of feeling like a slavering deviant, grew to crave acceptance. Surely he wasn't so unusual. He knew all there was to know about autoerotic asphyxiation, had read about those who had taken the game too far and were found surrounded by their sadomasochistic paraphernalia, or wearing women's clothing, or yes, even suspended from the front of a John Deere tractor. He wasn't into the practice himself. He had no interest in the reputed euphoria and cataclysmic orgasm that resulted from hypoxia, the lack of oxygen to the brain. But oh, to find a willing partner, to see that fear in her eyes, to hear those gasps and gurgles, to see the purple. Very Dark Thoughts indeed.

Trusting himself was something he couldn't bring himself to do. What if it went too far? What if there was another accident? No, there had to be another way. Somehow, he should be able to have it all and not suffer the consequences.

The answer came via the telephone. The women told him he wasn't so unusual after all, that many men liked to do just what he was talking to them about, and many women liked choking games. If others didn't understand, well, that was their hang-up. Dallas and Amber had enthusiastically reenacted the fantasy with him, and in the beginning, he was grateful. He wasn't strange. He could fit in. He could belong.

He had expected the phone calls to act as a buffer. By articulating his fantasies, by sharing them and getting release, he felt sure it would be enough. He felt sure he would be satisfied.

Instead, the Dark Thoughts grew worse. And more frequent. Instead of the relief he sought, he became agitated, restless and angry, the phone calls serving only to whet his fury, not satiate it.

Somehow Opal was able to loosen the constrictor grip his Dark Thoughts had on him. She understood the power of fantasy, knew that the most potent sexual organ was the brain. She showed him another way. Imaginative. Steamy. And almost as gratifying as his visions of deep purple strangulation.

He couldn't wait any longer. Tonight there would be opportunity, the plan be damned. And Sucia Island was rife with out-of-the-way places where he could get Paige Rowan alone. He packed the essentials in his knapsack—electrical tape, a couple of strong rubber bands, Hefty bag restraints, a heavy rock and a see-through plastic bag.

CHAPTER 45

One of Paige's minor wishes was granted. During the sunset beach barbecue that Denise and Bill had organized, Paul left her alone, preferring instead to attach himself to the Ellisons. The day's fresh air and exercise had given everyone bottomless appetites and they feasted on cheeseburgers, baked beans and apple pie. Paige lost count of how much wine she'd drunk but knew when she stood up that she'd overindulged. The sand pitched under her feet and she didn't dare look out at the horizon. A sudden southeast wind had begun to blow around the Finger Islands and water churned and frothed in the bay. Her head pounded like the surf, and the idea of returning to the boat and being buffeted around by lurching waves brought the peppery taste of tonight's cabernet to the back of her throat.

The indignity of it, Paige thought. She was already more notorious than she ever cared to be, and now she would add to her sterling reputation by vomiting into the fire-pit.

Shawn Ellison was game for a trail hike in the dark. "Got to work off those calories from dinner," he said, patting his trim stomach. Gaby told her husband he was nuts. Paige, too, was reluctant to push her aching body any further, and Chloe echoed the sentiment, so the three women elected to stay by the fire and guard everyone's dry bags. The prospect of scoring points with Chloe by the roaring fire was enough to make the *Madrona's* engineer, Rafe, decide to remain behind as well.

"Need to protect the womenfolk," he joked, pouring strong coffee into everyone's mugs. "Pirates could come ashore to rape and pillage."

While Gaby Ellison asked Rafe about one of his more frightening tattoos, the rest of the group managed to produce four flashlights from their bags and they set off for the entrance to the trails, wishing the others victory over marauding pirates. Paige accompanied the group to the isthmus between Echo Bay and Shallow Bay, where restrooms serviced the centre of the island and the nearby campground. Paul, to Paige's relief, kept his distance.

The group stopped to read the trail map. The Washburnes wanted to take the trail past China Man Rock toward Lawson Bluff; the rest of the men wanted to hike further on to Ewing Cove. Paige just wanted a quiet place to throw up in private.

She held onto one of the flashlights. "I think I'll join you after all," she told them. "But I'll catch up." Before anyone could say anything, she darted for the restroom. Behind her she heard Hardy's beer-infused giggle as Mercer told the group the admiral would blaze the trail.

She had barely locked the door when supper came up. She squatted at the toilet; even in her pathetic, drunken state she couldn't bear to kneel on the grimy floor. We'll drink them all under the table, she had told Chloe. Fine job she had done.

Eventually she was able to stand and her stomach settled. She guzzled bottled water and rinsed her mouth. Once outside again, she felt better, away from the fetid air of too many body odors and toilet smells. She thought at first of running to catch the others then in a split moment, decided to venture to the opposite side of the island. She'd endured enough of Hardy's giggles and his lapdog devotion to Mercer Wyatt for one day. And she didn't relish returning to the campfire to watch Rafe put the moves on Chloe. A few minutes' peace. Not too much to ask.

She had already seen Ewing Cove, but hadn't hiked to Ev Henry Finger and to the memorial erected to the man credited with being the driving force behind making Sucia Island accessible to the public. She had water and a flashlight. There were other tourists moored in both Fox Cove and Fossil Bay. She wouldn't really be alone. She headed east.

Paige shone the flashlight ahead of her on the trail, looking for humped tree roots or fallen twigs that could cause her to lose her footing. Tired as she was, within minutes she was glad she'd decided to venture out on her own and let nature work its wonders on her. She tried not to think about the last time she'd hiked—had it really been four weeks ago? She tried not to think about Amber and how she must have felt in her final moments, and she tried not to keep anger in her heart at a God who would allow such suffering for someone who had already suffered much. She searched her mind for happier thoughts, but even thinking about Joshua made her throat tighten with emotion. What would happen when her vacation was over? Would time away from her make Joshua feel differently about what she had done in the past? And what about Seraphina Greene? How long would it take before the people of Oregon forgot about her? How long could she hide on this island?

Once the police determined the identity of the body in the bomb shelter, there would be more headlines. More requests for interviews. More Fallon McBride. Paige's troubles were a long way from being over. She still had the True Gentleman to fear.

When Paige reached the high bluffs at the southwest end of the island, she sat down on a fallen log near the cliff's edge and listened. The southeast wind was kicking up offshore and it sent the surf pounding against the steep rock face. Paige envied the water and its power. She couldn't remember the last time she'd felt relentless, determined, confident. She'd been an obedient child growing up, even more obedient when she'd met Nicholas, and now she seemed to be carried along again, weakened by a battering wave of media curiosity, local gossip and the ominous shadow of a ruthless killer.

With Joshua, she had felt strong. But she realized now that her strength wasn't his responsibility. If their relationship was over, that didn't mean *she* was. She had to draw strength from within, wanted to, but felt that at every turn, some person, or some event, was draining what meager resources she had left.

Her eyes welled up and that made her angry. She couldn't cry. She refused to return to the others with a reddened face and swollen eyes. She needed to focus on the positives—she had a job she enjoyed, a boss she liked, a great place to live. She could afford to pay the bills, take a vacation. And Parker was getting better.

Others had it far worse. Perspective, that's all it took. An attitude adjustment. She took a deep breath and though she didn't feel a whole lot better, she was no longer near tears. She was ready to hike back to the others, in one piece, or as close to one piece as she could get.

Paige uncrossed her legs and reached out to steady herself when she became aware of something not quite right. Below, the surf continued to pound. The wind swirled around her but above it all there was something else. Another sound—someone breathing. Hard. Paige turned to look, but at once, a sharp pain exploded at the base of her skull. The ground around her spun, sent out bright stars, then went black.

CHAPTER 46

A DEEP GROAN. A LONG SIGH. *Another. Then:* "Wow. My God. Incredible."

Whap whap whap whap. The sound of Kleenex tissues being pulled from a box.

"For me too. As always."

"You don't mean that."

"Of course I do."

"If that were true, we would be together by now."

"But we are together, my darling."

"I mean *really together*."

"Soon. I promise."

"I can hardly wait. It's difficult."

"Dark thoughts?"

"Not when I'm with you. I need you so much. I don't want to be bad anymore."

"You're not bad. You couldn't be."

"I wish that were true."

"You are a gentleman. A pure and good gentleman."

"I want to be. For you, Opal."

What bizarre nightmare was this? The couple had been in Bora Bora, making hot sweaty love in their over-water bungalow while schools of tropical fish swam below them. Through a soot-gray haze, Paige had heard Lani's voice. But that couldn't be. Too much wine, she reasoned. And a pulsing, sick headache that would surely twist her scalp off. Her chest felt heavy, too, weighed down by—

Wait a minute. Lani's voice?

Paige's eyes snapped open. The pale face looming over her was blurred, as if submerged under water. She struggled to find her hands, but they were bound behind her. Wiggling her fingers beneath her buttocks sent jagged bolts of pain up her arms, their circulation cut off by the weight of her own body. Her ankles, too, were immobilized, and someone was sitting on her chest.

Her head was sheathed in plastic, a transparent bag held in place by a rubber band that pressed against her throat. Holes had been punctured near where her nostrils were, but with each greedy inhalation, she felt the bag adhere to her face.

Not enough air. She panicked, thrashed, fought to rid her shoulders of the weight of someone's knees bearing down on them.

"I get so hot when we talk I'm afraid I'll boil over."

"Me too. I get hot just thinking about your calls."

"In fact, I'm starting to get ..."

"What? Again? You're incredible. Insatiable. My insatiable gentleman."

Then the voices disappeared. Headphones were removed then someone crooned in her ear. "Hello Laurel."

Hot breath wormed down her neck. "Don't struggle," murmured the voice. "You've got plenty of air. At least, you will have if you tell me what I want to know. Where's Opal?"

She gazed up through the smudge of plastic as the face repositioned itself over hers.

Arlen Dale smiled back.

Opal's True Gentleman. All these months, working across the street from Paige, waving his cheery hello, tuning his iPod in, not to the Dixie Chicks, but to the sound of Opal's voice. Recorded conversations. Relived moments. Keeping his telephone lover real.

"I don't know," she gasped, hungry for air. "Somewhere east ... with relatives."

"You'll have to do better."

From behind, she heard the tearing of—cloth?

Arlen held a pair of scissors over her face. Shiny, pointy scissors. Sharp enough to slice the bag away from her face. Or pop an eye from its socket.

He used the scissors to snip at a length of silver tape. Now a piece of it dangled from his index finger. With her next breath, Paige knew what the tape was for.

She gulped air and held her breath. Arlen sealed the holes.

"Ever play that game as a child, Paige? See who could hold his breath the longest? Watch the faces turn purple? Did any of your little friends pass out? Did your parents warn you about playing such a dangerous game?"

She tried to rock her body, slide herself downward to separate the plastic bag from its rubber band. Arlen, skinny Arlen, was too heavy. Dead weight.

How to conserve air? Stay still? But shouldn't she fight? If she could only move the bag.

"Know the world's record for someone holding their breath, Laurel? Twelve minutes and forty-seven seconds. Can you believe it? Some guy from Naples. A free-diver. How long do you think you can last? You're already turning a lovely rosy shade. And it's only been ..." he calmly looked at his watch "... twenty-five seconds. Bet it seems a lot longer."

She tried to nod, tried again to slide her head about. She needed her hands. She needed air. Not much longer and she would have to exhale. Slowly. Save the breath. And once her lungs were empty ...

Slowly, taking care not to tear the bag, Arlen removed the tape from the holes. "To show you I can be a reasonable man, I'll give you another chance. A name, Laurel. An address. Where's Opal?"

She let out air. Breathed in. And again.

It didn't matter now. Arlen wouldn't let her live. He couldn't. She knew who he was, what he had done, what he was capable of. Amber. Jasmine. She couldn't give up Lani.

"Gone to Maine," she said, still devouring air as if saving it up, as if she could hold it in reserve. "Kennebunk, I think she said."

"Specifics, please. An address."

She hesitated. A good friend wouldn't easily divulge information. She had to be convincing. Buy herself some time. Wouldn't the others be missing her? Weren't they now on Echo Bay asking themselves where she was? How long before they came looking?

They would double back on their trails, and seeing no sign of Paige and Arlen, they would return to the beach, then begin heading east on Sucia. They would have to split up. Some would go toward Fox Cove, others to Johnson Point, and hopefully some would take the trail to Ev Henry Finger and find her. Soon. God, let it be soon.

"Please, Arlen. The others. They'll be coming. You'll be discovered. Take the bag off me and I'll tell you about Opal. Whatever you want to know."

"First things first, Laurel. Tell me exactly where she's staying. With whom. Or we can change the game. This time, as you're suffocating, I can describe to you all the lovely shades of purple you're turning."

Laurel. He was calling her Laurel. She had spoken to him before. On the telephone. Frantic, she searched her memory, her thoughts careening from caller to caller, so many of them the same, just voices and more voices.

Then she remembered. A client. A plastic bag. Her gasps for air, her choked cries growing hoarser, more desperate as she heard his own guttural sound of release.

"You're Orson," she said.

He smiled again.

Paige struggled to fill her lungs, the weight of Arlen's body bearing down like a block of concrete. Amber's death, Jasmine's, and soon, her own—none of this was about Opal. Opal was just an excuse. Arlen loomed over her now, doing what he loved most—choking women. Watching them suffocate. Watching them die. On the phone, as Orson, he had told her as much.

The phone whores had not provided catharsis for Arlen's sick fantasies. They may even have spurred him on. Desensitized after so much talk, Arlen hungered for the real experience. Dory had been wrong. The phone whores weren't vigilantes. They were inspiration, sick muses for someone's murderous desires.

Paige reached deep within, fought to grasp whatever filaments of nerve she had left. "No deal, Arlen," she said. "The bag comes off or I tell you nothing."

He eyed her curiously. "Not in a terrific position to bargain, are you?" He snapped the tape in front of her face, his expression at first amused, then angry.

Ripples of fear snaked along her spine, sent cascades of tremors through her. If the bag was sealed again, she would inhale, mouth open, suck the plastic into her mouth, try to bite a hole in the bag. Would it work? She prayed she wouldn't have to find out.

"And you're in no position to refuse." She forced a hardened edge onto each syllable, set her jaw rigid. It would keep her from blubbering, stuttering, crying. "Kill me now and you'll never find your precious Opal."

There was a long pause, an interminable pause. Paige focused on the tape, still snapped taut between Arlen's knobby fingers, still poised over the opening in the bag. She inhaled but her breaths were shallow. The weight of Arlen's body grew heavier on her chest. Her lungs wouldn't expand.

Paige swallowed. Closed her eyes. Wanted the grinning face before her to disappear in a puff of campfire smoke. How much time had gone by? And where were the others? How long before someone from the boat came looking?

He studied her now with parodied concern. "You're losing, Laurel," he told her. "You've figured out by now, of course, that you'll die anyway. And dozens more will too, if I don't find Opal." Then he laughed. It was a full, body-shaking laugh, cruel and mocking. "I think once I'm done with you, Dory and Sebastian will get a visit."

"You have to find them first," she gasped. She tried to slow her breath, deepen it. Couldn't. "Dory's no stranger to the streets. She can go underground for a long time. How long are you willing to wait, Arlen?"

"It won't be long. Our Ms. Dallas can't hide forever, not with a child, especially one as ... unique as Sebastian. How many seconds do you think Dory will wait once I put this plastic bag over her son's head?"

"No ..."

"Think about it, Laurel. If you tell me who Opal is, nothing will happen to Dory and that special son of hers. Their lives rest in your hands."

"Arlen, you won't get away with this. The others know we're both gone. They'll put it all together. If anything happens to me—"

"Don't be stupid," he hissed, several dots of his spittle landing on the surface of the bag. "All forty-eight mooring buoys on the island are full. There are tourists galore. No one will track your murder to me."

"Of course they will," she said, stalling for time, which she knew was running out. "We're from the same town. You'll be the first one they think of. Some tourists could come along at any second, find us like this and you're finished."

Arlen looked around. "But I don't happen to see anyone around, do you?"

"And when you find Opal, then what? She won't be able to save you from yourself. If you love her so much, you won't saddle her with that responsibility. Have you thought about that, Arlen? What your sick fantasies will do to Opal? What will happen when she finds out what you're really like?"

"She'll never need to know. We'll have a wonderful life togeth—"

"Opal can't change you!" she shouted, focusing on his face, only his face. "You can't run from who you are. I see it in your eyes, Arlen. You're a killer, plain and simple."

"And you're dead," he whispered. "Plain and simple."

CHAPTER 47

He had tired of the game, he said. Tired of her. It was over. Were there any last words? he asked.

"Yes," she told him. "There's someone behind you."

He laughed again. He wasn't going to fall for that old trick. The first blow caught him at the nape of his neck. Arlen grunted, fell sideways. He turned, shot a puzzled look at his adversary and struggled to his feet. The second swing of the kayak's paddle knee-capped him and he crumpled to the ground once more, his howls piercing the quiet of the forest. Birds flapped wings, scattered into the sky. The oar came at Arlen again, this time as a battering ram to his stomach and he rolled over, retched and held up a trembling hand. Retched some more, a spume of vomit hitting the ground beneath him.

Mercer Wyatt peeled the bag from Paige's face and snapped the rubber band from her neck. She sat up and gulped gallons of air while Wyatt released her hands and feet from their restraints. Unable to help herself, she burst into tears and fell into Wyatt's arms.

When she calmed down and broke free from his embrace, Wyatt waved a cell phone in front of her face. "I've already called the parks ranger. He'll be here any second. This bastard is going away. Nice job, by the way, raising your voice so I could sneak up behind him."

"How did you know to come here?"

"I wish I knew. Call it instinct, but something wasn't right about that man. I've been watching him from day one. He didn't seem to make eye contact with you. Barely spent any time talking to you, yet you worked across the street from each other? It didn't make sense. At first, I thought he was trying not to be cliquish, then I wondered if he was just giving you space because of everything that's happened out at your cabin, but after a while, it seemed like he was going out of his way to avoid you. Yet, there were times when I'd catch him staring at you when you weren't looking, and it just rubbed me the wrong way."

Arlen groaned, tried to speak. Vomited again. Mercer raised the kayak paddle and the groaning stopped.

"Tonight, when he left the hiking trail, I got an uneasy feeling. He had his knapsack with him, and I couldn't figure out why he needed it. Then he said he'd forgotten to pack his water bottle and wanted to go back for it. We offered to share ours but he refused. The more I walked, the funnier I felt about it all, so I told the others I was going back to check on Arlen, make sure he was okay. When I got to the campfire, Rafe, Chloe and Gaby were passed out. Drugged would be my guess. And you weren't with them so I assumed you'd gone off on your own. It was a crapshoot figuring out which of the eastern trails you'd taken, and Arlen was way ahead of me too. It's just dumb luck that I happened to pick this trail."

"And you brought that trusty weapon," Paige said, pointing to the kayak paddle.

"It was all I could think of, in a pinch."

Arlen was curled up on the ground, one arm holding his shattered knees, the other clutching his stomach. He blubbered like a child. Broken bits of sentences staccatoed through the sobs.

"... close ...had her ... bastard."

Paige saw the plastic bag nearby, fluttering among broken twigs and ran after it. In seconds she had it near Arlen's face. "How'd you like to turn purple, Arlen? I think Bettina Reid used to like mauve. Or maybe a nice violet for Sarah Lydell. You sick son of a bitch."

"Easy, Paige," said Mercer Wyatt, coming closer and crouching beside her. "He'll get what's coming to him. Everyone does, sooner or later."

Paige crumpled up the bag and shoved it into Mercer's waiting hand. She had to move away from Arlen Dale. Move before she killed him. She stood and turned to see the parks ranger hurrying up the trail. Then she whirled back to face Arlen, who was still whimpering. "Want to know the best part, Arlen? You still don't know where Opal is."

She turned away again and heard, "Paige! Look out!"

Arlen lunged at her but Mercer was quicker. From his crouched position, he hurled himself at Arlen's injured knees, knocking him off balance. Then came the sound of tumbling rocks and a piercing scream. Arlen's. Followed immediately by Mercer's shout. "Ah, Christ! No!"

The parks ranger reached the scene just as Arlen Dale lost his footing and went over the cliff, his long tapering fingers stretching skyward, grasping at nothing.

No one got much sleep on the *Madrona* that night. Arlen Dale's body had been lifted from the rocks and was taken from Sucia Island in a Coast Guard boat. Paige put in a call to Carolyn, who was also wide awake. Gregg was packing a bag, moving out, and she was busy throwing underwear and socks in his direction, not wanting him to leave anything behind.

"I'm sorry, Carolyn," Paige said.

"Some things are worth fighting for," Carolyn said philosophically. "This marriage isn't one of those things. Not anymore."

She told Carolyn what had happened on the bluff. Arlen Dale, the True Gentleman, was dead. She was safe. Opal was safe. Then Carolyn dropped her own bombshell—Chloe Grier was a cop, on the *Madrona* to ensure Paige's safety. Unofficially, of course, as a favor to Carolyn. The tall blond had vacation time coming to her; she was fit—an outdoor enthusiast. It hadn't taken much convincing to get Chloe to sign on for the excursion to the San Juans, particularly when Carolyn offered to split the cost of the trip. Paige, though, had thrown Chloe for a loop when she'd strolled up to the washroom and not returned as expected. Arlen must have wanted those not hiking to be out of commission so he spiked their pot of coffee, leaving him to pursue Paige while the rest walked in the opposite direction.

"Why would Arlen take such a risk, Carolyn? Anyone could have discovered us on that bluff."

"And he could have just as easily shoved you off the cliffs and wailed up a storm about you having lost *your* footing. To him, it probably wasn't risky at all."

Paige answered as many questions as she had energy for, and was told she could take the Coast Guard boat back to the mainland.

She refused. "I've got two days' vacation left," she told Carolyn, "and I really need them. I'm staying on the *Madrona*."

Denise made coffee and Bill poured shots of strong brandy all around, refilling Mercer Wyatt's glass as soon as it was empty. "I didn't mean to kill him," he said, his voice as shaky as his hands. "But he was going for Paige. I ... I just tried to stop him. And then he was gone."

"Parks ranger saw the whole thing," Bill Washburne said. "It couldn't have gone any other way. Go easy on yourself." He poured more brandy.

Paige spent the next few hours telling everyone on the boat about her previous line of work, the True Gentleman, and how she'd come to be Laurel. When she saw that no one was staring at her cross-eyed, looking awkwardly around the salon or clearing their throats, she began to relax. Then came a series of stories about some of her weirder and wackier callers. Hardy Litton blushed but laughed anyway, his high-pitched giggle making the others laugh along with him, or perhaps at him. It was awful to be carrying on like this, Paige thought. Someone had died tonight, yet she couldn't stop herself. Tension release. Even Mercer, working on his fourth brandy, joined in. The noise from the *Madrona* rang out across the bay, prompting boaters in the next cove to tell them to shut up. More quietly, Gaby and Shawn Ellison talked about the one and only time they dared to try a new sexual position other than their favorite few, and how Shawn ended up in the hospital with a sprained wrist. Paige could have kissed them both. Finally, she felt accepted. She'd rid herself of her childhood bullies, perhaps forever.

At three a.m. they all went below, exhausted and drunk, but Paige was still wired. She kept hearing Arlen's voice, that crooning True Gentlemanly voice, whispering in her ear. *Hello, Laurel.* She saw Amber's foot, that toe ring with the little blue stone. She was afraid to fall asleep. What if she didn't wake up? What if there was no more air? She filled her lungs until it hurt.

It was the last part of her conversation with Carolyn that finally enabled her to relax and touch her head to the pillow.

"How's Joshua?"

"He's fine," Carolyn had answered. "Parker, too. Better every day. And they both miss you."

"I miss them too," she said. "Very much. Tell Joshua I'll be home about suppertime on Monday."

"Everything will be all right now, Paige. Really it will."

CHAPTER 48

THE MADRONA LEFT SUCIA ISLAND the next morning with two less passengers. Sergeant Chloe Grier had boarded the Coast Guard boat the night before, accompanying the body of the True Gentleman to the mainland. There was little mention of the former occupant of cabin six except to say that no one had perceived Arlen Dale to be anything more than what showed on the surface—a scrawny, introverted man who worked in a kite store.

"We kayaked around the island together for hours," Paul said. "I thought he was a really nice guy."

Mercer Wyatt poured more coffee for everyone. "They always come across like your brother, don't they," he said. "At least, they do in books and movies."

"I didn't think Arlen was any more of a killer than I was," Hardy Litton said. His admiration for Wyatt beamed from his face. "But you spotted something strange about him right off."

"All that's important is that Paige is safe," was the millionaire's reply.

They guzzled water, compared hangover symptoms then headed for Stuart Island where they would hike to Lighthouse Bluff for a picnic. At the end of the day they would dip their paddles into the water for a perfect sunset view from their kayaks.

Several times during the remaining days of the trip, Paige found herself overcome with emotion. Only natural, Gaby Ellison assured her, after all she'd been through. Her traveling companions, strangers to her a week ago, really cared about her. Through the greatness of nature and the power of tragedy, they had grown closer, if only for a time. Once the holiday was over, all would go in their separate directions, promising to write, remaining true to that promise for a few months, then petering out as other memories, other bonds nudged in to take their place. Such an odd thing, she thought, the effect that slowing down and experiencing nature had on people. There were all so different, yet out on the water or trudging through the forests, they were so much the same.

She thought of the friendships she'd forged with Bettina, and Dory, and Lani. Embarking on what they'd thought would be an adventure and a financial answer to their woes, they created a solidarity that served, in part, to assuage any guilt one or more of them may have felt.

If we're all doing it, then it can't be wrong.

What would come of her years-long friendship with Lani? With the True Gentleman captured, could they go back to being best pals? A question nagged at Paige—if the situation had been reversed, if Lani had been the one with that bag over her head, what would she have done? Would she have protected Paige, risked her life?

Perhaps relationships were always in a state of flux, with people entering and exiting each others' lives as their needs changed. It made Paige think of Joshua and what would be waiting for her when she got home. For now, she had two more days to enjoy her shipmates' company and to savor being part of a team. It was also good to know that no one on board gave a damn about Laurel and what she had done, or about Seraphina Greene either.

Feasting on salmon on the last night of the trip, they all agreed there would never be another vacation like this one. "Some parts of it I could have done without," Paige said and Paul rumpled her hair, lightening the moment. During a private few minutes, he even apologized.

"I never meant to make you uncomfortable. Thanks for setting me straight. Friends?" He held out his hand.

"Sure," Paige said and shook on it.

By the time the *Madrona* reached Port Townsend on their final morning together, everyone had exchanged addresses and e-mails. There were a few tears. Cameras came out and Paige good-naturedly told them to let all their friends know they'd shared a boat with Laurel, she-vixen of the phone lines. Mercer Wyatt offered everyone a holiday on his estate just outside of Palo Alto. Same time next year.

"I'll never find the right words to thank you," Paige told him.

He just nodded and gave her a hug. "Take care of yourself and keep in touch."

The only hitch to the feel-good ending to the trip was when Paige walked to her car and saw Arlen's van still parked in the space alongside. Had Bettina ridden in that van, gone willingly with Arlen after falling for his romantic sales pitch? He had courted her on the phone. Flattered her. Somehow coaxed the truth from her about her size and told her it didn't matter. Bettina had bragged about James Lowrey. Her Thursday-night doctor. And she would have eagerly climbed into James Lowrey's van.

Damn you, Arlen. And Orson. And whoever else you pretended to be.

So much tragedy, Paige thought. All because of pretending. She turned her back to the silver van and unlocked her Outback. In five hours, she would be home.

CHAPTER 49

Joshua checked his watch again. 10:00. The *Madrona* had been scheduled to dock at noon. Even accounting for heavy traffic, a stop for a meal en route, Paige should have been home four hours ago.

He watched the local news. There were no reports of any major accidents on 101. He called the Port Townsend marina. Yes, the *Madrona* was in her slip, and had arrived pretty much on schedule, the harbor master told him. He hadn't seen the passengers disembark, but he had watched Captain Bill, his wife and another man leave the boat with their gear.

Parker sensed Joshua's edginess and refused his food. "Come on, boy," Joshua said. "You've got to get your strength back." He nudged the bowl under the dog's nose. Heated the food in the microwave. Added water until it looked like chunky soup. The dog wouldn't eat. Parker limped over to lie in front of the fireplace where he always waited for Paige to return. From there, he could hear her car pull up.

Joshua called his sister. "Something's wrong," he told her.

"You're not kidding," Carolyn sobbed. "My life's a fucking mess. Gregg and that henna-headed girlfriend of his are going to have a baby."

"Ah shit, no. Carl, I'm sorry. What are you going to do?"

"Have another drink. Pray that bitch gets big as a barn and never loses her pregnancy weight—"

He heard her blow her nose. "Help me first. It's Paige. She's not back yet."

"What? I thought you were expecting her around dinnertime."

"I was. The meal I picked up has been reheating since seven. I'm worried, Carl."

"Listen, Josh. You sit tight. I'll make a few calls and get back to you. Meanwhile, try not to worry. I know you will anyway, but—"

"I'm going nuts here," he said. "Call soon."

Paige awoke groggy and cotton-mouthed. The bare twin-sized mattress she lay atop rested on an unfinished wood floor. It was a big room—an attic, judging from the vaulted ceiling and heavy beams that crisscrossed overhead. A single arched window was high on the wall to her left, and slivers of sunlight streamed through slats in the exterior shutters. Directly opposite her was a heavy oak door that looked like it had been rescued from a speakeasy. There was a square iron grille at what she judged to be eye level, and the small spy door on the other side of it was closed. She jiggled the knob. Pounded on the door. "Hey!" She pounded again. Yanked the knob.

She was still clad in the tracksuit she'd worn the final morning on the boat, but her socks and sneakers had been removed. Her watch was missing, too. She strained her memory. She had gone to her car, seen Arlen's vehicle beside hers.

Arlen Dale. The True Gentleman. He was dead. She had seen the Coast Guard boat pull away, and Arlen's body had been on board. It was over. It should have been over. So what was this? What had happened?

Paige remembered unlocking the door to her Outback then—what? She hadn't been struck from behind. Her head didn't ache, and when she palpated behind her neck and skull, there was a tender spot from when Arlen had hit her, but no swelling. Chloroform? An injection of some kind? She didn't know, but still, there was someone else who meant her harm. Serious harm.

It wasn't that she was bound. Her hands and feet were free of restraints. She had plenty of fresh air to breathe, and the room, unfurnished save for the mattress, was clean and dry. But in the corner farthest from her, someone had left a roll of bathroom tissue and a large enamel pot—her toilet. Closer to the mattress, and far more worrisome, were the objects that sent sharp pinpricks of fear through her body—a jug of water, a loaf of bread, a flashlight, and a Bible.

CHAPTER 50

FALLON MCBRIDE CATAPULTED INTO THE story of Arlen Dale's death in the San Juans. Her screaming headline "Local Man Connected to Phone-Hooker Murders" made front page of the *Examiner*. Bettina Reid's landlord, Clark Beattie offered this quote: "You can never really tell about a person, can you?" Bettina's parents still claimed a colossal mistake in identity had been made. Their daughter could not possibly be the Amber being referred to in the article. "Our Bettina was a good girl. She could never do a job like that."

Ava Lydell, whom Carolyn spent the better part of an hour consoling, had moved beyond denial and was seething with anger at her daughter. "What could Sarah have been thinking, talking to all those dirty men? I'm trying to get past it, Sergeant, but I find myself imagining the most horrible things. How could she have been two such different people?"

She was a good actress, Carolyn thought. Just like Arlen Dale had been a good actor. No one in Cypress Village had seen him as anything other than a milquetoast kite vendor, an asexual string bean who listened to music on his iPod. But he was the True Gentleman, who had obsessed after Opal and recorded her voice. He was also Orson, who liked to choke women.

Local radio call-in shows were running wild with the topic of phone sex. Habitual users of the 800 and 900 numbers pronounced the girls they spoke to as everything from "nice diversions" to "hot hot hot." Married women called in to say they often engaged in phone sex with their out-of-town husbands to keep their men from straying while on the road. There were those who found the phone-sex scene too smarmy and professed that the people who called the sex lines were little more than pathetic perverts who couldn't score any other way.

Women who proclaimed to work the phone lines called in as well. "We're fulfilling a need," one said. "If there wasn't a market for phone sex, we'd be out of a job." Another said it was preferable that they listen to callers' dark fantasies than for their clients to act out their kinky desires on someone else. This way nobody got hurt.

Tell that to Sarah Lydell and Bettina Reid, Carolyn thought and shut off her car radio.

She was subsisting on peanut butter sandwiches, Starbucks coffee and painkillers. Paige had been gone for two days, and Carolyn was as worried as Joshua. Paige's tan Outback was still in the parking lot of the Port Townsend marina, the vehicle's doors unlocked. Carolyn had driven up to Washington State yesterday to confer with the local police. She questioned the harbor master, the captain of the *Madrona* and his wife, and Rafe, the boat's engineer. Each had said that during the last two days of the voyage, Paige was sociable and friendly, glad the ordeal with the True Gentleman was behind her. She had spoken openly about her former profession and no one was giving her any static about it. Everyone on board was getting along. None of them had seen Paige go to the parking lot. They had been busy cleaning up the boat, checking equipment, stowing gear. The three of them seemed distraught that Paige had disappeared. "She's been through so much already," Denise Washburn said. "I can't bear to think that something's happened to her."

Bill Washburn furnished Carolyn with the names and addresses of the other passengers. The Ellisons, he said, had been planning to finish off their honeymoon with a driving holiday in British Columbia and weren't due back in Calgary until the 7th, if he remembered correctly. Carolyn gave the Ellisons to Zig Takacs, who was trying to track them down through car rental agencies. Chloe Grier, eager to be involved in the investigation, had taken a commuter plane to Petaluma and had given Paul Kuzemchak the third degree, particularly since during the first few days of the trip, he had been overly attentive toward Paige. Paul admitted he thought Paige was good-looking and that he wouldn't have minded getting her into bed, but that she'd made it clear she wasn't interested, so he backed off. They had parted on friendly terms. Chloe was going to dig further. Just because Paul claimed Paige had forgiven him didn't mean it was so. Perhaps some former girlfriends might have details they were willing to share about the breadth of Paul's devotion.

Carolyn had spoken with Mercer Wyatt by phone, reaching him at his Palo Alto office. "It can't be," he told her, his voice still weary from all he had been through. "She was safe. That bastard is dead." Wyatt had left the boat ahead of Paige and had walked to the parking lot with Gaby and Shawn Ellison. To the best of his recollection, Paige and Hardy Litton were the only ones left aboard with the Washburnes and the *Madrona's* engineer. Paul Kuzemchak had been the first to disembark.

"And once you left the parking lot—"

"I drove straight back to my place in the village, dropped off my gear, opened my mail then flew back here. I got in around nine thirty, fixed myself a bite to eat and went straight to bed. All that fresh air, you know. Plus the long drive."

Carolyn had already contacted Astoria Regional Airport where Wyatt kept his plane. His story checked out. And Wyatt had boarded his Cessna alone.

Carolyn heard him sigh.

"Forgive me, Sergeant, but this is almost too much to take. Paige has already had one close call. That's what makes it so hard to believe she's missing now. Is it possible she's just taken a little more time for herself, extended her holiday, maybe jumped on a bus or train?"

Carolyn had already thought of that. Paige had been through more in the past five weeks than most people could cope with. Returning to Cypress Village after the attempt on her life would mean more hounding by the press, more stares from the villagers, more of everything that Paige didn't want. And there was Joshua. Paige still didn't know what to expect from him. It was understandable that she might want to postpone it all, give herself more breathing room, and steel herself for the next invasion of her privacy and possible heartbreak.

"Let's hope so," she told Mercer Wyatt and hung up.

But Carolyn knew better. Paige had told her how much she missed Joshua, missed Parker, and that she would be home by dinnertime on Monday. If she'd changed her mind, she would have called. And if escaping for a while longer was part of her plan, she would have taken her vehicle, not boarded a bus or train. Carolyn's biggest clue was the door to the Outback. Paige would not have departed from Port Townsend leaving her car doors unlocked. Even if someone she knew had come along and made the offer of a quick cup of coffee, she might have gone willingly, but she would have remembered to lock her vehicle. But Carolyn's every instinct told her that Paige had not gone willingly. She had made it to the Outback. Unlocked the doors. Then someone grabbed her.

It had been noon when the *Madrona* docked. For someone to have abducted Paige at her vehicle and to have escaped sight unseen, he would have had to be parked in the space beside hers. Or very close by.

Carolyn checked the address for Hardy Litton. Litton lived in Salem and worked as a salesman for a low-end furniture store. Chloe Grier had told Carolyn that Litton was a real piece of work—a quintessential nerd, clumsy, and more than a little dense, so much so that Chloe had wondered if it was an act. Carolyn wanted to see for herself. The two-hour-plus drive had given her back-stabbing pain. She swallowed a muscle relaxant with the rest of her lukewarm coffee and pulled into a visitor's spot in front of Litton's apartment building.

Hardy Litton lived on the sixteenth floor in a one-bedroom unit, the view from his sliding glass door revealing an identical building across a grassy courtyard. Litton had clearly taken advantage of his employee discount, his living room furniture plucked straight from the showroom floor, an unimaginative suite of mud-colored checks and pecan veneers. He ushered Carolyn inside and offered her ginger ale, which she took. Once she was seated, Litton spoke enthusiastically about his excursion in the San Juans and how much he wanted to return. It was several minutes before Carolyn could remind him that she was there to discuss Paige Rowan.

"Oh, yes, Paige," he said, absent-mindedly fingering a WWJD pin affixed to the collar of his sport shirt. "I can't believe it. I just can't believe it. Hasn't anyone heard from her?"

"Afraid not."

She got Litton to verify who left the boat first, and his story jibed with Mercer Wyatt's. Paige and Hardy had been the last passengers to leave the *Madrona*, but he had reached his car first and remembered driving off, honking his horn at Paige. When he looked in the rearview mirror, she was waving at him.

"I understand Paige spoke about her job as a phone actress," Carolyn said. "Not that we're judgmental people here, but didn't that strike you as odd, what she once did for a living?"

"Now that you mention it, yes," Litton replied, his eyes cast downward at his knees. "Paige didn't seem ... well, you know—the type."

"How did you feel after she told everyone about it?"

Litton reached for his ginger ale and drank. He dabbed at the corners of his mouth with pudgy white fingertips. "Okay, I guess. I mean, it's not illegal or anything. It's no one's business, really."

"Still, makes you wonder, though, I'll bet."

He nodded, looked out the window toward the next building where someone was standing on a balcony shaking out a mop. "Hard to say what makes people do the things they do."

Carolyn asked him about the other passengers. The Ellisons, he said, were nice. Very athletic, fun-loving, and they mixed well with the others. They weren't all googly-eyed like most honeymooners. In fact, Litton liked all the people on the boat, but he clearly had a warm spot for Mercer Wyatt, who did wonders for his confidence. "I've never gone in much for sports or outdoor activities, but he made me feel like I was as good as anyone else there, even when I goofed up. And he wasn't a snob either, like you'd expect from someone who's got that kind of money."

She spent close to an hour with Hardy Litton, and calculated that he might have looked directly at her for a total of three minutes. Carolyn wondered how many dates Litton had been on in his lifetime, thinking she could count them on one hand. She wondered, too, if he was really as laissez-faire about Paige's former occupation as he was claiming, or whether Hardy Litton would secretly yearn for his own little sex slave.

"Sounds like you really enjoyed your time on the *Madrona*," Carolyn said as she was rising to leave. "Doesn't all that outdoor adventure make you wish you had a little cabin of your own somewhere? A place where you could just get away from everything?"

Litton nodded, his eyes darting first at Carolyn, then at the door.

He wants me to leave, she thought. Nervous? Because she was a woman? Or a cop? Perhaps something else had set the man on edge.

"I'll never be able to afford another place," he said. "Not on my salary. But it's nice to dream."

"No rich relative to leave you a little nest egg, I guess?"

Litton chuckled. "Sergeant, in my family, I am the rich relative."

As Carolyn walked down the corridor to the elevator, she suspected she would be paying Hardy Litton another visit, if only to shake him up again and see what spilled out. She was certain he had unresolved issues with his sexuality, issues perhaps someone like Paige, with her salty banter and know-how, could help him with. Especially if he had a secret cottage or apartment tucked away somewhere. Litton didn't appear robust enough to swat a mosquito, but neither had Arlen Dale, and as yet, Bettina Reid's torso and limbs hadn't surfaced.

Except for the Ellisons, the police had questioned everyone who had been on the *Madrona* with Paige. That only left any number of former Saints who might hold a grudge against anyone with the surname Greene; a disgruntled phone-sex client who, like Arlen, had crossed over from dark fantasy to even darker reality; or perhaps someone closer to Paige herself.

First thing tomorrow, Carolyn would acquaint herself with Nicholas Bissonette.

CHAPTER 51

THE FIRST TWO PHASES OF starvation can occur during even relatively brief periods of dieting or fasting. After only one week of food deprivation, the body begins breaking down fat for energy. After several weeks, when fat reserves are depleted, the body switches to protein for its energy, which it gets from the muscles.

Paige had no concept of time. During her first few hours in captivity, she had scrounged around the attic, searching not only for a way out, but for a stone or nail or something sharp that she could use to scratch off the days on one of the wooden slats beside the mattress. Sun continued to filter through the shuttered window, and darkness fell, but she had lost track of how many times it had done so. She had read somewhere that people rarely died of starvation. Some infectious disease usually got them first.

The crusty baguette, half eaten now, was stale and hard. Her stomach didn't growl anymore. Her lips were dry and beginning to crack. She wondered how long it would be before her abdomen bloated like the infomercials showing Third World children, their faces covered in flies and scabs.

Just a dollar a day, the cost of a cup of coffee, would give little Aiysha the nutrients she needs to survive.

Though she'd always been meaning to, Paige had never sent her dollar a day.

She drank sparingly, cursing that whoever had brought her here had provided no lid for the wide-mouthed plastic jug. Her precious water supply, bit by bit, was evaporating. She removed her shirt and stuffed it into the opening of the jug. A person could survive for weeks without food, but only days without water.

And the bastard had cranked up the heat.

In those first few hours, she cried a lot. Now she was afraid to, desperate to conserve every ounce of bodily fluid. She was plagued by diarrhea and raced to the enamel pot, thinking the indignity of it to be the absolute least of her worries. She was drying up, withering like a crisp brown leaf.

From dust to dust.

She searched the attic, not even knowing what she was searching for. She crawled along the floor, examined each board like Braille text, fingertips brushing across wood, probing. She checked for loose slats. She did the same with the walls, knowing it was useless, knowing she wouldn't find anything. The only oddity Paige discovered in the otherwise unfinished room was a brand new phone jack. Useless without the phone she needed to summon help.

Still, her searching passed the time. Once in a while she hummed, crooned herself into a calm, lullaby state. She made lists. Her top ten favorite songs. The five places on earth she would like to visit. Famous people she would enjoy sharing a meal with. During those moments of mental exercise, she almost forgot she was hungry. And frightened.

She had no view to the outside. The shuttered window was high above. There were no cooking odors, no sounds of running water from a shower below, no rumble of a car engine starting up. Wherever she was, she was alone.

She thought about her captor. And her parents. Whoever had brought her here was reenacting the indoctrination ritual of The New Order of Angels and Saints. Had someone taken over her parents' church? Appointed himself to be the new spiritual leader? No. This was more than indoctrination. Her parents' ritual had been a weekend affair. Paige had already been here longer than two days. This was revenge, an ex-worshipper, getting even with the Greenes. Thanks to Fallon McBride, everyone in the Pacific Northwest was reminded that Paige was Seraphina Greene. Someone could have been plotting this scenario since the article appeared in the paper.

Then she grew tired of thinking, grew tired of trying to discover ways to escape when there were none. She lay on the mattress, tucked her knees against her empty stomach and closed her eyes.

CHAPTER 52

CAROLYN'S SCIATICA WASN'T THE SOLE cause of the pain in her ass on Thursday morning. Gregg Holt stopped by the house unannounced for his rowing machine, catching her as she was straining to zip up her slacks, her abdomen swollen with premenstrual bloat. They barely exchanged five sentences yet it was long enough for her to want to shoot out the headlights of his Escalade as it pulled out of the driveway, just to keep her skills sharp.

She wished that she were promiscuous, that she'd gone out last night and found some ripe college boy and brought him home, and that he'd answered the door this morning, towel wrapped around his waist and still smelling of post-lovemaking sweat. Maybe Gregg would call ahead next time, not assume she was alone and missing him. Instead of corrupting some handsome youth, she'd spent the evening with caffeine and case files and this morning, she had the puffy eyes to show for it.

It was a day made for confronting assholes. It didn't take long for Carolyn to size up Nicholas Bissonette as a self-centered son of a bitch. She located him at his gallery in the village where he was reigning imperiously over a frazzled work crew who were trying to put finishing touches on the interior. He made grand sweeping gestures with his hands, clicked his Italian shoes across the bleached floors as he pointed out where he wanted his spot lights directed. Various *objets d'arts* in ceramic and blown glass, the work of local artisans, were mounted on laminate pedestals. Framed acrylics graced the walls. The place smelled of fresh paint, new wood and money.

Carolyn's unannounced entry earned her a snarl.

"Excuse me," he snipped, coming toward her, "but the studio doesn't open for another week."

When she flipped him her I.D. he recoiled like a vampire being flashed a crucifix.

"What can I do for you, Officer?" His voice was less strident now, his arms still.

"Sergeant," Carolyn said. "A few questions for you, Mr. Bissonette."

"Regarding?"

She longed to squirt indelible ink on his form-fitting silk shirt. Instead she said, "Paige Rowan. I believe you once had a relationship with her."

Bissonette led her to the back of the gallery where he kept a small office. Boxes were stacked in corners. Shelves were still bare. He motioned toward one of a pair of black leather and chrome director's chairs. Once they were seated he said, "I knew Paige in Europe. We shared an apartment awhile."

"For nearly two years, according to my information."

"I guess that's right."

"And you split because …?"

Bissonette concealed his nervousness with haughty irritation. "Look, Sergeant, let's keep this moving along efficiently. As you can see, I'm very busy and that crew out there doesn't know a light bulb from a tulip bulb. I read the papers. I know Paige is missing, and because we shared a past, I'm concerned for her. But I don't know where she is. Now instead of wasting your time here, shouldn't you be out looking for Paige?"

Carolyn shot him a pinched smile and leaned forward in her chair. "This is an investigation, Mr. Bissonette, and I'm in charge of it. As busy as we both are, there are questions that need to be answered. We can do that here *efficiently*, or I can send a squad car over with lights flashing and siren wailing. The chairs in my office aren't nearly as comfortable. It's your call."

Some of the bravado slid from the man's shoulders. "We were young, Paige and I," he said, his voice lower still. "We grew apart. That's all."

"Did she ever tell you about her parents, the kind of people they were?"

"She was putting some distance between herself and them, that much was clear. From what she told me, they were overly protective, rigid, and their views about the modern world were pretty negative. Now that I've seen that TV program, I think Paige was being kind in her description. The Greenes sounded like complete head cases. No wonder Paige was so buttoned up when I met her."

"But you changed that."

He cleared his throat. "Paige wasn't the first girl to leave home and sow a few wild oats."

"And she sowed them with you."

Bissonette nodded. "We had some good times."

"But eventually she left you. Returned to the States."

"Like I said, we grew apart. People change."

"That being the case, why did you show up at her cabin a few weeks ago?"

His eyebrow arched. He paused for a breath. "Just looking up an old friend."

"And that old friend reacted how?"

Bissonette cast his glance over her shoulder toward the workers in the studio then to the pile of boxes against the wall.

Don't even think about lying to me, you bastard.

"Paige was surprised, but not pleasantly so. My visit was brief."

"And that was the last time you saw her?"

He seemed to consider his response again. "No," he said. "I went out to the cabin with an invitation to the opening of the gallery. You know, to show there were no hard feelings."

"And were there?"

He tried for a nonchalant smile. "Paige would have preferred that I had mailed the invitation. I didn't overstay my welcome."

"Not used to being told 'no,' are you, Mr. Bissonette."

He shrugged. "I'm the same as anybody in that regard, Sergeant."

"Your relationship with Paige was over years ago. Why, after all this time, would you be trying to make inroads again? And just so you know, I'm not buying the 'to show there were no hard feelings' story."

"Like I said, Paige and I had some good times. Maybe it's like that song, you don't know what you've got 'til it's gone."

"Of course you can verify your whereabouts for the 25th?"

"I was at home."

"Alone?"

"I'm rarely alone, Sergeant."

She was long past fed up with Bissonette, his smug riddles, his expensive clothes and his ridiculous furniture which offered her sore back no support. "And your companion can vouch for you?"

"Do I need an alibi?"

He was baiting her and she knew it. She also knew she was going to bite down hard. "Look, your former girlfriend is missing. And unless you can prove to me that you didn't climb into that fancy Porsche you own and scoot up to Washington State to meet Paige when she came off that boat, I'm going to be all over you like polyester pants. You don't open a place like this on money you make from painting greeting cards. Maybe you had something to do with Paige's disappearance and maybe you didn't, but I know there's more to you than this uptown gallery and I bet you don't want me to find out about it."

The air went out of his chest. "I lied," he said. "I was home alone. There's no one who can give me an alibi. But I didn't do anything to hurt Paige, Sergeant. And that I'll swear to."

She gave a relieved Bissonette a curt nod as she left the building. Inside her car, she called her doctor and managed to get a four o'clock appointment. She needed a cortisone shot and quickly. She couldn't afford to take time off, not now. They were short-staffed as it was and working sixteen hour days. One of the officers had already missed his wedding anniversary, his wife now sunning herself at a resort in Baja without him. Carolyn needed the job, needed to stay busy. The last thing she wanted was to be nursing pain from her bed at home. Her empty bed.

Besides, she wouldn't make lieutenant by knuckling under. She had to keep going. The job was all she had.

Chloe Grier called from the Petaluma airport. She would be on the next commuter flight back to Oregon without any dirt on Paul Kuzemchak. Ziggy Takacs had located the Ellisons in Victoria B.C., having tea at the Empress Hotel. They could offer nothing new. They'd told Ziggy they'd left the *Madrona* with Mercer Wyatt and walked to the parking lot with him, just as he and Hardy Litton had said. They looked forward to the reunion of the travelers in the coming year at Wyatt's place and said they hoped the invitation wasn't just talk. Everyone had gotten along so well.

Carolyn would see to it that Paige was at that reunion. She had to find her. Soon. She had already been missing for four days. There had to be a way to narrow the investigative field. Without that, the police would have to get outside help.

Following her visit to the doctor, she would go home, clear off the kitchen table and make a pot of strong coffee. Tonight she would focus, not on her pain, not on her soon-to-be ex-husband and his new family, but on Paige's journal. Perhaps Arlen Dale wasn't the only one who liked to play rough.

CHAPTER 53

Joshua fed Parker, who was getting stronger. It was as if the dog sensed the danger around him and knew he had to buck up. Joshua was the one cracking under the strain. Full of self-recrimination and shame, he'd tossed in bed every night since Paige had gone missing, kicking himself for being such a bastard. It shouldn't have mattered about Laurel. He knew that. His love for Paige should have been unconditional. Well, he was paying the price now, wasn't he? For not loving enough. For not getting it right.

He was doing a half-assed job at work as well, arriving late, leaving early, keeping to himself. His staff was understanding and compassionate, and they picked up the slack, coordinating volunteers, soliciting corporate sponsors, organizing the silent auction fund-raiser. He would be late again this morning. He needed to stop by his place to shower and change, check his phone messages. He was planning to squeeze in a visit to "The Great Outdoors" and talk to Paige's boss and her co-worker, Lukas. Carolyn would kill him if she knew, but he had to do something. He felt powerless in this agonizing search for Paige. He knew the police were logging in sweatshop hours. On the phone late last night, Carolyn had been on the knife-edge of breaking down. He had dug deeply for words of support.

"You're doing everything you can. Go easy on yourself. You'll find her tomorrow."

He heard himself speak the words, but even louder were the ones screaming inside his head. *Where the hell is she? And why can't you find her?*

Carolyn, being his twin, knew the thoughts he'd left unspoken. Just before hanging up, she said, "I'm sorry, Josh."

But it was he who was sorry. Paige had to come home, safely, and give him a chance to apologize. Meanwhile, what could he do? He didn't know where to search, and other than Paige's boss, he didn't know who to talk to. Carolyn had spoken to the passengers of the *Madrona* as well as Paige's ex-boyfriend. She had taken Paige's personal phone book and journal. Joshua's hands were tied. After a brief stopover at his place, he drove to St. Bartholomew's Church, slid into a pew at the back and prayed.

Lukas Rush blinked twice when he saw Joshua Latham come into the store. That he looked like hell came as no surprise. Paige's disappearance had to be wearing him down. He nodded at Luke who introduced him to his cousin, Sammi, who was filling in until Paige got back.

"Really sorry to hear about your girlfriend," Sammi said, her eyes wide. "I met her once and she seemed really nice."

"Thanks. Harry in?"

Lukas pointed toward the back of the store to a door bearing a sign that read: Staff Only. "Just knock and walk. Harry's inside."

Joshua moved to where Lukas pointed and when he was out of earshot, Sammi said, "I still can't believe what I've been reading about Paige in the papers. Was she really one of those phone-sex girls?"

"Looks that way," Lukas said. "Anyway, no big deal. Everybody calls those lines at least once, just to see what it's like."

"Even you, cuz?"

"A gentleman doesn't phone and tell."

"Well, probably pays more than this job. Her boyfriend's cute."

"Yeah, not bad, considering he was going to be a priest once."

"Priest?"

"Not kidding."

"Dating a phone hooker? Cool."

Lukas inclined his head toward the first customer of the day, a stout man who seemed lost between the Gortex vests and the snowshoes. Sammi moved toward him and Lukas went to the back of the store, where Joshua had left the door open.

"If I was the type to keep liquor in my filing cabinet, I'd offer you a drink," Harry was saying. "No leads on where Paige is?"

"Nothing," Joshua replied.

"I don't have to tell you, I'm as worried as you are. Paige isn't the type to just take off, not without calling. And she's never missed a day of work, not since she started here."

"I know, Harry. I'm going crazy with it. Still thinking about those passengers on the boat. How possible is it for there to have been someone else on that trip besides Arlen who had it in for Paige?"

"Seems far-fetched, I'll agree. I talked to Bill again last night. My brother says it's one of the best trips they've had. Everyone was a real team. He couldn't even speculate about anyone. Of course, who'd have thought Arlen capable of … well, you know. He worked across the street from me for five years. Matt Severs, who owns the store, can't believe it either. Thought Dale was a loyal employee. Hard worker. Got along with the customers. Matt had to close up awhile until the press cools it. Took off to his time-share in Idaho."

Joshua looked through the doorway at the kite shop across the street, blinds drawn, a CLOSED sign on the door. Lukas leaned back to avoid being seen.

"Have Bill and Denise taken another crew out?" Joshua asked Harry.

"Yeah. They run the trips until the end of October when Sucia Island closes then they take their own vacation. Building a second home on Salt Spring Island in B.C. Roughing it, they say, but I've been to the place. It's a little isolated but it's no shack. Thirty-five hundred square feet. It'll be a beauty when it's finished. But never mind that. I sure wish I could do something for you, Joshua. More importantly, I wish I could do something for Paige."

The two men spoke for nearly half an hour while Lukas busied himself near the open doorway, listening to their conversation. It became clear to Lukas from the way Harry was talking that he suspected Joshua was involved in Paige's disappearance. It made sense. In cases like this, police always looked to the husband or boyfriend. And Joshua was showing his miserable face all over town, proving to everyone how distraught he was, how much he missed Paige and wanted her home. Might not have taken much for an ex-seminarian to snap once he learned his girlfriend had been talking the nasty with strangers. A five-hour drive up the coast, meet the boat, 'hi Paige, surprised to see me?' then whomp. It could be done.

More interesting was that Joshua seemed suspicious of Harry. It was his brother's boat, after all. Harry had suggested the trip to Paige. He knew the boat's schedule. He'd taken the trip once or twice himself. Maybe he was even in league with his brother Bill. A killing partnership. It wouldn't be the first. And no one knew too much about Harry's comings and goings. He was a private guy.

What neither Joshua nor Harry realized was that whoever had taken Paige might have nothing to do with the *Madrona*. The boat's itinerary was available on the Internet. Anyone who knew Paige was going on the trip would also know when she arrived in each port and when the boat would dock in Port Townsend. And Paige had spoken often about the trip. Anyone could have met that boat. Hopped from island to island, watching, waiting.

By the time Joshua emerged from the back room, Lukas was busy helping a customer select a tent from a catalogue. "Think good thoughts, man," he said to Joshua as he made his way to the exit. Joshua nodded then Lukas caught Sammi's attention, directing his gaze toward another customer in the middle of the store. He wanted Sammi to watch the man. Sometimes theft was a problem, particularly the small specialty items like army knives, mini-maglites, travel clocks, hiking guidebooks. This guy, though, didn't seem interested in any of those things. He wandered aimlessly about the store for a few minutes, returning often to the rack of women's sweaters which he stroked with his fingertips.

CHAPTER 54

THERE WERE DRY PATCHES ON her skin. Her breath smelled like pears. She was dizzy, weak. She tried to conserve energy by lying perfectly still.

She was cold now, but there was no blanket or sheet. Nothing left for her to fashion a noose so she might, in despair and desperation, hang herself. The rafters were too high, and there was no bedpost, no furniture legs, nothing around which she could loop her shirt or slacks. Her shirt was still stuffed into the opening of the water jug. She removed it and put it on, though it did little to quell the shivers.

She had less than an inch of water left. If she drank it now, she might survive for a few more days. She was so thirsty. And dry. So very dry.

Carefully, so she wouldn't trip and spill what was left, Paige removed the jug from her sight, tucking it into a corner behind her. Out of sight, out of mind. Out of her mind.

The last of the crusty bread had gone yesterday. Or perhaps it had been the day before. Good news, she thought. A person didn't lose her appetite until the final stages of starvation. She was still hungry.

Diversion, please. More mental activity.

Favorite color: green. Favorite comedy: *While You Were Sleeping*. Favorite line from that movie: How do you get your potatoes so creamy? Favorite treat: boiled Maine lobster. Coconut cream pie. Buttered popcorn.

No, not food. Think about something else.

Things she hadn't tried yet. Surfing. Riding a horse. Sky diving. She didn't like heights much, but knew if she could somehow reach that shuttered window, she would smash the glass and jump. She didn't care how far it was to the ground, didn't care if her body folded like an accordion. Paige looked over at the window. Useless, thinking about what would happen to her if she leaped out. There was no way she could get anywhere near that window. It was a good ten feet from the floor, tucked snugly under the rafters. The walls, though constructed of rough wood, weren't rough enough to give her a good toehold. She had already tried. He had thought of everything.

Death. Wasn't there something else she could think about? She was much better off when she was thinking about food. How about movies with food in the title? *Mystic Pizza. Chocolat. Fried Green Tomatoes.* There had to be others.

Come on, brain. Keep working.

Wild Strawberries. Thank you, Fellini. And *Bananas.* How could she forget Woody Allen? *The Grapes of Wrath.* Nice to know fruit was well represented cinematically. She wondered if Kevin Bacon had been in any food films.

She tried to laugh out loud. A dry cackle escaped instead. Even her voice had withered.

Favorite people, she thought. That was easy. Joshua. And Parker. Her dog counted as people. Her friends from the boat—Chloe, the Washburnes, Mercer, the Ellisons. Paul Kazemchak? Hardy Litton? No to both. But yes to Joshua's sister Carolyn, especially if she was searching for her right now. And Uncle Spence. Dear Uncle Spence. He had always looked out for her. Could he save her this time?

I'm here, Uncle Spence. Your Angel Heart. I'm in trouble again. The biggest. Am I getting through to you? Can you please send someone to get me the hell out of here?

She wondered about hallucinations. She knew people deprived of sleep could experience them. And people locked in dark closets with no visual stimulation. But did starving people hallucinate?

She sensed something different about her surroundings and thought her brain might be transmitting a wonky signal, but then she realized there was someone in the house. It might have been the quiet closing of a door or cupboard, she wasn't sure. Then ever so softly, a creak of floorboards and what—? Stocking feet padding along the hallway? No. No one could hear that. Wishful thinking.

On wobbly legs, Paige moved toward the door anyway and pressed her ear against the cool wood. The labored breathing she heard was her own, the rapid heartbeat hers as well.

She felt a sharp tickle at her toes. A sheet of newsprint was being passed under the door. "Hey!" she hollered, her cry more like an amphibious croak. Paige pounded on the door. "Please! Let me out!"

Another sheet of newsprint scraped along the floor at her feet then she heard the sound of receding footsteps, floorboards creaking faster now and shoes making purposeful strides away from her.

"No! Don't leave! Why are you doing this? What do you want?" And finally, in a hoarse whisper, she asked, "Who are you?"

She waited, her ear against the door for what could have been minutes, but there was no reply. Beyond, all was quiet.

Paige stooped, steadied herself against the door and reached for the two pieces of paper. Clippings cut from newspapers. The first one was from the *Clatsop County Examiner* and bore Fallon McBride's byline. It was dated October 2nd. Was that today? Paige had left the *Madrona* on the 25th of September. Eight days. She'd been here at least eight days.

She sat on the floor by the door and read.

Bones Still Unidentified

```
The skeletal remains of a young male,
discovered in a local bomb shelter are
still a mystery.
    Joshua Latham, executive director of
"Friends for Families" found the bones
while searching for a lost dog on the
property belonging to Spencer Rowan, the
uncle of current resident Paige Rowan, a.k.a
Seraphina Greene. As yet, the skeleton,
which bears evidence of an untreated injury
to the fibula, has not been matched to any
Missing Person reports. Despite widespread
publicity and law enforcement cooperation
on a national level, the identity of the
skeleton continues to baffle police.
```

Forensic anthropologist Dr. Marion Hawley has determined that, in addition to the injury, the victim stood approximately 5'11". After examining the length of the femur and the amount of wear on the teeth, Dr. Hawley estimated the victim's age to be between 18 and 22.

It is believed that the victim entered the shelter with the intention of fulfilling a religious ritual instituted by Jerome and Millicent Greene, co-founders of the New Order of Angels and Saints. Former church member Eric Bowden believes the death to be accidental. "The Greenes wouldn't hurt anybody," Mr. Bowden told reporters. "I was no great fan of theirs toward the end, but no way would either of them leave a person in that hole to die."

Police have ruled the victim's death to be the result of an unfortunate accident. Forensic tests have determined that the unidentified individual entered the underground chamber, likely on a Friday evening, according to the dictates of the ritual, but was unable to be rescued by the Greenes, who were killed in an auto accident four years ago. Police continue to urge former members of the Angels and Saints to come forward with any information they may have concerning the identity of the remains.

In a bizarre twist to this story, police also continue to search for Paige Rowan, a.k.a. Seraphina Greene, daughter of the late cult duo, missing since September 25th.

A similar article appeared in the Portland *Oregonian* on the same day, with one striking difference: across the article, Paige's captor had taken a red marker and printed, "Figured it out yet?"

CHAPTER 55

Spencer Rowan stared out his window, something he'd been doing plenty of during the past few days. He wasn't looking at anything in particular, just hoping to relax his mind enough that it might conjure up something useful. He could still be useful, couldn't he?

He had never been one to fear getting old. He had worked hard all his life, building his real estate business. He anticipated retirement with relish and was eager to spend time at the cabin, go fly fishing with a couple of his friends. His dream had lasted six months then the stroke turned his golden years to rust.

His life was becoming one loss after another. He needed help with some tasks now, his hands not always obeying what his brain commanded. He could still chew a steak, but someone had to cut it for him. Last month, his bridge buddy Earl had died. Massive heart attack, right there at the dinner table. Spence's memory, too, had as many perforations as a paper doily, and right now, that was the loss that bothered him the most.

That, and the knowledge that Paige was missing and he was too feeble to round up a posse. He had been following the story in the *Oregonian* and on the news. To know that the niece he loved like a daughter had cheated death once only to disappear days later was like a hot knife through his heart. He was her only relative. He had to help. If he could. If it wasn't too late.

He vaguely remembered a visit from an officer not long ago but details of their conversation were sketchy, and that disturbed him as much as the newspaper folded in his lap. He looked down and reread the article that had been vexing him for days. The bones. Male. 18-22. With an injury consistent with a skiing mishap. Familiar. But why?

He closed his eyes, reached into the deep part of his mind where his memories were still clear. He recalled a story of a young boy, taking skiing lessons at some posh place—Vail or Aspen, maybe. And there had been something about an out-of-control skier—yes, that was it. Came barreling straight down the hill, screaming for his life. Plowed right into the boy as he was preparing to turn. Sent the kid hurtling into the glades and the deep, untracked snow. His bindings didn't release. Crack. He went down, his head missing the trunk of a pine by inches. He was lucky to be alive.

Now why did he remember that, of all things? What was so special about a broken leg?

Spencer's heart raced. Easy does it, came the warning. No sense going like old Earl. He didn't need another stroke either. The last one had robbed him of enough. If he stayed calm, took deep breaths and just didn't try so hard, he might be able to figure out what exactly it was that nagged him about those damn bones.

He returned his gaze to the world outside his window. Below, Emily Griffith was out for her afternoon constitutional, pushing the walker that her grandson had decorated with bright daisy decals. Vince Cerruti was sitting on a bench in the gazebo, reading. Vince was never without a book, even during meals. A trio of sparrows alit on the upper rim of the two-tiered fountain near the entrance to the building.

"Come on, Spence. It's that time again."

Lionel Weber stood in the doorway to Spencer's room, smiling broadly. Spencer liked Lionel, who treated him like a friend, not a patient. Still he wished he didn't need to depend on him for a bath.

"Scotch tasting tonight, remember?" Lionel said. "Room full of drunken widows—you want to be looking your best for that. Could be your lucky night."

Spencer rose from his chair, pushed it away from the window, and moved toward Lionel. "My friend, I could sure use some luck. A boatload of it."

CHAPTER 56

She did not move from the mattress. There was no point. The attic was dark. The water was gone. Since her captor had slid the newspaper clipping under the door—and how long ago had that been?—he hadn't returned.

Beyond the shuttered window, Paige heard the rain tapping its forlorn notes on the roof. Bitter despair lodged in her parched throat. Outside there was plenty of water.

A hole in the roof. Was that too much to ask for? A hole just big enough to allow the rain to leak in and quench her thirst. Keep her alive. She imagined tilting her face upward toward the water, opening her mouth, feeling the cool wet drops slide down her throat.

Figured it out yet?

She had tried. It was all about the bones. What did she know? What was there to figure out?

She had been in Europe when her parents had begun gathering worshippers, building their congregation of angels and saints. What had occurred on Uncle Spence's property while she was overseas had nothing to do with her. Her mother and father, had they lived, would have rescued that boy.

But they had died. And someone's death had gone unavenged. That was it. Paige was standing trial. Because someone needed to be held accountable. Quid pro quo. Tit for tat.

Someone had known she was going on the *Madrona*, knew what time the boat docked, knew when to strike. Who had she told? Everybody. She'd been so excited about the trip.

Joshua knew, of course. So did Harry and Lukas. Lani. And Dory. Had Nicholas somehow found out? Was she being held captive in the house he had bragged about?

Cypress Village is a small place, Paige. You won't be hard to find.

But Nicholas wasn't connected to the bones. Neither were the others. She couldn't focus. She was so thirsty, so hungry.

In the blacker-than-blackness, she detected movement, moiré waves of formless shadows at the edge of her vision. Oil slicks in the dark. She groped for the flashlight and slid the switch. The beam pierced the room, landing on the grille of the speakeasy door. The small trapdoor was still closed. No menacing eyes peered in.

Paige made a sweep of the room, checked all the corners but knew the attic was empty.

Yet the house was not. Somewhere below her, someone slept. Or lay awake in bed, reveling in the notion that his clever, sinister plan was succeeding beautifully. Perhaps even now he was imagining her death, calculating how long it might take, the position he would find her in, her facial expression. She should keep her middle finger extended, go out with a final "fuck you."

Giving up already, Angel Heart?

Dammit Uncle Spence, what would you do?

Perhaps there was a way she could turn the tables, torment her tormentor. She could stomp on the floor, keep him awake, drive him crazy until he came and unlocked the door. Angered, he could kill her sooner. Or worse, leave the house, not return until she was a pile of moldering bones.

She didn't have the strength to stomp anyway.

The night was cruel and endless, and Paige couldn't bear its darkness. The beam of the flashlight came to rest on the Bible, unopened throughout her captivity. She had avoided the book as she would a scorpion, but now her eyes needed some stimulus to banish the wavy optic hallucinations that were plaguing her. The Bible was the greatest-selling book of all time; there had to be a good story in it somewhere.

She opened the book at random, her gaze coming to rest on John, Chapter 6. The page was turned down at the corner, a perfect forty-five degrees. The miracle of the loaves and fishes.

Her hands, her feet turned to ice. Other pages were dog-eared as well. Matthew, Chapter 4. *After spending forty days and nights without food, Jesus was hungry.* Verse 16 was also marked. *And when you fast, do not put on a sad face the way the hypocrites do.*

Bastard. He had led her to passages about hunger. And food.

There were others. The wedding feast at Cana. The Passover supper. Jesus appearing to his disciples after his resurrection, instructing them to cast their net over the right side of their boat into Lake Tiberias. *Simon Peter went aboard and dragged the net ashore, full of fish, a hundred and fifty-three in all; even though there were so many, still the net did not tear.*

Mental torture. Because the physical agony she was enduring wasn't enough. Her captor needed to twist the knife, to inflict as much suffering as possible.

He had marked one more passage in the book, this one not indicated by a folded corner, but by a slender green ribbon. Paige opened to the text and read. And understood everything.

CHAPTER 57

CAROLYN NEEDED TO GET AWAY from her desk, where she'd sat since four a.m. She had already purged its messy surface of the framed photo showing her and Gregg sipping rum swizzles under a patio umbrella in St. Lucia. Fair-skinned Gregg got a flaming sunburn on that trip. Served him right, she thought. Too macho to apply a sun block and Gregg refused to wear a hat as well. He didn't have a hat face, he'd said.

The ergonomic chair Carolyn had requisitioned hadn't arrived and she couldn't bear another moment on her old desk chair, an armless swivel model that seemed to have it in for her. Her lower back was already aching. A full-blown sciatica episode was probably on its way. She needed to keep moving. The Mad Magyar was already gone, en route to question another disillusioned follower of the Greenes. They were like termites scuttling out of rotten logs now, and Ziggy suspected at least one of them smelled a book deal. Carolyn grabbed her jacket and was out the door minutes after Zig.

She arranged to meet Cassie Pepper at a café in the village. The young woman had phoned first thing this morning. Like Carolyn, she had spent a sleepless night, not only because of the storm but because of something she'd remembered about one of the former saints. "It's probably nothing," she said, "but I'll feel better telling you anyway."

The Cheshire Cat was an upscale coffeehouse tucked amid a cluster of boutiques and galleries in the village centre. It was too trendy, too quiet, and too small to be a cop hangout which was why Carolyn chose it. When she entered, Cassie was seated on a stool at the long breakfast bar enjoying a bowl of the owner's special granola. Carolyn sat beside her, shook hands and ordered a Sumatran blend, but passed on the fresh baked muffins. "You think you've remembered something that may help us identify those bones?"

Cassie shrugged. "I hope I haven't dragged you here for nothing," she sighed, "but there was this guy. He came to all of our meetings for about three months before Jerome and Milli—before the Greenes died. He was really into it all. He thought the Greenes were cool, that everything they had to say made sense."

"Such as?"

"Well, he thought the world was pretty screwed up, that people were worshipping the wrong things, that there was too much of a difference between the haves and the have-nots. He was all for a simplified life. He believed, like we all did, that if everyone scaled back, took only what they needed and shared the rest, we'd all be happier. No competition, no jealousy—you know, everyone is equal."

The world was going to hell in a goddamn hand basket, Carolyn thought. At least her world was. And Joshua's too, if Paige wasn't found quickly. It was Day 9, they were no closer to locating her, and sitting beside Carolyn now was the first nibble they'd had since the article on the skeleton had appeared in the paper on the 22nd. But Cassie Pepper, with her granny glasses and her hemp overalls, struck Carolyn as a fricking loon. She wondered if anything the girl said would amount to a dust mote. She only knew she didn't have any more time to waste listening to Kumbaya philosophy.

"And this guy—the bones ... what do you think the connection might be?" Carolyn heard the impatience in her voice and could imagine the scowl on her lieutenant's face, but Cassie didn't appear to take notice.

"Like I said, this might be nothing, but I remember him complaining because he'd gone jogging earlier in the day and his leg was killing him. He said he'd hurt himself once on a ski holiday and now his leg couldn't handle high impact exercise. I told him he should try swimming instead. Anyway, the article in the newspaper said the skeleton had an injured leg bone too."

That's right, Carolyn thought. Just above where a ski boot would be. One of the most common places for a fracture in skiers.

"Plus," Cassie continued, "he never came to the Greenes' funeral. And he was a really devoted follower, you know? So I got thinking, what if he couldn't come? What if something happened to him?"

Did she dare hope? Carolyn pulled out a pocket-sized notepad from her jacket. "Name?"

Cassie dipped her spoon into the granola then studied the array of baked goods beneath domed lids on the counter. "I've been thinking about it all night. Give me a minute. It'll come back to me. There were a lot of us toward the end."

Carolyn waited. Drank coffee. Had her mug refilled. "A description?" she urged. "Can you remember anything about him?"

"He was a lot taller than me," Cassie said after ordering a multi-grain muffin. "Close to six feet, I guess."

That much had been printed in the paper. Carolyn clicked her pen. The notepad was still blank.

"He always seemed a little sad, like he'd seen a lot. Was disillusioned, you know? But every time the Greenes spoke, he nodded, like he was right in their heads. He spoke up every chance he could, supported Jerome and Milli, but otherwise kept to himself. It was like he was afraid to trust too many people, like he was scoping us out."

Cassie broke her muffin in half, blew on her fingers and watched steam escape from the middle. "Oh, yeah. He had this crazy blond hair. Like—what's his name? He was my father's favorite comedian."

Carolyn bit her lip. Cassie was too young to be this forgetful. She wondered what drugs the girl had ingested before she'd found religion.

"Harpo Marx," she announced, triumphant. "He had hair like Harpo Marx. You know? Like something you'd scrub a frying pan with."

Carolyn was writing now as more details flew from Cassie. The boy never said anything about where he'd come from or what his interests were. Cassie didn't get the impression he was a student. Maybe a musician, she thought. He dressed sloppily—black jeans with frayed bottoms, oversized T-shirts, sometimes covered by a denim jacket or baggy sweater.

"Any tattoos, piercings, anything like that?"

Cassie shook her head.

"Callused fingers, maybe from playing a guitar?"

"Not that I noticed." She squinted, trying to squeeze the last drops from her memory. "Oh!"

"What is it?"

"His name. It was T. J."

"T.J.? What did that stand for?"

"He never said. Just told us to call him T.J."

"Last name?"

Come on, Cassie. This is it. Carolyn needed this from her. Just one more thing.

"I don't know," she said. "T.J.'s the only name he used."

CHAPTER 58

Joshua loved his sister. He knew she was a good cop despite what some of her colleagues thought of her. She had been busting her behind for the past year to rid herself of her Rambette image, created when she brought in a local surgeon on spousal abuse charges. The man's temper was legendary, and exceeded only by his arrogance. Jail was too good for him, the nursing staff at the hospital said. Carolyn saw the wife in Emergency, her entire face the color of eggplant, her eyes swollen shut, part of an ear missing. In the interrogation room, the doctor requested orange juice, snapping his fingers at Carolyn as though she were a waitress at a truckstop diner. In her zeal to procure an arrest, Carolyn ignored the request, and proceeded with the interview. The doctor, it seemed, turned out to be a diabetic—none of Carolyn or anyone else's business, he'd said later—but in court, it was concluded that the interview was conducted under extreme mental and physical duress. The case was thrown out. The doctor was free. All because of orange juice, and Carolyn's hatred for wife beaters. Even Gregg had been more embarrassed than supportive. Perhaps their troubles had begun then.

Joshua had reached his sister earlier and heard the exhaustion in her voice. She had spoken to someone who had given her a lead on the bones, and she couldn't talk long. Did Carolyn think the bones had something to do with Paige's disappearance? She wouldn't answer. Forget about the bones, he wanted to tell her. Concentrate on finding Paige. Alive.

There must be something he could do. When he left his office at 6:30, he had a plan of sorts. He looked up the number for S. Gardner, Paige's neighbor, who readily agreed to stay with Parker. He even consented to drive into the village to get the key to the cabin from Joshua.

Gardner arrived fifteen minutes later, looking weary and disheveled. He'd been out splitting logs, he told Joshua, and almost didn't hear the phone ring.

"Hope Paige turns up soon. Her Uncle Spence and I go way back. You could always count on him. Those folks of Paige's, though, now there's another story. I only met 'em a few times, but a bigger pair of wingnuts never walked. Kooks like that should be shot and pissed on, and not necessarily in that order."

Joshua had a ninety-minute drive ahead of him and was eager to be on the road. He nodded and pressed the key to the cabin into Gardner's hand. "I'll try to be back by eleven."

"I'll be awake." The man clawed a strong hand through his thick gray hair. "Get kind of edgy at night, living on my own."

Joshua felt sympathy for the man, indeed for all seniors facing their final years alone and he vowed that when Paige came home, they would keep in close touch with their elder neighbor, have him to dinner, even drive him in to Portland so he could have a long visit with his friend Spencer Rowan.

When Paige came home. Not if.

There was a minor accident on the Sunrise Highway so Joshua, caught in a line-up of rubberneckers, didn't reach Portland until nine fifteen. He spent another ten minutes cruising unfamiliar streets until he located the flat-roofed, stucco-and-glass home of Nicholas Bissonette. The silver Porsche was in the driveway. A single lamp glowed in a ground floor window to the left of the front door. Joshua parked his Jeep at the curb a few houses away, turned up the collar on his jacket, donned a dark baseball cap and sprinted across several newly mown lawns to peer into Bissonette's front window.

The man's living room was a magazine layout, a '70s-inspired space with a tan suede sectional sofa contrasting with carefully chosen ebony tables. A large black étagère dominated one wall. Aside from the minimalist furnishings and a few strategically placed *objets d'arts*, the room was empty. Joshua didn't know what he expected to find—a museum to Paige? A room filled with old framed photographs? Or perhaps Paige herself—bound to one of the straight-backed chairs and struggling to free herself from the restraints that held her captive.

Joshua wondered suddenly at the wisdom of his decision to check out Bissonette on his own. He knew very little about the man except what Paige had told him. He was a serial philanderer, heavy drinker, recreational drug user and asshole. Was he also a killer? Had he seen Joshua approach the house? Was he watching him now on some hi-tech security equipment?

So be it. If police were called, Joshua would tell the truth. Wracked with worry over Paige's disappearance, he had come to Portland to shake down Paige's former lover, to see what he knew. The papers were filled with news about Paige; the police would understand Joshua's need to take some kind of action. If he got the chance to explain. If Bissonette didn't shoot him first.

Joshua crossed the low front stoop to look into another plate glass window but he could only make out vague shapes in the darkness of the room, perhaps a dining table and chairs, but he couldn't be sure. He continued around to the back of the house, stepping quietly onto a large cedar deck. He nearly tripped on the cover of a hot tub wedged into a corner near a bank of sliding patio doors, catching himself just in time with a clumsy sidestep and a muttered curse. He followed the perimeter of the house, moving toward the only light source. Pale yellow glowed from a trio of long, narrow windows.

Nicholas Bissonette stood alone in the centre of the room before a large canvas balanced on a pair of wooden easels. He was studying his work, palette poised against one bent arm, paintbrush handle tapping against his lip. Through a partly opened window Joshua heard music blaring. INXS. "The Devil Inside." Bissonette's body rocked to the thumping bass line, not disturbing in and of itself, except that the man was completely naked. His penis was erect.

Paige had told him that Nicholas was an artist, at first living from day to day selling pen-and-ink sketches of noteworthy European landmarks and other touristy kitsch. From the Internet, Joshua learned that Bissonette had done some nudes as well but finally met with minor commercial success when he created covers for the resurgence of pulp detective magazines. In underground circles, he was also known for his skill as a porn cartoonist. Bissonette's forte, it seemed, was depicting women in pain. Still, the canvas he was working on here was life-sized, and he was working with acrylics. A special project? One that was better inspired by his painting in the buff?

And one that was clearly causing him arousal. Joshua wondered what was on that canvas and who Bissonette was painting it for. And what, if anything, this creep had to do with Paige's disappearance.

He retraced his steps to the front door, rang the bell and waited. *He's deciding whether or not to ignore it*, Joshua thought. *Figuring maybe whoever it is will go away.*

Joshua had no intention of going away. Not until he knew when Bissonette had last seen Paige. And how he was reacting to her being missing.

He rang the bell again. Moments later, the artist stood in the doorway in a thick velour robe, one hand jammed deep into a pocket. He looked annoyed at first then there was a flash of recognition.

"We were never introduced," Joshua said, "but I saw you at Paige's cabin one night a few weeks back."

Bissonette nodded. "I was being given the bum's rush, as they say. You are?"

"Josh Latham."

Neither of them extended a hand, and Bissonette made no move to step aside and allow Joshua entry.

"Nicholas Bissonette."

"I know. Paige told me."

"You're here because ...?"

"You know that Paige is missing."

"The entire state knows. Awful news. But that doesn't answer my question."

Joshua shot him a deliberate, shamefaced look. "I'm not even sure I can answer the question. Not in a way you'll understand. I'm just so worried. Paige and I ... well, we've grown pretty close. And I know the police are doing their best—hell, my sister is lead investigator on the case, but so much time has gone by and ..."

Bissonette, either sympathetic or embarrassed for him, gestured him inside. The foyer gave Joshua a clear view into much of the ground floor, an open-concept, modern layout with lots of reflective surfaces. *All the better to see myself, my dear.* The room at the back of the house, where minutes ago Joshua had seen the artist in his naked glory, seemed to be the only room that had a door. It was shut.

"So your sister is Sergeant Latham Holt," Bissonette said. "She questioned me at my gallery in the village."

A dark look came over the man's face as memories of his meeting with Carolyn resurfaced. Joshua could see that Bissonette had no fond remembrances of that encounter.

"I can appreciate you being at your wit's end," Bissonette continued. "Paige is a helluva girl. But I don't see how I can help you. Still, you've driven all this way. I can at least brew you up an espresso for the road."

He led Joshua down a wide tiled hallway into a gleaming white-on-white kitchen where he fired up the espresso machine.

"Nice place you've got," Joshua said. "Good to know that someone can make a decent living in the art world."

"I do all right."

Which is what Joshua couldn't figure out. Bissonette was opening a trendy place in Cypress Village. He drove a Porsche. While his house wasn't huge, it was in a chic neighborhood and could easily fetch high six figures. All this from designing magazine covers?

"You knew Paige in France," Joshua said. "Were you aware that she was Seraphina Greene?"

"I'd never heard of the Greenes or their so-called congregation. I didn't keep up much with Oregon news in Europe. Paige was always Paige to me, but she did tell me her parents were a little crazed. She couldn't leave her family fast enough."

"This disappearance though. You don't think Paige has just run off, do you?"

Bissonette seemed to consider his words carefully. He busied himself rooting in the cupboard until he fished out a thermal travel mug. At length he said, "You may not want to hear this, but yes, I think it's possible. Paige has always been a runner. She ran from home.

She ran from me. Maybe she wasn't ready for the kind of relationship you wanted. Was everything okay between you two?"

Joshua swallowed. "Like I said, we were pretty close."

"Still, maybe there's what you thought and then what Paige thought. I'm sure I'll be blue-lipped in the morgue and still won't have completely figured out what goes on in women's minds. I thought I knew Paige, too, but then she left me without so much as a word or note."

"Must have made you angry."

"Sure it did. I really thought we had something there. She sure fooled me."

"If you were so angry, why'd you come out to her cabin that night? She'd already made it clear when you telephoned her that she didn't want to see you."

Bissonette poured tar-black espresso into the travel mug and snapped the lid on. "I don't like loose ends," he said simply. Then, sensing how his words must have sounded, he added, "I didn't see any need for bitterness. There's no reason, after having spent nearly two years together, that Paige and I couldn't be friends."

"Things don't always work out the way we'd like. Listen, I won't take up any more of your time. Like I said, I honestly don't know why I came. I'm just grasping at anything, trying to get a handle on what could have happened to Paige."

"If I could help, I would," Bissonette said matter-of-factly. "But I've only seen Paige twice since I've been back in the States and neither visit amounted to a total of ten minutes. Still, I guess in a case like this, it's only natural to investigate the ex-boyfriend. Natural for you to be suspicious of me too." He smiled. "That's why you're really here, isn't it?"

Joshua shrugged. "I'm so out of my head I'm suspicious of everybody."

Another smile. "And yet statistics show that in cases like this, the villain is usually the victim's mate. So that would be you, am I right?"

It was Joshua's turn to smile, though it was the last thing he felt like doing. It would have felt more natural to smash Bissonette's head against his stainless steel refrigerator, a reaction they would have frowned upon in the seminary. Joshua accepted the espresso and asked to use the washroom before making the trip back to the village.

"Top of the stairs. Second door on the right."

Joshua took the mug, walked back into the foyer and set it on a console table. He climbed the open staircase and found the washroom door ajar, glanced quickly down the stairs and, not seeing Bissonette below, tiptoed along the corridor. There were two bedrooms on this level, decorated in tones of chocolate, beige and black. King-sized mattresses set on raised platforms. The closet doors were wide open. Paige wasn't in either of the rooms. There was a laundry room, too, since the house didn't appear to have a basement. If Bissonette had Paige, it wasn't in this house. Joshua ducked into the bathroom and when he emerged, he saw Bissonette waiting for him on the bottom step holding the coffee mug.

"Sorry to have troubled you," Joshua said. "I'm afraid I've embarrassed myself by coming here."

"Forget about it. I hope this all works out the way it should."

Not: I hope Paige is safe. Not: I hope she comes home soon. But: I hope this all works out the way it should.

Joshua heard the door shut behind him, wondering if the artist had bought his self-effacing act. He knew he wouldn't get far by being hostile and antagonistic though that might have felt more satisfying. His curiosity, though, had been piqued about the scene he'd witnessed before he'd rung the doorbell. What had been on that canvas?

He saw the lamp go out in the living room. Quickly he bolted around the house once more but now the elongated windows to the room where Bissonette had been painting had blinds drawn tightly over them. He would not discover the subject of the man's arousal tonight. But one thing Joshua knew for certain—Nicholas Bissonette didn't give a damn about anybody but himself.

It was some minutes later when Nicholas saw the black Jeep disappear up the street. The man was pathetic. Transparent. Foraging around upstairs, his footsteps on the ceramic floor clearly audible below. Looking for his poor, lost Paige.

Nicholas had purchased the house nearly six months ago, paying more than he should for it but, unlike the others he'd seen, this one had all the features he wanted. Good area full of upwardly mobile couples who were too busy to pay much attention to their neighbors. Lots of natural light. A large deck and patio plus hot tub for entertaining. And the one eccentricity that the realtor had been somewhat shame-faced to mention—a third-floor panic room, accessible only via a hidden door at the back of the master bedroom closet.

CHAPTER 59

With the help of the Mad Magyar and the other exhausted police, Carolyn once again rousted the angels and saints, this time asking them about a member known only as T.J. Several remembered someone with curly blond hair at the gatherings but one person thought the initials he went by were A.J. and not T.J.

"Like that race car driver," the worshipper had said. "A.J. Foyt." There was a moment's hesitation, then, "Or maybe it was R.J. But yeah, I remember the guy."

"Fuckin' bunch of wackos," Ziggy said when he and Carolyn compared notes.

It was 8:00 on Tuesday night. Normal people would be sitting in movie theaters or restaurants, tucking young children into bed, telling teenagers to turn the music down. Carolyn paced in front of her desk. A large burning fist pressed into her lower back, the pain so severe she wished someone would take a butcher knife and carve the spot out. If Ziggy wondered why she hadn't sat down for the better part of an hour, he didn't say. Carolyn needed to lie down, knees tucked to chest, but that wasn't going to happen any time soon. Pacing was the next best thing. Sitting would be excruciating.

"Tomorrow I'll pay another visit to Hardy Litton," Carolyn said. "Something about him made my scalp itch."

Ziggy sighed. "And I'll take another go at the ex-boyfriend." He checked the file on his lap. "Paige fluffed him off three times in his short, privileged life. Wonder how he feels about that?"

"Meanwhile we've got the bones and the elusive T.J. What do you think those letters stand for?"

"Thomas James. Timothy Joseph. Tucker Jonathan. Any of those combinations familiar to you?"

Still pacing, Carolyn shook her head.

"Trent Jacob," Ziggy continued. "Thaddeus Jehosephat. Christ, I sound punch drunk."

"Two hours' sleep will do that to you. Go home, Zig. There's life beyond this building."

"It's okay. I won't be able to sleep anyway."

"Well, here's a concept. Spend some time with your family. Maybe a little one-on-one with Ilona. You remember what that's like, don't you?"

"Vaguely. What about you? Gregg waiting at home with a pitcher of martinis and some Chinese food?"

"I doubt it. We don't share many meals now that he's moved out. Locksmith is coming on Thursday."

Ziggy leaned forward. Carolyn hoped he wouldn't stand up and hug her. She would crumble.

Instead he said, "Jesus, did you tell the bastard his timing is for shit?"

"I should have," Carolyn replied. "And I should have mentioned lousy timing to his girlfriend with the fertile eggs too."

"Ah, fuck." Ziggy hung his head. "Doesn't life suck sometimes?"

"Many times," she admitted. "Bringing Paige home will help balance the scale."

"I can stay, you know."

"No need. Go home, my gypsy friend."

Ziggy rose, and with a demonstration of both sympathy and affection that Carolyn appreciated, he tugged on her ponytail. "Try for some sleep."

"You too."

"And I'm sorry about—well, you know."

"I'll be fine."

With Ziggy gone and no one else paying her much attention, Carolyn bent over her desk and stretched out her back muscles. One more hour until she could take another pill.

Todd Jared. Tate Jeremy. Terry Joel. Who are you, T.J.? And please, God, will you lead me to Paige once I find out?

She grabbed the file that Ziggy had left on the chair, leafed through the pages as she resumed pacing. What was she missing?

The T.J. angle could be all wrong. Perhaps the bones found in the bomb shelter and Paige's disappearance weren't even related. Maybe it all circled back to phone sex. If Arlen Dale could discover the phone room, taunt Dory Getz, kill Sarah Lydell and Bettina Reid, what would stop another client from doing the same? It hadn't taken much for the True Gentleman to disguise his voice. Paige, as Laurel, didn't know she'd been talking to the manager of "The Sky's the Limit" those few times Arlen had called her.

But now Arlen was dead. And Paige had vanished. Teamwork? Did Arlen have a partner? Was there someone else looking for Opal, someone who needed the information only Paige had?

Carolyn set the folder on her desk, pulled Paige's journal from it and searched through the neat, slightly backhand penmanship. Angus. SPKG. Spanking, Carolyn assumed. And there were three check marks beside his name. There was the caller who'd passed himself off as insurance adjuster Orson, who turned out to be Arlen Dale. And three Bills. The captain of the *Madrona* had been a Bill, too. Bill Washburne. A client?

Come on, Carolyn. You're sleep deprived.

Bill Washburne was married. His wife Denise had been with him on the boat when the passengers had disembarked. And Rafe was with the two of them. No opportunity for an abduction.

Paige's journal was full of potential kidnappers. Anonymous clients using fake names. It could be any of them. Or none of them. But Paige, with her gift of sexy banter and empty promises of wish fulfillment, would be a perfect sex slave for someone who otherwise might never get the girl. Was there another Arlen Dale concealed somewhere in this book?

George N. PARA. STRP FANT. So George liked strippers. Wanted to hear how each article of clothing was removed. Wanted to imagine each gyration, each hip grind, as Laurel slowly, seductively, did her sexy thing. Maybe for George N. listening wasn't enough anymore. Could be that he wanted his own private dancer. For keeps. PARA. What was that? Paramilitary? Paraplegic? If the latter, he'd have needed a partner to abduct Paige.

Carolyn shook her head. She was really losing it. There was no shortage of hookers to accommodate someone like George N. Booking a gig like dancing for a guy in a wheelchair was easy money. Throw a few tunes on the boom box, peel off the clothes, wriggle on his lap a little, and go the hell home. No kidnapping necessary.

Maybe Ziggy was right. She should just go home, grab a shower, fall into bed. She smelled a little gamy. Her legs could use a shave.

But it was Paige who was missing, dammit. The woman her twin brother loved.

The phone rang. Carolyn paused before reaching for the receiver, afraid it might be Joshua.

No, nothing yet, Josh. I'm sick with worry, too. I'm sorry. I'm sorry. I'm sorry.

Mea maxima culpa.

She picked up. It was Spencer Rowan, Paige's uncle.

Different caller. Same bitterly disappointing message.

"I've remembered something," the man said, his voice garbled.

Sedatives?

"It may be nothing, but ..."

Shades of Cassie Pepper. Someone else singing the It May be Nothing blues. Great. Another wrong tree for Carolyn to bark up.

He told her about an article he'd read. Long time ago, he said, but he was fuzzy on the exact year. There had been a boy. An eight-year-old. The skiing accident had been very newsworthy at the time. The boy's picture had been in all the papers.

Carolyn waited, examined a ragged fingernail, straightened a pile of papers on her desk. She sat up when Paige's uncle mentioned a head of curly blond hair. Then Spencer Rowan, with startling clarity, announced the name of the young boy. Carolyn dropped the phone.

CHAPTER 60

"Because this son of mine *was dead, but now he is alive; he was lost, but now he has been found. And so the feasting began.*"

The parable of the prodigal son.

This time, there would be no feasting. The son was not coming home. He had died of starvation.

Paige would do the same.

She was dizzy almost constantly now, her body shaking with cold. It had rained again last night, the staccato droplets of water on the roof more cruel reminders of her thirst, her body's need for fluids. Her mouth and her tongue were dry. She had trouble swallowing, her saliva thick and gluey. She couldn't remember when she'd last peed, only that the amount had been little more than a trickle. Succumbing at last to wretched despair, she had gone on a crying jag. No tears fell.

She heard a noise in the hall, the metallic scraping of something being dragged across a floor. When the small door behind the black grille squeaked open, Paige wasn't surprised. He would come to watch. She rose unsteadily from the mattress and moved toward the pair of staring eyes, crinkled at the corners. Smiling eyes.

"Hello, Mercer."

Mercer Wyatt backed away slightly from the door so she could see his face. It was the same face she'd looked at that night on the boat when neither could sleep. He had talked about Taylor, how he had searched for him. But Taylor didn't want to be found, he'd said.

Mercer had set a patio bar stool in the hallway, and he hoisted himself onto it. Beside the stool was a matching table, part of a poolside bistro set, and on it sat a liter bottle of spring water, drops of condensation joining into rivulets that slid down the bottle and formed a fat puddle on the tabletop.

The millionaire had dressed for the occasion—dark slacks, a crisply starched striped shirt, a V-necked vest. He propped his elbows on the armrests of the stool, steepled his fingers and studied her.

Paige studied him, too. She looked at his hands, the same hands that had wielded the kayak paddle that had hobbled Arlen Dale, the same hands that had loosened the restraints from her ankles and wrists, untied the plastic bag that had nearly suffocated her. Hands that pushed Arlen off the cliff to his death.

Mercer had held her, offered her comfort when she could at last breathe again. On the boat, he appeared radically shaken by what had happened on the bluff. He drank. He cursed. He hadn't meant to kill Arlen, he'd said. The others had rallied around him, as much as they had for Paige, assuring him that he had no choice. To them, Mercer Wyatt was a broken creature, a sympathetic figure who had only wanted to protect Paige from her attacker. Protect her, so he could save her for this.

She could have asked him why, but it would have been a waste of precious energy. She already knew why. Instead she said, "How long have you been planning this?"

"Since you returned from Europe."

Nearly four years.

She must have telegraphed her surprise because he said, "I don't make rash decisions, Paige. Everything in my life has been carefully planned out. And some things, like this, are worth waiting for." He uncapped the bottle of water, smiled, and took a drink.

"I don't suppose you could have accounted for your wife getting cancer," she said, her voice hoarse and gravelly. "Or your son running away. Must be terrible to know there are still some things you can't control."

The millionaire's mouth pinched into a frown. He set the bottle down. "In your position, you can hardly afford to be sarcastic."

"In my position? You mean, if I play nice, you'll open this door and let me out?"

"Hardly."

"Then I guess I can say whatever the hell I want. In ... my ... position."

Mercer tapped two fingers to his temple, a mini-salute. "Touché. I suppose I should be more understanding. Irritability is, after all, a symptom of dehydration."

"You've done ... research?"

"Naturally."

It made horrible sense. Mercer had spent the last four years torturing himself with images of his son's final hours. Paige's punishment needed to fit the crime.

She tried to clear her raw throat, gagged instead. "Mercer. Please. Some water." She jammed her fingers through the grille, got her hands stuck at the wrists.

Mercer said nothing, but smiled his infuriating smile and took another drink.

Paige withdrew her fingers and leaned against the door. Eventually she forced out a whisper. "You told me Taylor still sends you letters."

"It's what I tell everyone."

"But you really think he's dead, don't you? You think he's the one they found in that shelter on my uncle's property."

"I know he is. When Taylor was eight, he broke his left leg learning to ski in Vail. He was a natural on the slopes," he said, his words filled with pride. "The instructors couldn't believe how quickly he caught on. They advanced him to an intermediate group by the end of our first week. Then some bumbling idiot from the beginner's group came rocketing toward him in a full-out schuss. He plowed into Taylor, sending him into the glades. My only son almost died that day, his head missing a tree by inches. He was lucky to escape with only a broken leg, the doctors said. It was a miracle there were no head injuries, not even a wrenched neck."

Taylor Wyatt had eluded death. As Paige had. But eleven years later, death caught up with him, took him away from his father for good.

"But news of that injury to the bod—Taylor's fibula just recently made the papers," she said, her words little more than faint puffs of air. "You told me about it on the boat. How can you say you've been planning this for years?"

"Because I've known Taylor was in that hole for years."

"What? H-how?"

Mercer sighed. "The head of security for my company, after months of searching, eventually discovered that Taylor was last seen in the company of your dear mother and father. We learned that they had organized some kind of cult, that Taylor was mesmerized by their charisma. I was flying up from California to convince him to come home when he disappeared and your parents' car crashed into that abutment. I told my man to keep searching, that the clue to Taylor's whereabouts rested with your parents. He spoke to some of the followers after the funeral, learned about the ritual, found out that your uncle had several acres of property just outside the village."

"Your security man found the shelter?"

"The third night he searched. Your uncle was already in the nursing home, and you never knew we were on the land."

"We? You were there too?"

"My trusted friend told me what he'd found, begged me not to come, said we should call the police. I was already formulating other plans. Imagine what it must have been like to discover my son's body in that horrible place, to see his skin falling away from bone, turning black ... and then to leave him there, alone."

"Why did you?" Her knees buckled. She grabbed the door handle to steady herself. "You could have called the police, given Taylor a proper burial. This could have been over for you years ago."

"But then it would have been over for you too. Hardly justice for my son."

"But my parents didn't leave Taylor to die," she gasped. "They wouldn't have. It was an accident. The police said so."

"I don't give a damn," he said through clenched teeth. "Your parents' death was quick. They didn't see it coming. How do you think Taylor felt, knowing he couldn't get out of that hole, his body shriveling to dust? Do you think he cried? Did he try to claw his way out, leap at those concrete walls until his strength gave out? Do you suppose he prayed, read that Bible hoping he'd find an answer in it?"

"I don't know, Mercer," she told him, deliberately using his name, keeping it personal. "You expect me somehow to atone for the supposed sins of my parents. And after I'm dead, will the score be even? Will this all be over for you?"

"It doesn't matter, Paige. This may not be right, but it is fair. Taylor ran away from his home, just like you did. But try to look at the bright side. I'm actually doing you a favor. I'm returning you to the loving bosom of your family. Seraphina Greene can lie beside her parents for all eternity."

He laughed then, and Paige, cloaked with another wave of dizziness, saw two grinning faces, split like some macabre funhouse trick with mirrors, the shapes blurring, separating, coming together again until finally, they melded as one.

"You look tired, Paige. And flushed. Perhaps you should sit down. Is it true the dizziness is worse when you're standing? I remember reading that somewhere."

Her legs were trembling, her throat full of sand. She stayed put, gripping the grille with both hands for support. "Mercer," she said, her breath coming in short huffs, "you saved me once. You can do it again. You're not a killer."

"No?" He took another long swig from the bottle then wiped the excess from his lips with the back of his hand. "Then you haven't been paying attention."

Paige struggled to remember. What did he mean? Her brain was fuzzy. She couldn't think, especially not with that smug grin before her, and that nearly full liter of water scarcely five feet away.

"Your head of security," she said at last, the realization settling in her empty stomach with a hollow thud. "You couldn't risk keeping him alive. Not if he'd helped you make the connection to my parents. He would have wondered why you didn't call the police, why you didn't remove your son from that awful place."

God, it hurt to talk. But she had to. Had to. "He would have wondered what you had planned," came her faint whisper. "Maybe figured it out. He'd have blackmailed you for the rest of your life."

"I believe the headline was: 'Palo Alto Man Dies in Warehouse Fall.' A shame, actually. Stuart was a good man. But dreadfully overweight. And ladders are so unsteady. Still, he did find my son. And he led me to you."

And died for his trouble, Paige thought. A means to an end.

"He tailed you for weeks. It didn't take too long to connect you to that phone-sex room, and my elaborate plan for getting rid of you began to take shape."

For a brief moment, the millionaire appeared wistful then he was laughing again, doubling over. He guzzled water, coughed, sputtered, drank more.

"What the hell's so funny?" Paige gasped again, her efforts to speak now draining what little remained of her energy.

"The part about me saving you," he said. "The police are going to give me a citizenship award for it. I love the irony, of course, but the really funny part is ..." He paused, sipped more water.

Dear God, he'd gone through nearly a liter in the short time he sat in front of her. She had made her own water supply last for several days. Right now she would kill for a mouthful. But she would have to get out first.

"... When Arlen had you pinned on those bluffs at Sucia? When he had that plastic bag over your head? I was watching from the trees. For a good fifteen minutes."

Paige gulped but there was nothing to swallow. She knew what was coming before Mercer Wyatt uttered the words.

"I could have saved you a lot sooner."

CHAPTER 61

THE BACKGROUND CHECK Carolyn conducted on Mercer Wyatt painted a grim picture. For every ounce of happiness in his life, Wyatt had paid with blood. His wedding, at age thirty to former model Brooke Schyler, had been a small, elegant affair, the joy of the day overshadowed by his mother's recent diagnosis with leukemia. The birth of his only son, Taylor Jamieson, was quickly followed by the death of Wyatt's father two weeks later. The obituary had read: "After a lengthy and brave struggle with lung cancer, James Benton Wyatt passed away quietly at home ... "

Mercer Wyatt went on to make his first million, and more millions followed. He became known as the "silent philanthropist," quietly giving back to the community wherever the need was greatest, supporting women's shelters, food banks, after-school programs for disadvantaged youth. He entered a 10K race for MS, volunteered once a week at a palliative care hospice, purchased a dialysis machine for the hospital.

It wasn't enough. His wife was already losing weight when the results of her Pap smear came back.

Cancer was devouring Mercer Wyatt's family.

After Brooke's death, Wyatt withdrew from the public eye, immersed himself in his company and hired a succession of frustrated staff to tend to his unruly son, Taylor. The man's fortune grew. His son vanished. Wyatt's life shattered.

The following spring, he purchased land just north of Cypress Village and had a massive log house built on the site. Weeks after Paige's parents died.

He must have suspected Taylor was in the area.

Carolyn grabbed her jacket and headed downstairs, trying to hurry despite crippling pain that shot down her leg. She'd foregone the muscle relaxant, wanted to be fully sharp and alert. Now was not the time for mistakes.

She started up her Explorer and pulled out of the parking lot at the same time as she raised Ziggy on her cell phone.

"Remember that advice I gave you about spending time with your family?"

"Yep," he answered. "Just about to pour myself a glass of chardonnay and head for the hot tub."

"Can you put those plans on hold? I need you. You're the only one who won't think I'm nuts. I'm running up to Mercer Wyatt's place. The skeleton. I think it belongs to his son, Taylor."

"What? Never mind. I'm already heading for my car. I'll call you back on my cell."

Carolyn didn't need to give Ziggy instructions to the Wyatt place. Everyone in Cypress Village knew where it was, perched alone at the top of Signal Hill, a wooded rise that had once been an ideal make-out place for teenagers who wanted a spectacular view of the Pacific while they drank, smoked up, and banged each other's brains out. Wyatt building on the land had done the police a tremendous favor.

Her cell phone rang.

"What the hell's going on?"

"The bones," she told Ziggy. "I checked. Taylor Wyatt broke his left leg skiing years ago. He's the same approximate age as those bones we dug up."

"Then why didn't his father claim them?"

"It's called getting even. An eye for an eye. Seraphina Greene needs to pay for what happened to Wyatt's son. Mercer Wyatt has to keep up the charade that his son is still alive. Can't have us connecting the dots from Paige's disappearance to Taylor's body."

"But he rescued Paige from that other creep. He saved her life. Now he wants to kill her?"

"Yeah, I know. Perfect, isn't it? Who's going to suspect? We give the guy a medal for his heroism and meanwhile, he's doing to Paige what he thinks the Greenes did to his son."

"Makes awful sense and it's a neat theory, but—" Ziggy paused, cleared his throat, "—how sure are you?"

Carolyn bristled. Her Rambette days were a long way from over, even in Ziggy's mind. "How sure can anyone be?" she replied, holding her temper. "Pretty sure. Reasonably sure. It's in my gut, Zig."

"Okay, but if you're right, then this guy is as fucking nuts as that Arlen Dale."

"Zig, if I'm right, he's worse."

"Listen, you're ten minutes ahead. Wait for me. And I'm calling for more back-up."

"I'm at the bottom of the hill now."

"You just stay put."

She snapped the phone shut, hoping that Ziggy would forget the speed limit and gun it to get here. Carolyn parked the Explorer beside Wyatt's old-fashioned mailbox and killed the engine. No sense in announcing her presence. She would head up the hill, scope things out first. Ziggy and the uniforms would be here soon.

The Aerie, the name Mercer Wyatt had given his getaway place, was a five-thousand-square-foot log home, small by millionaire's standards, Carolyn supposed, but perched on the top of Signal Hill, it looked majestic. Lamplight glowed in each of the multi-paned windows, homey, welcoming. Huge twenty-four-inch diameter logs supported the impressive front portico. Carolyn remembered seeing the massive logs being trucked through the village when the house was being built. People in town who'd helped with the construction talked about an interior bridge that connected the main house to a guest apartment over the carriage house. Was that where he was keeping Paige?

Carolyn checked her watch. Ziggy should be here any second now, though there was no sign of his car coming along the S-curve below. The road was dark.

She decided to begin the climb. She needed to move. Ziggy would catch up. Despite the blades of hot pain that shot down her leg, Carolyn found herself picking up speed until soon, she was running up Signal Hill toward the grand entrance to Wyatt's house. She wasn't fooled by the friendly gleam of the lamplight, the warmth of the rough-hewn timbers, the well-tended garden that seemed to beg visitors to slow down, take a look. Carolyn knew damn well this was the home of a monster.

CHAPTER 62

"Tell me, Paige, have you already resorted to drinking your own urine?"

Her empty stomach flipped. She needed to escape that horrible face with its self-satisfied smile, the perfectly garbed figure who taunted her from the other side of the door. Mercer had excused himself briefly, only to return several minutes later with another bottle of water. He had changed his clothes, too, wanting to freshen up, he'd said, and something else was different as well.

It was his voice. Where before Wyatt's tone had been clipped and business-like, now it carried with it the crooning low moans of a seducer. Whispers in the dark.

"It doesn't work," he murmured. "A person can't rehydrate by drinking urine. And I couldn't help but notice you've eaten all the bread. Sadly, you'd have been better off leaving it alone. Dry food needs water in order to be digested properly."

Mercer raised the new bottle to his lips and winked at her.

Paige turned away, the floor spinning beneath her. Her arms and legs cramped. She needed to lie down. Lie down before she fell down.

She would not give Mercer Wyatt the drama he expected. She would not whimper. She would not beg, nor would she promise she would do anything he asked. No gala performance. She would simply fade away.

Paige Rowan, peacefully in her sleep. In lieu of flowers, donations may be made to your local animal shelter or to causes benefiting wildlife conservation.

But this wasn't peaceful. She was in agony, every sinew and bone and organ burning and screaming for relief. For water. The mattress was just ahead. She bent down, reached out for it and collapsed.

"Just curious, Paige," came the deep sultry voice from the opening in the door, "but did any of Laurel's clients express much of an interest in bodily functions? What is the lingo they use in the trade? Golden showers?"

Oh God, no. She knew how he intended to play this out. She would not be allowed to go peacefully in her sleep. More indignity. More torture. Whether physical or psychological, she was too weak to fight either.

Paige heard metal scraping against tile. Mercer was dragging the stool closer to the door. At once, his smiling mouth appeared behind the iron grille. Then his eyes filled the space. She turned away, rolled toward the wall and focused her gaze on a spot straight ahead to where a tiny ant was disappearing into a crevice with what looked to be a crumb from the loaf of bread.

"Have you checked your skin lately, Paige?" he whispered. "Does it look wrinkled to you? If you tug at it, does it stay folded, seem to take forever to return to its normal position?"

Sweet Jesus, please make him go away. She had done nothing to deserve this. Had she?

Her parents had believed in a vengeful God, one who righted wrongs, gave sinners their comeuppance, sent forth floods and blight and pestilence until people got the message. Paige chose to believe in a benevolent, grandparent-type God, one who smiled at her from the sun sparkling through tree branches, one who made Himself known through the kindness of strangers, the good will of neighbors and friends, the unconditional love seen in the eyes of an animal. Whichever was the true God, where was He now and why wasn't He saving her?

"What about your fingers and toes?" he asked. "They're not turning blue, are they? Peripheral cyanosis is a very bad sign, Paige. A rapid and feeble pulse as well. Have you put your thumb on your wrist? Sometimes in cases of moderate to severe dehydration, the radial pulse is actually undetectable."

She hadn't checked her pulse, and now she was tempted but she refrained. Yes, when she'd looked at the skin on her hands, it was as if she'd grown older with each hour that passed. Her breathing, too, was rapid and deep. Mercer had done his homework. How long did she have?

"Your eyes look sunken as well," the damnable voice continued, purring through the door. "And how is your stomach? Other than empty, of course. Is it swollen? Bloated? I don't suppose you'd be willing to show me. No? How silly of me. You're all talk anyway, aren't you? Isn't that what you got paid for? Talking?"

Paige heard the sound of loud gurgling. Mercer was gulping water.

"Some men like their women curvy. Myself, I much prefer a leaner physique. Just think of all the aspiring models who would love to look like you do, wasting away, not much more than an emaciated, cadaverous shell. That heroin-chic appearance is still very *au courant*. Do you know there are actually anorexia websites that encourage women to strive for the look you now have? Yes, I must say, to me, you've never been more beautiful. I suppose that must sound strange to you."

She felt she could cry but resisted. Her body wouldn't be able to withstand the convulsive effort that crying would involve, and there would be no tears anyway. She bit her lip and tried to swallow, but there was no saliva.

"What am I saying? That probably doesn't sound strange to you at all. You've undoubtedly heard much odder things during a fifteen-minute telephone conversation. I'm right, aren't I?"

Paige squeezed her eyes shut, clapped her hands over her ears, but still the voice came.

"They must have been pigs, some of the men you talked to. Amber thought so. But she always enjoyed my calls. She thought I was a real gentleman."

What? Mercer had spoken to Bettina? Paige's brain was muddled. She couldn't think anymore. Too thirsty. Too weak. She must have heard him wrong.

"Amber sat by her phone every Thursday evening, anticipating my calls. Couldn't wait to meet me in person, the one man she was so sure wouldn't mind her looking the way she did."

It couldn't be. Mercer's voice. A British accent.

"A ripe, eager minx, she was. And wouldn't she do just about anything for Dr. James Lowrey?"

From somewhere within, Paige said, "You?"

In the dead silence of the night, more water gurgled down Mercer Wyatt's throat. "You can't possibly think that fool Arlen Dale killed those women." He paused, let the thought sit a moment then added, "That man probably couldn't dissect a frog for a biology grade. I, on the other hand …"

Paige thought of Amber, so eager for acceptance and so ripe for love that she would readily rush to meet her Thursday caller, an honest-to-goodness doctor who didn't care what size she was. Paige remembered that awful foot, placed deliberately so she would find it. Feel terror. Wonder every day whether she would be next.

"Arlen actually wanted to stop killing. That's what the quest for Opal was all about. I promised to deliver Opal to him. A promise, of course, that I never intended to keep."

Paige willed him to shut up. She wanted to shut down. How much longer before she died? And would she have to go mad first? She didn't want to know more.

The thoughts came forward anyway. Dory, fearing for her own son, subjected to hearing Amber's final screams. And Jasmine, begging for her life, crying out that she didn't know who Opal was. Paige looked along the floor and spotted the one item in the room that since her captivity she'd always thought wasn't quite right—the phone jack. The calls had been made from this room. Amber and Jasmine had died here.

And she would too.

CHAPTER 63

FROM THE OTHER SIDE OF the door came quiet laughter, mocking. "So easy to pretend to search for Opal and report to Arlen how close we were getting. Easy as well to stalk and torment Dory and her son, make Arlen think I was working on his behalf and that he was really in the game, a scant breath away from finding his beloved Opal." Wyatt gave a bored sigh. "A lopsided partnership, really. Arlen leaving me to do all the dirty work. Though I must admit, I can understand how someone as easily seduced as Arlen could become addicted to those phone girls. Having my security man Stuart come across Arlen and his idiosyncratic kink was precisely the scenario I needed, and it fell into my lap completely by accident. A quirk of fate, thanks to Stuart, a moonlighting job, a recorded conversation and the death of one Tammi Jean Flowers."

Tammi Jean Flowers. Where had she heard that name? She struggled for a memory but none came.

Wyatt was eager to fill in the gaps. Arlen Dale, it seemed, had ventured into Seattle for a sin weekend and met up with prostitute Tammi Jean, who agreed to play Arlen's purple game. She lost.

"My security man was already in Cypress Village looking for Taylor, but Stuart was always up for padding his wallet, so he put an ad in the paper and within days was doing some moonlighting for the owner of 'Sky's the Limit.'"

Wyatt explained that the kite store owner suspected an employee of stealing from him, so a hidden camera was set up, along with a recording device. It wasn't long before Stuart became privy to a series of nightly conversations with phone sex hookers, particularly those who willingly catered to the asphyxiation fantasies of one Arlen Dale.

Poor Arlen, who lived with his parents, could hardly make the calls from home.

At this Wyatt laughed. "You should have seen the gleam in Stuart's eyes when he told me about the little pervert with the choking fetish. I did some further digging and made the connection between Arlen and Tammi Jean. I began to see how Arlen might become useful so I arranged an accidental meeting. When it comes to liquor, Arlen's something of a lightweight and over the course of a few weeks, his lips became looser. I hinted at some fictional kinks of my own and Arlen confided to me his obsession with finding Opal. He truly believed she could cure him of those nasty dark thoughts."

Paige didn't want to hear anymore. Arlen was dead. Lani was safe. This should be over.

"It became tit for tat, you see," Wyatt continued. "I agreed to help Arlen find Opal. Calling Dory was my end of the deal. In return Arlen could simply keep me company, be like the son I was missing so terribly. To Arlen, our alliance seemed harmless enough. Then Bettina died and Arlen balked. 'You want to find Opal, don't you?' I said."

"Arlen didn't approve of my campaign of terror, but by then it was too late. I simply trotted out the name Tammi Jean Flowers and the little bastard's jaw dropped. 'I know you killed her, you fucking pervert,' I told him. There wasn't much he could do but watch the real game play itself out. None of this was ever about Opal, you know. It was all about you, Paige. The police look for a serial killer stalking phone-sex operators and guess what Paige Rowan used to do for a living? It was the perfect cover, and Arlen was the perfect marionette."

Once Wyatt heard from Dory that Paige worked the phone lines, information he already knew, he passed her name on to Arlen, hinting strongly that Paige could be the key to finding Opal. He ensured Arlen a spot on the Madrona and coached him to "do what needed to be done" in order to extract what he needed to know about Opal's whereabouts from Paige. That was the plan. Wyatt promised he would be there to help. What Arlen didn't realize was that he was never meant to survive. And though it was risky to confront Paige on Sucia Island, riskier still to abduct her from the parking lot in Port

Townsend, surely no one would suspect her captor was the very same man who'd saved her life on the bluffs.

"I've subsisted for the past four years on one thing only, Paige. Killing you. Tormenting and killing the phone whores was just ... foreplay."

She half turned, directed her feeble voice over her shoulder, still not looking at him. "But Arlen's dead. If I die, the police will know there's still a killer out there."

"There are always killers out there, Paige. It's the society we live in. But your disappearance will go unsolved. You might even end up being an Oregon folk tale, your story told around campfires. Laurel. Paige. Seraphina. They'll never find any of you. Just like they'll never find Amber. Only the parts I wanted found. Ah, the joys of having my own plane."

Again she turned to the wall, refusing to imagine the worst, yet unable to stop it.

I'll be dead by then, she reasoned. What will it matter what he does with my body?

"Do you know I haven't been with a woman since Brooke died? I haven't been interested. Yet now, curiously, I find myself with you, and some of those old feelings are starting to come back. This may sound strange, but I'm actually quite aroused." He laughed.

Then she heard the unmistakable yanking on a zipper. "Ah, come on, Paige baby, won't you turn around and look at me? I want this to be good for you, too."

She clenched her eyes shut once more, drew her knees into her chest, tried to hum, hoping to drown out the horrific sounds coming from the other side of the door.

"Farmer in the Dell." "Mary Had a Little Lamb." "Three Blind Mice." Ridiculous tunes. Childish tunes, and they were the only songs she could think of. She hummed louder. The sounds continued.

"Give me a little something, Paige," Mercer breathed, harder, faster. "I know you usually get paid for talking, but surely, just this once, you'll throw in a freebie. For a real gentleman."

...they all ran after the farmer's wife, she cut off their tails with a carving knife ...

"I'd much prefer to share this experience with you, come into the room and—"

In the distance, Paige heard a chime, then much closer, "Shit."

She rolled over onto her back as Mercer stood.

"It appears as if I've got company," he said, annoyed. "I'll just go and see who that is and get back as soon as I can. Don't go 'way."

For a brief moment, Paige thought Mercer would leave the little peek-a-boo door open but she heard his footsteps come closer again then the door slammed. She wondered how much strength she had left and whether she could summon up one final scream.

CHAPTER 64

TAYLOR WYATT HAD GONE INTO the hole for a weekend, and with him was a loaf of bread, three liters of water and a Bible. His water supply would have been ample, provided that the Greenes had returned on Sunday evening to rescue him. But they hadn't returned, and by the following Thursday, Taylor would have been in trouble. He had undoubtedly screamed for help. He would have wept. He might have prayed.

Paige had been missing for ten days. If Wyatt had given her no water, she might already be dead. But Carolyn sensed that the millionaire would be following the do-unto-others credo to the letter. Paige, like Taylor, would have been given a jug of water, but even if she had rationed her supply carefully it would have been consumed days ago.

If Paige wasn't at the millionaire's getaway on Signal Hill, Carolyn would need to get a tele-warrant, enabling Palo Alto police to search Wyatt's other residence. Yet, the closer she got to the Aerie's front door, the more she felt her instinct was correct. Paige was here.

Instinct? She could hear the lieutenant's growl in her ear. You went where? You did what? Because of instinct? By tomorrow morning she could be kissing all hope of promotion goodbye. One fucked-up career. One fucked-up body. One fucked-up marriage. Three strikes.

Then she was on Wyatt's front porch, standing under a gleaming halo of light and looking through a double set of French doors into a foyer and great room beyond. To either side of the vast space, the house angled off into symmetrical wings. There was an open kitchen and dining area to the right, and what Carolyn presumed to be a bedroom wing to the left. She saw no movement anywhere.

Carolyn rang the doorbell, heard the cathedral-like chime resound through the quiet night. When no one came, she pounded on the door, waited. She depressed the toggle on the large bronze latch, but the door was locked. She could easily shatter one of the glass door panes and enter, but again heard the lieutenant's cautionary voice in her head.

You need justification for entering, remember? Reasonable grounds. What did you see that led you to believe the Rowan woman was in there? What evidence did you have that Mercer Wyatt was committing an illegal act?

It wouldn't be that easy. Paige's purse near the doorway, her jacket slung over a chair—Wyatt wouldn't leave those things in plain view. Nor would the millionaire come to the door with a guilty look on his face and unburden his soul. He had been planning this since the papers had printed the nature of the skeleton's injury. Maybe even longer.

If it turned out that Wyatt was upstairs in the shower or even better, entertaining a female friend, Carolyn's days in law enforcement would be over. The millionaire would sue her ass just for sport, and Fallon McBride would have another front page scoop. There were worse things. Worse was Paige inside somewhere, dying or dead, and Carolyn standing outside second-guessing herself and doing nothing.

From the porch, Carolyn looked out across the property, scanning the darkness for a reassuring set of headlights but there was no sign of Ziggy, nor the approach of uniform patrol officers. Her backup was late. And she couldn't stand here another second.

Carolyn hurried across the veranda and around a screened-in porch on the right side of the house, skirted a peninsula of boulders then followed the angle of the kitchen wall to a side entrance. A pair of rustic lanterns flanked either side of the solid door which was sheltered by a domed roof perched on river rock columns. Above the overhang, Carolyn saw four windows, guessing that these belonged to the bridge that joined the upstairs of the house to the guest quarters. The windows were dark. A large three-car garage stretched further right toward a stand of tall cedars. There was a peaked roof over the central garage door. The guest apartment.

Something wrong there. Beneath the V-shaped angle of the roof there should have been a large window overlooking the front of the property and the vista below. There was plenty of room for one—even a pair of doors opening onto a balcony would have been in keeping with the architectural style of the house. Instead Carolyn saw an undersized window, a mere keyhole given the scale of the house, covered over by a set of shutters. No. Not right.

She stepped onto the flagstone porch. This time she didn't knock. When she tried the handle, the door opened. A keypad for a security system was on the wall to her right, but there was no monotonous voice coming from the speaker instructing her to disengage the alarm. It hadn't been set.

Carolyn found herself in a long gallery, dimly lit by an overhead pendant fixture suspended from huge rough hewn beams. An old pine church bench stood along one wall, a pair of black rubber boots beside it. At either end of the hall were matching French doors with arched tops, the one on her left leading into the main house, the one on her right opening into the garage. She tiptoed first to the left and peered once again into the millionaire's kitchen, checking for signs of movement. There was no indication that the room had been recently occupied; Carolyn saw no dirty dishes on the counter, no unplugged kettle, no pot on the stove cooling before being put in the dishwasher. The floor was showroom spotless. The stainless steel appliances gleamed.

She retraced her steps and tried the door leading to the garage. The handle moved easily. Paige entered and noticed Wyatt's black Range Rover. Was this the vehicle he had used to abduct Paige? Carolyn went toward it and shone her flashlight inside, the beam wandering over leather seats and plush carpeting, across the burled console, but though she searched for a telltale earring, hank of hair, or other indication of a struggle, there was none. Save for a few gardening tools hanging along one wall, the rest of the garage was empty.

Perhaps Wyatt wasn't even home. He may have gone into town in another car, or he might even be walking around Signal Hill, getting a dose of fresh evening air. He would leave the lights on to deter intruders, make the place look occupied.

No. If he was so worried about intruders, he would have locked the side door. He would have set the alarm.

Wyatt might be at the bottom of the hill, wondering whose car was parked there. He could be hurrying back up the slope to investigate.

A concrete staircase rose up in front of Wyatt's vehicle in the corner of the garage and without hesitation, Carolyn began the climb. The uniforms would be here soon, she told herself again. And Ziggy.

Then there was no more time for thinking. She had found reasonable grounds for entering. At the top of the stairs, tipped on its side, was a woman's Saucony running shoe. By the time Carolyn cracked open the door at the top of the stairs, the lights in the hallway were on. Mercer Wyatt, or someone, was here.

She unholstered her gun, felt her heartbeat rev, ready for overdrive mode. No person with anything worth stealing would leave doors open. Nor would Wyatt, holding Paige for ten days, be so careless as to leave one of Paige's sneakers in plain view. He was playing a game, throwing her a crumb, reeling her in. Trap. TRAPTRAP*TRAP*. It was a set-up, and Carolyn knew it. Which could only mean that Paige was somewhere inside.

Gun drawn, Carolyn hovered at the entrance to the bridge, that windowed hallway that joined the house to its guest quarters, and tried to slow her breathing. Her fingertips were freezing, her torso slick with sweat. When she at last eased her head into the corridor, she saw that it was empty. At one end more light glowed from a massive ceiling fixture—the loft space over the great room. But to her right, Carolyn's gaze was drawn toward a heavy oak door, the wood several shades darker than the other doors she had seen in the house. It was a foreboding, hideous door, one that belonged at the entrance to a dungeon, its great black iron hinges and pockmarked surface completely out of character with Wyatt's getaway dream house.

On it, at eye level was a small hinged door. For peeking in? At what? Carolyn knew that whoever had designed the home wouldn't have chosen such a monstrosity. Mercer Wyatt would have purchased the door for reasons of his own. Reasons that were making the small hairs on the back of Carolyn's neck rise. She turned carefully to look down the stairs behind her, then again at the loft area. Perhaps she had time. Perhaps Wyatt was indeed trekking down the hill, wondering about the Explorer parked by the mailbox. Perhaps he was calling the police right now, reporting an intruder. Five minutes. It was all she needed. Look through the trapdoor. See if Paige was there. If yes, rescue. If no, run like hell the way she came in.

She moved toward the door, ducked under the bank of windows in case Wyatt was outside, though her now pounding heart told her he wasn't. Still in a crouch, she spun and glanced behind her, half-expecting to see a shrieking madman spring from the doorway at the far end of the hall. Carolyn reached the door and turned one last time, weapon balanced on her forearm. Then she was standing, opening the tiny trap door. When she shone her flashlight inside, she bit down hard on her lip and choked off a sob.

The stench of human waste wafted through the small space, bringing bile to her throat. Paige was lying on a mattress, motionless, pale, perhaps already dead. No. Carolyn wouldn't believe it. It could not end like this.

She tried the latch, whispered to Paige to hang in there, told her that she was safe, that help was coming. Then something slammed her from behind. A cold, hard fist near the middle of her back. No, not a fist. And not cold now. Hot. Like a blow torch. Searing, crematorium hot. And God, she hurt. Felt herself melting on watery knees. She sunk to the floor and turned. Mercer Wyatt stood at the end of the hall, gripping a Smith & Wesson revolver. He was smiling.

CHAPTER 65

Carolyn hated fairgrounds, carnivals, amusement parks, each with their oily sweet smells, their screeching noise, their sticky pavement and the popping and pinging of amateur shooters hitting revolving ducks and other harmless targets to win gaudy gifts for girlfriends. Why was she thinking about that now? Lightheaded. Woozy. Losing it.

At the end of the corridor Mercer Wyatt raised his gun. She was trapped against the speakeasy door, the exit to the garage too many steps away. A long shooting gallery. A sitting duck. Ah, so there was a connection. He fired, catching her in the right shoulder, another flaming arrow of pain boring through her flesh.

She returned fire but Wyatt disappeared around the corner, waiting, she knew, until he thought she would be too incapacitated to render him harm. Her shoulder was bleeding, but when she glanced at her stomach, she saw nothing. No exit wound. No blood. The bullet that had got her in the back was lodged somewhere in her body, caroming off bone, taking detours. Bad news. Hemorrhage. Infection. A coin toss to see what killed her first.

Carolyn wasn't going to sit here and let it happen. Nor was she going to give Wyatt an opportunity to blow her head off. Her only shelter was behind her. How was that for clear thinking?

For a split second, she removed her gaze from the end of the corridor and glanced at the door latch overhead. She closed one eye, raised a wobbly left hand and tried to steady it with her almost useless right arm and shot at the latch. Just as another shot screamed down the hall, Carolyn tumbled into the room.

Paige had somehow dragged herself off the mattress and was inching her way along the floor toward the far left side of the room, smart enough to stay clear of the doorway and the path of bullets. A zombie. The crawling dead. Carolyn went toward her, half walking, half kneeling, her own body a mass of fiery pain.

"Hurt," Paige whispered, lifting a trembling finger to point at Carolyn's shoulder. Her voice was scratchy, a death rattle. "Blood."

"Flesh wound," Carolyn muttered, hazarding only a glimpse of those sunken eyes, the slack jaw. She heard Paige's breath, coming fast but deep. Rough shape. *Don't think about it.*

Carolyn winced. Sat down. God, it hurt to breathe. Wyatt's first bullet had punctured a lung. The least of her worries. "He's coming, Paige. Any second. I'll need your help."

Hollow eyes blinked. "Name it."

Carolyn pulled a knee to her chest, struggled into a position with Paige at her right, both of them near the door. "Shooting arm's no good. Take my hand."

Carolyn had her Glock clutched in both hands, wrists balanced on her knee. White-hot rods of pain flashed up her arm, and pain a thousand times worse pulsed through from her back, growing larger, spreading, consuming. A body engulfed in flame.

"Close your hand over mine," she whispered. "Index finger on top, like that." She felt Paige's grip, shaky over hers, then Paige's other hand came up underneath.

"Not ... steady."

"Save your strength. He comes through that door, you just squeeze, squeeze, squeeze. We're going to shoot that son of a bitch. Use every bullet if we have to."

They waited. Listened for footsteps. A squeak of floorboards. Something that would tell them the monster was approaching. The house was quiet.

Worst case—that Wyatt would do nothing, simply wait for Carolyn to bleed out here, that he would let Paige die. Also bad—that he would play this waiting game, knowing that Carolyn would eventually have to emerge, and in doing so, place herself once again as an easy target to be picked off at the end of his shooting gallery.

Wyatt was an organizer, a diabolical adversary. This scenario had not figured into his overall plan. He would not, could not remain passive for long. He would come to them, look first at the mattress. Carolyn and Paige would wait. As long as they could.

Interminable minutes ticked by. Carolyn bled. Paige edged closer to death. Both clutched the gun.

Carolyn stared at the door, at its huge black hinges not more than seven feet away. The door would swing toward them. She imagined she saw it move then realized she was dizzy. Too much blood pouring from her shoulder. More pouring out inside her. She thought she felt Paige's thready pulse against her own wrist then decided that couldn't be. She could barely feel the gun in her hand.

Suddenly the room grew tomb-quiet. Paige was holding her breath. The door flew open, Wyatt's S & W appearing in the opening. He looked straight ahead. They were below him, to his left.

Take the shot, Paige. Squeeze. Take the goddamn shot.

The air exploded in a fog of cordite and an enraged Wyatt screamed, spun toward them. Carolyn felt the press of Paige's finger once more as another shot rang out, this one finding its mark. The millionaire went down, clutching his leg. Femoral hit. Nice teamwork.

Wyatt still had his gun. Carolyn shifted her knee, squinted down the barrel of the gun. She whispered, "Again," and Paige squeezed.

The shot blasted a ragged hole in Wyatt's hand and the millionaire released his weapon. From the corridor came the sound of an army of pounding feet. Carolyn was dimly aware of a choir of glorious noise—the percussive snap of handcuffs, the static radio call for an ambulance, and the best sound of all—Ziggy Takacs entering the room and saying, "Well, fuck me."

"Watch it, Sergeant," Carolyn whispered on a gasp of exhaled air. "There are ladies present."

In the ambulance Carolyn spoke to the EMT who was trying to stanch the flow of blood from her shoulder wound. "When we get to the hospital, ask the surgeon to do something about my herniated disc. He'll be poking around in there anyway."

"You got it, Sergeant."

"But not before he looks after my friend over there. She's the important one." Carolyn turned to face Paige, already hooked up to a network of tubes and hoses. "She makes it, you understand? She makes it."

CHAPTER 66

IN SOME MEDICAL CIRCLES, IT'S known as "the Golden Hour," that crucial sixty-minute window during which a crack trauma team finds and tries to repair the damage caused by a gunshot. For Carolyn, the clock started ticking the moment Mercer Wyatt's .22 caliber bullet ripped through the flesh of her back just left of the midline.

The trauma surgeon and program chief were garbed in green scrubs by the time Carolyn was wheeled into the trauma bay. A paramedic recited her vital signs to the assemblage of nurses, technicians and surgeons. Then there was a warp-speed bustle of activity—blood samples were taken for cross-matching, central lines were inserted for transfusions and fluids; the x-ray tech took rapid images looking for broken bones that might give a clue to the bullet's path. The surgeons log-rolled Carolyn, checking under dressings to assess her injuries.

Once the bleeding was stanched and the team ensured that her airway remained open, it was time for Carolyn's next challenge: the operating room and survival of surgery. Massive cutting would be needed to determine the bullet's damage—there could be tremendous blood loss which would trigger a sudden plunge in body temperature and arrhythmia. She wasn't out of the woods, not by a long stretch.

Carolyn was swathed in a bear-hugger—a Michelin-man puffy, motorized blanket that circulated warm air—and the team went in and performed damage control, looking for life-threatening injuries. Then they sutured her up and allowed her to recuperate. The next day, if she was stable enough, they would go in again.

The rosary was clenched in Joshua's fist but he'd stopped relying on the beads seven Hail Marys ago. Prayers were erupting from his heart now, jumbled bursts of words that ricocheted around his mind like so many pinballs.

O God, in Your divine mercy, let them both be okay. Name your price; you know I'm good for it.

Beseeching. Contrite. Then despite his best efforts, the anger seeped in. His fingers tightened around the rosary.

Why did this happen? Neither of them deserved this. And furthermore, how could you have let me be such an asshole?

"No need to panic, Josh," Carolyn had said when her gurney wheeled past an hour ago. "They're just going in for a look-see. I'll be back in a couple of shakes with the bullet on your dinner plate."

She'd been pale, short of breath, her clothes soaked with blood. Seeing her like that made him lose it. Tears fell and he couldn't wipe them away in time.

"Don't wimp out on me now, favorite brother. I'll need you later to wait on me, and don't think I'm not gonna milk this for all it's worth." She smiled, a crooked, forced smile then she disappeared through a pair of swinging doors into the OR.

He felt a searing hot fire in his gut as if he'd been shot himself. He clutched the burning spot, willing his sister's pain to come into him.

Bring her back out, good as new. Please? God?

The rosary beads were forming oval indentations in his fingers now. Joshua loosened his grip, leaned over and used his other hand to smooth Paige's blanket, brush stray curls from her face, caress her cheek.

"Come on, Paige," he said, his voice soft and close to her ear. "Parker and I need you. If you wake up, I promise not to be such a jerk anymore. I've talked it all out with the man upstairs and we know what needs to be done. So come on back, would you?"

He planted a gentle kiss on her forehead, another one on her lips. He listened for a groan, watched for a fluttering behind her eyelids but there was nothing, just Paige's soft breathing. Careful to avoid the I-V tube, Joshua eased back onto the chair.

He had spoken to the doctor earlier. When Paige was admitted to the hospital, she had been in serious condition. Her eyes were sunken, her pulse was thready, her blood pressure was low and she was lethargic, coming close to fainting more than once. The doctor spoke about abnormal skin turgor, Paige's skin tenting when pinched and taking its sweet time falling back into place. They'd infused a saline plasma drip immediately to replete her blood volume. They closely monitored her electrolytes. Beyond that, the somber doctor offered little else. "Stay quietly beside her," he told Joshua. "Say some prayers, if that's your thing." That's when Joshua began his bargaining with God.

A nurse entered, clad in pale blue, her jet black hair woven into dozens of miniature braids at the end of which dangled a myriad of pastel beads. She took Paige's blood pressure and temperature, checked her I-V.

"She's sleeping so much," Joshua whispered. "Is she okay?"

"She been through a lot," the nurse said, pure Montego Bay. "Sleep what she be needing now. But don't worry. BP is good. Temp is good. Still, you stick around. When she wake up, we start oral rehydration, get rid of that pesky I-V. Maybe you can feed her some Jell-O or rice pudding."

Throw me a lifeline, he thought. Give me something to grab onto. "Is she okay?" he asked again.

"Forty-eight hours, tops, she be good as new." The nurse patted his shoulder. "Pretty special little thing, her helping that lady cop shoot that son of a bitch millionaire."

"Yes," Joshua agreed, "she is pretty special."

CHAPTER 67

On the 13th, Atelier Bissonette opened to mixed reviews. The arts columnist from the *Examiner*, eager to promote area talent, pronounced the gallery "exciting," and the work of the artist "innovative, edgy and evocative." Other critics from further afield weren't quite as generous with their praise, one citing Nicholas's work as "trite, humdrum and not frameworthy." Nicholas quoted the good reviews verbatim for Paige when he saw her on the street two days after the opening. He told Paige that if he mounted a large ripe turd on a pedestal, he could probably convince someone to buy it. Paige didn't crack a smile. Nor did she accept his invitation to dinner. Or drinks. Or a ride down the coast in his Porsche. He told her she would change her mind once she got over the shock of everything that had happened to her. She told him to go to hell.

Days later, Nicholas's gallery was Atelier Fermé. A small article in the *Oregonian* that evening mentioned a raid on a Portland home in a quiet, upper-middle class neighborhood. Nicholas's panic room turned out to be a pharmaceutical warehouse, storing everything from Quaaludes to heroin, so now his house and car would be converted to cash to cover his astronomical legal fees.

Paige returned to work. The busy fall season kept her mind occupied during the daylight hours but at night, she jumped at shadows. Weekly appointments with a psychiatrist and a supply of antidepressants helped her cope with the darkest moments when ghosts of Nicholas, Arlen Dale and Mercer Wyatt came creeping. Nights were long and sleepless, even with Joshua beside her. She dreamed of Taylor Wyatt, desperately trying to claw his way out of the shelter, his mouth wide in a silent scream.

Though her new number was unlisted, Paige could hardly bear the telephone's ring, wondering if somehow, one of her former clients had found her and the horror would begin again.

Carolyn was recuperating in Paige's guest bedroom, and Paige didn't like to leave her alone any longer than necessary. Carolyn was steeling herself for months of rigorous therapy for her arm. She still tired quickly and got short of breath when she tried to overdo it. She couldn't face going home; she had already decided to sell the house, claiming during a New Age moment that bad karma caused by Gregg's toxic aura still lived in the place. Gregg had sent flowers to the hospital, her favorite peach-colored roses along with a generic get-well-soon card, but Carolyn had given the roses to the patient in the neighboring bed. "Maybe these'll cheer you up," she told the woman, who'd just had a hysterectomy. "They don't do a thing for me."

It seemed natural for Paige to offer her guest room to Carolyn. Joshua's sister had saved her life, going against every police voice in her head to follow her gut and the feeling that deep down, all was not right inside The Aerie. Too, Carolyn's moving in made it easier for Joshua to keep his eye on both women; he was spending most of his non-working hours at the log cabin, tending to his sister, repairing his relationship with Paige. He was doing fine with both.

Fallon McBride had scooped herself another mega-story with the arrest of Mercer Wyatt. The millionaire was recovering from his bullet wounds as well, though not nearly with as much success as Carolyn. His right hand was almost useless, and the bullet from Carolyn's gun had sent a spray of shrapnel through Wyatt's body. The metal shower was nowhere near his vital organs, but a femoral hit could be just as deadly. Wyatt had lost buckets of blood and was dealt another blow hours after being admitted to the ER—the amputation of his leg. His suffering was just beginning. He would be tried for the murders of Sarah Lydell, Bettina Reid, and Stuart Plumb, head of security for Wyatt Enterprises. Fallon McBride would be in the courtroom. So would Carolyn, Paige and Joshua.

The bomb shelter bones were positively identified as belonging to Taylor Wyatt. They were buried in a grave next to his mother, Brooke. A handful of people attended the ceremony—Cassie Pepper, some police officers, a few of the millionaire's loyal executives. Stock prices in Wyatt's company took an abysmal plunge; in retrospect, Joshua was glad he hadn't bought shares when it had gone public nearly six years ago. Others weren't so lucky.

With the real True Gentleman safely behind bars, Dory and Sebastian returned to the village, as did Lani. Both women had telephoned Paige; she had seen their numbers come up on call display and hadn't yet returned their calls.

Where's Opal?

Amber and Jasmine were dead, at least in part, because of Opal. Sebastian had been in danger, Paige's breath nearly snuffed from her, all because Opal had pushed the sexual buttons of a killer. She had told him he was a good person, a true gentleman. She had made him promises, promises she had no intention of keeping, promises that should never have been uttered. What she should have said was, You're a miserable sick fuck. It's what they all should have said. Paige would live with monumental regret for each and every time she'd played into some caller's dark fantasy. How many more Arlens were out there, concocting scenarios that equaled or even surpassed those dreamed up by his alias, Orson?

She wondered how many evil seeds had been planted simply because one of them had opened a door to a shadowy realm of depraved thought. The door should have remained bolted shut. Some wishes should never be fulfilled. Yet each of the women had given permission for their callers to embrace their most secret desires, to abandon conventional constraints that prevented them from fulfilling their sexual destiny. Call enough numbers and any client was bound to hear that what he was thinking, what he felt like doing, was perfectly acceptable.

She wanted to burn her journal. Carolyn stopped her. There were lessons to be learned from the stories and characters contained within, and Carolyn said Paige should be the one to write about them. Uncle Spence agreed. "You're already notorious, Angel Heart. This won't go away because you want it to. May as well take some of the mystique out of it. Tell your story, Paige. Laurel's and Seraphina's too."

CNN wanted an interview. Paige held out for a book deal which came six days later. She would donate a portion of the advance to Joshua's charity.

They lay together, Paige nestled in the crook of Joshua's arm. Parker, sensing the end of the afterplay, whined from the throw rug at the foot of the bed. "Okay, you hobbled old mutt," Joshua said, "get up here." On cue, eighty pounds of dog leaped onto the bed and wedged between the two of them.

Parker, another victim of the New Order of Angels and Saints.

"Carolyn's looking a lot better, don't you think?" Paige said.

"On the outside, yeah, but I can't help worrying about what's going on underneath. She's got to be worried about her arm. Since grade school, she's only ever wanted to be a cop."

"You know your sister. She'll bounce back, better than ever. Meanwhile, we'll help her through the rough patches."

"What about our rough patches, Paige? Are we over them? Will we be all right?"

"We're getting stronger every day. All of us. That's promising, don't you think?"

Joshua nodded, held her closer. "I'm still beating myself up for being such a jerk, Paige. I just wanted to be one of the good guys."

Paige thought about Mercer Wyatt, Arlen Dale, Nicholas Bissonette and all those clients who once whispered in the dark. She snuggled in, wrapped her bare feet around his and sighed, the weight of the past weeks beginning to melt away.

"Go easy on yourself, Joshua. You are, without a doubt, one of the good guys."

Knowing that, she was at last able to drift off into contented sleep.

THE END

ABOUT THE AUTHOR

After teaching elementary school for several years, Brown's thoughts drifted to murder and in 2001, her firs *Wickedness* was published by Doubleday Canada. It was an Arthur Ellis Award for best first crime novel and ha take blood thinners very worried. Cathy's second thriller *in Madness*, was published in 2004.

Critics have claimed that Cathy "writes a slick, st tale" with a "sinuous plot as her stories gallop to a clir mentor Eric Wright says "Vasas-Brown seems to hav knowing how ... she's here to stay." *The Victoria Times-C* "Vasas-Brown hits all the right notes." Though Cat described as a writer who "shows a talent for great go very soft spot for animals (and she likes people too). quality time with her two cats, Spike and Arthur, and s company of the four felines no longer with her—Sherl Moriarty and Holmes.

When not writing, she enjoys traveling, skiing, in playing cards, cooking and going to rock concerts. She ha to dance as if no one is watching. Cathy credits her lat giving her a love of music and puzzles; her late mothe with an appreciation for nature and the gift of storytel husband, Al, gets an A-plus for simply being the best pa exciting journey.

OTHER BOOKS BY CATHY VASAS-BROWN

Every Wickedness
Some Reason in Madness

PREVIEW: THE MONITOR

"We get so much in the habit of wearing disguises before others that we finally appear disguised before ourselves."
—François de la Rochefoucauld

PROLOGUE

August 25, 2012. North Cascades National Park, Washington State. 2 p.m.

HE REFOCUSED HIS BINOCULARS AND smiled. The five were all in place now, the eldest and stoutest of the group having made several granddaddy stops along the mountain trail before finally joining the others on the wide ledge. The climb was steep but nothing they couldn't manage. He had made sure of that.

It was a marvelous day for a celebration. The sky was a vivid ultramarine, teased with spun wisps of clouds. Tufts of yellowed grass jutting from the side of the rock face barely moved in the still, cool air. Earlier in the month, when he was searching for the perfect location, he had flicked pebbles, like so many marbles, over the side of the cliff and swore he could hear each one as it bounced its way into the valley below. In the distance loomed the twin peaks of Mount Triumph and Mount Despair, and to the east, the ripsawed crags of the Pickett Range. He had heard that the first climbers of Triumph had ascended the peak by following five mountain goats to the top, enduring a volley of falling rock loosened by the animals from the path above. An amusing picture, he'd always thought, expending all that effort only to be conked on the head by a hailstorm of stones. A perfect Wile E. Coyote image.

Today's hikers had fared much better. They had been well prepared and well educated. They drank plenty of bottled water en route, having learned that giardia, a naturally occurring organism, could contaminate the most pristine looking stream, river or lake. Though symptoms of the parasitic infection wouldn't appear for days, no one was risking a sudden attack of diarrhea while trekking to the summit.

Once again, he looked across the chasm at the group. They would be feeling the sun against their faces as they congratulated each other. One of the two women, barely out of a training bra and still battling acne, laid out a blanket on the smoothest section of rock; the other female, decades older, poured red wine into five plastic glasses, then arranged a mix of flowers into a crystal vase. They had each brought their favorites— white roses and lilies, yellow daisies, irises, and cushion mums. The older woman had brought elegant stationery as well—nothing too feminine, she had promised—and a clipboard.

There was plenty of food, too. Baguettes, cheese, fresh fruit, and—why the hell not?—a bag of Lays potato chips and a dozen Krispy Kreme donuts, which they devoured. And they had music. Some Bessie Smith, a little bluegrass, Pink Floyd's "Comfortably Numb"—this from the heavyset man—and a selection of tunes by The Cure provided by the bearded man wearing the torn denim, the one who least appeared to be in a partying mood. "No offense," he wrote last week when they'd all chatted on-line, "but I've gotta get into my own zone."

No offense taken, they'd posted back. They would respect what he needed to do.

They settled on the blanket, circling around a fat, scented candle the young girl had removed from her backpack. The final male in the group—well-built, ruggedly attractive, and HIV positive—fished a joint from his shirt pocket and lit up. They all smoked. They finished the wine, played more music, talked. The girl, looking nervous, leaned toward the stout man then they both stood and executed a passable waltz along the ledge, treading carefully. At the end of their dance, the man gave his partner a courtly bow. She raised her hand to her mouth. A shy giggle.

Some wrote. They wedged their completed pages beneath the candle that was much shorter now. The man in denim looked briefly at the others then reached forward, pinched out the flame. The party was breaking up. A fastidious group, each of them began to repack belongings into knapsacks but the candle remained, the papers and flowers, too. And there was a framed photograph, added to the still life by the older woman.

The sun eased around the valley. Now it shone directly on the spot where they gathered. The group was on its feet. The women embraced, then the men. Except the one in denim who waited in silence.

They lined up, shoulder to shoulder. Boy-girl-boy-girl-boy. They joined hands. They faced Mount Despair. Seconds later, they stepped over the side in a perfectly choreographed swan dive, the sun not on their faces now, but at their backs as they plummeted to the rocky valley below. Exactly as instructed.

CHAPTER 1

November 25, 2012. Cypress Village, Oregon

Carolyn Latham, who dropped the Holt part of her surname when her husband dropped her, had been enjoying the first decent sleep she'd had in months when her bedside phone rang. Groggy, her mouth filled with what felt like duck feathers, she rolled over onto the stuffed animal that had become her constant bedmate. With the mini-halo of a 4-watt nightlight to guide her, she groped for the receiver. "Whosit?"

"Who else would call you at this hour?" came the voice from the other end. "It's your favorite gypsy."

Sergeant Zygmunt Takacs. 2:30 a.m. This couldn't be good.

"You gotta come, C.L.," he said. "It's ugly. Worse than ugly."

Ziggy's next comment made Carolyn jolt upright. It couldn't be. "Where did you say?"

"You heard right," he said. "I'll be waiting for ya."

Carolyn went to her closet, felt around for denim, grabbed her jeans and stepped into them, the waistband inches too big now. Then she went to her dresser, flicked on the lamp and grabbed thick socks and the warmest sweater she could find. Maybe then she could stop shaking.

The Aerie. That's what Ziggy had said. Four teenagers, no ID, and a rented Neon filled with charcoal fumes parked in the driveway of a millionaire's getaway home. Carolyn shivered again. The place was cursed.

Minutes later she had located her hiking boots and started up her Explorer, pointing it in the direction of Signal Hill.

There were days when she still had to baby her arm. She favored the left one for mundane tasks—carrying groceries, pushing a vacuum cleaner, washing windows. She saved the right one for bigger things—writing out police schedules and shooting practice. Even an act as simple as waving to someone across the street could evoke that now familiar twinge, that constant reminder that she wasn't the same, not since a Smith & Wesson had ripped a hole in her shoulder, just about a year ago. At the Aerie. There were times too, usually in the middle of the night, when Carolyn would take shallow breaths, afraid that a full inhalation would elicit a searing chest pain, even though her doctor had assured her that her punctured lung had completely healed.

So that was good news. Better news? The bastard who'd shot her was in jail.

The road at the base of Signal Hill was lined with cars by the time Carolyn arrived. Now, to add to her already flesh-crawling shivers was a core-deep rage that threatened to explode when she spotted reporter Fallon McBride's white Ford Escape among the vehicles. Yellow tape stretched across the entry to the estate's driveway, but it would take more than the words CRIME SCENE DO NOT CROSS to deter Fallon. A croc-filled moat might slow her down, but not for long. Carolyn hoped some well muscled cop was ushering McBride away from the scene now, hopefully with a Taser aimed at her ass.

Partway up the hill, Carolyn was met by a sweet-faced patrol officer. He introduced himself as Ben Mitchell, first on the scene, and despite the chilled November air, he wiped sweat from his brow. "It's bad, C.L.," he said using her initials too familiarly, since he was brand new to the force and they'd hardly spoken. C.L., she reasoned, was a much better moniker than her previous handle, Rambette.

"One of 'em's no more than fifteen." The officer talked a nervous streak the rest of the way up the hill, filling every silence. "Two guys. Two girls. And something else? They're all dressed up. I mean really dressed up. Guys wearing suits. Girls in long gowns with their hair done. Like a prom night gone wrong, you know?"

Keep talking, Carolyn thought. Keep talking so you won't see me shake. Won't see that I'd rather be anywhere than here.

"Serious about dying, too. Had enough charcoal on that hibachi to cook sausage for an entire Eye-talian family reunion. Put electrical tape around the inside of the doors. Taped over the vents, too. Car was sealed air-tight. Pretty effective gas chamber, but you'll see for yourself."

Carolyn didn't want to see it, didn't want to believe that not one but four teenagers had decided that life wasn't worth the trouble. She didn't want to face the long night ahead, knowing that eventually she would be knocking on doors, telling worried parents their child wouldn't be coming home. Carolyn, so preoccupied with her ex-husband's impending marriage, and especially his new baby, had trouble enough finishing sentences these days, frequently halting in mid-stream, even mid-word, her thoughts fragmented, jumbled. How would she ever find the right words when she looked into those parents' eyes?

"I'm sorry to have to tell you that ..."

"There's no easy way ..."

"I'm Sergeant Latham, and I'm afraid I have some terrible news ..."

Lame, lamer, lamest.

The long gravel driveway curved and the Aerie came into view, a custom-built river rock and shingle house, the same five thousand square-foot hellhole where she'd been ambushed by a lunatic. She quelled a series of shudders that scudded up her spine and wondered how many aftershocks she would have to endure. She had pulled through. She was in one piece. Wasn't she?

"No wallets, no ID," Ben Mitchell continued, nudging Carolyn back to the present. From one hellhole to the next. "It's like they wanted to disappear."

"No," Carolyn said, finding her voice. "If that were true, they wouldn't have come here. Wouldn't have dressed up."

She took the flashlight Mitchell offered. Even before she approached the car, saw the bodies, she knew. "This is about punishment. These kids are sending a message."

"Ah shit. Son of a bitch. Goddammit."

"You disagree?"

He was looking over her shoulder. "How did that parasite get up here? I stopped her at the bottom of the hill, told her we were securing the scene."

Carolyn whirled around to face the object of Ben Mitchell's grimace. Fallon McBride, looking too well-groomed, too trim, too exuberant for this hour, was trying to coax a statement from Sergeant Zygmunt Takacs and a grey-haired couple standing next to him.

"I've got nothing for you at this time, Ms. McBride," Carolyn heard Ziggy tell the reporter as she drew nearer. "And if you continue to get in our way and disrespect both this crime scene and the job of the police, I promise you'll be writing the recipe column for a paper somewhere in the bleakest, most God-forsaken corner of Alaska."

"And Sergeant Takacs will have the full support of his department, Ms. McBride," Carolyn said, now close enough to see Fallon's sooty eyelashes, long and thick enough to look good without mascara, damn her hide. "What we can tell you right now is that you will accompany Officer Mitchell here back to your car and you will leave this area." She ushered McBride a good distance away from Ziggy and the couple.

"You know I always cooperate with the police, Sergeant," McBride said, smiling too widely, her teeth perfect. "But you have something I can print?"

"Oh, sure. It goes like this. You'll write that four unidentified youth have been found in an isolated area north of the village. Police are investigating and trying to determine the identity of the teenagers—" Carolyn squinted through the darkness to peer inside the car, her throat tightening as she beheld the four still figures before looking away again "—two males and two females. What I do not want is a headline on the pages of the *Examiner* with the word 'suicide' in it. And nowhere in your article will I see a description of the method by which these young people died."

"Oh, really, Sergeant. Why don't you just write the article for me?"

"If I had the time, I would. What I'm asking you to do is accept a degree of responsibility. I know what you've seen here, Ms. McBride, and I'm pissed that you've seen it. But what I don't want is to be awakened from a sound sleep on another night and have to do this all over again. Exposure to suicide methods in the media can do a lot of damage, and copycats we do not need. There's a vast difference between reporting the news and providing some depressed reader with a formula for dying. Do I make myself clear?"

"Looks like we've all got our work cut out for us," was Fallon's only reply then she obediently followed Ben Mitchell back down the long driveway, her sculpted behind proof that the money for her gym membership had been well spent.

Carolyn felt a sickening thud in her already hollow stomach. If Fallon put her mind to it, she could be trouble.

"Sergeant Latham," Ziggy said when Carolyn turned toward them, "this is Gary and Noelle Lynch. They live on the adjacent property, about a half mile down the road. They called this in."

The Lynches had their backs to the vehicle. Mrs. Lynch looked ready to heave. Her husband kept his arm protectively around her waist. They told Carolyn the same thing they'd told Ziggy. They'd been returning from seeing a movie around midnight when they spotted a red Neon turning into the Aerie's driveway. They didn't think too much about it at first, figuring that the absentee owner must be paying someone to watch his property. But about an hour later, when they let their dog out for a pee, they noticed the car was still parked near the house and none of the Aerie's lights were on. They wondered if they should do anything about it, thought maybe it was a couple of teenagers up there making out, just like in the days before the owner had built on the land. Ignoring it didn't sit well with Mrs. Lynch, so they decided to check things out and found the car, with its four occupants dead.

"We didn't touch anything," Gary Lynch said. "I had my cell with me and we called right away."

Ziggy had been thorough. Carolyn had little else to ask the couple, so she thanked them for their time and helpfulness, assured them they had done the right thing and could not have known when the Neon made that turn into the driveway that the intent of its passengers was something so dreadful. They felt guilty nonetheless.

"We should have checked it out sooner. Should have been better neighbors."

Carolyn told Ziggy she would walk the couple back home, though the Lynches insisted they were fine. Carolyn's wishes overrode their insistence; she wanted them to follow the same path down the gravel drive that Officer Mitchell and Fallon McBride had just taken. It wouldn't do to have the Lynches take a short cut through the brush and wooded area, attaching scraps of wool from sweaters and hats to bare branches which the officers might misconstrue as evidence.

They had barely turned to go back down the drive when Carolyn stopped dead. She had almost missed it. If she'd been talking, distracted, she would have. To the right of the driveway was a stand of Douglas fir, their needles still glistening from the early evening rain. But among the evergreens the ground had been disturbed, the wet grass trampled into a rectangle. She tried to suppress a shiver. Could not.

Carolyn remained rooted to the gravel, about six feet from the spot. She spun around and looked toward the house as another seismic ripple traveled up her back. Her mind was clear now. If she stood on the flattened spot she realized that Ziggy, standing beside the Neon, wouldn't be able to see her. She would be protected by the dense fir branches.

Had someone else been protected too? Earlier tonight, had someone stood—or perhaps even sat, on this very spot?

At once she crouched and swung the flashlight's beam in a slow arc beneath the trees. About twenty feet ahead, near the trunk of one of the evergreens, she saw it. Cautioning the Lynches to remain where they were, Carolyn ducked under the low branches. She crouched at the base of the tree and with gloved hands, picked up a fat cork from a champagne bottle. The cork was clean, not muddied by the elements, not wet. And it had been a rainy week.

Someone had sat here, celebrating. Recently. With a bottle of Dom Perignon.

One of the four in the car? Police would check for muddy shoes, grass stained-clothes. If they found neither, another possibility existed.

Someone had watched those four young people die.

Made in the USA
Charleston, SC
29 August 2014